True North

Also by Jim Harrison

FICTION
Wolf
A Good Day to Die
Farmer
Legends of the Fall
Warlock
Sundog
Dalva
The Woman Lit by Fireflies
Julip
The Road Home
The Beast God Forgot to Invent

CHILDREN'S LITERATURE
The Boy Who Ran to the Woods

POETRY
Plain Song
Locations
Outlyer
Letters to Yesenin
Returning to Earth
Selected & New Poems
The Theory and Practice of Rivers & Other Poems
After Ikkyū & Other Poems
The Shape of the Journey: Collected Poems

ESSAYS
Just Before Dark
The Raw and the Cooked

MEMOIR
Off to the Side

JIM HARRISON
True North

A Novel

Grove Press
New York

The quotations on pages 298–299 from Elaine Pagels's *The Gnostic Gospels*
were quoted by Pagels from another source *The Nag Hammadi Library*
by James M. Robinson, copyright © 1977 by E. J. Brill, Leiden,
The Netherlands, published by HarperSanFrancisco.

Published simultaneously in Canada
Printed in the United States of America

FIRST EDITION

Library of Congress Cataloging-in-Publication Data
Harrison, Jim, 1937–
True north : a novel / Jim Harrison.
p. cm.
ISBN 0-8021-1773-2 (hardcover edition)
ISBN 0-8021-1774-0 (limited slipcase edition)
1. Family-owned business enterprises—Fiction.   2. Upper Peninsula (Mich.)—
Fiction.   3. Conflict of generations—Fiction.   4. Fathers and sons—Fiction.
5. Lumber trade—Fiction.   6. Michigan—Fiction.   I. Title.
PS3558.A67T78 2004
813'.54—dc22   2004040449

Grove Press
841 Broadway
New York, NY 10003

04 05 06 07 08   10 9 8 7 6 5 4 3 2 1

To Judy Hottensen and Amy Hundley

True North

Father was wailing. I deduced from the morning sun and moving flotsam that we were drifting slowly southward with the force of an unknown current. He slumped on the back seat of the wooden rowboat and I leaned forward grabbing his shirt to keep him from pitching overboard. Both of his hands had been severed at the wrist and the stumps had been tightly bound with duct tape. His normally withered forearms now bulged with an unsightly color. When they had pushed us out from the estuary on a falling tide before dawn I had been given only one oar. When I clearly noted this at first light the humor wasn't lost on me. I was equipped to row in circles with my left hand. The thumb of my right hand was missing and the pain lessened when I raised it high. In the early light I had seen a green or loggerhead turtle and took my thumb someone had stuffed in my pocket pitching it toward the beast but the turtle had submerged in alarm misunderstanding my good intentions. By midmorning the shore had arisen and I could see the coastline south of Veracruz. The current was carrying us toward Alvarado. My father woke from his latest faint. His face was too bruised for clear speech and now rather than wailing he bleated. His eyes made his request clear and I pushed him gently over the back of the boat. It was quite some time before he completely sunk. I would study the stinking fish scales and bits of dried viscera on the boat's bottom and then look up and he would still be there floating in the current. And then finally I was pleased to see him sink. What a strange way to say good-bye to your father.

Part I

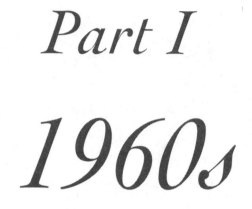

1

My name is David Burkett. I'm actually the fourth in a line of David
Burketts beginning in the 1860s when my great-grandfather emi-
grated from Cornwall, England, to the Upper Peninsula of Michigan which forms the southern border of Lake Superior, that vast
inland sea of freshwater. This naming process is of no particular
interest except to illustrate how fathers wish to further dominate
the lives of their sons from the elemental beginnings. I have done
everything possible to renounce my father but then within the chaos
of the events of my life it is impossible to understand the story without telling it.

My father was so purely awful that he was a public joke in our
area but with his having moved to Duluth so long ago the jokes had

become quite stale, truly ancient, and were now being raised to life only by older men, mostly retired, sitting near the breakwall in the public park next to Lake Superior watching boats they never boarded going in and out of the harbor.

Perhaps it is strange for a victim of evil to see this evil become more local folklore than a vital force, but then I was a temporary victim abandoning both my parents at age eighteen when I had the strength of my anger though I admit my sister Cynthia at age sixteen beat me to the punch by a full month. Cynthia got herself pregnant by her lover, a mixed-blood Finn and Chippewa (Anishinabe) Indian, the son of our yardman, who was a senior to her sophomore, and a star on the Marquette High School football team. At the time, 1966, for a girl of Cynthia's social standing to get herself pregnant by an Indian boy would be the same as a girl from a prominent Mississippi family becoming pregnant from an affair with a black man. In animal terms Cynthia could be likened to a wolverine, the most relentlessly irascible beast in North America, whereas I, in my teens, was more an opossum who wished to be a bear. Not oddly, it was a grotesque and unprosecuted crime committed by my father that drove us away, but then I have to work up to this dire event.

I'm too impatient to start at the beginning, and besides, no apparent god knows when that might be. I'm averse to the mirror in my cabin toilet, having long ago unscrewed the single lightbulb, but since the toilet is on the north side of the cabin and heavily shaded by a clump of fir trees I never see myself anyway in more than dimmish light. I don't dislike myself but there's enough left of the outward thrust of jaw to remind me of my great-grandfather, my grandfather, and my father. More than a trace of luck came along when my mother's small facial features moderated my own so that the old-timers in Michigan's Upper Peninsula didn't directly turn away in muted fear and nervousness. All but a few of the younger citizens, say those under forty, have forgotten the specifics of who we were.

I'm not going to trap myself here. I wasn't quite eighteen years old when I declared my intentions to Lake Superior on a stormy night near the grave of an old Indian on Presque Isle that I wasn't going to use up my life thinking about myself which seemed to be the total preoccupation of my schoolmates and all the adults I knew except Jesse, my father's aide since World War II, Clarence, and my uncle, my mother's brother Frederick who lived in a cabin way down in southern Ohio across the Ohio River from eastern Kentucky. Fred had been an Episcopalian priest in Chicago who had lost interest in his calling a step ahead of his parishioners losing patience with his terminal eccentricities. He survived on family money and a small pension from the church given for his general mental incontinence. Fred told me when I was sixteen that modern man at the crossroads mostly just stayed at the crossroads. This notion is fine in itself but more importantly Fred taught me how to row a boat on lakes and rivers. He built one for me in two weeks during a hot Ohio June, lifted and secured it in the back of his pickup, and then we drove north straight through to Au Sable Lake near Grand Marais, Michigan, launching the boat at dawn, breaking a bottle of Goebel's beer over the bow, but then Fred became confused over the names we might use to christen the boat. Fred owned an obnoxious dog, a mixed Airedale–bull terrier he had named simply "No" so I suggested "Yes" as a boat name because when we finally rowed the boat out on the lake that summer morning Fred had to forcibly detach No's teeth from the oar and I wanted to put a positive feeling on the experience. Fred subdued the dog and said the name Yes would be "banal." Fred liked to imitate the questionable behavior of his poor white neighbors but he was a learned man, his cabin stuffed with books. He broke another Goebel's bottle over the gunnel and christened my rowboat "Boat."

It was then that a male loon flew near us disappearing into the mist at the west end of the lake with that circular and querulous cry which after a long silence Fred likened to the laughter before death of an insane saint. All of Fred's frame of reference was Christian though he thought of it as a religion that hadn't "panned out" and after three beers would present a long and repetitive argument that the religion of his calling had done more harm than good to the world. This point was a precarious teeter-totter that daily haunted him but after too many beers and a nap he would withdraw his blasphemies because I was thinking of the ministry at the time and he didn't want to discourage me. How better could I renounce both my father and my own Western preoccupation with self than to take up a primitive form of Christianity? Of course my father ignored this right up to the point that I also refused the family tradition of Yale and enrolled instead at Michigan State University and then he knew that he had truly lost me, not that he seemed to care.

This is a case where mere fact isn't instructive. I had taken over the rowing and we were close to shore moving through reed and lily pad beds with the dog growling intermittently on the shore. It was already warm at eight in the morning and a slight breeze kept the clouds of mosquitoes enshrouded in the forest. Fred was peeling a hard-boiled egg drawn from the cooler and dosing it with Tabasco. I had just asked a mawkish theological question about Mary Magdalene, a query about forgiveness attached to this woman in part because I was a virgin at sixteen and imagined Mary Magdalene to be a haunted seductress, her robes parted wantonly for those who took interest and gave her a few coins. This boat incident took place over thirty years ago and I see the bits of eggshell floating on the shaded water. Fred was tired and irritable from driving north all night.

"That's your main problem," he said. "You can't have religion without belief. You're just using your religion to decorate your life to protect you from your father. It's like your mother flying down to Chicago to go to a dress shop, say something pastel pink for Easter when the Lord was said to arise. That's no better than your dad driving from Marquette to Duluth to fuck one of his fifteen-year-olds. What I'm saying is that you can't be playing around with your Christianity like it was a tool kit to keep you going. How does that make you better than your dad? Right now you'd give your left nut for an hour with Mary Magdalene." Fred was making light of my recent religious conversion wherein my soul was *saved* at the fundamentalist Baptist church, an event that offended my family's Episcopalian sensibilities including Fred's.

The landscape turned reddish and I pulled hard on the oars and hit shore in a snake-grass reed bed. The dog understood my anger before Fred and barked loudly. I jumped out of the boat and headed into an alder thicket that immediately tripped me three times because my body was trying to move faster than my feet. I think I was yelling "fuck you" and even now my voice feels boyish and cracking with dry sobs. Two weeks before on the day I hitchhiked south from Marquette my sister Cynthia had been sitting on a blanket out in her special corner of the yard near her disused playhouse. I was in the work shed next to the garage where Clarence our yardman often stayed, and where he slept on an old leather couch. I was near the greasy workbench careful not to touch it in my Sunday suit. I was on my way to the Baptist church while my parents were dressing for a later service at the Episcopalian. I was checking to see if Clarence wanted to trout-fish that afternoon. Many Chippewa are large men and so are the Finnish and Clarence was half of each. I once saw him unload a four-hundred-pound woodstove from his Studebaker pickup and carry it into this self-same shed.

One June Sunday morning through the stained window above the workbench while we were talking about where we might fish in the evening and had decided on the Yellow Dog we saw my father walk across the yard and approach Cynthia who was now doing calisthenics in a bathing suit which the prig in me thought far too brief for Sunday morning. He must have said something truly awful because Cynthia grabbed a large wooden stake that propped up a rose trellis and swung it at Father hitting him in the chest, hip, and knee before he could retreat to the back porch where Jesse was standing on the steps. Father was hobbling but Jesse made no move to help him. I made a move toward the work shed door but Clarence grabbed my arm. Jesse brushed off my father's pant leg where the dirty end of the garden stake had soiled them. I looked back at Cynthia who was now reading a magazine as if nothing had happened. She was fourteen at the time, ruled her own world, and kept her bedroom door locked.

I went out the back door of the work shed and down the alley to the street where Jesse now stood by the old Packard waiting to drive my parents to church. I told him I was going to hitchhike or take the Greyhound down to Ohio while my parents were at church. When something went wrong with my family I always fled for a week or so. Jesse's real name was Jesus Tomás Sandoval but the people around Marquette couldn't accept the occasional Mexican custom of naming a son Jesus so he was called Jesse by everyone except my father, who called him Sandy, a private joke that had never been explained to me. They had met at basic training for World War II near Houston and where Jesse had come north from Veracruz when he found out you could earn citizenship by fighting for the United States. They fought together, I think at Corregidor and the Philippines under MacArthur, and my father had quite literally bought Jesse's life what with his becoming a faithful manservant, "amanuensis," bookkeeper, valet, travel agent, and whatever to my father. Jesse was efficient rather than subservient while my father's appearance was such that if you saw him in a bank or airport you'd think there's a man who knows what he's doing, always well groomed and tailored, checking his watch as if time was of consequence, a shell actually on which the culture had slowly painted all of the characteristics of a WASP cock of the walk, an alpha white male, while inside there was only a decayed question mark, a living grave soaked with booze and desires so errant that all but a few people wished to run from him.

I told Jesse my intentions only because I didn't want my mother to launch a search party, or sit there in her nest in the breakfast nook in the kitchen with the table stacked with books of reassurance, from theosophy to the further reaches of domestic double-talk.

Jesse was faithful to my father and I don't recall a single word of criticism to anyone else though once I was in the basement and could hear a conversation in the den up a furnace vent, and then Jesse was brisk and trenchant trying to reason with him.

I was simply going to head down the street but Jesse reminded me that I was wearing my Sunday suit. I was confused of course. Seeing your sister beat on your father with a club is an uncommon experience. I thanked him and shook hands good-bye in case I didn't return before he left on vacation. Every year I could remember Jesse went home for the months of July and December to Veracruz where he had a wife and a daughter. It was less a vacation than a stipulation for his continuing services. Jesse had relatives that grew coffee up near Jalapa north of the city of Veracruz but still in the province. My father would complain about his departures, actually whine because he was quite lost without Jesse and disliked Clarence as a driver because he drove so slowly. My father had accumulated a number of drunken driving tickets and the family name and political influence couldn't get his license back after he passed a dozen violations. The complaints were meaningless anyway because my parents spent most of the summer at an old-money club about fifty miles north of Marquette and December took them to Florida. It's odd but I've never been able to refer to my father as anything but "Father" while my childhood friends had actual "Dads," many of them quite wonderful, though Fred has often reminded me that in Clarence and Jesse I had dads who were better than most anyone had. The biological collision of parenthood meant nothing to him, even though his sister was half the quotient.

Back to the lake which I couldn't find though I'm fairly good in the woods, especially so when I was sixteen and overconscious of where I was headed. That morning, however, I had mostly thrashed through the underbrush in an enraged state. Fred had said despite my religious beliefs which I thought profound that I was no better than my father whom I loathed, and deserved loathing, or better than my daffy mother about whom I was beginning to have doubts. For instance Cynthia and Father would carry on these brittle, acerbic conversations when my mother was down in Chicago three or four days a month to get a physical condition she called "phantom pain" corrected. My father and I believed in the reality of this infirmity probably because it was suggestive of our own mental ills. Cynthia, however, had told me that the doctor mother was seeing had been a friend of hers when she was at Stephens College and he was a poor kid at the University of Missouri. I couldn't accept this though I didn't inquire how Cynthia knew it to be true. Cynthia merely asked that if you were married to Dad (she called him that) wouldn't you seek outside comfort? A young man can accept a father's unfaithfulness but a mother's is definitely in a much higher category of pain, but then Cynthia added that she didn't mean that they were necessarily sleeping together. She said that my helpless young male imagination construed any male-female relationships as sexual. That Sunday morning when I went back into the house to get out of my suit, nodding to my parents as they came down the steps to go to church with my father still limping from his daughter's assault, I packed a small bag and then went out in the yard to say good-bye to Cynthia who had been joined by her friend Laurie. I simply couldn't understand how she could do what she had done and not feel confused and remorseful. Not a chance. They were singing Beatles songs then laughed at me because I always reddened when Laurie was in her bathing suit, a two-piece flesh-colored suit only slightly less daring than a bikini. I stared off at the lilacs and Cynthia said, "Don't feel badly. You didn't do anything. Dad should be locked in a zoo." And that was that to a fourteen-year-old girl who tried hard to make her brother as tough as she was. Far later when I was a graduate student in theology in Chicago taking a course in Oriental religions I read a Japanese twelfth-century philosopher who said, "No changing reality to suit the self." Cynthia, Clarence, and Jesse were experts at reality while mother, father, and myself were tormented speculators in the area of self-deceit and Fred was a tightrope walker between the two worlds.

By noon I had reached a steep hillside from which I finally could get a firm sense of my location. I had climbed several trees in the lowlands but couldn't get high enough to see anything more than other trees and I hadn't paid enough attention to the position of the sun when I was first lost to have it be of help. Now I could see miles to the north to the beige and lumpy outlines of the dunes that abut Lake Superior, all too many heartless miles away. My bug repellent was in a kit in the rowboat and my face was so swollen by mosquitoes, blackflies, and deerflies I could see only in a squint. My mouth was dry as dust and my stomach rattled with hunger. I had smeared my face and bare arms with swamp muck which helped with noxious insects. Blackflies, however, had made their way well up my pant legs. The mud poultice had been shown to me by Clarence

one evening when we were fishing the Yellow Dog and had forgotten our insect repellent. We built a smudge fire and fried some
trout. Clarence always packed along bread, salt, an iron skillet, and
a baby-food jar of bacon grease. I can't say Clarence was wise in
any orthodox sense. At one time he was a famous bar fighter in the
Upper Peninsula but one day his wife took the two children and
went back to her parents' home near Ontonagon. Clarence decided
to kill himself and jumped off the pier with a cement block tied to
a leg but down on the lake's bottom while running out of breath it
occurred to him all he needed to do was quit drinking, not kill himself. My father who used to bet on Clarence's more organized fights
with his equally despicable cronies hired Clarence when I was about
five years old and soon after that I was taught to fish. Around the
smudge fire on the Yellow Dog I heard the only story with which
I could directly connect Clarence with religion. When he was in
the Korean War and it was January several of his friends had lost
toes to frostbite and Clarence began to worry about his own. One
dawn after he pulled the boots off a crying soldier friend and some
toes came with the boot he shot a "gook" running out of a hut.
Clarence took off his own boots, slit open the dead man's stomach,
and stuck his feet among the warm guts until they began to cool.
He still lost the little toe on his left foot which he saved for his
medicine bag. The problem was that the Chippewa are expected to
have respect for the dead so years later Clarence was still worried
about the method with which he had saved his toes. It was especially hard after shooting and gutting a deer. He told me that since
he was half Finn he thought it was the Finn in him that forced him
to save his toes. It was ten minutes sitting there around the fire
before it occurred to me that I was supposed to make a judgment.
It was a strain but I said I had heard that it was hard to walk well
without toes and perhaps that Clarence's gods knew how badly he
would need to walk in the future. After the night of struggling with

the knot in the black cold water and nearly drowning Clarence
would take off walking for hours in the woods when he felt he had
to have a drink. Later in a theology class I brought up Clarence's
religious questions but my fellow divinity students found them
repellent.

After I had rested on the hill for a half hour Fred's surly cur
No showed up and began growling and barking at me. Fred's can-
teen was wrapped around the dog's neck and I detached it after a
struggle laughing to think that the dog owned some of my sister's
character. It was after I drank the water that I realized what Fred
probably meant about the failure of religion. He knew I went to
the Baptist church in part to piss off my parents. He didn't know
that I had read the New Testament a dozen times because I hadn't
been brought up to read it. Fred was more interested in the long-
term socioeconomic aspects of Christianity and lacked confidence
in such basic matters as the Resurrection which I believed in irra-
tionally because I had lost faith in rationality.

All the way following the dog back to the lake I felt light-
headed, even amused by the blisters on my feet. When I fell behind
the obnoxious dog would bark and wait for me, stopping where I
had peed in the morning and giving me a knowing look. Maybe I'm
only an animal in human clothes, I thought. Only a month before
when Laurie was sleeping over Cynthia had teased her into opening my bedroom door and mooning me. I knew they had been drinking beer and smoking pot. This was the sixties and marijuana had
made its way into all the nether regions of America. I was sitting at
my desk reading C. S. Lewis, the door opened, and there was Laurie's
bent-over nude butt. Then she was gone. I virtually swooned like a
Victorian lady. When I said my long nightly prayers I was unable
to dismiss the image of Laurie's butt. Most of me viewed her butt
as satanic but when I told Fred while we were building the rowboat in Ohio he laughed and said a butt can be lovely but not

satanic. I was already having trouble with my Baptist minister who startled me by disapproving of C. S. Lewis, also Mozart who had helped so much in lifting me out of depression.

It was years before the full comic volume of that day reached me. It was five in the afternoon before the dog and I reached the point on the shore where I had leaped from the boat. I was crestfallen when Fred wasn't there but then I heard him hollering from the dock at the launch site a half mile up the lake. I waved and the dog took off, and then I floundered into the lake rinsing off my mud-caked body before I noticed that Fred had left the rowboat behind for me.

At the campsite Fred joked that an eight-hour walk had been good for my health. He fed me three hot dogs and a can of warmed-up beans, then bathed my blistered feet in hydrogen peroxide. In defiance of my vows to be unlike my father I drank a bottle of beer. I fell asleep and awoke weeping from a bad dream at midnight. Fred stoked the campfire and made coffee. I was embarrassed over my tears and hobbled down to the dock and watched the moonlight glistening on the placid water. In my dream Laurie was thin, red-eyed, and bald, obviously terribly ill (ten years later when I visited her in the Marquette hospital where she was dying of breast cancer she looked similar and I remembered the dream). I composed myself, a state that lasted at best no more than a few minutes, then walked back to the fire, turning to see that the dog who had followed me was still on the dock and apparently staring at the moon, a possible metaphor for man's relationship to God, or so I thought at the time. I mentioned this to Fred who said, "That's pretty good." I asked Fred if he thought that I was a prig and he answered "probably" which destroyed my short-lived composure. "Prig" is what Cynthia called me the day after I confronted her about teasing Laurie into her errant behavior. The word "prig" wasn't used in the U.P. but then Cynthia read a lot, especially long nineteenth-century English novels by George Eliot,

Jane Austen, and the Brontës that I didn't care for. Cynthia had said, "I'm tired of having a prig for a brother. All you do is read and mope around disapproving of the world." It had truly pained me to discover that at age fourteen Cynthia was no longer a virgin. Neither was Laurie for that matter. They had selected two boys, one of them Clarence's son, Donald, who was a bright but tough athlete who affected insensitivity in public but in private—we had grown up together—was a wonderful companion.

I sat there by the fire trying to listen to Fred, who poured whiskey in his coffee, rail on about the treachery of governments, the chicanery of the Catholics, the sodden stupidity of the Protestants, but I wasn't listening. I was trying to figure out how not to be a prig, how to stop thinking about myself, how to enter real life, the dimensions and specifics of which I had no idea. I kept thinking of a quote in the nightmarishly confusing Book of Revelation that ended the New Testament that said, "I would that you were either hot or cold because if you are lukewarm I will utterly cast you out." A prig was lukewarm for sure.

Over thirty years later while recapturing all of this I become again a tenuous and hormonal prig somewhat frightened of the night, Fred's dog, the glitter of the moon on the water, the power of Laurie's bottom jutting in the door, the madness of girls, the Book of Revelations, my drunken and perverse father, my mother so densely surrounding herself with fluff that she was a ghost, how sometimes I prayed on the hardwood floor on my knees for the clarity of pain. This far away I seem to have exhausted all my fears though I can re-create them.

"Where are you?" Fred asked, bringing me out of my reverie. "There's a sure way to stop being a prig. Just figure out what's wrong with your family and avoid doing likewise. That doesn't mean doing nothing. That doesn't mean walking around with your head up your ass."

There was an immediate visual image of a man trying to get his head out of his own ass. Fred was close to drunk but that didn't keep me from taking him seriously. It was the first truly important night of my life. Despite my aching bones and blistered feet I sensed a possibility of strength, of a mission that drew solace and the chance of success or victory from the fire, from the dog, from my fellow human Fred, the night, the bright moon and stars, even the owl we were hearing intermittently. This sounds vaguely absurd now but then so many changes in the direction of our lives come as a result of accidents, happenstances, the slightest pushes in any direction, and on the more negative side the girl you met at a gathering you didn't want to attend who infected your life to the extent that the scar tissue will follow you into old age.

2

We woke at midmorning not having turned in until dawn when Fred tipped over backward asleep and I rolled him into his sleeping bag and spread insect repellent on his face.

"Don't believe anything I said last night," to which he added, "What was the last thing I said last night?"

"You said that I couldn't comprehend what was good until I comprehended what was bad." I wanted to take a walk but looked in despair at my blistered feet.

"Disregard that. It might be true but it's dangerous."

I had heard rumors that one of the matters that had displeased Fred's parishioners had been his excessive interest in black culture, including an affair with a prostitute which made his wife cut and run after only three years of marriage. Fred had told me a number of times that he was sick of white language and could "no longer operate on that level of discourse," a matter of which took me years to understand.

We gave up our heavy talk and spent two days rowing. In my own life strength has come from unfolding, subtracting, rather than adding. We simply took turns rowing the new boat. I didn't have a fly rod along which robbed me of the chance to show off my expertise to Fred, and also to myself, a skill often becoming a trifling and dishonest thing (Clarence always teased me about making long casts when short ones for were called for—he'd say "stop fishing with your dick"). Fred had a battered spinning rod and we trolled enough to catch a few bass and pike to eat. On the two overwarm afternoons we hiked out on the massive Grand Sable Dunes having discovered that the insects were averse to this sandy terrain. It was hard walking but there were shaded sandbanks of blooming wild sweet pea and sea rose, and wild strawberries which we'd eat despite the sand embedded in them. On the highest edges of the dunes you could sit and simply stare down at the icy clarity of Lake Superior, or look far out to sea and note passing ore freighters. The ore freighters irritated Fred because that was the business his and my mother's father was occupied in to the point that Fred claimed he and my mother were but an afterthought in their life in Lake Forest just north of Chicago. I tried to tease him about the freighters saying "I thought we were supposed to meet this head on."

"You are. I couldn't."

There was a tinge of redness in his face not caused by the sun and I wished I hadn't said what I had said, dispelling the sense of the idyll, the sand dunes, and Lake Superior growing dullish with the mood change.

"My sister is no longer a virgin," I said idly, trying generously to change the subject from Fred's torments to my own.

"That's no one's business but hers. Cynthia is fourteen years old going on fifty. She's the only honest human in the history of your family." To Fred young Cynthia was a heroine of specific dimension. From an early age, say about seven, Cynthia had a pungency and lucidity of speech that nearly everyone except her friends found nerve-racking. She had been encouraged in her precocious reading by a gay (a word not yet used in the sixties) teacher out of the University of Michigan who my father had managed to get fired by framing him, an incident that began at the age of twelve her campaign, somewhat merciless, of revenge against Father.

"It's natural for me to worry about my sister. Didn't you worry about my mother when she was young?" I asked lamely.

"Not really. I had the reverse of you. She was two years older and a mean-minded girl which she covered with a patina of good manners. She got nicer after Richard died."

I never knew my father's younger brother, Richard, who would have been my uncle. My parents' families were both members of the Club, north of town, an elaborate social retreat for the mogul families of the Midwest containing seventy thousand acres of lakes and rivers on Lake Superior. Many of the members were from Chicago and Cleveland with backgrounds of timber and mining and Great Lakes shipping. When I was about ten and heard the rumor that my mother was first in love with my father's younger brother I discounted it. The child's refusal to accept confusion in his parents' lives is a good protective measure. At that age parents are still gods though growing smaller by the year. Richard had supposedly drowned but those who told me this never appeared to be totally convinced.

On our third evening at the campsite, actually the summer solstice, the warm air seemed to gather a yellow tinge to add to its unnatural

stillness. Fred claimed he could feel the drop in barometer in his
eyes and ears. The sun had sunk behind the dunes on the day of its
farthest northern course but then it grew suddenly darker. Fred
immediately started to pack up our messy campsite. We began to
hear deep thunder and wind to the west and our vigilant dog trotted down to the dock to threaten the oncoming storm. We were
packed and finally in the pickup when the first stiff blast hit and
the truck shuddered. Not liking thunder the dog shrunk to the floor
and curled around my feet.

We found a slightly shabby tourist cabin on a hill in the village of Grand Marais. There was a kitchenette and two bedrooms
barely larger than closets with an obligatory set of deer horns. Fred
looked around fondly saying that the cabin held "romantic memories." My essential but I hoped waning priggishness doubted that
as there was a scent of beer, mouse turds, and fish in the air, and
the cabin walls shook in the storm as if there was a question that
they would hold up. Fred stood puzzled in the kitchenette and I
could tell he was trying to remember which of the bedrooms had
created the memories. He shrugged when the dog No made the
choice for him, sprawling across the pillows and growling for general reasons.

Fred poured himself a whiskey and asked if I wanted one. I
shook my head and took a shower to get ready for the inevitable
trip to the tavern. Fred claimed he liked taverns for the "plain
speech" and their admirable lack of Episcopalian patrons. When I
came out and Fred took a shower I tasted his whiskey and poured
myself a small one. My mother thought of her brother as a "problem drinker" but close observation led me to believe that he drank
less than she did. While we built the rowboat he drank two beers
before dinner and that was that, and we were up at dawn to beat
the heat, while my mother's daily two martinis were in the direction of the outsized. Fred's two beers made him relaxed and quite

happy while my mother's two martinis had no visible effect one way
or the other except to pacify her errant mind. When Father was
there he shook their martinis in a silver lidded container over his
shoulder as if he were creating a masterpiece or a ritual without
which polite society could not healthily proceed.

At the tavern the owner called Fred "Preacher" from past familiar-
ity but when I was introduced the owner became a little stiff and
formal. After all it was only eighty years before that my family had
finished laying waste locally to a half million acres of white pine.
In the mid-sixties the virtue of this was not in question, and the
grandeur of the destruction had been mythologized in story and
song. Fred ordered a whiskey and though only sixteen I was served
a beer as if it were unthinkable for the owner not to do so. I looked
old for my age, was just short of six foot, and had to shave every
morning but the reason I was served was my name and as the
evening progressed the word got around the fairly crowded tavern
and many people, usually middle-aged or beyond, looked over at
our table where Fred was buying drinks for two lumpy women in
their thirties one of whom was eating a snack of french fries with a
ladle of gravy on it, a localized Upper Peninsula custom. A retired
logger and trapper who had to be in his eighties and quite drunk
stopped by our table to say hello to Fred, but then he looked at me
and joked, "I met your grandfather and great-grandfather, the biggest thieving assholes God ever allowed to live." There was silence
in the tables around us but I only said "that's probably true" and
the ambient chatter began again. I was embarrassed to be looked
at as a young potentate and wanted to leave but Fred was making
a speech to me about language, drawing my attention to the nature
of what those around us were saying about weather, sport and
commercial fishing, alcohol, mosquitoes and blackflies, love and

adultery. By comparison, Fred maintained, nothing in my father's language was causally related to anything he might actually feel or with any accuracy to the world around him. My mother was close behind him. Their language was wry, ironical, and loaded. Throughout this the two women sitting with us gazed around in puzzled boredom that they didn't try to conceal, then the storm knocked the lights out and everyone cheered. The owner lit two lanterns and in the dim light Fred was kissing the woman closest to him. The other woman had disappeared and I got up to leave but when I reached the door the lights came back on and I nodded at two college-age girls at the door who were drinking pop and watching their seniors with amusement. "Why leave?" asked the prettiest who wore a tight, scanty T-shirt. Lacking an answer I shrugged and went out in the rain. I intended to sit in the truck but No went berserk when I touched the door having decided he didn't recognize me. I walked the mile or so to the cabin in the rain and wind, listening to the roar of Lake Superior rather than thinking long thoughts.

In the middle of the night there was loud banging at the door which was stuck because of the moisture rather than locked. I was slow to respond and Fred shouted at my window. I jerked the door open and was startled to see him with the college girl in the scanty T-shirt. It was the prig in me that would think that Fred in his mid-forties couldn't come home with a girl so lovely. I was standing there like a geek in my underpants and she winked and laughed.

Back in my room I suspected it might be a long night and actually prayed that they were drunk enough to fall asleep promptly. No such luck. The thin wall between our rooms seemed to amplify rather than muffle the sounds of their lovemaking. I had nothing to read but the small leather-bound New Testament (King James Version) I had carried in my pocket for a year and half since being "saved." I flipped through Thessalonians and Colossians, but nothing St. Paul had to say could compete with next door's sexual racket. This was definitely Boy Christian hearing a world he hadn't made, had no part in, and wished for the time being to keep remote to avoid imagining dire consequences as extreme as his parents' marriage. My fishing friend Glenn, a poor kid, had papered his tiny room entirely with Playmates of the Month from *Playboy*, and when we sat there at his desk tying our Muddler Minnows, Adams, and Fan-Winged Coachman fishing flies, I would glance up at the wall amok with tits and butts, feel my loins squirm and face redden, then despondently go back to tying trout flies.

This experience, however, was unequaled and I put away my New Testament for fear that it too could hear the groans, slurps, whimpers, the soprano shriek of "fuck me harder," the dog's bark. I turned off the light and could make out Laurie's bottom in the wall created by the wind-swung streetlight near the entrance to the cabin. My door opened and Fred shoved the dog in my room with a "sorry." Finally after more than an hour by my watch I could hear their alcohol snores and both dog and I were able to sleep.

I slipped out very early for a walk with No. The wind had subsided clocking around to the east and though the air was coolish there were still rumpled whitecaps on Lake Superior. The sky looked washed, glistening blue, and the sunrise made my tired heart ache. No led the way downhill on a path through alders and dogwood to the beach, a path he evidently knew. Fred would come north in the summer for a month or so, stop briefly to see us, go up to the Club for a necessary visit to his old father and a maiden aunt who moved into their log lodge as early as the snow would allow them, usually in early May, then as soon as possible Fred would retreat for a few weeks each in Grand Marais, a shack near Whitefish Point, the

Canadian Soo, and then he would drive north all the way around
Lake Superior through Wawa and Thunder Bay, on to Duluth
(a city he loved), to Houghton, back to Marquette to see me and
Cynthia, take an overnight hike with Cynthia near the McCormick
tract in the Huron Mountains, back to Marquette to avoid Father
and have lunch with Mother, then back to Ohio by Labor Day.

To be frank I admired him beyond all other men, followed by
Jesse and Clarence. Fred was the black sheep who was so black
everyone had ceased talking about it. He was a fact of life I anticipated with as much joy as I could muster every summer. By the
time I was ten I was welcomed to walk with Fred and Jesse from
the monstrosity of our old house out to Presque Isle for a picnic.
For the first few years the two of them would lapse into Spanish
when they didn't want me to hear what they were saying, but then
by the time I was fourteen I was allowed to hear everything. For
instance, last summer Jesse had paused, looked at me and then at
Fred, and said that wealth was like the breast of a pretty woman
but there was no woman attached. You had to make up the rest
yourself. Fred thought that inheritance taxes should be ninety-five
percent while I kept thinking of my recently acquired Baptist experience and the preacher saying, "Idle hands are the devil's work
tool," or something like that, my father obviously being a case.

I got back to the cabin on the hill in an hour and Fred's beloved
was standing in the yard brushing her wet hair. "Isn't it beautiful,"
she gestured at the landscape with her hairbrush. "You should've
hung in there last night. My friend was horny as a toad." Naturally
I envisioned an actual toad, but then managed to think of the other
girl standing near the tavern door. My stomach flipped over the idea
that I had been that close to losing my virginity or not. She offered
a hand without the brush and I could smell Ivory soap emerging

from her T-shirt and swinging breasts. She seemed to be exuding steamy heat from her shower. "Cat got your tongue?" she teased and I shook her hand, still not having managed a word. Fred saved me, calling us for breakfast.

Robin was her name. She and her friend were from Livonia near Detroit and had just graduated in teacher's education at Central Michigan, then headed north for an "adventure." She hugged Fred when she said this then let the dog lick egg yolk with a small piece of bacon off her spoon, and continued using the spoon on a bowl of Cheerios. Both Fred and the dog seemed to be smirking. Robin slurped her coffee and then drew a wrinkled joint from her purse, lit it, and drew deeply, her breasts jiggling with her cough. I naturally turned down a drag, but Fred shrugged and took a puff. "I'm on vacation," Robin fairly shrieked. Fred sensed my discomfort and pushed the pickup keys across the table. "Could you come get me in a few days? I'll give you a call."

3

I was passing through Munising and halfway home before my composure fully returned though I recognized for the first time that this composure couldn't be a significant item if it took a full hour to come close to the condition. It meant only that I had succeeded in keeping the world from intruding on the pickup cab. The paper mill in Munising was changing shifts and a dozen cars were pulling up at a tavern for the morning beer. Two heavily laden logging trucks were parked out front and with my windows open there was the heavy scent of torn bark and tree sap that reminded me of Robin after her shower. In stoned enthusiasm she had hugged me tightly good-bye and as I went up the hill out of Munising toward Au Train it occurred to me that it had been a full year of my new fundamentalist religion and I hadn't hugged a girl in that period. The last had been the previous June when my buddy Glenn's girlfriend, a big Finnish girl our age, had hugged me next to our campfire on the Middle Branch of the Escanaba River after I caught a brown trout of at least three pounds. She was far too burly for my taste but I admit that I became excited when she embraced me. She and Glenn would split a six-pack he had swiped from his dad, and I'd drive us home from fishing in my late-model Ford my mother had given me when she bought a Buick. At fifteen it was illegal for me to drive at night on my learner's permit but my parents were too distracted to be aware of this. Anyway, after fishing I'd drive the hour back to Marquette and Glenn and his girlfriend would make out in the backseat and I'd turn on the radio loud to drown out the very audible sounds of Glenn getting a blow job, an act beyond my ken. She had said loudly several times that she didn't want to get "PG." When Glenn came off he'd kick at the front seat and I'd yell for him to stop.

I was short of making the turn in Harvey when I pulled off at an uninhabited beach and dozed for an hour. I couldn't have had more than three hours' sleep and I felt giddy looking at Marquette a dozen miles west along the shore. If I had picked up my binoculars off the seat I could have seen our home looming in the trees on Ridge Street above the harbor. The week before I had gone south to Fred's in Ohio I asked my Baptist preacher what it meant when Jesus said, "Work out your own salvation with fear and trembling," which clarified it as more an individual thing rather than a group effort. The passage sounded strenuous and cruel to me. The preacher was always sucking on hard candy lemon drops and popped a fresh one when he said, "We worship together but we die alone so we have to work real hard to keep our faith on the right track." This struck me as a lame exegesis but then the preacher was deeply enmeshed in the problems of his hell-raising oldest son who we could

see out the parsonage study window smoking a scandalous cigarette while he washed his car. He was tall and somewhat fat and
sold condoms and beer on the side, all in all a poor advertisement
for his father's religion though in the folklore of the Upper Midwest the sons of preachers were always problematical items. Many
thought the preacher's wife to be too attractive to be suitable. She
was a southern woman (Missouri) and her silken voice struck us
as sexual. Her breasts were protuberant and when she lifted her
angelic chin for a solo of "Fairest Lord Jesus" my body hummed
with the lowest chords of the church organ. When I had been baptized by immersion with several others in a big metal tank with
underwater steps she had helped her husband and her wet white
dress was distracting. I had grown up going to St. Paul's Episcopal Church a mere three blocks down the street from our house
though Jesse still had to drive my parents as my father put great
stock in what he called "family traditions."

It was strange driving into Marquette that late morning because,
though I had been gone only a little over two weeks, the city looked
different to me, somehow more attractive and interesting with all
of the old buildings on the hillside in fairly good repair. I felt a twinge
when I passed the Peter White Library because this man stood in
noble contrast to my own questionable ancestors as did the relatively benign Longyears. So did Mather who actually believed in
educating loggers and miners, a revolutionary concept among the
robber barons of the nineteenth century.

When I pulled in the alley behind our house because I knew
my mother wouldn't abide her brother's ratty pickup parked in front
I stopped near a clump of blooming lilacs and wondered about my
change in feelings. I admitted silently to God and Jesus that I had
enjoyed my forbidden beers, and hoped someday to sleep with

someone like Robin, that I no longer wanted to go to the Baptist
Church, that I wished to slip upstairs to my room and listen to my
Mozart and my Sonny Terry and Brownie McGee and Joe Turner
records Fred had given me, and to avoid my parents, and that if
Laurie ever exposed her butt to me again I would lunge at her
like a timber wolf would a fawn. In short, my mental weather had
made a change as radical as the storm that had recently hit Grand
Marais. I meant to give myself to my mission of finding out what
went wrong with my family, or find out if it was ever right in the
first place beginning with those big-eyed, jut-jawed portraits in
my father's den.

Sitting there staring into the dense clumps of lilacs I didn't feel
a trace of irony over this youthful epiphany. I supposed years later
that a sixteen-year-old is still unformed enough that his path is elas-
tic. He is not yet as rigid as the iron railroad tracks that adults find
themselves moving on. At sixteen you can still jump off to the left
or right, go backward, or simply fly away. It all had the purity and
simplicity of feeling I had experienced at age twelve when I had
helped Clarence dig a garbage hole at the back of a garden for a
rich old lady down the street. When we were finished she gave us
lemonade, Clarence five dollars, and me a single dollar bill. We were
hungry and walked down the hill to a workingmen's diner I was
forbidden to enter. My mother didn't want me to have a trace of
the U.P. Finnish accent. My dollar paid for a delicious hamburger
and a bowl of potato soup. This relationship between labor and food
when you are terribly hungry made a distinct impression on my
frivolous young mind. It was wonderful. At home my mother would
have served me Campbell's tomato soup and an American cheese
sandwich. I imitated Clarence and put hot mustard on my hamburger and a liberal sprinkle of black pepper on the potato soup.
Walking home up the steep hill I felt manly for the first time. When
I walked into our house my mother hissed "you're dirty" and I was

a fragile boy again. There was certainly no point in telling her that I had earned a dollar on my own.

I was distressed when Clarence came out of the work shed and Jesse came down from his apartment above and neither made a pleasant commotion about my new rowboat. Clarence's eyes were red rimmed and Jesse was somber. I felt my heart thump assuming someone dear to us had died but instead it was a dire family crisis, what my father after several martinis liked to call a shit monsoon. Mother had gone off to a normally daylong bridge game but then felt oncoming sniffles and returned home early to discover Cynthia and Clarence's son Donald making love on the living room carpet. Mother had fainted and Cynthia hadn't called the doctor. My father, mother, and Cynthia were waiting for me in order to start a family conference. My father had even gotten the state police to look for me in Grand Marais. My mother was insisting that Clarence should be fired. Jesse explained all of this while Clarence looked at me imploringly. He had worked for the family since just after World War II. The imploring look grieved me and instead of stumbling toward the house I strode. Cynthia was in the kitchen making a batch of lemonade for the meeting. She rolled her eyes, grinned, and gave me the thumbs up. Her smile irritated me slightly though I quickly admitted to myself that she was the master of difficult situations. She whispered, "If they fire Clarence we both leave." I nodded in agreement.

My father sat at the head of the dining room table with his chin in his hands, his elbows firmly set, his eyes half closed as if almost irretrievably lost in thought. Cynthia and I referred to this as his "Wise Old Owl" position which he assumed during the rare family conferences, a function that a therapist in Chicago had recommended to my father who, we sensed, rather liked the drama of it all. My mother sat beside him playing with several handkerchiefs, her face tilted, trying to manage the appearance of a mother in a war-torn country looking for her children.

"I was called away from an important board meeting at the bank to deal with this," my father began but with insufficient conviction to trap us.

"If you fire Clarence we're both leaving," Cynthia said flatly.

"Cynthia!" mother said in a thin sob with a tinge of the Judy Garland diction that told us the doctor had sedated her. Both she and my father looked at Cynthia as if totally unprepared.

"Clarence is no more at fault for his son's behavior that you are for Cynthia's," I said judiciously.

Cynthia glared at me with fake hate and flounced from the room. I got up and stood between my parents, hugging each with an arm in commiseration for the monster daughter they had to deal with. They slumped against me and my father actually asked, "O God, where have we failed?" with a tinge of radio baritone. I stood there proudly feeling that any compromise was worthy if it saved Clarence his job. Cynthia returned with a tray of lemonade and when my father said, "You're not to see that young man again," she gave off a high trilling laugh.

4

It was another two years before my family achieved complete disintegration. Unfortunately my stance at the family meeting made my parents ignore Cynthia and concentrate on me as a possibly fair-haired boy which Cynthia thought quite funny.

The effort and aftereffects were worth it when I immediately returned to the work shed and told Clarence that there was no problem. He slumped to the sofa and Jesse leaned on the workbench soiling the elbows of his always impeccably white shirt. At that moment Laurie came up the back sidewalk wearing a new, extremely brief bikini, waved to us through the window, and Jesse said "Caramba" in relief. Clarence ignored Laurie, shook my hand, and said, "Thank you. I know it was you." My ears tingled in

embarrassment and then finally we went outside to inspect and ad-
mire the rowboat. Since Jesse was from the coastal city of Veracruz
and knew his boats he was a little critical pronouncing the rowboat
"more than serviceable," an expression he got from my father,
whereas Clarence thought the boat wonderful. True old "Yoopers"
(citizens of the U.P.) like Clarence aren't big on details. Much of
the local workmanship is a bit hurried with the shortness of good
weather and the winter often seven months long with high below-
zero winds off Lake Superior, and the snowfall regularly exceed-
ing two hundred and fifty inches, a lot for a sea-level city. Some of
the big houses were built with imported labor. I had been told that
the workman for our own home had been brought by my great-
grandfather from Sussex in England. One of the Longyears had
liked her home so well she had had it moved stone by stone from
Marquette to Brookline, Massachusetts, at considerable expense.

Jesse was summoned by a buzzer and a half hour later while
Clarence was still discussing the position of the oarlocks my father
came out to say good-bye. He and mother had decided to go up to
the Club a week early, I supposed to avoid Cynthia but he said Jesse
wanted to start his summer vacation early. I was always curious
about my father's propensity to fib even when nothing was at stake.
He glanced over at Cynthia and Laurie in the corner of the yard
and shrugged. I dutifully went inside to say good-bye to my mother
who scarcely noticed me in her sedative haze. She was flapping
around giving old Mrs. Plunkett elaborate instructions on how to
take care of us and the house. She pointed at an empty windowsill
and said, "Water the flowers." Mrs. Plunkett was the maiden aunt
of one of Mother's bridge partners and hailed originally from Iron
Mountain, where there's a large Italian population. We loved Mrs.
Plunkett because she was daffy and cooked us Italian food which
was a delicious and startling contrast to the anemic WASP food my
mother fixed. Mrs. Plunkett watched television, played solitaire,

sipped at cheap jug red wine that Clarence kept her supplied with,
and cooked. My mother never allowed pizza, catsup, or garlic in
our house but everything was possible with Mrs. Plunkett, including supplies sent via United Parcel Service from Iron Mountain. A
full day before my parents would return all the doors and windows
of the house would be opened and Cynthia and I would help Mrs.
Plunkett by spraying down the house with room deodorizer to
banish the smell of dangerous food and condiments.

Clarence and I took the rowboat out to the Dead Stream for its local
launch. It was too early in the afternoon for serious fishing. This
far north there's still a trace of light at eleven o'clock and the last
hour before dark was always the best for trout. Clarence said a striking thing about rowing that I've always valued, the upshot of which
was that he liked rowing because you were approaching life backward. You could clearly see the past, and you glanced quickly at
the future over your shoulder mostly so you wouldn't run into
anything destructively immovable. Too much of the future was
predestined by the behavior of others for you to be in control. The
most you could hope for is to be ready and attentive. These aren't
Clarence's exact words. Like many mixed-blood Natives I've known
Clarence spoke slowly and drew word pictures out of what was at
hand: birds, water, weather, shapes of clouds, trees, the comic behavior of people. "Just like today," he said. "At noon I was fired,
gut shot by my son who's stuck wings to his dick. He doesn't fight
like I did at his age but he thinks there's a whole world out there to
fuck like a buck with a dozen does. Then about two o'clock you
got me my job back." This took about a half hour and a mile of
rowing to say and he laughed about his son because what we can't
control is often comic. Luckily we caught two decent-sized brook
trout. Mrs. Plunkett was very fond of trout and would clasp her

hands and look upward as if in prayer when I brought home trout. She would eat a small portion of spaghetti or lasagna, then turn to her sautéed trout. She cooked many kinds of spaghetti, all of them previously unknown to us.

When I got home from rowing with Clarence I drove Jesse with his single suitcase out to the airport for his flight to Chicago, thence to Mexico City, and a short flight in the morning to Veracruz. When I dropped him off I wanted desperately to go along and had been asking him for years without knowing I was being insensitive. Simply enough, he deserved to get away from all members of our family.

Another front came through with two days of wet cold weather. I spent them at the Peter White Library, canceling a fishing campout with Glenn which would have meant trying to start fires with wet wood and drinking beer in a cold moldy tent.

Of course I didn't know where to begin at the library and Mrs. Mueller (the assistant librarian I knew vaguely) at first thought I was interested in genealogy. I said I wanted to know precisely what my ancestors had done in the Upper Peninsula and she joked that it would take me a couple of years. There was a lot of material in locked bookcases in my father's den but then I didn't want to snoop around looking for a key for fear of finding more of the pornography I had seen years before when I was ten of so. Of course I also didn't tell Mrs. Mueller about my secret mission to discover the sources of evil. I mostly read background stuff about mining and the timber industry in the nineteenth century and looked out the windows at the rain, and imagined my father with his cronies from Cleveland and Chicago up at the Club sitting around the lodge fireplace drinking and belittling in virulent terms Lyndon Johnson's Great Society project. Mrs. Mueller was fairly stocky with flaccid arms but I still felt a buzz when she brought books and articles to my desk because her peculiar flowery perfume was similar to the scent Laurie—who had been spending a lot of time at our house in my parents' absence—wore and emerged from her skin when she and Cynthia danced to Beatles tunes on the oak floor of the dining room. To please Mrs. Plunkett I'd play gin rummy with her for a while in the evening, positioning myself so I could see Laurie dance which though it enervated me was worth the bother.

On the second rainy morning at the library I was in a storage room with Mrs. Mueller. She was trying to find follow-up material on an aborted court case dealing with the State of Michigan against my great-grandfather who had timbered twelve thousand acres near Ontonagon that he didn't own. The state's prime witness had disappeared, reemerging years later as a streetcar conductor in Chicago. I was propping up Mrs. Mueller who stood on a shelf about three feet up and was digging through a file carton on a higher shelf. When I helped her down she slid through my arms and my hands paused an extra split second on her ample, flubbery breast. She didn't try to wriggle free. "It would be fun but it's out of the question," she said. Her hand dropped and she gave my penis a twitch and laughed. Evidently I said, "I'm sorry," but I couldn't hear my own voice. "Don't be sorry. It's just normal," she said, hurrying through the door of the storeroom. Looking back there's something preposterous about the amount of sexual desire in a sixteen-year-old. There I was trying to research evil with a very hard dick for a burly married librarian with three children, as far as you could get from the girls I had carefully studied on the pages of Cynthia's *Seventeen* magazine. This lust was all down there on the level of a joke I had overheard one of my father's cronies tell about an old logger whose girlfriend was a milk bottle full of pork liver. The change in me was that unlike a few weeks before I didn't pray to God that he would remove my lust. I hadn't given up on God and Jesus but had abandoned the idea that divine force was likely to banish my desire.

The rain disappeared and early on the third morning Mrs. Plunkett knocked on my bedroom door to say that my uncle Fred was on the phone. I put on a robe to conceal the usual erection and trotted downstairs. In the mid-sixties it hadn't yet occurred to people to put a phone in every room though Cynthia had had one installed in her own room with her own money against my parents' wishes.

"Come and get me. I've been rode hard and put away wet," Fred nearly shouted.

"What's that supposed to mean?"

"It means I'm a tired, physically abused horse. Or pony."

I started to pack immediately but then Cynthia caught me in the kitchen and decided she and Laurie would come along. I said no because I was taking Fred's pickup and the boat and there wouldn't be room for all of us in the pickup cab on the way home. After two days of cold rain and library work I desperately wanted to row my boat on Au Sable Lake if only for an hour or so. Laurie, who had slept over, came into the kitchen in her nightie and I naturally altered my decision. Cynthia noted this change of heart with her patented crazy little laugh. Laurie's oldest brother was in the air force in Mississippi and had sent her a number of blues records that they had played late into the night so when I prayed on the cold air register I was hearing music from people who deserved to pray. Since my recent religious waffling I had stopped praying for the salvation of my parents which seemed as unlikely as my lust suddenly taking a powder. I mused on this and some troublesome dreams at the glass-topped breakfast table where Laurie ate her oatmeal and fruit with energy, and through which I could see her tan legs and her spare hand when she gave the inside of a thigh a scratch. She was a superb swimmer and tennis player, cheerleader, courted by our best athletes, but tormented by her freckles. Usually she treated me as if I didn't exist, or was merely a piece of furniture to walk around. She chewed her nails constantly and did poorly in her studies, and smoked as much marijuana as she could get her hands on though it was of poor quality and known as "Indiana Red." She had extended fits of depression and took the same pills, downers, that the same doctor had prescribed to me for the same reasons only I threw mine away and Laurie took hers which made her mumble disconnectedly at times like my mother. Cynthia returned to the kitchen and told Laurie that I was looking at her legs. Laurie spread them and stuck out her tongue. I told her not to worry, that I wouldn't fuck her at gunpoint, a sentence so uncharacteristic of me that they were both startled. I was tempted to walk out of the kitchen like John Wayne but in truth I was far closer to Montgomery Clift. In the Upper Peninsula you would be far better off imitating John Wayne but I suspect that Montgomery Clift wasn't that way because he wished to be. Marquette, in any event, wasn't the kind of place where a young man would want his classmates to know that he needed pills to get through the day. Pills and any other kind of drug were okay for the students from Northern Michigan College (now a university) but then many of them were from southern Michigan below the straits of Mackinac and we supposed that if you lived in Detroit you needed to be narcotized.

Out by the work shed where the pickup was parked Clarence was concerned that I was taking along Cynthia and Laurie but I said that we would be back by evening. Standing there petting my rowboat as if it were a dog I drifted off into a near trance wherein my sight became more intense and utterly vivid so that all of the various flower beds Clarence had planted became uncomfortably lurid. I could hear the girls singing from an upstairs window and it seemed I could see the sound drifting into the heavy clumps of lilacs. I scuffed the dirt with a boot toe and unearthed a penny from 1903. The penny was incomprehensible. I looked up at scudding and whispy clouds and I had the feeling I was seeing too far in space. I made an effort to draw back from this strangeness by staring at the girls as they came out of the screened back porch but they didn't help when they broke into dance steps similar to those used by black music groups. A lump formed beneath my breastbone and I felt a desperate urge to be ordinary. Clarence patted my shoulder as if to awaken me. I was frightened when I turned the key in the truck's ignition. The expression "to lose your mind" haunted me and I wondered that if I got out of the truck and lay facedown on the grass I might recover my equilibrium. Laurie was beside me and Cynthia said, "Let's count our money." We had ninety-one dollars between the three of us and this counting helped.

The girls sang Beach Boys tunes on the entire two-hour trip. I was upset when we reached Fred's cabin on the hill and Donald was waiting there in his old blue Chevy. It was a setup and I said, "Goddamn you, Cynthia," then my stomach felt stricken because I had used the Lord's name in vain for the first time in memory. Cynthia and Donald took off and Laurie and I stood there for a few minutes watching a group of ravens quarreling up in a tree which diverted me from my anger at Cynthia. Laurie said she was going to check and see if the harbor on Lake Superior was warm enough to swim and headed down the hill.

    I knocked before entering Fred's cabin not wanting anymore surprises, but Robin wasn't there. Fred looked bleak and exhausted sitting at the table drinking coffee and reading a book. The cabin was in disarray with four pork chops congealed in a pan on the stove

and a grand collection of beer cans and bottles spilling out of a garbage bag.

"Don't mix drugs, alcohol, and younger women," Fred said in
mocking imitation of a sage.

"I don't feel I'm in danger." I poured myself a cup of coffee,
squinching my nose at the odors of stale beer, sweat, perfume, an
ashtray full of marijuana roaches. I should have known my timing
was off but I stood there and poured forth my lack of progress in
my mission to find the roots of evil in my family, also my recent
religious doubts. It was immediately apparent that not only was
Fred not listening carefully but he obviously didn't recall his part
in the inception of my mission. This put me in the emotional framework of my early childhood when my father would promise to take
me sailing, fishing, or hunting but never did. Fred waved a book at
me, an historical study of black Indians that he had been reading
down in Ohio when we were building the rowboat. He began talking about the book but my head was heated by embarrassment and
I couldn't quite hear. I suddenly felt quite alone on earth when I
thought I had a firm ally. Gradually I could hear Fred talking about
black and Native intermarriages in southern history, and then it
occurred to me that Fred wished he was a black Indian rather than
what he was. He put his head on his arms on the table, spilling his
coffee, which had been mixed with whiskey. And then be began to
snore.

The reality of the day wasn't shaping up very well, I thought.
It was clearly time to row the boat, but then halfway down the hill
I saw Laurie on her way back. She was teary because the harbor
water was too cold to swim. I told her to come with me because Au
Sable Lake would be warm enough and she could swim while I
rowed. Her tears went away and she cheerily sang the Beach Boys'
"In My Room" as if I weren't there. She helped me launch the boat
and I rowed about a mile west down the lake where there was an

unoccupied cottage and a nice beach. She got out of the boat and
stripped to her undies throwing her T-shirt, sandals, shorts, and
bra into the boat with me. She didn't mind me looking because of
her happiness over swimming so I went ahead and looked, amazed
at the pinkness of her nipples in the hot sunlight. She swam off
straight across the lake toward the dunes so I rowed in another
direction not wanting her to think I was crowding her. I rowed in
a big circle and after half an hour she headed back to the beach and
so did I. It was too boggy near shore so she waved her hands at the
insects and waded back out to a shallow sandbar where the water
was only a foot deep. She was shivering when I approached and
she said, "Come on in." I took off my clothes except for my underpants, got out of the rowboat, and pushed it toward shore. I sat
down in the water next to her and began to rub her shivering body,
quite startled to feel how solid her body was when she looked so
soft. She straddled my lap facing me and hugged me for warmth. I
was sweaty from rowing but then I thought so what? In my rubbing I was avoiding her breasts and bottom and she teased "you're
missing the good parts." I slid my hands under her panties and felt
her cool solid bottom and then I passed my thumbs across her pink
nipples. She stood up abruptly and took off her panties. I leaned
forward and planted a French kiss on her pubis and she laughed
and sat back down on my lap. "We don't have a rubber so you're
going to have to pull out," she said matter-of-factly. She guided me
and at first I couldn't get in but then suddenly I could. The sensation was so startlingly warm that I had to push her backward because I was instantly coming. "Look, thousands and thousands of
babies," she said pointing at my semen in the water. She rinsed the
head of my penis and got back on and this time it took a lot longer
before I flopped back to disconnect us. I lay there half-submerged
with my heart pounding and she looked around the lake and said,
"I'm hungry." By the time we dressed and I rowed back to the truck

she was dozing. She fell asleep in the truck and in town after I bought her hamburgers to go I put one under her nose which partially woke her up though she tried to eat it before it was unwrapped. She sleepily admitted that Mrs. Plunkett had made them stop playing their Mississippi blues records at four A.M. and they'd gotten extra energy by taking the last of their diet pills which I assumed to be Dexedrine.

Fred wasn't at the cabin and there was no sign of Donald and Cynthia. Fred left a note for me to meet him at the tavern. I put Laurie to sleep in my room but then she didn't want me to go. She was teary again and I lay back next to her wondering what was expected of me. The cabin was very warm and she had taken off her clothes but I found her tears antisexual. I still had something left of the good feeling of no longer being a virgin but this was being lost in her tearfulness. She hugged me so strongly that I nearly lost my breath and then she fell asleep. A scant half hour later by my watch, she was awake and we were making love again. I was worried because I wasn't sure if I had withdrawn quickly enough. She went back to sleep but I was starkly awake leaning on an elbow and memorizing her body, confident that my good luck wouldn't last and I would return to my state as a lonely prig.

I heard Fred come into the cabin and I dressed and slipped out the bedroom door but Fred caught a glimpse of Laurie's body on the bed. His eyes widened but he graciously said nothing. He unpacked a bag of groceries and started to cook dinner. It occurred to me that we would be late and I should call Mrs. Plunkett. Fred announced that he had "tapered off" with a few beers at the tavern but hadn't eaten in twenty-four hours. He smelled so sour I moved away from the stove where he had discarded the uneaten pork chops and started a fresh batch. Laurie smelled sweetly of fresh lake water and the odor of sun was in her hair. I asked Fred what happened to Robin. She had taken off with a college boy late the night before so he had gotten drunk in sheer relief. He would visit his relatives up at the Club tomorrow then go back to Ohio and return to his books with joy. "You can only take so much reality," he said. I offered to trade my Ford for his pickup but he said I'd be getting a raw deal and that we could simply switch for a while. I couldn't imagine my parents allowing me to buy a pickup but I needed one for my rowboat. I wondered what had happened to the dog and Fred stomped on the floor and yelled "No," explaining the dog hadn't liked Robin so had dug a tunnel under the cabin for a retreat. The dog appeared at the screen door and when I let it in it shot for the garbage bag and rooted out the old pork chops. Fred decided not to notice and poured a chopped onion and a jar of baked beans over the chops in the frying pan, the kind of meal a famished bachelor makes with an air of culinary victory. It didn't look appealing so I went in for a nap sliding onto the bed quietly in hopes of not waking Laurie.

Cynthia and Donald showed up around ten-thirty just before dark. I didn't hear them enter and Cynthia caught us making love. She shouted and laughed and I covered my face with a pillow for want of anything else to do to handle the situation. Donald had wanted Cynthia to meet his cousins so they had driven over to the Chippewa reservation near Brimley to the east toward Sault Sainte Marie. Donald had to get home for work the next morning and Laurie got her things to go with them. Cynthia sat on Fred's lap and told him about the reservation while smoking a joint. Donald was intrigued by the idea that there were black Indians and Fred loaned him the book. I walked out to Donald's car with them thinking that Laurie might wish to kiss me good-bye but she didn't.

5

When you're sixteen your world is small and events easily conspire to make it even smaller. You have glimpses of greater dimensions but this perception easily retracts. Eros enlivens another world but not the simple world of masturbatory trance. Laurie lacked the simplistic charm of a magazine photo. In fact I had quickly consented to my own thought that she was as complicated, maybe as fucked-up, as I was. Naturally during the act of love you're undisturbed by reality, a grace note I also found in trout fishing, but then lovemaking and fishing don't manage to dominate your life like you wished they could.

When we got back to Marquette at midmorning the next day I had my first real quarrel with Fred. A year later he would dismiss this falling out but it was a stomach churner. On the way home I had halfway agreed to drive up to the Club with him for his annual overnight visit, but then my preoccupation with Laurie overwhelmed me and I couldn't bring myself to go. Fred kept a suit of clothes at our house for this occasion and he stood there in my bedroom looking idiotic in a Haspel summer suit, rep tie, and button-down shirt angrily trying to change my mind. I had actually gotten dressed but then was suddenly covered with sweat at the idea of seeing all of those people, including my parents, that I didn't want to see. Fred stomped off leaving the dog with Cynthia who in turn left the dog with me. I decided to walk out to Presque with the dog but it decided to stay with Mrs. Plunkett who was chopping garlic in the kitchen. I called Laurie who said "I can't talk now" and hung up. The dog and Laurie made me feel abandoned.

On my walk toward Presque Isle (with a lump in my throat) I made a minor impulsive move that was to figure large in my life. I turned down a street on which Glenn's shabby house stood thinking of my mother's list of approved dogs which didn't include the Labrador I wanted, only small yappy breeds, and saw Glenn and his dad loading equipment. They were surprised to see me because I always called first, another pointless sign of good breeding that had been drummed into me. There wasn't a nitwit male alive that I wouldn't call "sir."

Glenn's dad was a small-time cement worker and contractor. They were headed over to Iron Mountain to do curb construction for a month or so. Glenn's dad, named Herb, was a little leery of me because of our difference in background but said jokingly he was a shovel man short of a full crew if I needed work. Glenn ticked off the rivers we could fish in the evenings. I found myself saying that I would know by first thing in the morning if that was soon enough. Herb gave me the number of the tourist cabin in Iron Mountain and off they went.

I continued on to the tip of Presque Isle then circled around the west side of the peninsula and back toward home, a three-hour walk loaded with sappy feelings about Laurie, the kind of emotional schmaltz that makes country music so sodden. I made a detour to avoid passing the Baptist church what with the odors of the sin of fornication on my skin, not a small item after a year that included baptism, prayer meetings, and my prolonged and devout study of the Bible. I consoled myself by thinking that fooling with girls didn't seem high on Jesus' agenda of the forbidden, and while St. Paul was doubtless a good man he tended toward dreariness. This sort of waffling is typical of young fundamentalists looking for an angle in which they may behave as they wish. The true ethical question was whether Laurie was of sound mind, let alone me. There were all those common idioms dealing with sanity—was someone dealing from a full deck, or did they have both oars in the water? Both Laurie and Cynthia, though fourteen, seemed older than me in all respects, but with close contact some doubts had arisen. They both belonged to the raciest crowd in high school, young people who by virtue of their character were popular, the sons and daughters of the prosperous, successful athletes, and the very attractive whether male or female. So-called old money was in a rare category by itself, with two friends of my childhood being sent away to Groton and Kent. Both Cynthia and I threw major tantrums at the merest suggestion that we might be sent off to boarding school.

I admit that every few months I had doubts about my own willful behavior, especially since I got "religion." I even discussed the problem with Cynthia who made no pretensions toward being fair-minded but in this case paused ten minutes, putting down her Jane Austen, and talked it over. "Of course we're hopeless. What else could we be? We come from a long line of snotty criminals on both sides. Dad's an alcoholic pervert and mother's a goofy pill head." I said righteously that we didn't have to be like them and

she agreed because she had no intention of being like them. There
was the idea, she added, that our willfulness was part of our character, and it made the people in our family what they were, and
would make us like we wished to be and hopefully that would be
better than our "worthless" parents. This conversation had taken
place only the month before and I was startled at the time about
her sharpness on the matter no doubt gotten from the maturity of
her reading which contrasted with her errant behavior. Cynthia was
clearly the leader of the "bad girls," the free spirits in her crowd,
despite the fact that she had just finished her freshman year and
others were older, and some of them seniors.

When I reached our front yard Laurie and Cynthia were there
sitting on the lawn dressed for a party in the skimpiest of clothing.
This was the age of the miniskirt. Laurie merely nodded at me and
then Donald pulled up in his car with Brad who was headed to
Michigan State in the fall as a football recruit. Laurie and Cynthia
got in the car without so much as a backward look. Twenty-four
hours before Laurie had told me in the hot cabin that I was her
"all-time love" and now I was there shuffling my feet in the grass
with the dog No barking at me from the front porch as if I were a
stranger.

I went inside, packed my duffel for Iron Mountain, and had a
glass of a red wine called Cribari with Mrs. Plunkett. The wine
tasted syrupy but the aftereffects were pleasant. I played double
solitaire with Mrs. Plunkett who for reasons about which I didn't
inquire wore elbow-length white gloves. I cautioned myself against
a second glass of the red wine not wanting to fall into the family
trap of habitual sedation. Mrs. Plunkett seemed as distracted as I
was that evening and must have drunk a half dozen glasses in an
hour before she burst into tears telling me that I shouldn't have
Laurie for a girlfriend because there was an outside chance I was
related to her. I didn't believe this because I didn't want to. Of

course my father was a renowned philanderer but when I had asked
Jesse about a gossip item years before he had said ninety-nine percent of all gossip was speculative. My parents were of an antique
age, in their early forties in fact, but Laurie's mother had had her
son who was in the air force at fifteen, then had Laurie after she
was married at twenty-one. An amazingly high percentage of girls
in the Upper Peninsula managed to get pregnant before marriage,
and if marriage wasn't an option simply had the babies anyway.
Abortion wasn't a popular option in the mid-sixties in this area, and
since so much of the U.P. is Scandinavian and French-Canadian
there wasn't the social onus on pregnancy found in many parts of
the country, say in the Bible Belt.

I went to bed early, at ten, fairly stewed but able to dismiss
Mrs. Plunkett's familial gossip. Laurie's brother owned a conceiv-
able resemblance to my father but not Laurie, whose mother at
thirty-five would dress up to look like Marilyn Monroe for New
Year's Eve parties, and every male in the region felt called upon to
express his desire for her at one point or another. Laurie's father
was an "outsider," a professor at the college, and likely free from
hearing much of the local talk about his wife who was originally
from the neighboring town of Ishpeming.

Before I went to bed I made a pass around the den thinking of
breaking into the cabinets, or into the desk where all the drawers
were locked except the innocent top drawer. I knew my father
owned some pornography from my early poking around but then I
liked pictures of nude women excluding those pictures of men
fucking them. I knew there were ledgers and journals in the cabinet beginning with those kept by my great-grandfather and eventually I would break in and make copies but that could wait. Right
then I was feeling like a drunken young crackpot rather than a man
with a chosen destiny. After all, in trying not to spend my life
thinking about myself I had become more self-involved. And while

beginning my project to uncover the evil in my family my own behavior had some question marks. There was the idea that even if
making love to Laurie wasn't a dire sin, but merely the resolution
of a biological urge, when you rubbed two young people together
you had a real mess on your hands. Clarence and Jesse listened to
a country-music station while having midmorning coffee out in the
work shed. I never cared for the music but it was impossible not to
be haunted by Hank Williams singing "Lovesick Blues." Older,
sensible senior boys headed to the prostitutes in Hurley, Wisconsin, and avoided local messes. Not me.

It was about three A.M. when I awoke from a heavy, half-drunken
sleep and sexy dream to find my penis was being sucked on, and
simultaneously smelled Laurie's scent mixed with a warm lilac odor
from an open window. I was instantly angry with her and made the
weakest effort to push her head away but then I had never experienced this daring physical act. Afterward I could smell my own
semen on her breath when she whispered that we would always be
"secret lovers." At first light, soon after five, I got up to go to Iron
Mountain, quickly dressed, and then looked back at Laurie nude
on her tummy in the tangle of sheets. I quickly made love to her
without taking off my work clothes but she gave no indication of
being awake. The idea that I could think straight had never been
more remote.

I wanted to get away very early before Fred arrived back from the
Club and changed his mind about the temporary swap of my Ford
for his pickup. He would anyway be in a bad mood. My mother
always bird-dogged her "little brother" around the Club during his
annual overnight visit in order to placate any quarrels he started.

Unlike Fred I had already figured out that the proportion of absolute assholes remained constant in any social class. Fred loved to
bait Republicans but in relatively subtle ways. He told me that the
year before my father and a group of men had gathered sitting
before a fireplace in someone's twelve-bedroom "cabin" with their
snifters of old brandy talking about Tom, Art, Kim, and Bob. They
always used first names for Thomas Dewey, Arthur Vandenberg
(a former senator), Kim Sigler (an ex-governor), and Robert Taft
from Ohio. Given enough to drink there would be stories about the
bizarre sexual tastes of the Kennedys and Lyndon Johnson. Fred
had interrupted with an absurd and lengthy lie about how he himself had made love to Angie Dickinson who was a devout Episcopalian in her backyard in Beverly Hills and how they had been
viciously attacked by her pet peacocks. I was amused thinking it
would be far simpler not to go to the Club in the first place, but
then Fred had lost most of his immediate inheritance in his divorce
over his affair with the black woman in Chicago and had to depend
somewhat on the kindness of relatives. I know it goaded him that
he couldn't figure out how to be totally self-supporting.

By noon I had located Glenn and his dad Herbert in a run-down
cabin near the Menominee River a few miles west of Iron Mountain. The river was big and slow and we launched my rowboat and
tied it to the small, rickety dock. We sat on the picnic table sorting
through our trout flies and ate a sandwich made of Italian cold cuts.
A lot of the miners around Iron Mountain are of Italian descent,
people my father referred to as "guineas" (Irish were "micks" and
since there were very few blacks in the area except out at the Sawyer
Air Base they were largely spared his language).

We left Herb sleeping off a hangover on a lawn chair and
drove over to the Fence River northeast of Amasa and Crystal

Falls. Midday isn't normally a good time for trout fishing but the weather was warm, still, and cloudy. Brook trout are simpleminded so it's always best to walk a distance from an easy access. I had heard about this particular stretch of the Fence River from John Voelker, our only famous Marquette area resident, who was a Michigan Supreme Court justice and had written the novel *Anatomy of a Murder.* Jimmy Stewart, Lee Remick, and Ben Gazzara starred in the movie version which was directed by Otto Preminger. Out of curiosity I had gone to a reception at the Club to meet these people with my parents and when I shook Lee Remick's lovely hand my insides had jellied. I knew that Judge Voelker disliked my father but he didn't hold it against me and gave me many trout fishing tips.

My father owned plenty of barely used fishing and hunting equipment, plus various sailing outfits though our sloop barely ever made it out of port except when two young men were hired to take it up to the Club just north of Big Bay. He needed all the equipment for the outings he took with a real wealthy friend and Yale classmate from Duluth, Minnesota, named Seward, who Cynthia had described as "another pervert." I noticed in the spring when this man had visited that he paid special interest to Cynthia and Laurie dancing to *Hullabaloo* on television, affecting a special interest in the program. He and my father both made a fetish out of fine French wines which they drank with dinner after loading up on gin martinis. When I stole a bottle of French wine Glenn said, "This shit doesn't have enough sugar in it."

We caught a half dozen brook trout and saw an osprey. It had always been a toss-up for me whether I'd rather be an osprey or a dog, with the osprey winning because it spent its life looking for fish to eat. My mother had gone through a period when she believed in reincarnation but was disappointed in my choices. The proper one was to want to come back as the king of England or a French count. I stood fast in favor of the osprey.

*   *   *

Thus began the best two months of my life up to that point, and perhaps since. The manual labor, which was mostly digging and building footings for the cement curbs, was an unalloyed freedom from my problems and abstractions. Within ten minutes of starting that Monday morning I was back within the pleasure of helping Clarence dig the garbage hole. I made four dollars an hour, which was more than enough to pay for my share of the cabin and food. Glenn's dad had taken up with a sassy waitress from an Italian restaurant, Ventana's, and twice a week we would splurge there rather than cooking at the cabin. We would order spaghetti with enormous meatballs and sausage, or spaghetti and steak if we felt flush. Most of the time, though, we'd eat a hurried meal at the cabin so we could take off trout fishing on the long summer evenings. The hard work made me tired the first two weeks but after that I was in good enough shape not to be drowsy during the evening's fishing, though one evening when I dozed off on the bank I awoke to find a bobcat staring at me from across the narrow river. On Saturdays we'd go farther afield over to Bruce's Crossing where we'd fish the Middle Branch of the Ontonagon. I was the driver because Glenn in the same manner as his father was always drinking beer when not actually working. This habit pretty much shitcanned his life, as they say locally, by his mid-thirties.

I suppose it was simpleminded to take so much pleasure from the elementary economic principle that work directly equals food and a bed but I was earning my own keep for the first time and sensed the possibility of independence from my parents. I loved my sagging bed in the cabin, the linoleum floors, the drizzling shower, the food that always seemed delicious because you were very hungry, the excitement of finding new streams to fish.

Only three things went wrong during those two months and they seemed minor at the time, though one of them proved not to

be. In the middle of the second week a young lawyer from the firm
that handled our family stuff showed up and it was embarrassing
to talk to him with other workers watching from a distance. Of
course my parents had sent him over. I told him I was fine and he
wondered if I needed money or anything. I said no and went back
to digging so he drove off in his MG. The other laborers except
Glenn and his dad thought I was in some sort of trouble.

The second item was a mixture of the good and bad. Glenn
and I had met some local high school girls at lunch at a hamburger
stand. We asked them to go to the movies that evening but when
we picked up my date at her parents' small bungalow her father, a
miner with crippled legs from over near Republic, was quite upset
when we were introduced and he caught my name. Standing there
before their front door which had a stack of cement blocks for steps
he asked me to repeat my name and where I was from. I did so and
felt sweat arising all over my body. His dowdy wife stood right
behind with her arms crossed but looking sympathetically at her
daughter who stared down at the ground. "I don't think you have
good intentions toward my little girl. You come from a bad family,
you bring her straight home after the movie."

Her name was Polly and we didn't go to the movie but drove
around with four of us in the front of the pickup, then took a walk
in the twilight on a country two-track. I was so self-conscious that
it felt like my insides had shrunk. Polly was a happy-go-lucky girl
and at the same time quite intelligent. In fact she was smart like
Cynthia but without the abrasive edges. When she tried to apologize for her father by saying that his legs hurt all the time I said
that her father wasn't wrong. I said that any self-respecting union
man should have shot my grandfather and great-grandfather and
then she said, "Then you wouldn't exist." We laughed about that.
"Why not your father, too?" she asked. "He never did much of
anything except spend money. There's no reason to shoot him. At

least I don't think there is." Polly was graceful and I had never met
anyone so serenely pleasant. She kissed my cheek when I dropped
her off and we met the next four days at the hamburger stand for
lunch after which she had to go over to Escanaba with her mother
because her grandfather had had a stroke and they couldn't afford
to keep him in a hospital. We exchanged a few letters and then faded
away from each other but only for the time being. Polly had a
strange off-brand beauty to her, and a peculiar way of talking from
being half-Finnish and half-Italian. I knew my father would have
loathed her but that wasn't what made me adore her. She simply
didn't have any neurotic twists, no half-demented hidden sorrows
in her character.

The third thing that went haywire and that I chose not to believe was when Donald drove Laurie and Cynthia over to see me one
Saturday morning in early August. I was irritated because I had had
no success rousing Glenn from his sleep in order to pack up and go
up to the Porcupine Mountains for an overnight fishing trip and now
the plan was being interrupted. Donald was evasive and wouldn't
quite meet my eyes. I asked him as a pissed-off favor to get Glenn
out of bed and pitch him in the river. He did so with Glenn yelling
"you fuckin' Indian." This was funny but only for moments. Cynthia
and Laurie approached me from the other side of the cabin yard and
Cynthia blankly said, "Laurie missed two periods since late June.
We'll know before school starts after Labor Day."

"How do you know it's me?" I asked with an intended air of
cruelty. Being a secret lover does not discount all the others.

"Because you're the only one she screws who is stupid enough
not to use a rubber," Cynthia hissed and Laurie turned away.

"And she's stupid enough not to take the pill." I walked over,
got in the pickup, and drove off with Glenn yelling and chasing the
truck in wet underpants. I stayed away for only a half hour, unable

to bear my own stupid cruelty. Simply enough, driving away wasn't Christian.

When I reached the cabin they were sitting in the yard drinking beer and smoking a joint. I walked over and took Laurie by the hand and led her to the rowboat.

"Don't drown her," Donald yelled and Cynthia slapped him.

We rowed quite a while before I could say anything and she was no help sitting there in the back seat sniffling and red-eyed, looking suddenly smaller and younger than her years so that I felt deceived by her previous somewhat coolish confidence about life, her imitation of Cynthia's flippancy when she didn't have Cynthia's mental equipment.

"I'm sorry," she finally said, and then sobbed. "I mean I don't know for sure." More sobs.

I couldn't imagine that I had fathered a child. It was out of the question despite biological facts. Once in a private experiment I tried to put on a condom I got from Glenn but it seemed both silly and bizarre. While rowing I glanced at Laurie's tummy in her pale blue shorts and decided it was impossible that there was a living piece of me inside those blue shorts. As a goofy alternative I felt sexually aroused and suggested that I pull the boat up and we make love in the woods.

"I don't feel up to it." Her voice was especially small leaning over the boat's gunnel to look at her reflection in the dark water. Now she looked lovely again with a leg stretched out for balance. The rejection somehow spun my mind back to the Gospels. The mind is capable of bad timing.

"I got this feeling you're not pregnant." Reassuring a waif was definitely Christian. "I've read up on the subject and there are a lot of reasons a girl can miss a period."

"Two. I missed two since Grand Marais."

"There are a lot of reasons a girl can miss two periods. Physically active girls in gymnastics or who run marathons miss periods," I recalled from reading about medicine in *Time* magazine.

"I've been in three tennis tournaments this summer," she said hopefully.

By now my head was throbbing and I had to go to the toilet though there was a slight feeling that I had convinced myself.

Back at the cabin Laurie kissed me good-bye before they drove off. While we packed for our camping trip Glenn, who had heard the whole story from Donald, said that he could easily find ten guys that had screwed Laurie so there was no way that I had to bear the responsibility by myself. I rejected this nasty idea without saying anything. Unlike other teenage males I couldn't get angry at Laurie's apparent promiscuity because I had known her since we were little children and I simply didn't know if the very popular word "love" had anything to do with us. I certainly couldn't run away because I was already in Iron Mountain. Asking advice from my father or the Baptist preacher was out of the question and Fred was back in Ohio, and besides he might still be angry at me. Clarence wasn't a possibility, partly because he had several illegitimate children from his wilder days and I knew from comments that he tended not to take middle- and upper-class concerns very seriously. His main ambition was to put food on the table. Once when I went to a fish fry at their ramshackle house in the woods, really a trailer with additions, I couldn't sort out the children, grandchildren, who belonged to whom. Some looked more Chippewa and some looked more Finnish. I had Jesse in reserve and idly wondered what the Mexican attitude to the problem might be. As the years passed he had taken on more responsibility and several times a month he would put on a trim blue suit and visit the accountant, the broker, the bank, and the legal firm. Once when I was twelve and we had visited one of my father's cousins in Palm Beach on spring vacation my father had introduced Jesse as a "whiz" or a "jack-of-all-trades." I hated the place except for the two days Jesse had taken me up to Stuart to go deep-sea fishing. I caught a sailfish which seemed the most beautiful creature I had ever seen. Other than that I followed sanderlings down the beach and noted how they would reach a certain point then fly out over the water returning to the point on the beach where I had first encountered them, and then there would be a new group of them. Cynthia never had any problems wherever we went. She read and danced. Once in New York City we were in a fancy hotel only an hour when Cynthia found a girl her age down the hall who also wanted to practice dance steps. It occurred to me that dancing for Cynthia was the same as the pleasure I took in manual labor or fishing. Maybe everyone was better off in a state of physical exhaustion.

Our trip began as a bust with a cold rain off Superior, and a screwed-up carburetor in the truck when we reached Ontonagon. I had lamely left my money in my suitcase back at the cabin. This disgusted Glenn who said that I didn't know the "value" of money, then regretted it and apologized. Of course he was right. Cynthia and I directly received fifty bucks a week from a small trust set up by my deceased grandmother on my mother's side. She had disliked and distrusted my father and had no intention of letting the money be funneled through his office. She wasn't very likable herself though she had a black man, Sam, who worked at her home in Evanston who would take me to museums in Chicago, also to Brentano's bookstore where I could have any books I wished. I also got to have a pizza and once went into a black restaurant and met some of Sam's friends and relatives. Anyway, I stored my money in my room what with having an aversion to going into banks, and now I had none to speak of.

So our asses were in a sling. We stood in a gas station drinking pop and watching it rain while a mechanic determined that it would require fifty dollars to get a carburetor from the junkyard and install it. We had only twenty-five between us and the gas station wasn't inclined toward credit. I was brain limp from dealing with Laurie or I would have figured it out sooner. My dad had a third cousin, named Sprague, an old bachelor who lived near Ontonagon who we saw only at rare funerals at St. Paul or in Evanston or Lake Forest. He was cranky but talked to me because of our common interest in fishing. My mother said he always wore the same suit he had had tailored in London in the 1920s. He seemed to dislike everyone in the family and there was the joke that he came to funerals only to make sure that so-and-so was dead. I called him and then put him on with the station owner who then told me the truck would be ready by dinnertime. Sprague sent over his hired woman, an enormous Finn, in a wood-paneled Ford station wagon from the late forties. The car was rusted out around the fenders and the woman drove it at top speed, slamming on the brakes at stop signs and then accelerating as fast as the car would go.

Sprague's house was large and gabled and had been past due for a paint job forever. He was more gaunt and frail than ever which made his Burkett jaw look larger. He shuffled when he moved around the den showing us a large collection of Indian blankets, pottery, and weapons from the Southwest where he spent the winters near Tucson.

The fried-chicken dinner was good but the conversation was harsh with Sprague railing against our family's "shameful" behavior in the 1880s and 90s in the timber era. "They cut twenty thousand acres they didn't own just west of here," he said, pointing at the wall. I said I had been looking into the matter and mentioned a number of details that pleased him. He hadn't touched his dinner and the huge Finnish woman, Nelmi, pushed the full plate toward Glenn who, though slender, could eat as much as anyone.

"I'm on my way out," Sprague said, then pinched my arm. "No one's had muscles in our family since the last century. You're breaking the mold."

"I've been behind the shovel for two months," I said, then with no hesitation told him a little about my project about finding the source of evil in my family.

"You're naive as hell. Do you think you can be honest when you have their feed bag around your neck? I taught school until I was forty-five then gave myself over to leisure, you know, fishing and travel and collection stuff, all the while convincing myself that most big money is dirty. Now I believe that some is a lot dirtier than others. We were people of immeasurable greed. We suffocated a hundred children up in the Keweenaw and don't you forget it."

"There's not much evidence one way or another from that long ago," I offered. "I've researched this and the newspapers said it was simply panic."

"Bullshit. If you're going to dig, dig deep. It was murder. The goons yelled *fire* in a crowded hall. That's murder."

That was that. Nelmi brought out a bottle of brandy and a pencil and paper. Sprague poured a large glass for himself and small ones for Glenn and I, and then drew us an intricate map for fishing including the combination to a gate lock saying it was only about a hundred acres but to fish where a small creek emptied into Superior, and after that there was a good beaver pond up the creek behind the cabin. We were welcome to stay in the cabin but there was "nothing" there. He also said he would ship me a carton of "research" material. He shuffled out on the porch with us to say goodbye looking at the sky critically and noting that the breeze had clocked around to the south. "Your father was only good at war, do you know that? Afterward he mostly spent money." I nodded though in fact my father never mentioned World War II and belonged to

no veteran's organizations, though Jesse had told me that if he had
stayed in the service he would have become a general. This was
impossible for me to believe though it later occurred to me that if
there was no vast stretch of land, big as some states, to devour you
could thrive only in a global war.

Sprague's cabin was unlocked and eerily empty though immacu-
late. It was about twenty by twenty with a small fieldstone fireplace,
a single bed, and a table with one chair. On the table there was a
typed card for intruders that read, "There's nothing here so don't
bother looking." There was no stove, toilet, pump, or any other
amenities. Glenn said, "This spooks the shit out of me," so we went
fishing for hours and camped down near the beach. I had noticed
that the cabin was perched on a hillock in such a way that you could
only see Lake Superior out the front window.

      The property was pristine with huge white pines and some
hardwoods shading the ground so that there was little understory
except the alders around the beaver pond. The land was bisected
by a small clear creek and when we reached the mouth we ducked
back having seen a school of coasters which are lake-run brook trout
and not very common. We were jittery when we rigged our fly rods
and flipped a coin for the first cast. Glenn won and caught a two-
pounder and then it became apparent that the fish weren't gun-shy
so we could both cast. We caught a dozen before dark and released
all but two which we kept for a midnight snack and ate with a six-
pack of beer Glenn had stowed in the cold creek. The northern lights
were astounding, whirling sheets and cones of rose and green and
bluish lights so strong they gave off a tinny metallic sound. Glenn
said that if we had some pussy it would be the most perfect night
in the world. I pretended to agree in the general enthusiasm but

inside I was relieved not to have thought about Laurie in half a dozen hours.

It was cool and windy in the morning with Superior too rough for the coasters. We fished the beaver pond with success and then I took a walk to work the creaks out of my body gotten from sleeping on the beach. Behind the cabin in a grove of hemlocks I was startled to find a simple gravestone partially covered with moss. My curiosity overcame my good taste and I scraped off the moss and read:

AMANDA SWENSON BURKETT
October 7, 1913–June 12, 1937

Sixteen-year-olds aren't good at mortality and my skin prickled. I went back to fishing but without energy as if the property had become an immense mausoleum.

It's almost appalling to think that a busted carburetor could make a specific difference in one's life. We got back to Iron Mountain on Sunday evening and I wrote a thank-you letter to Sprague. I made bold mention that he had promised to send some information. I wanted to ask about his peculiar cabin and the gravestone but then thought that neither was any of my business. I added a number of gratuitous comments about the nature of ancestral wrongdoings. Few sixteen-year-olds are wise enough to squirm at their pomposities. I had not yet come to consider that my arrogance in attacking this enormous project was simply another family trait.

On Monday morning Herbert woke us at five A.M. He had lost his sassy waitress and come to his senses. He was clearly panicked

over the idea that we were well behind on our work and in a few
weeks he would lose both of us to school. We began to work ten-
hour days, and then included Saturday which precluded our weekend fishing trips. In the last week our hours went up to twelve. The
other workers earned time and a half for overtime but Glenn and I
stayed unfairly on straight time. Glenn had an ugly quarrel with
his dad one night when they were beered up. Glenn swung and hit
Herbert a glancing blow that teared up his eyes. Herbert threw
Glenn through the screen door into the yard. I turned up Marquette
public radio until Brahms, not my favorite, was booming through
the cabin.

There was nothing left of me after working twelve hours and
eating too much to keep going. This was definitely the flip side of
manual labor where all the good feelings were lost to exhaustion.
It occurred to me to quit but I didn't want to go home until the
last possible moment. I took to drinking too much beer in the
evening like Glenn and Herbert and talking as stupidly as they
did under the influence. I also hadn't touched the half dozen books
I had promised to read for extra credit. My English teacher, Mrs.
Schmidt, had told me that I was her only student who wasn't utterly disappointing. I closed my duffel so I couldn't see the European novels she wanted me to read by Stendhal, Hamsun, Céline,
Gogol, Dostoyevsky, and Alain-Fournier. In short I felt dumb as
a stump.

The Friday evening before I left I ran into Polly on the street.
I was well oiled from drinking a whole six-pack after we had finished work, and then Herbert also had snuck us whiskey in the
darkened booth of the Italian restaurant. I walked off with Polly,
with Herb and Glenn yelling that they would leave without me
for the cabin.

We went to the city park but I was too drunk to talk intelli-
gently though naturally I told her I loved her. Given my condition

she thought this was very funny which made me angry but only for moments because I suddenly threw up. Polly helped me wash up at a drinking fountain and then I fell asleep for an hour or so sitting in the grass leaning against a tree. She was still there when I awoke so I walked her home. I had never felt stupider, a record I was to break several times in the ensuing weeks.

6

Laurie was pregnant. I found this out minutes after driving up the alley that Saturday. While I was talking to Clarence and Jesse, who said I now looked like a boxer, Cynthia came out of the back door of the house and told me right in front of the others. I felt a little dizzy and then suddenly coarse.

My parents and a lawyer met with Laurie's parents that Saturday afternoon and that evening she and her mother took a flight to Chicago. My father didn't say a single thing but my mother was absolutely disgusted holding her drink in the kitchen, saying, "The fruit doesn't fall far from the tree." I supposed that the tree meant Father.

Laurie returned within a week from Chicago and never mentioned her abortion when we took a walk out to Presque Isle. She started to a couple of times but couldn't talk. She pretended to be quite angry because I had throttled her halfback boyfriend Brent the first day of gym class when he confronted me. I had no idea how to fight so I threw him down and got him in a choke hold.

I had gained a bunch of weight and muscle and an assistant coach suggested that I go out for the football team because I caught the ball well when we played touch football in gym class, but then we had too many good players in the end position so they made me a middle linebacker, a fine way for a young man to vent his anger. In the fifth game of the season on a frozen field in Sault Sainte Marie I broke my left ankle which was put in a cumbersome cast. After the cast was taken off in January I rebroke the ankle coming out of the Peter White Library onto an icy sidewalk. I spent a month in my room in a state of clinical depression with Cynthia bringing home my schoolwork.

I wasn't the only news in the family. A week before Christmas while my father was visiting his Yale crony Seward in Duluth they both had been arrested for "consorting" with underage girls. It certainly never made the Marquette newspaper, and it wasn't a family crisis because my mother fled for Chicago to be under the care of her phantom-pain doctor. I must say that my father handled it with aplomb, not missing his annual tradition of having a hundred roasts of beef distributed to the poor so they could have a "proper" Christmas. My own knowledge of the prosecution of my father's crime was thirdhand, if that, but by February he was off for six weeks to a medical facility for alcoholics outside of Minneapolis, a plea bargain with the judge. I've always found it odd in American jurisprudence that the punishment for certain crimes is mitigated if the perpetrator is drunk. I'm also certain that a goodly amount of money went to the parents of the underage girls. Jesse was busy that winter

driving my father to Duluth though he also made two trips alone.
Mrs. Plunkett left the dining table in tears one evening when
Cynthia said, "They should put the fucker in jail," meaning our
father. After he got out of the alcohol clinic he spent most of the
winter in Florida.

After two months in Chicago my mother returned for a week
in March to discuss my father. I don't know what she expected us
to say. Cynthia kept glancing down at a novel she was reading by
Alan Sillitoe. For want of anything better to say I offered that she
and Father should try six months of counseling before making such
a big decision about divorce. Cynthia looked at me in astonishment
and I realized that she had also read Ann Landers that day in the
Detroit Free Press. That evening Cynthia told me that she suspected
that Mother looked so nice because she was having an affair in
Chicago. "At her age?" I said loudly, and Cynthia said, "She's only
forty-three and as usual you don't know shit."

When the cast from the second severe break came off I was
put back in the hospital because my ankle hadn't healed properly.
An orthopedic surgeon would decide the next morning whether to
operate and then put me back in yet another cast. It was an unusu-
ally warm March evening and the whole town was melting from
two hundred inches of dirty snow. Cynthia brought me in a portion of Mrs. Plunkett's lasagna and a full jar of red wine. Cynthia
had recently found the hiding place for the key to my father's wine
cellar and we had been availing ourselves to some bottles. "Lynch-
Bages 1953," she announced pouring into a spare water glass. There
were "get well" cards from my father and Laurie with his postmarked Key West, with a note that said, "Fishing is great" which I
doubted. My ex-minister from the Baptist church stopped by on
his pastoral rounds of the hospital. He gave me a fresh Gideon copy
of the King James Version of the Bible. I introduced them and
Cynthia sat down gravely as if hanging on every word the minister

said. She was on her way to a party and her miniskirt revealed a lot of leg if not more. The minister had begun a longish wandering metaphor of Christianity as both a militia (onward Christian soldiers) and an athletic contest (the race goes to the swift). Cynthia lit a cigarette which even then was questionable in a hospital room and I thought I caught the odor of cannabis in her Old Gold filter. She plainly unnerved the pastor and would have likely upset any man except her brother.

Late that evening with moonlight flooding the room I got up and dressed having pretty much decided against an operation and more months in a cast. I had been reading Dostoyevsky's *The Possessed* for extra credit in Mrs. Schmidt's class and had reached the part where Krylov bites Stavrogin's ear in a dark room. The novel, among other things, had shown me how infantile my search for the source of evil in my family had been. I had continued the project by reading background books on the timber and mining industries, and exchanging several letters with Sprague who had sent along a carton of material from his corner of the family. My last letter had gone unanswered and I wondered if he had died.

I sat down by the window and stared at the moon making sure I had reached the right decision about leaving the hospital without the ankle operation. I stared at the moon so long that my mind went quite blank to everything including the passing cars, the hospital sounds (a dropped bed pan in the hall and a male orderly saying "damn"), and the contradictory voices in my own mind. In the furthest corner of my brain, however, I realized that I was helplessly experiencing the same sort of trance I had gone through in the alley behind the work shed near the lilacs though this time I was less frightened about losing my mind. Time became foreshortened and I could see the moon move. It was hyperreal and at the same time soothing to "lose" my mind. Toward the end my brain visited several locations including the cliff over Lake

Superior where my father's brother Richard had fallen and died, Sprague's "nothing" cabin west of Ontonagon, and a lovely stretch of the Fence River where I had fallen asleep while fishing. The difference was that I was seeing everything much more vividly than when I had actually been in these places. I had visually recorded them with much greater clarity than I had thought possible and there was the delicious freedom of not thinking about myself to which I had aspired. In the last few moments of the trance I had moved to the shadow behind Polly's ear and then to the back of Laurie's knee beaded with lake water. I lost the moon when a nurse on her rounds interrupted me with "why aren't you in bed?" and I answered "because I'm sitting in a chair," which she found amusing. A few minutes after she left I slipped out of the hospital. I noted by my watch, I had spent hours in this strange state, that it was nearly six A.M. and the diner downtown would be open. I had a slight limp from the bum ankle and was careful what with melting snow and puddles having refrozen in the night so that parts of the sidewalk were miniature skating rinks.

Clarence was there with two of his trapping buddies. During the winter Clarence ran a trap line and when the moon was big he could check it at night. He told me that he needed the extra money to feed grandchildren and he was hoping Donald would get a football scholarship so he wouldn't have to chip in. Clarence waved me over to their table and I was amazed how much these scruffy men were eating but supposed that walking all night on snowshoes would make you pretty hungry. One of the other men called Bobber was darkly Indian and had recently healed slash marks on his face. He saw me looking and humorously explained he had an argument over a woman down in Rapid River. After eating their breakfasts the men dozed on their chairs waiting for their day jobs to start. Clarence would often cat nap and Cynthia and I would try to sneak up on him unnoticed but never succeeded. Jesse joined us wearing an overcoat and blue suit and carrying an alligator-skin briefcase he had brought up years before from Veracruz. Despite his dark color everyone in Marquette seemed to like Jesse for his ready smile and impeccable manners. He was thought to be razor sharp on business matters though he didn't seem to care if he was wearing his blue suit or the white jacket my mother demanded when he served at her tea or cocktail parties.

After his coffee and donuts Jesse nodded me outside and on the street asked me why I wasn't at the hospital. Clarence had already said, "I thought they were going to cut on you today," after his friend Bobber had explained his own scars. I told Jesse that I needed a break and couldn't bear to be back in a leg cast, and then he smiled, shook my hand, and said that late the evening before he had gotten a phone call from a lawyer in Ontonagon and I had inherited a cabin and property from cousin Sprague.

I stood there tingling and then walked up the steep hill and down Ridge Street to our house where I got in the pickup and drove to Ontonagon to see my second home. I was now a landowner and the feeling was nearly as extreme as losing my virginity. I could now totally escape my family and live on fifty bucks a week. I was now seventeen and a free man. Absurdly, I sang the current civil rights anthem "O Freedom" in my awful voice. I was an hour out and west of Champion when I noted the heavy snowbanks along the road and it occurred to me that I might not be able to get close to the cabin. I drove on into a gathering blizzard which was a near whiteout by the time I reached Ontonagon. The last two miles of the county road up to the property gate were unplowed and covered by immense snowdrifts formed by the wind off Lake Superior. I sat there counting my money with the engine heat ticking away and the truck shuddering in the cold wind. I had enough to buy snowshoes or

perhaps hire someone to haul me out to the cabin on a snowmobile
though the latter was improbable because snowmobiles are designed
for trails and when I got out of the truck I sunk into my waist beyond the end of the plowed road. The snow also made my questionable ankle ache as if there had been a nail driven in it. Despite
the disappointment my heart was still full when I drove back to town
and found a motel. It didn't make the cabin less mine that I might
have to wait until late April or early May to see it again.

I stood in the motel room for a while looking at the blizzard
out the window then walked over to Sprague's house but it was
dark and closed up tight. I couldn't remember his housekeeper's
last name, her first was Nelmi, nor could I figure out standing
there on a residential street in the blinding snow why I wished to
see her anyway. I was cold and exhausted and went back to the
motel room, drew an easy chair up to the window, then fell asleep
staring at the frightening whiteness of the world. It was clearly a
blank canvas on which you could paint your life if you cared to.
Just before sleep I imagined sitting at the cabin window and
painted the interior of what would be my cabin, including the front
window from which the only visible thing was Lake Superior and
the line of the horizon, but there was the nagging idea Fred had
explained that as a putative Christian I had to learn how to function in the world before I earned the right to retreat. Fred joked
that one had control of the world when sitting on the toilet but
that was a limited venue.

When I awoke late in the afternoon the snow had stopped but
the wind had further lifted so that the window rattled and Lake Superior in the distance was rumpled. I took the ubiquitous Gideon
Bible from the dresser and it seemed almost too heavy to lift. There
was a single piece of motel stationery in the drawer and a ballpoint
pen near the phone. I wrote:

1. God created the cosmos billions of years ago then departed leaving everything up for grabs.
2. God probably doesn't monitor our activities with our genitals.
3. Jesus was the son of God but then he said in a mystifying passage so is everyone else.
4. You can separate the words of Jesus from the rest of the New Testament and see that most of it is add-ons for the convenience of the temporal church.
5. The Church seems to encourage people to be evil. Fred says this is to ensure the Church's power.
6. Fred says that when he sees a politician who has further crushed the poor pray in public he wants to pick up a gun.
7. When the Church wedded itself to worldly power it lost its actual connection with Jesus.
8. Laurie no longer will speak to me. I told her I had bought condoms. She is seeing a psychologist counselor who told her to spend a full year without fucking anyone. Cynthia has settled down to only Donald. I still say my prayers including my wish to stop thinking about fucking Laurie but this hasn't panned out. It's the most pleasure I've ever had and now it's gone. It's easier to write about sex than God and Jesus. Glenn pointed out a kingfisher last summer and asked aloud, "Who made that up?" On the way back to Crystal Falls a bluebird flew into the truck radiator. We stopped and the bird was stuck in the grill, its eyes still flickering. Then its eyes closed for good. Glenn asked, "Why did this have to happen?" I said, "Birds will never figure out cars." It is startling how light in weight birds are. I crossed a ditch, slipped through a fence, and dug a small hole with my hands. I was already kneeling so I

prayed, "God take the spirit of this bird to heaven." I put a stone on the bird's grave, thinking that I kill lovely fish and eat them.

9. Why did God allow evil people like my parents and their ancestors to be created? Or me for that matter.
10. I think I'll call Polly in Iron Mountain. Is this a good idea?

I had used both sides of the piece of paper so I called Polly. She was depressed because her dad was in the Veteran's Hospital getting another operation on his legs that were crippled in the mining accident. My family had started the mining company in the nineteenth century. We were still big stockholders though the stock wasn't going to be worth much anymore according to Jesse. I didn't say so but I believed my family would have been better off broke.

I asked Polly if I could drive down to Iron Mountain and see her. She told me I was nuts because the weather was awful. I was lucky enough to follow a series of snowplows but it was slow going and I didn't make Iron Mountain until eleven in the evening. I sipped from a pint of schnapps Glenn kept under the truck seat and ate a ham sandwich. When Polly came over to my room she said she had told her mother where she was going and her mother had said, "My father hated your dad because he was only a miner. This is just the reverse." Polly thought this was funny but then she was always in a good mood. Much later I found out this condition was called "hyperthymia" where the victim is always happy. We talked and necked on the bed and she told me she wasn't going to go "all the way" and never had. I asked why and I proudly drew a condom from my wallet. "That's not the point," she said. "I'm not sure about you." It turned out she had a cousin in Marquette who called her about the gossip surrounding Laurie's abortion and later my father's "problem" in Duluth. I had the unvoiced feeling that it would be nice to live in New York City where not everyone knew your secrets like they did in the Upper Peninsula. She declined a sip and I finished the rest of Glenn's schnapps in two gulps. I had recently read the disturbing *Brothers Karamazov* and it dawned on me that I was all three brothers plus the idiot half brother in one body when I wanted to be the holy younger brother Alyosha. I was downcast but then she announced that we could fool around and within a few minutes I was nude and she was down to her panties which she said would stay on until she "tied the knot," a peculiar idiom for marriage. I wasn't prepared for the nudeness of her nudity. It was almost too much of a good thing, as they say, and compared to Laurie, Polly was soft and lush and with breasts large enough to be embarrassing to her. We did everything but the final connection and I easily admitted to myself that it was more fun that way. While I gnawed at her panties I felt too much of her teeth and when I winced I heard a muffled "sorry." She became spasmodic and flopped around in slow motion and I was briefly afraid that she was having some kind of seizure. I had to massage a cramp out of her foot and was delighted at the fullness of her laughter. I was as happy as I had ever been and I laughed myself which was rare. When she left I stood by the door in my underpants letting the icy wind cool my body. I told her that I loved her and she gave my dick a yank and said "you just love coming off" and her laughter enclosed the snowy parking lot. I stood there until she drove off in her ancient Plymouth with the tires spinning in an icy moan.

In the morning she stopped by for a scant fifteen minutes on her way to school. She wore a pleated skirt and her legs were very cold to the touch compared to her vulva which seemed like a miniature electric heater only soft. I shuddered when her icy hand touched my penis so she substituted her mouth. She said, "It was my first time doing this last night and here I'm already doing it in the morning," then laughed. Afterward she wondered how I could miss school so much and I said that they scolded me but that I always got all A's so they didn't push it. I was a junior while Polly was a senior. Her principal told her she was a sure thing for a tuition scholarship at Michigan State down in East Lansing and that she was sure she could earn her own room and board. As usual the struggles of real people embarrassed me. When she left I returned temporarily to a maudlin state. What the fuck was I doing toying with this lovely young woman but then I decided I would marry her in a minute. This posed a specific problem as I had already decided that I never wanted to father children. I was convinced that I should do my part to stop my family's genes from spreading in the world. I was supposedly smart according to the tests but then, strangely enough, my father had graduated magna cum laude from Yale and my mother had done very well too all of which proved that intelligence could be a suspicious factor. When my father pointed out his diploma on his den wall to visitors I always wanted to offer that "this man would be better off if he was dumber, the world would be a better place," and so on.

7

My parents returned in early April from their separate locations both looking tanned and comparatively fit but then a tan can cover a multitude of sins. Mother had been in Bermuda, and father in Palm Beach and Key West. He had actually gone fishing and had many photos of sailfish, tarpon, and bonefish to prove it. Always the young detective I noted certain consistent elbows, knees, thighs, backs, bathing-suit-clad butts but never the face in the photo. I couldn't fault him on his taste but only hoped she was vaguely adult though I knew the age of consent varied from state to state with Mississippi at the lowest at fourteen.

Cynthia wept that Mrs. Plunkett was gone but then recovered in a few days. When not in school that winter and spring I spent

most of my spare time at the library though my mission had become
a little stale in the welter of historical fact and county and regional
maps. Twice a week after their arrival my parents drove down to
Escanaba for reasons of privacy and visited a marriage counselor.
I allowed myself a shred of hope. After all one can't help but love
one's parents even though this love seems to emerge mostly from
the closeness and dependency of early childhood. Cynthia had
taken to spending time with Donald's aunt back in the woods over
south of Au Train. Cynthia told me that she liked to help this
woman, a full-blood Chippewa, but with two young grandchildren
whose mother had died from alcoholism. Cynthia wasn't allowed
in Clarence's house because he was fearful over his job. One late
night Cynthia told me that Father had tried to "tinker" with her a
couple times when he was very drunk. I said I had guessed that
the summer before when I saw her whack him with a garden stake.
She was amused when she thought about that particular scene. Occasionally I am appalled by her toughness. I can't quite believe it.
When I asked Fred about it he admitted he had also been puzzled
and asked a psychiatrist about Cynthia. The psychiatrist said though
it was impossible to accurately make a long-range diagnosis that
perhaps one out of ten thousand young women were that resiliently
strong. He had never run into one in his practice for obvious reasons
but had seen the condition referred to in professional literature.
Fred added that there is really no pathology to study in the strong
and mentally healthy.

    We were corresponding again after our spat of last August.
Fred held out the prospect of my helping him teach disadvantaged
kids how to read and write, a government project inelegantly called
"Catch Up." With my gimpy ankle there was no chance I could
return to the serene life of a manual laborer. Glenn had anyway
reached a dead end having lost his driver's license on two drunk-
driving charges only three weeks apart. The social services people

decided to dry him out under lock and key. It had been over two years since Glenn had visited our house. He said he didn't like the way my parents looked at him though they were polite. I decided not to correct him. In truth people like Glenn simply didn't viably exist as humans to my parents. We had a falling out on the first day of trout season in late April, normally the happiest of times. It was a cold rainy day and I could spend only ten minutes at a time wading in the river without my ankle becoming unbearable. Glenn called me a "pussy" in a genuinely hostile way. I chided him for having a pint of schnapps in his creel because if he got caught he was back in what he called the "zoo" under lock and key. "Fuck you rich kid," he yelled glugging at his schnapps. He drank the whole pint within an hour, then fell face forward into the Middle Branch of the Escanaba. I went over my waders saving his sorry ass. He fell asleep in the truck when I drove him home. He was shivering violently in his sleep and when we reached his place he fought me off when I tried to help him into the house bloodying my lip. Glenn was my only close friend. Everyone else was an acquaintance. When he was about ten his mother had taken off with a transferred enlisted man from Sawyer Air Base. Herbert with Glenn along had chased them all the way out to a Strategic Air Command base in North Dakota but she wouldn't come back.

By mid-May and near the end of school, my junior year, my mind began to fail me. I had ten spiral notebooks full of material on my project without touching the carton Sprague had sent me. Mrs. Schmidt had me read *The Stranger* by Albert Camus and I'm not sure it helped what with my propensity to fall into characters until I was close to suffocation. I had loathed *Catcher in the Rye* thinking the hero to be a wimp though, of course, it was the insufferable resemblance of my character to his however slight.

An uncommon early wave of heat came in May and I further delaminated. For instance, after my mumbled prayers at night I'd turn my bed light off and on a hundred times to make sure everything in the room was in its proper place. I think that's why I did it. The degree to which I had failed in my secondary project of not thinking about myself stunned me. I gibbered in a letter to Fred who was alarmed enough to write back immediately to say that I should stop everything except rowing the boat which I hadn't done yet this spring. He said that there was no political solution for the disease of greed in my family, past and present. I sounded like a young version of Karl Marx wired on lysergic acid. I could tell he wasn't really joking. How could I at age seventeen expect to figure out the nature of greed when the world's great philosophers hadn't been decisive on the matter? Maybe I should buy a recording of "Pomp and Circumstance" and play it around the clock. When you're aiming at the big thing you have to take care of the little things. In short, Fred wasn't gentle.

Even my parents untypically noticed my slump and insisted on seeking professional help though what they meant were the magic pills they used. Fred had said that people of inherited wealth largely had nothing to do while all the others mostly didn't like what they were doing to make a living. Life had clearly become an impasse.

I noticed with mild sadistic pleasure that my father was having financial problems. The den door was always closed and you could hear his shouts of "buy" or "sell" while he talked on the phone. Meanwhile my mother had commissioned a private detective to follow Cynthia after school and confronted her at dinner over the fact that she was still seeing the forbidden Donald. Cynthia said, "You could have saved money by asking me." My father who was fueled by his martinis tried to lighten the atmosphere by saying that since Donald was half-Finn and half-Indian he could be called a "Findian." Nobody laughed but him. I looked down at my whitefish that had been baked into white cardboard. Along with Cynthia I had been losing too much weight since the departure of Mrs. Plunkett. I had also given up fishing and drinking. It was mid-May and I hadn't caught a single rainbow or brown trout, and my experience with Glenn two weeks before had made drinking unattractive.

I was oddly charmed by my parents' silly efforts in my behalf. To my surprise Jesse picked me up after school on Friday saying he needed to talk to me. Jesse always minded his own business on personal matters and I could see my father's assignment was difficult for him. He began by saying that mine was the time of life that I should also be dancing, having a few beers, and chasing young women. I was studying too much and it was "hurting" my head and my unfortunate experience with Laurie shouldn't be allowed to poison women for me. Why did I like only "old time" music and never go dancing? I tried to explain that I didn't like rock and roll though I didn't go into my private theory that both modern music and television were the "soma" Aldous Huxley spoke of in his novel *Brave New World*. My schoolmates listened to thousands of hours of rock and roll and it had obviously scrambled their brains. Jesse said that when we got home he would loan me some records from Veracruz and perhaps I would like them. I had heard his music faintly from the windows of his apartment over the garage during warm weather. Jesse was so discreet that it was never loud enough to truly hear it and you felt only the slightest throb of the marimbas.

We had a nice dinner at the Mather Inn during which he told me I also must have my ankle operated on because I couldn't limp through my life like an old man. I said maybe later in the summer because when school got out I was heading down to Ohio to teach poor kids how to read and write with Fred. "Teaching poor kids will make you feel worse," he said then got up to use the lobby telephone.

After dinner we drove around the block twice in the twilight passing an attractive but rather bulky girl who was leaning against a lightpole reading a magazine. "Do you like her?" Jesse asked. "She's a present from me to you." I thanked him and said I had a girlfriend over in Iron Mountain. "A girl way over in Iron Mountain can only be in your head," he shrugged.

When we got home there was a note from Clarence saying he would pick me up for fishing at six A.M. I played some of Jesse's Veracruz music and again I admit it made me feel better. I called Polly to see if I could drive over to see her and got a knife in the stomach. Her little sister had found some of my letters and showed them to her father who was still convalescing and would be forever. She couldn't see me "up here" under any condition but she was starting at Michigan State early this summer to make sure she had a job in the kitchen of a dormitory. I could see her in East Lansing in June. That was that.

Perhaps Clarence was less wise than Jesse. It's hard to tell because he wasn't verbal and in our culture if you're smart you better say something smart or at least catchy. I had wanted to go down and fish the confluence of the Middle Branch of the Escanaba and the main river but Clarence had only a few hours because my mother liked our yard to look like a golf green and he had to mow before she threw a baby shower for a friend's daughter.

We were an hour out on the Deadstream with me rowing before Clarence said anything at all.

"I heard you was down in the dumps."

"I guess so."

"I figured. I bet you can fish your way out of it. Or row. A body gets restless if it doesn't get tired."

Absurd as that sounds it's true. After a couple of hours Clarence had to get back for mowing but I returned, made a sandwich, and rowed until midafternoon. When I got home I called Laurie and asked her to go to a movie and she said "why not?" I hadn't seen much of her since Cynthia was spending so much time with Donald. We went to an early movie, the seven to nine, and saw *Picnic* which she liked and I didn't but I avoided saying so.

After the movie there was a warm rain but barely more than a sprinkle. We went out to Presque Isle and walked up the west side keeping an eye on the yellow glow of the setting sun behind the darker clouds of an approaching storm. She had broken up with her halfback boyfriend Brent who was unhappy about her abstinence. "I hope you didn't call for that," she said. I said only that I had seen her hitting tennis balls with her coach and I was lonely to talk to her. "I can beat him this year," she said proudly. I had a lump in my throat and apologized for what had happened the summer before. "You didn't do it by yourself," she said shyly. "I just thought boys carried rubbers." I joked that I did now but hadn't used one yet. She nudged me toward a thicket. "It's too wet for my skirt. You get on the ground." I did and we necked for a while and then naturally I tried to put the condom on backward and it popped into the grass so she helped. The light was still yellowish and it had begun to rain in force and then it got darker. I brushed a mosquito off her bare hip and she said "thanks." Afterwards when she was lying on top of me despite the hard rain she said, "It's strange how much fun it is when you do it because you really want to." Now there was thunder and I had my mouth open to catch rain because my mouth was dry from exertion. I was idiotically trying to figure out if I had done the right thing. I had my hands on her crouched knees and suddenly thought, this is her knee not my knee, and I am not the center of the universe. She is she and I am I. It sounds just on the edge of stupid but it wasn't to me, as if I had previously thought myself the hub of an old-fashioned wheel and all others were spokes emanating from my core. Lying there looking up at an occasional flash of lightning my mind spun with the consequences of these thoughts. I slipped my hands around Laurie's rain-wet butt as if it was a marvel which it was. She had a tiny penlight and inspected the condom for flaws, giggling as she did so. We made love again. Back in the dome light of the pickup she was a radiant waif. We were as wet as if we had been swimming in our clothes.

When I got home my father was watching the Stanley Cup hockey playoffs. He was a little drunk but affable. When I was younger we would watch the Detroit Lions or the Green Bay Packers play football but neither of us was much interested so we stopped. In the eastern U.P. men follow the Lions but to the west where the U.P. is contiguous to Wisconsin they are Packer fans. My father thought of football as a military metaphor, a kind of fake war. I sat down on a couch and drank a beer. He looked at my clothes dripping on the floor as if waiting for an explanation but I offered none. He said it was sad to hear that my friend Glenn was having problems. He sounded sincere and without the usual ironic backspin and I replied that Glenn was a kamikaze drinker. Of course having spent a couple of years in the South Pacific during World War II "kamikaze" had a special meaning to him. He turned to me gravely and said, "It can be a terrible disease. I started loving alcohol when I was fourteen. My brother Richard could take it or leave it." His hands waved at some invisible point in the air. For a unique moment I felt compassionate. "I hope it's not a problem for you," he said. He was staring at me and I said I didn't think so. I averted my eyes to a locked book cabinet of my mother's first editions of Robert Frost, as if anyone in Marquette would steal them. I thought of Frost as tedious but my mother had seen him perform several times when she was in college and loved his work. She was

disappointed when Frost consented to read at the Kennedy inau-
gural. "I heard Robert Frost was mean when he was drunk," I offered. My father took this comment quite seriously and said, "Then
he could be mean when he wasn't drunk. I still regret the dog." He
was referring to an incident when I was in second grade. My father
had a nasty bulldog at the time because of his sentimental attach-
ment to Yale. The dog severely bit the hand of a little girl classmate
of mine and her father, a county road worker, came over and shot
the dog on our lawn. My father got the man fired and they moved
away from Marquette. I knew that he had paid to get the girl's hand
fixed but so what? At that moment I wanted him to regret an incident with Clarence but there was a question of whether he remembered it. Once a few years back when he was red-eyed and drinking
in the morning he was yelling at Clarence out in the flower garden.
Clarence was kneeling over a bed of flowers and my father tried to
kick him but Clarence caught his shoe and upended him. I saw it
from the bedroom window. I was uncomfortably pleased.

I finished the beer and said good-night. My father smiled.

"Tell the young lady to trim her nails."

"Pardon," I said but he was pointing at my shoulders. There
was a little blood coming through my shirt on both shoulders from
Laurie's fingernails tightly holding on. I was too embarrassed to
say anything. Maybe he thinks I'm like him, I thought.

8

It's hard to admit cowardice even when you're trying to be completely honest. I mean that however young I was at seventeen I liked to think of myself as a man and this experience turned me back into a boy for a single night. A few days after my falling out with Glenn I drove over to Ontonagon one afternoon to see the property Sprague had willed me. I was alarmed at the outset because within the severity of my depression I seemed to have tunnel vision and driving west on Route 28 in early May I was unable to enjoy the first pastel greens of spring. It was similar to driving through the kind of large pipe they use to construct water mains. My breath was periodically short and I couldn't swallow properly as if there were a lump of coal beneath my breastbone I would never be able to dislodge.

When I neared the cabin there were still patches of snow in the woods which were stark and bare with few signs of spring this close to cold Lake Superior. I unpacked my stuff and was surprised how cold the cabin was. In my haste I had brought along two peanut butter and jelly sandwiches which I didn't ordinarily like and a can of sardines and crackers, but had forgotten anything to drink. I didn't have a container for water so I went down to the beach and knelt drinking directly from the lake which was flat and slate gray in the twilight, eerily calm. In my haste I had forgotten a flashlight so I quickly gathered pine-twig kindling and deadfall branches to build a fire among a jumble of rocks in front of the cabin. I also cleared out a fairly even place near the fire and put down my sleeping bag. I had also forgotten a pillow but could use my duffel bag. It was too late to start fishing, especially without a flashlight. I tried to figure out why someone had left a pickax leaning against the front steps of the cabin. There had been tracks on the road coming in and someone had known the combination for the gate lock. I was a bit spooked and began to think about how black bears fresh out of hibernation occasionally but rarely kill and eat people, or so I had heard from Clarence who had told me how a drunken Indian had fallen asleep and been eaten near the Soo. I felt embarrassed when I strapped on my great-grandfather's long-barreled Colt .44 pistol. My father had given it to me for decoration for the mantel of the fireplace in my room. Glenn had got hold of some shells through a cousin and we had shot it a few times but were discouraged by the kick and the deafening noise.

It was now twilight and I lit the fire with difficulty. The deadfall limbs were still damp from snowmelt but I recalled seeing a few white pine stumps on a hillock to the west of the beaver pond. I took the pickax to try and separate some slabs of wood from the stump, but when I got around to the back of the cabin I saw that a small round hole about a foot wide had been dug near the grave of Sprague's young wife. There was a pretty fresh mound of dirt and I inappropriately dug with my hand until I found a small Indian pot that I had seen in Sprague's den. It contained his cremated ashes and tiny bits of bone I could feel with my fingers in the gathering dark. I might have known, I thought, feeling ashamed. I re-covered the hole and hurried up the hillock with the pickax and managed to gather some slabs from the ancient stumps. They got my fire going to a comforting roar which would dry out the damp limbs. I would have to use my wood sparingly to make it last as it was too dark to find more.

I looked down at my hands which were dirty from the grave dirt and finally admitted why I had brought along the pistol. I was thinking about killing myself. I felt dizzy and sat down on my sleeping bag. I took out the pistol and examined it in the firelight. It looked utterly unfamiliar but it was loaded. Curiously, I was vain enough to decide against the mess that would be made if I shot myself in the head. The target would have to be the heart which was thumping rapidly. I looked up at the stars which were thick above the firelight. I knew my constellations but at this juncture of my life the stars meant nothing to me. I massaged my sore ankle thinking that it was about to escape this irritating pain. I was disturbed by the suicide cartoon images with the comic caption of "good-bye cruel world." Did I wish to hurt my parents or merely remove myself from their world? For a few weeks now I had begun to suspect the character of my loneliness. I must relish it because it simply wasn't that hard to make friends in the easygoing north, though in truth people similar to my own nature were hard to find. I thought of Clarence and Jesse and Cynthia and Polly and Laurie. And Fred. I was closest to Fred in terms of mental companionship and it was only a month before I'd see him in Ohio. I added a slab of dry white pine, the skin gray but the decayed wood an ocher color. Why save wood if you're going to shoot yourself? I stood up. I wasn't going to take it sitting down. I stumbled on a stone and barely caught myself at the edge of the fire. I burned my thumb and knew I should soak it in cold water. Should I bother? I looked to the east and saw the white crescent top of the moon, two days before full, beginning to rise out of Lake Superior. My burned thumb hurt like hell and I scrambled down the slope and soaked it in the creek. Since I was about ten my parents had allowed me to walk along the beach on nights the moon was in its larger phases. My daffy mother believed that the study of nature was a good thing though any details were quite beyond her. Half up and throwing a skein of light between us, the moon was as white as Polly's panties. Goose bumps arose when I heard a rustling up by my campfire. I drew the pistol and crawled slowly up the bank and saw a tiny year-old bear of perhaps fifty pounds scooting off with my paper bag of peanut butter and jelly sandwiches. Luckily the slender container of sardines fell out of the sack. I stood there puzzled about what I should do and watching the big moon light up the world with the shoreline in both directions becoming visible. If I shot myself I clearly wouldn't be able to bring Polly here, she of the white pant-ies. Was this enough to keep me alive? I tried to remember where in the Bible it said you shouldn't kill yourself. I had two allies, Polly and Jesus. I had an iron heart and never cried but right then I began to sob like a truly hungry baby. I wanted to throw the pistol out into the lake in case I changed my mind but then maybe a much larger bear would arrive looking for food. For a moment I thought I felt the moon herself beckoning me toward life.

9

When I left Marquette the first week of June there nearly was a song in my heart, almost but not quite, a tribute to the mercurial nature of my emotions. After the wet evening with Laurie and my suicide night I returned to the earth from wherever I was. I fished and rowed and studied for finals which were a pushover. I varied my listening to somber music with Jesse's records from Veracruz, the distinctly Caribbean rhythms quite literally entering the body so that if you listened to the music late in the evening it entered your dreamlife. I shocked Cynthia by actually buying records by Otis Redding and Wilson Pickett which were a soul tonic compared to her Beach Boys and Beatles. My parents were wrangling over the visits to the marriage counselor of which my father described as "fatiguing" though he had nothing else to do except brood about his pratfalls on the stock market. The evening before I left they quarreled, of all things, about reincarnation. My mother had made pot roast at my request, one of the few dishes she made well, so I could pack pot roast sandwiches for my trip. They were getting ready for their summer at the Club in the big lodge my grandfather had built that to me had all the charm of a morgue. I was watching them closely but not listening carefully to the reincarnation quarrel about past and future lives, the logic of which was lost in the usual martini haze. My mother was making, as always, an attempt to stay high-minded while my father joked that in a past life he was a stray dog that got run over by a Model A Ford and in a future life he would return as a toad or a guppy. During dessert (tapioca pudding) I doubted if my father had ever considered suicide. He had an unfounded belief in the innate superiority of his bloodlines. In short, it was a good time to leave town, and that's what I did.

Early the next morning I had a good-bye breakfast with Clarence and Jesse at the diner. I was anxious to get going but Cynthia wasn't an early riser and I knew she was spending the night with Donald at his relatives near Au Train, a scant hour to the east. Jesse was thinking of bringing his daughter Vera with him when he returned in August after vacation. He thought of English as the language of the future and he wanted her to learn it fluently. I said I'd help coach her before she started school since teaching kids was to be my new profession. Jesse was an exception to my mother's basic racial prejudice. She adored him and since she had basically given up on the captious Cynthia she thought it would be pleasant to have a girl around in whom she could instill the "proper values," whatever they might be. It seemed to me that my father had always been in rapid decline while my mother's was gradual. I often wondered why she hadn't bailed out of a marriage that had been thought to be a brilliant piece of social matchmaking. I knew that Cynthia from about the age of ten had begun advising my mother to run for her life. I also knew she had enough of her own money from her family so the question is why didn't she leave? It was years before I began to understand what muddy waters many marriages swim in.

In the village of Au Train I stopped and studied the map Cynthia had given me and then headed south until I found a ramshackle house, really only a shack, in a forest clearing. A baleful mongrel sat on an open porch rumbling a growl and a big woman came to the screen door whose holes were plugged with a dozen cotton balls to keep away flies. She said that Donald and Cynthia had driven over to Bay Mills that morning. She had a round, brown, shiny face, and a soft, melodious voice. I went in for a glass of lemonade and she talked while she carved the head of a cane from an alder limb. There was a stack of canes near her worktable and she insisted on giving me one that had a lacquered loon's head handle, my favorite bird. "I seen you limp on the way to the house," she said, rejecting my offer of payment though there was a sign that read "canes five dollars" out by her mailbox. "Do you stay in the winter?" I asked, looking at the flimsy walls on which there were stretched pelts of beaver and otter and a single bobcat. "No, I go to my beautiful home on the ocean in Florida," she laughed, then patted my hand as my face reddened. There was an urge to stay there and be her errand boy or whatever. When I reached my pickup I impulsively stuck twenty bucks for my new cane in her mailbox. She was watching from the porch and waved. I suspected she was in her mid-fifties or more but when I drove away I thought how grand it would be to have this woman as a mother or lover. She had said with a twinkle that Cynthia was one of the toughest bitches in the world and Donald was lucky to have her as a girlfriend.

Bay Mills wasn't that far out of the way, though I was anxious to get to East Lansing to see Polly. It had the specific poverty of any Indian reservation though the people didn't act poor. I wasn't as tired as Fred was with what he called the "white lie" where everyone was suffocating in white bread doing white things in the white world. It was ultimately a beautiful place on Lake Superior and of course I wanted to stay there and be part of something which might have been a portion of Cynthia's motive with Donald. I found them frying up a mess of illegal pike at his great-aunt's house. We ate the mess of fish which were delicious in the late spring that includes June this far north. It was a warm day with a south wind and we ate lunch on a picnic table out in the yard. Cynthia had her portable tape player and Indian kids were dancing around to Aretha Franklin's "Respect." I found Aretha's strident voice almost frightening but the kids didn't. One little boy did Indian dance steps to the black music and they all begged Cynthia to dance with them. She did and I was curiously proud of her for finding another life. She and Donald were fond of each other to a degree that I poorly understood. I told Cynthia that I was stopping in East Lansing to see Polly and she teased me about my evening with Laurie who had gone off to a big-deal tennis camp in California soon after our evening. There was an awkward moment when I realized that within Cynthia's ethic you weren't supposed to have two girlfriends at once. Donald teased her and she slapped at him and then he danced with her holding her straight above his head and she pretended she was doing a swan dive through the air. Even more so than his father Clarence, Donald was massively strong and agile. After his coming senior year of school Donald was a sure thing for an athletic scholarship to a college. On the track team he always won both the shot put and hundred-yard dash, a rare combination of strength and speed. Some people were troubled that as a mixed breed he was dating the most socially prominent girl in town but then every location has its classic Greek chorus muttering, chattering, moaning in the background.

I had a nightmarish time finding Polly's room in East Lansing. It was the day before graduation and the town was crowded and I had had little experience driving in heavy traffic. A squad car stopped me after I drove down a one-way street the wrong way but the cop was sympathetic when he learned I was from the Upper Peninsula and the equivalent of a "hick." He admired my rowboat and I gave him some tips on fishing locations for his vacation. He also led me to Polly's rooming house a few blocks from the campus. It was a discouraging place, an absolute mess with students moving out for the summer, beer bottles and trash in the yard and on the porch and in the halls of the house. Her tiny room had a broken lock but she wasn't there. It was somehow neat and squalid at the same time.

I drove over to the Kellogg Center and finally got to talk to her on the loading dock behind a huge kitchen. She was working a twelve-hour shift in preparation for a huge graduation banquet and smelled not unpleasantly of carrots, onions, and celery. She told me not to hug her because she was sweaty. She got off in eight hours but I could tell she would be too tired for anything and would have only six hours to sleep before she was due back to help on another banquet. I then made the mistake of saying I had a pocketful of money and wanted to help her rent a larger more pleasant room. She was smiling as always but a little offended. I couldn't think of another move so we kissed good-bye. I was disappointed and the world looked unreal as a comic book when I drove away. A hundred miles south I very much regretted not having stayed. It was our first chance to sleep together and the idea it would have been actual sleep was fine by me for the time being.

10

I drove through the night arriving at Fred's in Ohio the first faint light of Saturday morning. I didn't want to wake him so I pulled off at the beginning of his long, rutted two-track driveway. It was sprinkling with a promise of real rain so I spread my sleeping bag under the back of the truck, rubbed on some mosquito dope, and slept for a few hours, waking when I saw bare black legs to the knees wearing sneakers, and heard a voice say "come on out, boy."

Her name was Riva and she described herself as Fred's "aide" in the Catch Up program which she pronounced "catsup" with a twinkle. We walked down the two-track and it dawned on me that Fred had found his black Indian. She was from Sapulpa, Oklahoma, and was part Choctaw and part black. She said, "I didn't join the counterculture, I am the counterculture." She was homely, tall, and thin but managed to be sexy through her grace of movement and abrasive humor. She wouldn't put up with a single moment of the white guilt posture. After my first morbidly unsuccessful day of teaching I mopingly said, "They try so hard. I'm not sure I deserve to live on the same earth." Riva exploded. "Cut that bullshit. That's all ego jive. You're here to improve their reading and writing five percent in two months, maybe more but probably less. Why think about yourself in that bullshit way? You got your head up your ass, boy. You're suppose to be helping these kids and you can't do it with your head up your rich ass, kiddo."

My face burned while Fred laughed. We were cooking hamburgers, rather Riva was because she thought Fred's cooking to be beneath contempt. I wanted to run and hide in a thicket but that would only be fulfilling her low opinion. Fred with two degrees from the University of Chicago, plus a divinity degree, was the director, but Riva as his aide quickly ran the whole show. She was a graduate student at Ohio University a couple of hours away. The other two teachers beside myself, both from Ohio University, were Ed who was Jewish and from Pittsburgh and Lila, a bright, plump, whey-faced girl from Columbus, Ohio, who was irritated at me because her boyfriend would have had my job if it wasn't for "nepotism," or so she said. I felt so awkward I couldn't respond. All five of us taught two hours in the morning and two hours in the afternoon in a group of shabby Quonset huts owned by the county that had neither heat for a cool morning nor-air conditioning for the hot days which were in the majority. In addition to orchestrating our meals Riva also made lunch for the thirty-five kids though we all pitched in in our various incompetent ways.

Fred and Riva separated the kids in five groups of seven with me getting the twelve-year-olds, the oldest, who were thought to be largely hopeless. Riva administered a diagnostic test the first day, and another would be repeated halfway through the program, and then a final test the last day. (Midway my kids showed the least improvement with Fred's next to the bottom. Ed's were at the top, with Riva second and Lila third.)

I lived in the pump shed attached to Fred's cabin. He had whitewashed the floors, walls, and ceiling, and I had a cot, night table, and reading lamp and shared a bathroom with the lovers Riva and Fred. I would have preferred to join Lila and Ed in their small cabin down the road but there wasn't enough room. Riva made a lot of noise during their lovemaking which caused discomfort during my sleeping and reading. We didn't start teaching until ten in the morning so I fished early for bass and catfish and also would often fish in the evening. I took Ed with me once but he didn't like to eat fish so didn't get the point. Lila went with me several times and I admit we had a minor romance in physical terms. This was the mid-sixties and Lila had a friend who sent her regular letters from Haight-Ashbury. Lila felt she was missing everything in this backwater and she doubtless was. She got a "dear Jane" letter from her boyfriend and turned to me for comfort. "Any port in a storm," she said which while not complimentary alleviated our loneliness. Ed pretended to be jealous but in fact he and Lila quarreled all the time.

I wasn't homesick for my home but for the north with its vast forests and cold rivers and trout. In the first month I drove Lila all the way to Athens three times to see movies. We watched *Alfie, Blowup,* and *Who's Afraid of Virginia Woolf?* I liked the first two and loathed the third because it reminded me of my parents' cold-hearted quarreling. Fred thought Lila was leading me around by the nose and I was too much the young gentleman to say that she was passionate about giving blow jobs. I'm not sure what it meant, if anything. She was also explicit in her teaching me how to go down on her, a practice in which each woman seems to have her peculiarities.

Fred was irked that I had brought along a carton of books and monographs on logging and mining. One hot evening we sat at the kitchen table and he and Riva traded blows on my intellectual short-comings. Riva was less likely to see evil in Fred's economic terms. She was a graduate student in sociology and when I had blithely told her about my project she began to make a book list that included Marcuse, Paul Goodman, and Oscar Handlin. Fred insisted that I read Schopenhauer, Nietzsche, and a whole string of theologians including Niebuhr whom I had already tried but found too dry. They both agreed that my approach toward evil and socioeconomic ills was too narrow and that I would devour myself before I really got started. Riva was merciless about Fred's theological background. She saw religion as a wonderfully primitive impulse. Riva didn't drink but was an expert at rolling big joints. She would sing fundamentalist hymns like "Washed in the Blood of the Lamb" or "Power in the Blood" ("wonder working power") to piss off Fred. I could understand the idea that if I started with too narrow a base I would simply topple over. Riva teased me by saying that I was included in her definition of the human species, "males and females, usually between one hun-dred and two hundred pounds, mostly fueled by resentments that burst out in wars, divorces, lynchings, wife beatings, motiveless murders, and the stomping of the poor because they are the easiest to stomp." She was that unique human who could remain lucid and energized while smoking marijuana. One night she delivered a per-haps hourlong lecture on what happened to the Indians of Oklahoma since Andrew Jackson that left Fred and I in tears. The story con-tinued right up to the year before when some white teenagers on a lark shot her family's only milk cow. At the time I was pleased with the help Fred and Riva gave me but also disappointed because I wanted to write a short, excoriating family history and be done with it, freeing me to go on with a less obsessive life though I had no idea what shape that might take.

Curiously, it was my students who helped me to stop thinking about myself for the time being. Riva had quickly figured out that nearly all of the students arrived hungry but that our budget would cover only lunch. Ed was particularly upset about this and called his parents who shipped from Pittsburgh large cartons of this Jewish bread called challah that had eggs in it. The kids loved it and since I needed my ample pay like a hole in the head I went to a supermarket and bought local hams and blocks of cheese so that each morning when the kids arrived there was a big platter of bread, ham, and cheese. Ed joked that he wouldn't tell his Orthodox parents about the ham.

My class was comprised of a terribly thin mulatto girl, two Latino boys whose parents were farm workers, two white boys and a white girl from across the river in West Virginia whom I had difficulty in understanding, and a very short girl whose legs had been bowed by the disease of rickets. Her name was Marli and I still keep in touch with her more than thirty years later. She runs a public radio station in Kansas. I admit that teaching was the first sense I'd ever had of what they call "community." There was something wrong with every one of my students whether hearing impairments, obvious malnutrition which made them small for their age, various other maladies caused by this malnutrition, one of the West Virginia boys stuttered, and the West Virginia girl was sexually precocious. I called in Riva to deal with the latter. I overheard Riva saying, "You can't be showing your ass to boys for a nickel." I was amazed at the general lack of complaint or whining though I later figured out that they didn't complain because there was generally no one to listen. You either kept your chin up and you would fall apart. They were shy and friendly stoics. Marli who was barely four feet at the age of twelve joked that she would never have to deal with boys bothering her, and when I couldn't laugh she patted my hand as if I were the one who needed sympathy.

11

I always date the beginning of the end of my family to the morning of the Fourth of July when I slid into second base. We were playing softball in the public park during a picnic for all of the kids. Anyway, I had beaten out a cheap single, there was an error, so I took off for second and made a slide I probably wouldn't have tried if I hadn't had a few beers. Second base had no give but was spiked there firmly to prevent theft. My bad ankle simply crumpled with flesh tearing from bone, and bone splitting from bone. Within a minute I fainted from pain.

My mother arrived by late afternoon and I was flown in a small hospital plane to Meigs Field in Chicago, then taken to a hospital for orthopedic surgery early the next morning. I was being injected with Demerol and don't recall much of anything until I woke up in a recovery room. My mother was standing there with the doctor who supposedly treated her phantom pain. He bore a resemblance to my father though his face was relatively unlined and in the times I saw him in the next few days he was always witty and smiling. Barely soon enough for my taste I was flown up to Marquette with my mother and ensconced on a bed in my father's den so I wouldn't have to get to my room upstairs. Cynthia, Clarence, and my father welcomed me. Jesse was still on vacation in Veracruz and I had pretty much convinced my mother that she and Father should return to the Club. I wanted only to read in privacy and have Mrs. Plunkett take care of me. My mother babbled on how she and Cynthia had redecorated a guest bedroom for the coming visit of Jesse's daughter because the garage apartment was too small and a young lady shouldn't have to sleep in the same bedroom as her father. Cynthia rolled her eyes at that one.

By morning they were all gone, my parents to the Club in their crisply expensive summer clothes, and after they left Donald picked up Cynthia to visit relatives on Sugar Island near Sault Sainte Marie. Mrs. Mueller from the library visited after I called for some fresh material. She admonished me about some "radical" books I had asked for but she was joking. She held my hand for a few minutes and I, absurdly enough, got an erection which she noticed by the rising sheet and let go of my hand. "I'm flattered," she said, getting up to go. I was a bit dazed by my pain pills but at the moment Mrs. Mueller evoked all the errant mystery of sexuality. How I longed to embrace her big chest and plump butt so that my heart beat faster in its confusion. Years before Cynthia and I would laugh when my father's bulldog would hurl himself drooling against the fence when a certain female mutt would walk by. Sometimes she would back up to the fence to receive an eager lap or two. My year of devout Bible study had called sins names but had certainly failed to explain them. Meanwhile we young Christians yearned, wheezed, ached, and throbbed just like the heathen.

Fred sent me a mournful and comic letter. He had asked Riva to marry him and she had replied, "Are you fucking kidding?" He also told me to read Christopher Smart, William Blake, Walt Whitman, Henry Miller, and Allen Ginsberg's "Howl" to "broaden" myself and I duly added them to my book list. Fred included a page of condolence from students that contained "you shouldn't have slided into base" and "if you send me a bus ticket I'm a good nurse, love Marli."

After two weeks in the den I was surprised that I still wasn't inclined to feel sorry for myself. At first I ascribed it to the pain pills that I was taking in diminishing numbers. I imagined the consequences of the metal screws in my ankle and wasn't particularly disturbed. I doubted if they'd keep me from fishing. I finally, though, attributed my lack of self-pity to my previous summer's labor in Iron Mountain but more so the teaching job in Ohio. You leave home and it dawns on you that the world bears little similarity to home. I remembered in Iron Mountain one late Friday afternoon when Herbert was handing out our pay and Clyde, a simpleminded older laborer, was talking how he was taking his wife and family camping and fishing on Lake Gogebic. His wife and four kids showed up in a junky old DeSoto and a little boy brought Clyde a cold beer and Clyde yelled "we're going to have a party." Glenn had said contemptuously that he had seen Clyde, his wife, and all four kids in a rental boat all at once fishing bluegills with dollar cane poles. Herbert had told him to shut up. And the kids in my class were so bravely woebegone that nothing short of my death could equal their misery. I returned to listening to Mozart and Beethoven because you couldn't very well listen to Otis Redding, Aretha Franklin, or Ray Charles when you were unable to move.

❊   ❊   ❊

One morning in late July I was dreading the arrival of my parents that afternoon. They were returning from the Club to welcome Jesse and his daughter Vera who were coming the next day. I was fond of my privacy and had persuaded Mrs. Plunkett to move the television into the kitchen so I wouldn't have to hear the game-show shrieks. I was in a mild codeine haze when Laurie suddenly showed up at the den door. She was home on a three-day break from her tennis camp and looking for Cynthia. I found the Au Train number of Donald's aunt and give it to her. She leaned over the desk in a short summer dress talking to Cynthia and I was heartlessly aroused. She turned to look at me while she talked and raised her dress up to her waist with her other hand. I reached for my crutches but then she hung up the phone and asked if I had a rubber and I told her they were upstairs in my desk drawer. I lowered the single hospital bed from its sitting position. I could hear Laurie chatting with Mrs. Plunkett in the kitchen and then her footsteps going up the stairs. I thought my dick would break. When she came back down she said she had found a bunch of fifty-dollar bills in the drawer and was charging me one. She closed the sliding den doors and took off everything except her bra and sneakers. Her legs and arms were very tan but her bottom and tummy and chest were white from her tennis dresses. She was careful of my cast which went up to my knee and straddled me. It was over in moments but she managed to get me up in fifteen minutes or so, a biological feat reserved for young men. Her body was as hard as a muscular boy and I wondered about the long-term effects of eight hours of tennis a day. Afterward we both fell asleep and were finally wakened by Cynthia opening the door and shrieking "sluts!"

Jesse and Vera arrived the next morning quite tired from taking the Mexico City to Chicago red-eye and the early connecting flight up to Marquette. My father, mother, and Cynthia stood there in the living room welcoming Jesse and Vera while I sat on the sofa crutches in hand. She was only a little over five feet, not as dark as Jesse, and had lovely though irregular features, a high forehead, and a slightly Roman rose. She wore a pale green dress, white anklets, and shiny patent-leather black shoes. She curtsied and bowed during the introduction. She looked down at me slumped on the sofa and offered her hand calling me "señor." She was twelve years old and smelled slightly of vanilla and cinnamon. She was obviously very tired and my mother and Cynthia took her up to her room. My father and Jesse went out to the back porch to talk out of my earshot. I had been distracted when Cynthia and my father were standing next to each other. She had become taller in the past year, perhaps five-foot-ten, and though her features were much finer than his she bore a strong resemblance to him. She's his flipside, I thought, smelling the cinnamon odor left on my hand by Vera who I couldn't help hoping would be good for our family.

We had a fine evening with only one sour note and in the morning Jesse drove Mother and Father back up to the Club. We had a good dinner with my father expertly grilling steaks. Vera had slept all afternoon and then become quite vivacious around dinner, speaking a limited pidgin English with Cynthia helping out because she had had high school Spanish. I showed Vera a textbook Mrs. Mueller had gotten me that was especially directed at teaching Mexicans the American language. It was slangy and up-to-date rather than formal and it seemed a good idea to start her on a level common with the culture. I felt nervous when flipping the pages of the book because Vera leaned into my shoulder but supposed that she was only trying to be friendly.

The unpleasant moment had come later in the evening. Cynthia had pushed aside some throw rugs and she and Vera were teaching each other dance steps on the bare maple floor of the dining room, both of them in shorts and sleeveless shirts. I was reading in my bed in the den and my father was reading and watching television in the living room. He was having the usual number of nightcaps and I finally noted he hadn't turned a page in his book. I came out of the den on my crutches to get a glass of cold water and ice in the kitchen and noticed that my father had lined up the television on its wheeled table so that he could watch the girls dancing. There was Veracruz music on the stereo and Cynthia was closely following Vera's intricate samba steps. I paused to watch Vera's sensual grace and the way her body moved fluidly as if she had fewer bones in it than we had in the great north. My father laughed and said to me, "What a sweet little butt," which seemed in bad taste. I was relieved when he and Mother left in the morning.

12

Later I figured out that we had exactly twenty-one beautiful days together that August. Cynthia and I would trade off teaching duties, an hour apiece each morning, Mrs. Plunkett would cook us lunch, and then the girls would go to the beach and I would return to the den. One day my reading of one of Sprague's journals enraged me and I moved back up to my room. I also was craving exercise and went up and down the stairs on my crutches until I was sweating hard and no longer pissed off. One morning after three or four days of this routine Vera insisted that I come along to the beach. We were in the middle of our once-in-a-summer heat wave so that Donald's preseason football practice had been moved to early in the morning. I agreed and Donald carried me from the car to the water's edge where the girls spread a blanket and towels. It's very hard to walk in loose sand on crutches but it was still embarrassing to be carried. I weighed about one-seventy-five but it was no problem for Donald. Vera's brief bikini was a little unnerving but the fact that she was only twelve offered enough cold water to prevent any conscious lust beyond the occasional moment. Her tummy was still rounded and her breast slightly conical but other than that she had a woman's body. When other boys on the beach would stare or walk too closely Donald would merely give them a baleful look and they'd scatter. Once when Donald and Cynthia were off walking Vera got out of the water and stood over my dozing head dripping water on me and then sat down on my chest uncomfortably close to my face. I resolved then that I would wait at least four years and then travel to Veracruz to see what could be done.

In our culture certain sexual moves are forbidden though less so in the cities in recent years. In Marquette at the time a senior boy could go out with a sophomore girl but a freshman girl was pushing the envelope. A man beyond high school years was gambling on legal problems if he fooled with high school girls though it was admissible for some of my female senior classmates to date college boys. A Lolita episode in Marquette would mean prison but in the further reaches of the countryside it wasn't unheard of.

By the end of the first week I was uncomfortably and stupidly in love with Vera but felt cool and collected about keeping it on a high level, say in the arena of what I had read about Dante and Beatrice. I was a teacher and she was the sacred vessel of my learning. That sort of thing. She was a quick learner and began to mimic Cynthia's lilting, playful patterns of speech. I struggled for a framework to put her in that was biblical in its isolation from so-called lower desires. A little sister came closest to working though flat on her blanket on the beach with her knees drawn up and a few hairs peeking out from a plump pubis shielded by her bathing suit exhausted the soul's finagling on the subject.

One late afternoon while Vera was dozing sprawled on the sofa Cynthia motioned to me to follow her out to the back porch. She said that it was easy to tell that Vera was becoming infatuated with me and I should try to be a little cool toward her. I readily agreed and stopped going to the beach. I became more distant and acted perplexed with the difficulty of my project. In the evening except for a gin rummy game with Mrs. Plunkett I'd go into the den and close the door to baffle the music. One late afternoon when I was about to enter my room I heard a fire truck and went to the hall window. Vera came out of her room wrapped in a towel and stood beside me. When the fire truck passed she turned and walked away with the towel not covering her bare bottom, turning at her door to smile. That night she and her father demonstrated some old-fashioned dances of Veracruz. Jesse was skillful and austere showing us something he called "danzon," a type of close dance performed a couple nights a week in the square of the city of Veracruz. Later when we were cooling off on the screened back porch and Jesse had gone to bed in the garage apartment Cynthia and Donald went off for a walk. I didn't want to be alone with Vera so I started to get off the porch swing with the help of my crutches. Vera kissed me goodnight and put her tongue as far as possible in my mouth. I paused a moment too long before pushing her away. I made my way upstairs with my head ringing. Within minutes she knocked on my door and I locked it.

My parents came home the Wednesday evening before Labor Day weekend, nearly a full week before their usual return from the Club. Jesse quickly disappeared after bringing in their luggage and carrying it up to the master bedroom. My father had a black eye and a fat lip and my mother's eyes were red from crying. She went out to the back porch with a stiff drink and my father followed her with a larger one but not before giving me a manic grin and saying, "I got the best of the asshole." He also paused to watch Cynthia and Vera hurry upstairs as if he were judging a dog show. I went into the den but through an open window I could hear them quarreling on the back porch. Their voices were muffled but I deduced it was something about her refusal to loan him money for a "margin call" on the stock market. It must have been an emergency because it had been one of Jesse's blue-suit days and when he had returned from downtown his face had been perceptibly grave. He hadn't changed his clothes before driving off north to pick up my parents.

I turned on some music on the radio to drown out the ugly voices and my father's shouts of "you goddamned bitch." I heard my mother come back into the house and go upstairs. I felt trapped in the den but wasn't sure how to make my escape when my father came into the living room. I eased out the den door but my father ignored me as he filled a water glass with brandy. I slipped on the first step of the stairs and my father quickly pulled me up by the elbow but it was as if he couldn't really see me.

I couldn't sleep and struggled to read a ponderous Thomas Mann novel without getting the names straight. I took an unnecessary codeine and a hit from a bottle of schnapps I had in the desk drawer. At about two A.M. I heard a truly piercing scream from down the hall. I woke to discover I was sitting at my desk. There was another scream and I grabbed my crutches and went out into the hall where Cynthia and my mother were already standing outside their bedroom doors. My father came stumbling out of Vera's room with his large, partly erect dick sticking out of his underpants. I thought I saw blood. I wobbled on my crutches and sat down on the floor.

Cynthia went in her room, dialed her phone, and started yelling at the police. My mother followed her and tried to grab the phone. My father went in his bedroom and quickly came out with his clothes and lurched down the stairs. Jesse who had heard the scream came in the house dressed only in his pants and raced up the stairs. My father ran out the back door and I heard my mother's Buick start.

It was a full hour before a policeman came and then it was the chief of police accompanied by the senior member of the law firm our family used. We had sat in the living room in a tableau of silence except for Cynthia who said several times "I'm going to kill him." Vera wore one of my mother's robes and she sat on the sofa with Jesse's arm around her shoulder. Jesse tried to take her out to the garage apartment but Cynthia wouldn't let them go. I sat at the dining room table holding my mother's hand.

When the policeman and lawyer arrived they were nearly overcome with embarrassment. I could see that some kind of delay or cover-up was already in progress. The lawyer poured himself a drink and it was decided that statements would be taken in the morning. Cynthia was hysterically angry. Jesse and Vera refused to say anything. My mother wept. I shivered. Cynthia ranted. I stayed up until dawn with her when Donald arrived. She left without luggage.

By the time I got up at midmorning quite groggy from my codeine sleep—I had taken two more—Jesse and Vera were gone. My mother sat at the dining room with a suitcase beside her. Clarence came in, took the suitcase, and drove her to the airport for the noon flight to Chicago. Clarence avoided looking at me. I went over to the sofa and fell asleep not wanting to be upstairs and out of ear-shot in case the police came for a statement. They never did.

Before dinnertime I awoke and heard Clarence mowing the lawn which didn't need it, and then he came and asked if he should call Mrs. Plunkett and I said not for the time being. I knew that she was headed down to Kenosha for Labor Day weekend and I didn't want to interrupt her vacation. We went to the diner and I had a hamburger and potato soup. When Clarence dropped me off back at the house I wondered if it wasn't like the house had burned down with all of us in it. No. We were still here, wherever they had gone, but it was likely we would never be all together again which was just as well.

Part II

13

Laurie died just before dawn three days before the summer solstice. I didn't want to be in the room but I was at her insistence. She touched her three-year-old daughter's hand, then her mother took the child from the hospice room. Laurie's husband, Brent, sat dozing by the corner window, the lilacs outside all bleached out, frazzled and dead. He naturally didn't want me around but Cynthia took him to a nearby tavern and gave him a lecture while I took the three-year-old daughter named Clemmie for a walk. Laurie's breast cancer was aggressive, rapacious, as it often is in younger women. She was twenty-five and told me that she had known it was happening for several months before she had gone to the doctor. Why, I had asked? She was depressed because she was divorcing her husband having discovered that what she had wanted was a baby not a husband.

The week before she died and when she was still coherent we talked out our entire lives because I had seen little of her in nearly ten years. We'd talk for an hour or two and then she would nap. I'd kiss her bald head good-bye feeling her skull beneath my lips, and remembering that I had dreamt so long ago of her arriving at this condition. How could this be? Obviously our souls are more accessible to our unconscious. This was far from the strangest conclusion I had come to at age twenty-seven.

She was so placid in the last week of her life partly, of course, due to the IV morphine drip. Her voice was so thin I had to sit close to the bed. She teased me about my "cheap" clothing, my masquerade as a normal person. She was delusional enough to suggest that she should never have had the abortion but that we ought to have run away together despite the fact that I had been sixteen and she fourteen. "They do it in other countries," she said. I tried to keep her talk of "what might have been" to a minimum by changing the subject as deftly as possible. I avoided her husband by leaving before he came in after work, and coming back late in the evening when she called. That way I also missed her parents, especially her father who had said, "She could have been a great tennis player," when in fact Laurie had quit the game when she was twenty. Her halfback had graduated from the local college and had become a "top notch" real estate salesman who was brusque to everyone except customers. Fred had described his type as the "new Americans" of which there were more every day.

When Laurie touched her daughter's hand with a forefinger and her mother gathered up the child we looked at each other and I saw the sight disappear from her eyes. She didn't so much die as withdraw, and her body under the sheet was still but there was an aura of departure that made me feel cold despite the warm room.

Instead of pressing the button to call a nurse I listened to an aspect of emptiness I hadn't heard before as if her passing had stopped all other sound. I'm sure it couldn't have been more than a few moments but time had collapsed. When it was over I had nothing left about which to draw conclusions. My incomprehension was total. She was here and then she wasn't and though I understood the biological fact of death the whole ballooned outward from the mute sum of the parts.

I walked for a couple of hours thinking of nothing because I had exhausted my capacities. I hadn't awakened her husband before I left the room. Out on Presque Isle I passed the thicket where we had made love on a rainy night, then turned back toward town. I met Clarence and Jesse at the diner and simply nodded when they looked at me questioningly. I thought of calling Cynthia from the pay phone but it could wait. She had lain in bed with Laurie and they chatted as if the inevitable was worthy only of being ignored. They even sang a few songs, but then Cynthia had to go home to Sugar Island near Sault Sainte Marie. She and Donald now had two children, a boy of eight years and a girl five. There was absolutely nothing in their small home on St. Mary's River to indicate her past except a photo of Laurie and me in my rowboat and one of Mother as a teenager.

Clarence still took care of the yard though I had doubts about what sort of paycheck he was drawing. I knew he was at least sixty-five though he didn't look it. After that night when the house had emptied out and there was only me left Clarence had continued his job as if nothing had happened, whether mowing, gardening, raking leaves, shoveling snow before daylight, fixing the refrigerator or furnace, cleaning ice out of the eaves troughs. That winter of my senior year of high school I was sure he was having an affair with Mrs. Plunkett who was staying in the guest bedroom. One moonlit predawn I had seen her from my window making her way back to the house from the work shed. Six days a week Clarence arrived at around five A.M. and when it was cold he'd start a fire in the wood-stove in the work shed. Having put in his eight hours at our house he'd leave early in the afternoon for the marina when he worked as a handyman in the summer and repaired boats in a big shed in the winter. When I was about ten and beginning a strenuous effort to understand the world I asked my father how Clarence could possibly work sixteen hours a day. "He supports a lot of people," he said, as if Clarence's labor was nothing in particular. This was my first clue well before my project started that the alpha predators in the lineage from which we came didn't have contempt for the ordinary workingman, they simply ignored him.

Jesse was another matter altogether. Why he came back to work for my father after the rape of his daughter was utterly be-yond me, and a horrid incident five years before during the last months of my marriage to Polly had taken a degree of warmth from our friendship that has never been restored. What happened is that I had just entered the seminary in Evanston at Seabury-Western that fall and by mid-October our marriage had disassembled. It was my fault because I had admitted a month after we married the year before when I graduated from Michigan State and she was work-ing on a master's in education that I had no intention of ever fa-thering children. I actually lied and said I had a spermatic cord torsion which was true, from an accident, but the lie was in not say-ing it was easily correctible. She let this slide for a while but when we drove north to have Christmas with her parents her father was very direct when he said how much he looked forward to having grandchildren. In married housing at Michigan State we were sur-rounded by couples with children and Polly was painfully envious. She maintained her good humor to protect my feelings, but then I finally admitted when we moved to Chicago the summer after graduation that my sterility was correctible. Our apartment was too small to say this kind of thing aloud. I insisted that the males in my family for the last hundred and fifty years didn't constitute the kind of bloodline that should be perpetuated. Since Cynthia already had given birth twice Polly couldn't accept my refusal.

Like many others I'm somewhat doubtful on the matter of repressed memories but then I certainly have no talent in the somewhat bruised arena of psychology. When I think of my four college years it's never on purpose. For instance, if my feet become wet with slush on the streets of Marquette in March I am effortlessly taken back to trying to negotiate the crowded sidewalks of Michigan State University's campus between class periods. The pallid beiges, grays, and greens peculiar to government building interiors sweep me back into the same institutional colors at the university and you have to wonder what malign imaginations devised such ugliness so in contrast with the beauty of the landscaping of the campus influenced by its justly famous horticulture department. Visual ugliness seeps into the soul and is banished only by an extraordinary teacher of which I cherished only three, possibly four, or a few books discovered in the sepia anguish of the library. Not oddly you fall back on your sexuality in desperation. One day I stooped before a bottom shelf in the library and removed a book which gave me a clear view of the other side where a coed was sitting on the floor in a wool plaid skirt raised a bit and her legs apart so I could see her vulva packed tightly in white cotton panties. It was akin to touching an electric fence. I left the library, cut my next class, and drove home to our horrid apartment in the huge married housing complex. Polly was hard at work writing a term paper at the kitchen table and refused to make love until I quite literally broke into tears. "O you big baby," she said, and leaned over the table with a text still before her. She cooked poorly and kept repeating fried chicken livers or meat loaf or fried indistinguishable fish. The level of discourse in a sociology text would upset my

stomach and only sex would heal me. We took to having pizza twice
a week and having sex both before and after the pizza. In short, I
utterly loathed college but still cherish the teachers who gave so
much of their enormous minds. Two of them, Weisinger and Jaffe,
were Jewish and from New York City. They had come to our in-
tellectually pathetic interior and saved my sorry neck. Only these
men, pizza, and sex with Polly could raise me from my collegiate
doldrums.

By early October we had pretty much disintegrated. Everything had gone wrong. After a single month I could see that preaching in an Episcopal church wasn't going to work for me though I
intended to see the year out with that curiously destructive brav-
ery of the midwesterner who never quite knows when to cut and
run. We decided to drive north to the cabin I had inherited from
Sprague and talk it out. Before our marriage I had lived there for
as much as three months at a time in a state of self-congratulatory
ascetic withdrawal but Polly on her two visits with her character-
istic honesty had found the place "creepy, scary, eerie." She didn't
see the point in the essentially barren room and the small cooking
shed I had clumsily built out back. She found the grave of Sprague's
wife unpleasant, feeling that the dead should be buried with other
members of the human race. I had taught her to love classical music
but when she tried to bring along her battery-operated radio I said
that I didn't allow music at the cabin at which she tossed the radio
from the back of the truck and it splintered on the sidewalk. We
were north past Milwaukee before she said a word and by then she
had used half a box of Kleenex. Well north of Green Bay I turned
off on a gravel road and we took a walk which made it worse. We
had forgotten the sandwiches I had made and she screamed, "I have
to have a baby you selfish son of a bitch." She ran down the road
and I couldn't catch her with my bad ankle which would never be
good for anything but walking.

We were temporarily saved by a golden afternoon once we entered northern Wisconsin and the Upper Peninsula. The popple and aspen had turned yellow while the conifers stayed green and all the hardwoods were shades of red and gold. We were nearly emerged from our slump near Bruce's Crossing and I idly said that maybe we should abandon Chicago, move up here and buy a farm. She laughed at the idea of us as a farm couple, turning in the seat, and I could see up her legs under her skirt. This usually aroused me but I felt nothing. Unable to leave this absence of desire alone I pulled the car off on a wooded two-track and tried to make love to her without success. This had never happened to me and I was so frustrated my eyes became misty. Polly was becoming increasingly confused and we sat there in the emotional flipside of the glorious Indian summer day in our homeland. The lump in my throat was enlarging and Polly looked like she wished very much to be elsewhere.

The worst by far was yet to come. We had a quick early dinner and drove out toward the cabin. I had bought a bottle of whiskey which was unusual because I rarely averaged a drink a month after having had a hard time with alcohol as a college freshman and realizing I was in danger of falling into the family trap.

When we reached the gate it wasn't my gate. It was a new, wider galvanized gate with a heavy padlock and the two-track beyond it had been graded and expanded and my favorite oak tree had been cut down. Polly said nothing and I was shocked to the point I nearly vomited. I climbed the gate and trotted down the road in the twilight. The porch had been torn off my cabin and a new one was being built. In place of my cookshed there was a prefab garage that contained a big generator for electricity. Steps built out of railroad ties made a path down to Lake Superior. Out in back the gravestone was gone and the beaver dam taken out so the pond was drained.

It was nearly dark when I started back to the car. Polly met me halfway and when I stumbled and fell she helped me up. I drove to the house of the old Finn who checked the cabin every week and had done repairs for Sprague. His wife said he was at the tavern and did I want my stuff, meaning my cooking utensils and sleeping bag and a carton of books. I loaded them into the trunk and drove to the tavern. Naturally I had guessed what had happened but it didn't make me feel less murderous. Tad and three other old Finns were playing euchre. He looked up and said blearily, "Your dad sold it in August." I wasn't capable of more than a murmur but said, "It wasn't his to sell."

It was a grotesque night on the phone. Polly finally got another room at the motel. I drank most of the whiskey and vomited all over myself when I tried to sleep. I tried to call my father who was in Italy with his crony Seward. Jesse wasn't at home but he had left a number of a motel in Duluth and there was no answer there. I called my mother in Evanston who knew nothing of it but said, "I'm so sorry." I called my father's main banker and the head of the law firm in Marquette and neither of them admitted knowing anything. All of our family papers of any consequence, including my own, were stored at the bank and readily accessible to my father and Jesse who also had power of attorney in most matters. I finally got hold of Jesse at around midnight when I was very drunk. He said only that he couldn't bear to tell me in July. I hung up thinking how easy the crime had been to commit in that my father was David Burkett III and my legal name was simply David Burkett. I passed out, vomited, choked, and slept. At first light Polly helped me clean myself up. She drove most of the way to Iron Mountain where I dropped her at her parents' and proceeded to Marquette. My throbbing hangover was the least of my discomforts. When we kissed good-bye in front of her parents' house I knew it was truly a good-bye kiss. She might still love me like you would a mad dog if it was

your own but it was definitely time for her to give up my ghost. In
my senior year at the university when we had been living together
before our marriage she had looked at me in a coffee shop after a
movie and asked, "Are you ever going to be all right?" I had said,
"Of course, darling." The fact that I wouldn't be what she called
"all right" until I finished my project was becoming obvious to me.

In Marquette the president of the bank kept his distance but
the senior member of the law firm spent a full hour with me considering the options. It was obvious to him that the title company
was liable in that they had guaranteed to the buyer that the seller
was the sole owner of the property. If I wished to pursue the matter the title company would make sure that my father was pros-
ecuted. The buyer would get his money back and I would eventually
get my cabin back after a couple of years' pursuit. "These things
take time," he said. He also said that my father had been a "disappointment" to him for a number of years, referring to alcohol and
sexual charges plus my parents' divorce. With all of this in mind,
plus the transaction of his sailboat in Chicago against which there
was a troublesome Marquette lien, the "right" judge might give him
several years in prison. The question was, of course, was I as a son
comfortable with sending my father to prison? Did I want the cabin
back in its recent condition? He represented my father not me but
he was willing to tell my father that if I wasn't given the sale price
he was certainly in danger of prison time. There seemed to be some
waffling here as I knew that a member of the same firm looked after
the interests of Cynthia and myself.

I went back home to think it over. Mrs. Plunkett was there
and fixed me lunch during which I drank a big water glass of her
awful wine. I saw through the kitchen window Jesse pulling up out
in back. I drank another big glass of the wine and went out to con-
front him. He and Clarence were standing there talking and I began
yelling "how could you do this to me?" I yelled until I was hoarse

and then I lay down on the lawn and fell asleep. It was a cool day and Clarence covered me with a blanket. That evening Jesse tried to convince me that he knew nothing of my father's intended sale of the cabin until it was completed but I didn't really believe it, not that my belief mattered to anyone involved. I remembered one evening when we were still in high school and taking a walk downtown Cynthia had joked that she knew Jesse was stealing money from our father. This pleased Cynthia and certainly didn't bother me.

14

Now five years later I return back to the diner the morning Laurie died in June of 1975. I had been up all night and been sapped by the power of death. Both Clarence and Jesse had liked Laurie very much. I told them she had died peacefully then suddenly put a hand on Jesse's hand. I wanted our friendship to be like it was before my father had sold the cabin. Clarence told me he had recaulked my rowboat and painted it dull blue so I could be further invisible. Jesse like Laurie and Cynthia asked me why my face was wind-burned. I had been camped out since the first of May mostly in Chippewa and Mackinac counties figuring out my ancestors' path of destruction. In courthouses I would pretend I was writing a book on the glories of the logging days which made clerks very cooperative. They would direct me to the ancient local men and women who could still remember the last days of big logging. The real treasure troves were at the local historical societies where you could see photos but the old people with their stories were essential. You needed the stories to put a human face on what had happened. Statistics and maps by themselves were suitable only to talented academics.

To be frank I had been periodically unstable ever since my divorce from Polly. Maybe the events of our marriage presaged its doom. Later on I thought of myself as a parasite on the body of Polly's essential happiness. In a marriage the melancholy and depression of one partner will often win out over the happiness of the other. Polly had been saving for college since she was twelve, and then still had to take loans. My grandparents on my mother's side established a college fund for Cynthia and myself which covered tuition and living expenses plus a hundred dollars a week for miscellaneous. Not much really, but enough, and a great deal in Polly's terms. What she thought of as "easy money" made her uncomfortable. I had always been a family joke because of my lack of interest in spending money so I wasn't the direct source of Polly's unrest. At our small wedding in Iron Mountain my mother, Clarence, Jesse, Cynthia and Donald, and their two small children attended but my father wasn't invited. My mother adored Polly and gave her a two-carat blue diamond ring she had inherited, plus a check for twenty-five thousand dollars that Polly was to manage to get us over what mother called the "bumps." This amount made Polly hysterically nervous but I said that my mother thought of me as absentminded about money, adding that mother must spend that much money on clothing every year. This wasn't, of course, the sorest point in our marriage but we could resolve it only by never talking about it. At Michigan State the year before our marriage I had been notified that my father had spent the trusts in his care for Cynthia and me.

It meant little to me, partly because I had guessed as much, and there was the good side of the absent money, distancing me further from my father's sins against the family. I warned Cynthia on the phone but she only laughed with the usual "fuck the nitwit." She had taken a high school equivalency test and despite caring for two young children was going to college in Sault Sainte Marie (the "Soo" they call it up here) to get a teaching degree for a promised job at the Bay Mills reservation. The comic aspect of their elopement had been all the muttering and grief in Marquette over losing Donald as a quarterback. In my senior year of high school after the family implosion I had to hear about the school's loss of Donald nearly every day as if I were partly at fault.

My mother was crushed over the divorce. Polly continued teaching in a grubby southside grade school in Chicago. She and my mother, in fact, became friends however unlikely that seems. My mother insisted she keep the nest egg which Polly tried to give back to me. Nothing could have meant less to me at the time. When Polly married a teacher the year after our divorce my mother attended. I should add that within a year after my mother was away from my father she had largely recovered through the efforts of an analyst. She lost her taste for heavy drinking and pill popping and though she was still a little fragile mentally she had become pleasantly human rather than one of those upper-class Judy Garlands. She lived in a nice old house in Evanston with a childhood friend, another divorcée. They were both what I called "all-star docents" at museums and libraries. She was appalled when I teased her about her doctor friend thinking she had gotten away with her phantom pain and understandable deception. He was still her boyfriend but she told me she had no intention of ever getting married again. It took a couple of years but she and Cynthia finally developed a fairly warm mother-daughter relationship, mostly on the basis of the grandchildren. I had become their only shared problem. By spring after my initial separation from Polly I entered what is thought of as a clinical depression though I viewed only it as being perplexed over the human race. Cynthia came down and Fred arrived from Ohio after I slugged an alderman on Clark Street who was leading his wife from a restaurant to their car by the ear. I probably shouldn't have interfered but she was screaming. I admitted that I resisted arrest strenuously. If my mother's family hadn't been highly placed in the Chicago area I would have been in real trouble. I had to do six weeks of in-house care at a psychiatric clinic north of the city. It all reminded me sadly of my father's plea bargaining but then one night in the Cook County jail was more than enough. I got pretty badly beaten up at the scene of my crime and my purple face helped with the judge. After I got out of the clinic it was agreed that I should let Fred keep an eye on me for a while in Ohio.

15

Actually, I'm being a little coy. Polly anchored me to earth and without her I floated in unpleasant ether. To admit that I was unstable is a euphemism. Once I sat at my kitchen table for two days and nights without sleeping or eating. I drank water, looked out the window, and peed. It was March, always my most problematic month. I was supposed to be writing a paper on the "liberation theologians" but had been stuck for weeks on the first sentence, virtually paralyzed by my thinking on the project. I found myself wishing I was Jewish, black, or Indian so I would have something valid to complain about instead of being a child of privilege.

When Fred retrieved me in May Cynthia had suggested that I might come live near her and Donald but I said that if I lived near impoverished Chippewa I might shoot myself. I said this in jest but she broke into tears and I assured her that I'd never do such a thing if only because it would make her unhappy. Theology school made me remote from the Gospels but I recalled that I shouldn't hurt people.

An odd, fateful thing happened the late afternoon before Fred and I left Chicago. We were coming down the steps of the Newberry, a private library of which Fred had long been a member and where we had been checking on the Upper Peninsula's early Native history, when we met a striking girl who approached us as we were trying to hail a cab. She was tall, slender, and wore a short summer dress in a pale yellow print. She held a tray of small boxes of matches and introduced herself as Vernice "the little match girl." It was so bizarre and we were both foolishly smitten. She wanted five bucks per box of matches and we both bought two. I rarely smoked but this seemed a good time to start. We were supposed to meet my mother and her roommate for dinner at the Cape Cod room at the Drake Hotel but we had time for a drink. I'm very slow in such situations. Actually I have no talent for it at all, but I felt a little glimmer of desire for the first time since I'd broken up with Polly six months before. Fred, however, thought of himself as a prime lothario despite his bulbous nose and pot belly. We went into a tavern and I had my first martini in memory while Vernice had a cautious iced tea and Fred stuck with the safe territory of beer. Vernice admitted her real name was Sharon but she wrote under the name of Vernice because it was more dashing. Her accent was similar to that of my student the diminutive Marli. She was from far southern Indiana but wanted to be a "city poet" so she moved to Chicago. She sold matches from about five to seven every evening after men sometimes had drinks and felt generous. She rotated her route to pass the better office buildings, cocktail lounges, and convention hotels and these two hours a day easily supported her poetry

writing. Fred was impolite enough to ask her if she ever got propo-
sitioned and she said "dozens and dozens of times." She laughed
and gave us a card with her name and numbers. Fred beamed but
Vernice said that the number was for the Salty Dog, a saloon. We
sat there a full hour listening to this fascinating girl and then it was
time to go so Fred asked her to join us for dinner. She said she would
like to but couldn't. Fred had been power drinking beer and acted
the cad by offering her a hundred-dollar bill to come with us and
she said coldly, "I make an honest living, Sir." She was headed to a
reading by the California poet Gary Snyder, who was one of her
favorites, and wouldn't miss it for the world. Fred was crestfallen
and went off to take a pee. Vernice then gave me a card adding her
actual phone number. I said I was leaving the next day and she said
"whenever," kissed me on the cheek, and was out the door leaving
behind her fatal lilac scent and the acute memory of her hazel eyes
and flossy hair. When she had gotten up to leave the bar I noted
the slight sound of the bare backs of her knees detaching themselves
from the red plastic chair seat. Irrational as this might seem the
sound drew me back to Vera getting up from a metal lawn chair in
her bikini one day so many years before. I had stood there deciding
to avert my eyes but then turned to watch her climb the porch steps.
When she opened the screened door she had quickly swiveled to
wave at me and perhaps to see if I had been watching.

The good-bye dinner with my mother went fairly well. I disliked
the effects of the martini with Vernice and so sipped a little wine
but Fred plunged on. He also knew my mother's divorcée friend
and acted comically seductive. She pointedly asked him why he was
pretending he wanted to make love to her when he was lucky if he
could find his dick to pee. My mother thought this was very funny
and Fred said wistfully that he was sure he'd be able to do the job

by the next morning. After dinner we went out to the Drake's main entrance and there sat a new yellow Chevrolet pickup, a gift from my mother to improve my spirits. The pickup immediately made me homesick for my rowboat and the north. There was an uncomfortable moment of clarity when I stared at the epaulets of the doorman opening the vehicle door. What in God's name was I doing in this particular time and place? My sense of dislocation was absolute. I hugged my mother who felt very small in my arms. Fred was kissing the hand of my mother's divorcée friend which amused a bellhop. I looked up at the night sky above the hotel marquee quite lonely to see stars which are scarcely visible in country terms in Chicago's ambient light. I shivered though it was a warm night. I found myself praying for sanity.

16

The trip back to Ohio with Fred began poorly. I tried to awaken him at six A.M. to get an early enough start to beat the traffic but it was hopeless. He hugged the couch with snores and dream growls and whimpers, his flaccid body knotted up in the sheet. I had given away most of my nice clothes to a group of panhandlers the week before so I had only one suitcase. I found a tiny agate earring of Polly's and was surprised by how much it upset me. The earring aroused me and I wondered how it could bring me back to a sexual earth along with my meeting with Vernice the day before.

I went for breakfast and brought Fred back a large coffee and bagel. We finally left at ten in the morning and Fred soon fell asleep rather than helping me navigate out of the city. He had recently been working with his old girlfriend Riva on another program for the rural poor but looking at him slumped in the seat and drooling it was difficult to see how he could help anyone, certainly not myself. I found a radio station that played country music to charm him back awake but he slept the three hours to Indianapolis waking near the outskirts and actually saying "what a beautiful day." We stopped so he could buy a quart of cold beer and then we began a mild quarrel.

I idly said that I hoped to get my personal problems out of the way so I could resume my project. Fred said that it was obvious that the project was my only personal problem and it might be immediately helpful if I drove up to Duluth and shot my father in the head. This threw me off balance because I had considered murdering my father a number of times since the night he had raped Vera. This urge had developed at one point to reading a gun magazine because I remembered that my friend Glenn's father Herbert owned a .223 rifle with which he claimed he had shot crows at four hundred yards. I loved crows and the idea of shooting one repelled me, but not so shooting my father.

While we were having lunch at a diner Fred decided it would be of considerable help if I promised him that I would read *Don Quixote*. I had to let this one pass because when I read the novel for a senior honors course at Michigan State I had noted the disturbing similarity to my own project and I didn't feel up to talking about it there in the truck. There is nothing less pleasant for a college senior to admit than his own humorless absurdity. I dropped the course and didn't take honors in English. My adviser, Weisinger, the most purely wise man I had ever known, convinced me to abandon my obsessions with Thoreau and Melville and leaven my sodden brain with reading Trollope, Chekhov, and Isaac Singer. Polly was delighted with the difference this reading made in our day-to-day life but I fell again with Joyce's *Portrait of the Artist as a Young*

Man when it occurred to me that my own obsessions were similar to the young men who wished to become novelists or poets.

We stopped for gas in a small Indiana town and the station was near the railroad tracks and an extremely poor neighborhood. A chubby little black girl with a dirty bandage around a bare foot stood nearby watching us. I turned away but felt my stomach jiggle with sympathy, empathy, or compassion. I had never quite figured out the precise difference between the three. I heard Fred talking to the attendant as I stared at a sorry-looking cornfield at the edge of town. The corn was stunted and pale and would never be knee high by the Fourth of July. The little girl walked around the front of the pickup to where I leaned against the hood. She said "my name is Lena" and curtsied. Her toes that peeked out of the bandage were swollen and I felt nauseous. I had no idea what to do and called Fred over. She was the attendant's daughter and had stepped on a nail sticking out of a board. The attendant was embarrassed and said, "She'll be okay." Fred said that he was a secret agent for the FBI and handed the man a fifty-dollar bill telling him to take the kid to a doctor. We would be back the next morning to make sure he had done so. The man said "many thanks" and we left.

It was a half hour down the road before we said anything but then Fred launched into what I first considered an attack on me but then I understood as heartfelt. He said that while it was true that my father's people were big-jawed predators who violated and denuded much of the Upper Peninsula I knew the effects only abstractly. I should take a close look at the human race which isn't fairly seen at Marquette High School, Michigan State University, and a year at theological school which Fred called a "fucking tea and sherry party." I lamely defended myself by saying that I had read a great deal and had talked to retired loggers and a few old miners. He drank the rest of his warm beer and laughed at that. He said I hadn't really noticed the aftereffects of the depredations

my family had made. The small "junta" of my family and other alpha
predators encouraged the miners and loggers to mythologize themselves including the thousands who had died in logging and mining
accidents. At this point he became a little irrational and repeated
the story of how the Chicago police had murdered the black activist
Fred Hampton. I tried to get him back on track by saying that
every wealthy Upper Peninsula family didn't have a malignant
past. Look at the Mathers, Peter White, the Cohodes, and many
of the Longyears. Fred had become intent on ranting and wanted
to stop for more beer but I refused. My mother had warned me that
Fred had borderline high blood sugar and had promised her that
he was no longer "sipping" beer all day long. Fred yelled "fuck it,"
then abruptly fell asleep leaving me to navigate the late-afternoon
Cincinnati traffic by myself. I was getting tired by the time I found
Route 52 which ran southeast along the Ohio River. Most of the
river towns were woebegone but I found them quite wonderful after
the interstate highways. Rivers are decidedly female and I began
to think of what Vernice's body might look like and got my first
daylight hard-on in six months, my tunnel vision expanding to take
in far more of the life around me that my mind had buried.

17

Looking back it is easy to see that Riva saved my sorry ass and Fred's too. The easily perceptible linear thread through our lives causes a basic misunderstanding when we tend to give the same weight to years, months, and days. The briefest moments can have an explosive power that overwhelms the time around them including what preceded them. We had arrived at Fred's in the last of the twilight. Riva had fixed us ham hocks, butter beans, and turnip greens knowing that I loved her kind of country fare. When we were still a half hour out I stopped so Fred could buy a six-pack. He also bought a pint of whiskey and I dreaded the idea that the rest of the evening would become unpleasant when he chugged half the pint.

I had a single beer, cautioned by the thought that this sort of power drinking occurred on both sides of my family.

Riva was angry at Fred. He had a few bites of supper then went over to the corner, finished the pint, and went to bed. She looked at me balefully and explained that Fred had passed out in a near diabetic coma the month before and had promised his doctor he would keep his drinking to two beers a day. I simply threw up my hands at her interrogation. Fred had gone to Chicago to help me out but at least part of his motive was the freedom from Riva to get drunk.

"I've had enough of this dumb motherfucker." She got her empty suitcases from the whitewashed pump shed where I was going to sleep. "Did you manage to get your head out of your ass?" She rubbed my shoulders and laughed.

I told her that I had noticed some signs of life in myself. I avoided my project and told her how my peripheral vision had widened when I got on Route 52 out of Cincinnati. She liked that and told me an appalling story of how when she was a senior in high school her basketball-star boyfriend had gotten drunk and "cornholed" her so that she had to have rectal stitches. She had spent a full month sleeping in a closet and three months after that had refused to go to school. "No one knew but I knew and the doctor and nurses knew." The boyfriend went unpunished because of his basketball stardom. She was a senior in college before she could stand to be around a man again, "a short, fat, white boy," she laughed.

Riva got up and fumbled in a desk drawer finding a letter I had left behind when visiting on spring vacation of my senior year in high school. It was postmarked Key West and was a furious note from my father written after he had learned that I had turned down my acceptance at Yale and instead had chosen Michigan State. It was incomprehensible to him that I had broken a family tradition.

The letter was a drunken and abusive scrawl. I was destined to be "worthless." I suddenly found myself telling Riva the story of the night my father raped Vera which I hadn't told Polly or anyone else. I didn't leave anything out and included Jesse leaving with Vera the next morning, my father's escape to Duluth, Cynthia taking off with Donald, and my mother's departure to Chicago. I began weeping, stood up, and turned to the wall to try to control myself. On the wall Fred had arranged a number of prints of Walker Evans's photos of the Great Depression in Alabama. My mind played a trick and imagined a photo of Vera so I turned back to Riva who was in a reverie over my story. She put in a Buddy Guy eight-track and like any bright but confused white man I envied his ability to turn terror into song. I struggled to get our conversation away from myself and asked if she was really going to leave Fred. She looked down at the suitcases on the floor and kicked one lightly. She said she had been with Fred for six years and it wasn't getting any better. She had turned down a good job in Washington, D.C., the year before to stay with him and now regretted it. She felt obligated to finish their current summer project. Fred was good at getting grant money from government agencies. He'd brandish his elegant education and spiritual commitments. She turned back to me.

"Fred told me your daddy done stole your money," Riva's grammar was normally impeccable unless she was speaking of emotional issues.

"I don't give a shit. His money's rotten."

"You might care someday," she teased.

"I get a hundred dollars a week from my mother's family."

"Baby, you're poor."

"Not for what I'm doing. I can get by. If I go flat broke I can go to graduate school. That's paid for." This reminded me to count the money in my suitcase. "It doesn't cost much to do what I intend to do."

We were still talking well past midnight. Riva told me that in
regard to my project I shouldn't follow a narrow route of inquiry.
If I didn't have a broad enough base the whole thing would suffo-
cate me. Good social anthropologists poked around for years in
societies before they drew conclusions. This sounded like good
advice to me but then she made a suggestion that wrenched my gut.

"You should go down to Mexico and try to make it right for
that young woman. You should try to get her forgiveness not for
your father but for yourself because I can tell you see yourself as
somehow tied to it. If you can't do it alone maybe you can get your
sister to go along."

I felt like I was swelling up and constricted at the same time.
I had to assume that Riva was correct but the idea of doing what
she advised gave me the sense of being catapulted into space. I was
too much a lightweight to risk my sanity. My brain began to jitter.

Riva lit a joint, turned up the music, and asked me to dance
with her. I was slow to get beyond a shuffle, then absorbed the
idea that I had a woman in my arms again. We were the same
height and I saw how her eyes faded into the music until she escaped her mind. It took me longer but I made it. She felt me becoming erect and laughed, pushing her hips into mine, then drew
away shaking a finger at me and saying, "I'm going to find you a
woman tomorrow."

We were sweating heavily and had just sat down when Fred
opened the bedroom door and walked quickly into the kitchen like
a windup toy. He knelt down and drew a tequila bottle from under
the sink and started sucking on it. He stopped to say "I can't sleep"
and then started again by which time Riva knelt next to him and
tried to get the bottle away. He pushed her and she tipped over. I
got there and reached for him and he hit me in the face with the
bottle cracking my lip. Now I was angry and wrestled the bottle
away from him and threw the tequila so hard that it went through

a front window and smashed on the cement floor of the front porch. I turned around and swung at Fred but missed and was glad I did. He looked at me like I was unrecognizable and scurried back into the bedroom. I was dripping a lot of blood on my shirt from the cracked lip. Riva wrapped a paper towel around an ice cube and held it to my lip. It was clear that another member of my family was headed to a clinic.

Riva started singing "Some Enchanted Evening" and I laughed, infatuated with her resilience. It was an unlikely time to think of it but I remembered my father's sharp wit which seemed to have passed on to Cynthia but missed me though I obviously suppressed it. Before my religious period starting in my fifteenth year I thought of life as basically comic.

Riva fetched herself a sheet from the bedroom and disrobed to her bra and panties. I turned away with that peculiar hollow feeling in my stomach while she did so. I spread the sheet more evenly on her body and rubbed her shoulder. "Sometimes a good thing would be a bad thing," she said with her eyes closed, and then curled on the couch in a mockery of sleep.

It was short of five A.M. and I had been asleep for an hour when Riva shook me awake. Fred had been moaning and flopping around but she couldn't really revive him. She had called his doctor who was worried about a diabetic coma so rather than wait for an ambulance we put a mattress in the back of the pickup and loaded him like a very large sack of potatoes. Riva was worried he would become conscious and frantic so I duct-taped his wrists together and also his ankles.

The sun was just rising when we reached the small hospital in Gallipolis on the Ohio side of the river. A doctor, nurse, and attendant were ready and Fred was wheeled off. The doctor told Riva

to call him at midafternoon so we drove back home and went to
bed. When I got up about ten Riva had her bags packed. She made
me breakfast and said she was moving down the street until the
program was done in August and then she was leaving town. Her
dark face glittered with anger so I said nothing. She was wearing a
light summer robe and I stared at her fanny when she leaned over
to close a suitcase. She turned around and I'm sure my face reddened. She was suddenly amused and asked how long it had been
since I made love. I said eight months since I had broken up with
Polly in late October. She said her own body had been pretty lonely
for too long. We were both still for a full minute before she closed
the distance to where I sat on the chair. I nuzzled her chest and
she put a breast in my mouth as if feeding me. Two hours later
we were still on the sofa and she was rubbing aloe lotion on my
sore penis. "Sometimes a good thing can be a good thing. We
deserved it," she said.

I had that curious golden feeling I'd gotten when working
behind a shovel in Iron Mountain. It may not be socially correct
to say that black women are better than white women at making
love but Riva was in my own modest experience. She heated up
the leftover ham hocks and butter beans while I called my mother
who suggested Hazelden up in Minnesota. She would cover her
"little brother's" recovery tab. I had learned from her that Fred
had been more generous than necessary with his first wife and
also that he gave away a great deal of his inherited money to needy
people and charities.

While lunch was getting warm Riva talked about how alcohol
easily becomes a culture's treat but then without effort in excessive quantities falls into becoming a culture's hiding place. There's
no physical place for most of us to hide so booze is the next best
thing. She naturally had sympathy for the dirt poor who drank too
much but not for people like Fred. She had never been able to de-

termine the true character of what she called his "heartache" or if it was merely a biochemical case where he drank because he started drinking. I told her how my father thought of himself as a northern gentleman to whom three martinis before dinner were nearly an obligation and how after dinner he might "brandy off," as he called it. That amount might have worked but at least twice a month there were binges.

Without thinking I doused my food with a vinegar hot sauce, then groaned when it hit my cracked lip and Riva applied another ice cube. I opened her robe for a look and then she sat on my sore dick until we broke the chair and ended up finishing on the linoleum floor. She said that since she was forty and I twenty-four we were a perfect match but this was the last time.

When we arrived at the hospital the nurse told us that Fred had become conscious and after a long conversation with the doctor had decided that he wished to live. Fred had talked to my mother but had turned down Hazelden opting for a clinic connected to a hospital up in Columbus. He would be voluntarily locked in for a minimum of six weeks.

When we entered Fred's room he looked awful but was smiling. "I had a drug-induced dream that you two were fucking," he said. "Of course we were," Riva teased while I broke out with sweat. He had a tablet and was writing his good-bye to his first love drinking. He had started at ten years of age with sips in his parents' pantry. "I guess I got out of hand," he said. "I was supposed to help you," he said, clutching at my arm.

18

I drove north at dawn feeling liberated enough in body and soul to begin my life in earnest. I knew this feeling would become tenuous occasionally but for the time being I was going to ride it. I had exiled myself in a marriage that was punishing for Polly, and further betrayed myself with a return to religion in the form of a thin and abstract devotion. How soiled and tawdry poor Jesus was compared to the theological school where the self-interest of the human intelligence smothered prayer, and the abstractions in the history of theology were a virtual fire extinguisher on the Gospels. I had envied my fellow students whose faith was profound but whose minds were evidently orderly enough to make formal studies remote from this faith.

There was a temptation to close my eyes while driving and thank God for the gift of a skinny black woman who was far wiser than all but one professor in my life, but then it had often occurred to me that the possible wisdom of my teachers had always been strangled by the institution. Being at the university through the deaths of Robert Kennedy and Martin Luther King Jr. ending with the more recent Kent State butchery had often made academic studies seem problematical and remote. How upsetting to see your professor break down in tears in your Chaucer class the day after King was murdered. My return to religion was a defense against the insanity of the time, a way to avoid standing there simply screaming like the girl in the famous Kent State photograph. I recalled the day when I was a junior at Michigan State and Cynthia had called to say that she had heard our ex–paper boy had died in Vietnam. He was a poor kid and never seemed dressed warmly enough in winter when below-zero winds blew in off Lake Superior. His name was Larry and Cynthia slipped him extra change and also food. He was none too bright but did well as a distance runner in high school track. I remembered seeing him standing in front of the pool hall when he came home from his marine basic training. He put a face on an insane war. I knew that Cynthia had had a goofy girlhood crush on this boy thinking it heroic the way he lugged his big canvas bag of newspapers up the snowy hill.

I was absurdly happy when I entered Michigan just north of Toledo though I was already lonely for Riva. She was going to stay the two more days Fred needed at the hospital then drive him up for his hoped for cure in Columbus. He had friends in the area who would visit him, especially a Zen adept named Claude who had quit drinking after taking a particular vow the name of which I've forgotten. I'd witnessed Claude and Fred in mild arguments over whether any religion could properly be removed and adapted away from its homeground, whether it was any of the forms of Buddhism or Christianity. The Germans tended to make Christ Germanic, the Americans made him a kindly glad-hander, and so on throughout the world. It wasn't a pretty picture when the Spanish killed everyone who wouldn't become Christians in the conquest of Mexico. Fred would counter with the question of what a solo Zen student was doing in Columbus, Ohio. Claude defended himself by saying that his practice was an "attitude" not a religion. Both his father and his brother had committed suicide and he wished to avoid this family trait. Claude and Fred gave themselves headaches when they arrived at the obvious point that we were colonialists in America with a religion of Judaic source. We couldn't very well adopt a religion from any of the more than five hundred American Indian tribes. Was religion without faith possible? It was a relief when they lapsed into their love lives in the manner of long-term cronies. This was years ago but Fred had always said it was Riva who glued his life together more than his religion and I wondered what he would do now that she was leaving. I knew I had to evolve my own private religion or I'd be in danger of falling off the edge of the world. Fred and I both had been startled that afternoon in the Chicago tavern when Vernice said that as a poet she had discovered it was her own story that was true.

I felt exhilarated in the early evening when I crossed the vast Mackinac Bridge into the Upper Peninsula. I made it to the Soo just before dark but missed the last Sugar Island ferry. I went to a tavern for a hamburger and beer then parked near the ferry dock and slept in the truck. It was a cool night and my sleeping bag was tucked safely away in Marquette so I awoke several times to start the truck and heater. I was bothered by the idea that I had committed adultery with Riva but finally let any guilt slide off into the night when I watched a huge ocean-bound freighter with a Duluth name heading down the lakes then east toward the St. Lawrence Seaway. The guilt couldn't amount to much if it could be dispersed by a freighter.

19

I meant to stay a single night with Donald and Cynthia but it extended into a fine week when I helped Donald dig up and retile their septic tank field. We'd fish for lake trout, whitefish, and perch early in the morning and then be behind the shovel all day long. We also dug footings and hand-mixed cement to build new porch steps. It was tough going but the exhaustion was wonderful. It was also fascinating to be around my nephew and niece. The boy was as gentle as Donald and the girl impulsive and headstrong as her mother. I felt some regret that I had decided never to father children. Cynthia also had three dogs, mixed-breed mutts, to make up for their absence in our childhood. There was also a seven-week-old female pup left from a litter, a Labrador and sled dog mix, that slept with me on the living room sofa. The little girl had named the pup Carla and on my last day with them it was decided that I should own the pup. Naturally I refused. This was at dinner and the pup had a gift ribbon around its neck.

"You're the loneliest asshole in the world. You need a dog," Cynthia said, closing the issue. Before dinner she had shown me a letter she had received from a lawyer in West Palm Beach, Florida, asking her to write a letter in support of our father's good character to be presented to a judge. She had called the lawyer out of curiosity and was told that my father had made an "understandable" mistake and had seduced a Cuban girl who was under the legal age. Under further questioning the lawyer had argued that for a white man it was impossible to determine the age of a dark-skinned Cuban girl. Cynthia told the lawyer she needed the prosecutor's number to help him build his case and the lawyer hung up on her. We stood there near the stove while she was cooking dinner with a wave of melancholy sweeping over us. It was then that I told her of Riva's insistence that we go to Mexico and apologize to Vera. Cynthia said that she and Vera still wrote to each other and that we had a seven-year-old half brother. At first I was unable to absorb this. Cynthia said that there was no reason for her to go but I should if it would make me feel better though I should think it over first. She then asked me if I wanted to see a photo of the boy Vera had sent and I said no. I asked if our father knew of the child and she said Jesse might have told him.

I left Sugar Island and the Bay Mills Indian community with a pup named Carla and the knowledge of a half brother I'd likely never see. I had called Riva the night before to see if she had an idea of what I should do and she said that given the situation I might have to "grow some balls" before I went to Mexico. I also made a late call to Vernice after everyone had gone to bed. She was sweet and friendly on the phone and I said that it occurred to me that she might like to come up to the Upper Peninsula for a vacation. "When?" she asked. "As soon as possible," I said, envisioning her lying on my green sleeping bag like a water lily on the surface of a northern lake. "I believe in words," she said, "write me a letter and tell me who you actually are on earth. I felt drawn to you in the bar or I wouldn't have given you my phone number, but you must describe yourself and what your intentions are in life. The other day an attractive man offered to take me to Paris. I've always wanted to go to Paris and I've probably read more about Paris than most Parisians but I believe more in people than in places, and have learned not to bow to my whims. For instance, when I first met this man on Michigan Avenue he was wearing a wedding band and the next day when we had a drink the ring had disappeared. He blushed when I said that Winnetka was an odd place for a bachelor apartment. So, no lies please. Pretend you're on your deathbed, which we all are, and tell me the truth." I said I'd write the letter but had sweaty doubts that I'd come up with something attractive enough to get her on a plane. "Try," she said. End of conversation. I sat there on the couch with the puppy, little Carla, next to me and speculated on the mysteries of women. The phone call would have made any man seriously consider becoming a monk.

I was off in the morning after Cynthia cooked me some illegal venison for breakfast. Donald tried to pay me a hundred bucks for my week's digging but I refused it take it. I certainly had never seen Cynthia so happy. She kissed me good-bye and handed me a baby blanket for Carla.

The pup cried for a while but I petted her tummy while driving and she fell asleep. As I drove west toward Marquette I felt firmed up with the green rumpled landscape appearing wider as it had begun to reveal itself outside of Cincinnati on the way down along the Ohio River. I began to question if I still believed in Christ's resurrection and decided after two hours that I did. Anything was possible on an earth that creates for itself such a fabulous landscape of forest, swamps, and rivers. I tried to recall a German philosopher we discussed in theological school who had said, in effect, the miracle is that the world exists.

Passing through the small town of Harvey on the outskirts of Marquette I noticed a restaurant that specialized in turkey dishes and had a good memory of my father. When Cynthia and I were quite young we liked turkey sandwiches. Late on Saturday mornings when we were doubtless driving our mother crazy my father would take us to the restaurant and all puffy-eyed would drink some coffee and smoke cigarettes while we ate. Afterward if it was summer we'd go to the beach east of Harvey, toward Au Train, and my father would doze on the sand while we played. Once, despite being dressed nicely, Cynthia who was about five at the time walked out in the water up to her neck and wouldn't come back. My father said, "Do something about her," but I couldn't. One morning soon after that she poured out much of his liquor in the kitchen sink and he spanked her, she disappeared and by dinnertime the Marquette police and hundreds of citizens were looking for her. I actually knew where her hideout was but didn't say anything because I liked the idea of pouring the liquor into the sink. About a block from our house lived a woman who owned a nasty German shepherd and Cynthia would often curl up in its doghouse. Just before dark I told my mother this and the policeman who retrieved Cynthia got bit by the dog.

When I reached the back of our house I developed an insufferable knot in my stomach. Jesse was kind enough to bring me the camping gear from my room. Clarence and I loaded the rowboat.

The next day Jesse had to fly down to Florida to bring my father a number of books and other items in jail. We didn't discuss the issue other than for me to say that I knew about it and hoped that my mother didn't, but then Jesse said she had paid for his lawyer. Clarence became philosophical about how much trouble a man's brainless dick could cause. I knew that my father still owned a great deal of land down between Witch Lake and Amasa and asked Jesse why he didn't sell it. He said it was because my father owned so much land jointly with his dead brother Richard and he couldn't bear to sell land Richard had loved. He added that land was the last thing that you sold which I viewed as ironical what with my missing cabin. I felt both puzzled and sympathetic toward these two men who continued going through the precise motions of maintaining a family that had disappeared. Frank Lloyd Wright had said that the rich became janitors for their possessions but it occurred to me that they mostly hired out that job. Fred liked to say that people who had nothing to do had nothing, that the long-range product of greed was emptiness.

20

I admit that when I left Marquette I felt as if I were fleeing the scene of a crime, but then the actual scene of the sequence of crimes was embedded in memory so that there was nothing to be done with it. I couldn't write a proper letter to Vernice because if I were truthful I would probably scare her away. Instead I would concoct an earnest description of my curiosity about what my family had done to what Henry Schoolcraft, an explorer early in the nineteenth century, had described as one of the most stunning, albeit foreboding, places on earth. Longfellow had never visited the Upper Peninsula when he wrote his *Hiawatha*. He had merely cribbed from Schoolcraft and the descriptions of Louis Agassiz. Vernice might be interested because it was concerned with poetry though I, in fact, loathed the poem. Peter White and the early Marquette fathers assumed that they cared for the Natives right up to letting them dance in the Episcopal church but that didn't stop them from moving the Natives out of the way of imperial progress. There are limitations to virtue.

The simple truth was that as a young man approaching my mid-twenties I had an overwhelming need for the opposite sex and I certainly hadn't the strength to oppose this desire. What I could oppose with whatever remnant of Christianity in my soul was picking on a lovely vulnerable creature like Polly whom my melancholy obsessions had nearly devoured. Vernice was unlikely to be susceptible. Unlike my father I intended to control the damage I did.

The only thing distracting about Vernice was that in my two-hour encounter she had reminded me of my English professors and so did our phone conversation. These professors appeared to believe that if you got the language right all other unpleasant considerations would simply go away which was not far from my own unvoiced belief that if I could balance things in my head reality would cooperate when there was no apparent connection.

That first June night in the village of Grand Marais I found the cheapest small tourist cabin for temporary quarters and unpacked my valise of maps. The knotty pine desk was too small so I spread several of the maps on the floor and knelt there. Some of them were quite old and I had to be careful as the edges would crumble. My family's business activities had spread across most of the Upper Peninsula but I decided on the middle section rather than east or west for a beginning because I had so many good feelings about the area from rowing the boat with Fred to my first lovemaking with Laurie on a sandbar on Au Sable Lake. I intended to walk all summer

long but starting slow in order to give my ankle a chance to build
its strength. I casually drew a grid map of a twenty-by-twenty-mile
area that included expanses about which I had already read.

It was still light at ten-thirty when I walked down to the tavern for
a sandwich having forgotten all about dinner. I talked to the bar
owner Mick, a very large rusty-haired man, about brook trout fishing places. I had met him before and knew he had been a timber
cruiser so would have ample knowledge of the places I needed to
explore. I had decided to masquerade as a graduate student for
reasons of privacy, the simple idea that my ambitions were too ill
formed to share with another human. Anytime I had mentioned
them before it was like describing a dream that was vivid to me but
of no interest to anyone else. Fred, of course, was an exception
though not a solid ally. After my Chicago fight with the police and
my enforced therapy I had been quite angry at a psychiatrist for
talking about my "obsessive compulsive" tendencies. Concealment
was certainly in order. I had also pitched my prescription of lithium
within minutes of my release. When a cop tears out a handful of
your hair so that the roots bleed it is understandable that you resist.
Being secretive comes naturally to the mammalian species.

I agreed on a meeting place to fish with Mick the next evening
then walked out in the gathering dark. A big yellow moon was rising in the east and I walked down to the harbor beach then east
toward the cabin. I felt cleanly exhilarated that my disorderly ap-
prenticeship was over and that I was beginning my life's work
though I had already hoped I might finish it in ten years or so. I
was still young enough to think in the grandest of terms.

I continued down the beach past the path to my tourist cabin
toward the estuary of the Sucker River a mile or two distant. The
moon's sheen on the water followed me as I walked for reasons not

clear to me. It occurred to me that my own point of view was unique
on earth but this was not a comforting idea. Wherever I stood and
looked I was the only one there. The few sounds of the village di-
minished, and I mostly heard my feet in the damp sand, and then a
loon call ahead in the estuarine area. To the left far out in Lake
Superior the lights of a freighter made their slow passage to the
west. I heard a coyote out on a forested promontory called Lonesome Point and single dog answering the coyote from the village.
My heart fluttered when I flushed a plover from a thickish stand
of beach grass. There was a dense smell of wild roses mixing with
the odor of cold water.

I was disturbed for a few minutes recalling the idea that if I
actually thought I was looking into the heart of evil in my family
I ought to include their sense of Christianity which they viewed
as a further entitlement for their conquests, and that my great-
grandfather coming out of England in the mid-1880s had also been
to India and Africa but gave up those fields as being too full and
competitive with others of his kind. Old journals are often fascinating but his were mostly filled with his speculations on business
opportunities, accounts, and overweening notations on his faith in
his own particular destiny intermixed with biblical verses and his
profound faith and trust in God. He believed but did I?

Luckily the tingling thought of Vernice and the presence of
the moon overcame the arrogant old bastard. I would try to write
her early in the morning before I set off in search of a camping spot.
I'd also have to count what money I had in my duffel bag, a repellent process. A month ago a Chicago psychiatrist asked what I hated
aside from the obvious police (the left side of my face was still blue)
and I errantly said "money" and when he tried to track this back
into my life I stopped talking. When Jesse had asked me how I expected to live on a hundred dollars a week he was apologetic about
my bilked trust. If my father ever tried to sell land there was a court

order to the effect that he had to return to me the sum for which
my cabin had been sold. This had been engineered by the embarrassed title company who confused David the third with just plain
David. And in a private moment at dinner at the Drake my mother
was concerned with her usual "I'm always there for you" but I escaped by saying that I was thinking of going back to Michigan State
for graduate school in history thus providing me with funds to live,
albeit simply, as long as I was enrolled even if I stayed at the university until I died. It was all so squalid with the ready assumption
that I deserved to live without lifting a finger in my own support.
It made me think of hardworking Clarence as Saint Clarence, but
Jesse less so as he was involved as a messenger in my father's financial shenanigans and nonresponse to Vera's rape. Frankly I
wanted to be useful in this life and that could be defined only by
work, not good intentions.

My immediate downfall was the moon. I lay back and stared
at it for an hour consciously trying to avoid one of my daffy trances.
I knew what the moon was but not what it was for, anymore than
I understood a bird or bear. There was a frightening image of my
mother's face as a yellow moon. It was before a costume party,
their Midsummer Night's gala up at the Club, and my mother was
in her bedroom with us dressing up with her face as the moon out
of which emerged fiery spangles. I was just out of kindergarten
so Cynthia wasn't quite four. Cynthia cried and tried to tear away
the moon masque. Mother pushed her away and Cynthia's head
bumped against the corner of the bedstead. Mother's red lip-
sticked lips emerged from the yellow moon face smelling of piney
gin. Her robe was thin and white with her sizable breasts perk-
ing out. Cynthia screamed "shitty shitty shitty" and mother rushed
out and father came in dressed as the Lone Ranger which didn't
frighten us because we knew the Lone Ranger. This did not stop
Cynthia from continuing to scream "shitty" and my father said to

me "take care of her" though there was a nanny who drank and chewed Dentyne with sharp snaps to cover the smell. Grandfather's "cabin" was large with at least twelve bedrooms with fireplaces and a motorized conveyor belt to carry wood into the basement and a small man who couldn't talk to carry wood to the rooms when there were many guests from Chicago. Cynthia led me to a room where we could watch the party out in the yard where ugly pink tents were set up. I told Cynthia to stop saying shitty so she said "pissy." We heard mother walking from room to room calling out "good night children" but we didn't answer because we didn't want to see her. We played Crazy Eights by the window hearing that Glenn Miller kind of music while hundreds of costumed people danced and drank. The nanny brought up hamburgers and Cynthia threw hers out the window onto people on the lawn below us. "What's that?" a woman yelled. Later we heard steps in the hall and hid in a closet. A man in pioneer leather clothes and a raccoon hat quickly screwed a woman dressed as Little Bo Peep on the bed. When they left I was upset but Cynthia jumped up and down clapping her hands and laughing. I think I was upset because the woman was the mother of a boy I knew and the pioneer guy wasn't her husband. Cynthia came to my room to sleep and locked the door with one of many keys she carried in a small red purse. One morning she had put an earthworm in Mother's coffee. I had a gold railroad pocket watch that read three A.M. when we heard Mother stumbling outside rattling the door to come in and tuck us in but we didn't answer.

It was the same summer at storytelling time when a college kid hired for that purpose had us seated in a pergola, maybe two dozen kids, and told us that we all had an animal who lived within us and told us what to do. It was this animal who controlled and dictated our bad behavior. It was hard work to get rid of this animal and that was why we had to obey our parents and go to church. It was meant to be a scary story and the narrative was couched along a line wherein a naughty little boy's animal grew so large it devoured him.

Sitting there on the beach in the motherly moonlight I realized that I had never reached a point where I actually disbelieved in the existence of this animal. It was probably still there wrapped around my spine. This way lies madness, I thought, listening to the rush of the river over gravel as it braided itself out into the bay. I also never asked my mother a half dozen critical questions that had frequently absorbed me, among them what truly had happened to my dead uncle Richard whom Fred told me she had loved to distraction. I would also ask her why she feigned weakness to deny any accountability for her behavior while we were growing up. And why since she had her own money didn't she leave my father after I was born, and then Cynthia, when his behavior was acknowledged to have become out of control? But then even the slightest personal question had made her flutter a hand in front of her face as if it held a fan. Didn't she know that her avowed phantom pain medically referred to those who had lost limbs and felt pain in the specific area of their absence? When I was twelve I chanced to see her standing naked near her dresser one morning and thought her the most beautiful creature in the world. My cock stayed intermittently hard for days and felt as if it were leaking despite the fact that I knew this desire was wrong. Fred told me that her beauty began to decline the moment she decided to marry my father. Fred also told me when he was quite drunk that he had caught my mother and her college roommate nakedly entwined. He told me this when I was in college and though I was shocked I researched it and found that it wasn't all that extraordinary. Humans are unable to discover unique behavior in their own species. When I was supposed to read Matthew Josephon's *Robber Barons* for a history course, a book dealing with capitalist predatory behavior in the nineteenth century, I dropped the class because I didn't want to think of other descendants in my same position. We want to keep our wounds as lucidly unique as possible, though sitting there on the beach I began to see it as a vain effort. I recalled seeing a book titled *Father of the Atomic Bomb.* Maybe I just wanted, absurdly enough, to take control of the past that was so directly painting the landscape of my present life. There was a glimmer of the idea that if I could see and understand this past clearly enough I could throw it away.

By the time I left the estuarine beach I was pleased to see the northern lights but they turned out to be the first signs of dawn. I had finished with my rational thinking and stared at the moon until I had the illusion that my eyes were detecting its slow, steady movement. The moon gradually had ceased being my mother for which I was thankful though the animal wrapped around my spine remembered my mother's body. My mind was able to replace my mother's body with that of Vernice. There was a vaguely uncomfortable resemblance which I dismissed. Becoming erect I rolled over and tried to fuck the sand which I don't recommend. I pressed my face against the sand which was a little damp with dew and imagined it the loveliest pussy on earth and I didn't care whose body owned it. I dozed and when I awoke to full morning light there was a rare piping plover quite near my left eye acting curious about this sleeping interloper in her home.

21

I was ashamed about forgetting Carla whom I had put in the truck before I walked down to the tavern the evening before. Clarence and Jesse after admiring the pup had found a small sky kennel to put her in while I slept and then had given me a few dog-raising tips I hadn't listened to. She bolted into my arms when I opened the pickup door. For lack of food she had chewed on the upholstery of the new truck, and shit and peed all over the seat. Rather than write my intended letter to Vernice I fed Carla puppy chow with warm milk and then cleaned up the mess. Carla was still irritated at me for leaving her alone all night so I held her while I drank coffee and studied a local map. I felt drowsy from my night on the beach but was more eager to get started than for a nap. I packed a small knapsack with a notebook, sardines, crackers, cheese, water, and a sack of puppy chow for Carla.

An hour later I was on the Kingston Plains, an area Fred had shown me years before. This was to be the first of 123 straight days in the field, a tribute to my mania rather than my good sense. The main feature of the Kingston Plains was the thousands of acres of white pine stumps, some of them very large, which had been cut at waist or chest height probably during the winter when it was easier to skid the trees out on snow-covered trails which they dampened to form ice so that the draft horse–drawn log sleighs could be more easily pulled. Earlier they had used oxen but oxen, unlike horses, had to be lifted totally off the ground to be reshod while horses could be reshod one foot at a time.

I had walked less than a mile among these stumps when I noted that Carla was no longer trotting alongside me. I turned around and there she was about thirty yards behind, curled up and sleeping. That was fine because my bad ankle already hurt from stumbling on the beach in the night and my ankle wrap and tape were back at the cabin. I sat down against a nearby stump and watched her sleep, gradually lifting my eyes to study the landscape around me.

A very quiet voice was saying "stupid" in my left ear. I remembered a fellow student in an American literature class who had returned from a summer in Haight-Ashbury in San Francisco with his head shaved. Many of us more orthodox creatures were envious of this daffy young man in his tie-dyed shirts and ragged trousers. Even sorority girls were drawn to him. The previous year he smoked dope constantly and drank a great deal but now along with his bald head he neither drank nor smoked and had become a vegetarian. One autumn afternoon I walked along the Red Cedar River with him and he told me he was "having satoris thick and fast," *satori*, a Zen term meaning an awakening that clarified his own true nature.

Leaning against the stump half asleep I was having one of my own, a girlish lisp whispering "stupid." Aside from the slightest smattering of knowledge the landscape was incomprehensible other than the sleeping Carla.

I took out my notebook and drew an absolute blank with my poised ballpoint. The "stupid" I was hearing wasn't contemptuous, just true. I had flushed a number of sandhill cranes when I drove down the two-track into the area and now one was returning with its curious and loud prehistoric honk and squawk. Carla leapt to her feet and scooted to my lap for protection. I felt thoroughly comic. I had been in similar areas hundreds of times on the way to trout fishing but then your mind is on the approaching river and chances of luck and far less so on the landscape around you.

I swiveled around until I had completed a 360-degree view, suppressing any anger I felt over the idea that they might have left a few trees for those in the future to look at. Maybe to try to imagine the trees was like asking a contemporary Lakota to imagine a million buffalo. There was an eerie sense of the gray stumps as ghost trees and I planned on visiting the area in the full moonlight. There is a beauty in desolation because that's all we have, I thought, the land shorn of its native self with the soil far too depleted to reenact its former glories.

Despite these melancholy thoughts I was relieved of my "self" and my head felt lighter than I could remember. I flopped over on my side at the same moment the sandhill crane squawked again and Carla buried her nose in my neck with her butt aimed at the air, her little tail curled downward in fear. I felt no less stupid than minutes before but it had occurred to me that this could be corrected by study. I had read a hundred books about God and couldn't remember a single thing of import, but the heart of nature and greed were far more accessible. I remembered coming home from college and Clarence asking what I was studying and when I said English he said, "I

thought everybody knows English?" It helped when I added literature though I said "stories" because Clarence was quite a storyteller
though he could neither read nor write. Being a mixed-blood he knew
hundreds of both Chippewa and Finnish stories that were so long
they exasperated Jesse whose tales of love and death from the province of Veracruz tended to be terse though poetic.

Of course I had high school and college courses in many aspects of the natural sciences but they didn't enable me to put together the whole picture of what I was seeing around me. It had
long been obvious to me that I wanted to know too much, perhaps
more than anyone was capable of, and my religious conversion at
fifteen was mostly a powerful desire to know God. Once on the way
home from trout fishing my friend Glenn had said, "People don't
know why they fuck, they just do it." I learned in my anthropology
course that people prayed in every single culture. But where did
the urge to know everything come from? In my case it started close
to home by wanting to know everything my ancestors had done in
the Upper Peninsula. This seemed to include everything bad my
father had done to our family. For the time being I had to exclude
everything bad my family had done to the population of the Upper
Peninsula because that meant my project would slop over the edges
of my known world.

My immediate response to these thoughts was to put on some
more mosquito dope because my sweat had washed off the previous application and all manner of bugs including blackflies and
deerflies were coming in to feed. I got up with a twinge in my ankle
but Carla decided to continue sleeping. I opened a can of sardines
and that enlivened her. We shared the whole tin and I carried her
back to the truck slowly. On the way I began counting the visible
stumps until I reached the truck, then wrote in my notebook "547
stumps." The world had opened up for me in a significant way,
however untraceable.

❊   ❊   ❊

I reached the cabin by midafternoon and loaded the rowboat. The temperature was in the eighties with a south wind driving the cooler air of Lake Superior to the north. It was tempting to sleep but my mind was a whirl of reality rather than self-concern. Perhaps I was reaching my youthful ambition of not spending my time thinking about myself. On the way back to the cabin from the Kingston Plains I had conceived of a new kind of prayer that didn't attempt to make exceptions for myself from the human condition but was a simple request to understand the world and consequently what was happening to me. To this I added a request to not get greedy about the matter because it had dawned on me that the sin of greed was deeper than money. At the end of the prayer when I was turning into the cabin's driveway I was startled by a teenage girl walking toward the village in the shortest of shorts. My modest speech to the creator of the universe was interrupted by a butt in blue shorts. So it goes. She turned and smiled, then came back and gave Carla a pat on the head before continuing on. She smelled like Ivory soap.

At Au Sable Lake Carla was upset when I launched the rowboat and then went swimming. It was clear she didn't understand what a lake was. Cynthia had likely kept her away from the dangerous St. Mary's River. I caught her with some difficulty and off we went in the rowboat with Carla heading under my seat. After a half hour she emerged and stood with her paws on the gunwale watching the oars and the passing water. I thought that she probably felt in cognitive disarray as I had on my first trip to downtown Chicago. We usually landed at O'Hare and then were picked up to go to my father's mother's house in Lake Forest, but when I was seven we landed in a private plane at Meigs Field and drove through the heart of the city which tightened my stomach and put a lump in my throat. Naturally Cynthia was delighted by it all.

Back at the cabin I took out stationery and began my letter to Vernice partly to keep my mind off the girl who had walked past a couple of hours before.

Dear Vernice,
I know that the odds on this aren't good what with our having spent only two hours together but I think of you often. I can't begin to answer all of the questions you posed on the phone when I was over at my sister's on Sugar Island near Sault Ste. Marie. If I did so I would have to write a relatively eventless autobiography. As a poet you depend on the vicissitudes of your consciousness, your self-awareness, and the infinite variances of your perceptions, while I'm mainly occupied with studying the social and economic history of the Upper Peninsula. This may very well not sound interesting to you but it ties in with an ancestor who came over from England four generations ago and he still seems to have a profound effect on my life. (It's hard to look for skeletons in the family closet because they are all skeletons now.) There was certain questionable economic behavior on my father's side while my mother's family was involved in the Great Lakes shipping industry in transporting iron ore to Cleveland and also the steel mills of Gary, Indiana.

I sensed you were interested in me and I in you, or you wouldn't have gambled on your phone number. Should you care to get out of the heat of Chicago this is a beautiful area. You might also like the puppy my sister Cynthia gave me. I like blues music and jazz much better than rock and roll. I don't cook well but I can catch trout for you to eat. I'm not too knowledgeable about your profession but at Michigan State I liked Wordsworth's "Prelude," Walt Whitman, and

Allen Ginsberg's "Howl." My only real contribution to the world of poetry is to send you money for a ticket.

Yrs. truly, David

What stilted, underwhelming bullshit! Stored in my brain cells was the sound of her thighs detaching themselves from the plastic seated chair in the Chicago tavern. This actually made my dick hard sitting there in the overwarm cabin. I took three one-hundred-dollar bills for her ticket from the stack in my duffel and put Carla in the sky kennel which made her break out weeping. I made the post office minutes before closing and sent my letter special delivery, then walked down to the tavern for a hamburger. It occurred to me that I could save a lot of money if I learned how to cook beyond the U.P. basics of frying this or that. It had been disappointing to discover in restaurants that no one cooked as well as Mrs. Plunkett. Besides my being hungry, every female on the street or in the tavern between the ages of fourteen and seventy looked somewhat desirable. The girl who stopped to pet Carla was playing partners pool with three friends and a dozen men lined up along the bar watched while pretending it was of no particular interest. Her friends called her Shirley and when she bent over in her tight blue shorts and brown legs a young logger yelled "bull's-eye" and she turned around a gave him the finger. When the game was finished she came over to me to say hello and ask how Carla was doing. My mouth went dry and I swallowed a bite of food with difficulty. She said she worked nights in the bar but would be glad to babysit Carla sometime if I wished. Mick came up from the basement with dirty hands from fixing a coolant pump. Shirley left to play another game and Mick said we had better hurry with our fishing because a big front was coming in from the west. We packed our gear in his rickety old Jeep because he said the road was too narrow and brambly for my "pretty pickup." The Jeep had the interesting feature of a hole in the floor so that you could see the road passing down near your feet. Before we headed to the river we drove down to the pier to see if the front was visible. Lake Superior was fairly peaceful but far to the west there was a rumpled black line and Mick figured we had about an hour and a half or two to fish before the "shit hit the fan."

It is utterly soothing to fly-fish for trout. All other considerations or worries drift away and you couldn't keep them close if you wanted. Perhaps it's standing thigh deep in a river with the water passing at the exact but varying speed of life. You easily recognize this mortality and it dissipates into the landscape. If there are flying insects and trout are feeding on them you fish with dry flies. If there's no surface activity you fish with streamers which imitate minnows or with nymphs which imitate the insect larvae that emerge from the streambed and float along with the current.

We were well down in a semi-gorge with steep clay-and-sand banks sprinkled with cedars. I had felt a moment's hesitation wondering if I could climb back up with my bad ankle but there was a succession of deep pools below made by deadfalls which formed logjams. In a riffle corner below one I could see brook trout feeding and I couldn't resist. It was very warm and still in the gorge and there were clouds of mosquitoes around my head. After an hour or so I heard the wind far above me and saw branches swaying. Mick waded toward me from downstream with a nice rainbow of about three pounds which would normally have made its way back to Lake Superior well before late June. I kept two brook trout, enough for supper.

On the half-hour drive through the woods to the river I called out the names of trees and got about seventy-five percent right, what is contemptibly called a gentleman's C. I intended to ask Jesse to send my largely unopened field guide books my mother bought for me when I was wearing out the Bible. Despite her evident imbalances she often sensed my own tangents and tried to correct them. With tree varieties, maple, also beech, birch, oak, and hemlock were easy while white and red pine, jack pine, spruce and fir were dicey, and so were the bushes such as sugar plum, dogwood, and chokecherry. When I put on my hip boots I thought for the first time that it was a little strange that we choose not to know all the ingredients of where we live.

Mick hauled me the last twenty feet up and over the edge of the bank when my ankle turned rubbery. By then the sky was dark an hour before sunset and the wind gusting to fifty knots. A deadfall had come down and we stopped while Mick took a chain saw out of the back of the Jeep and cut the two-track clear. When we came out into an open marsh we saw lightning hit a tamarack and burst into flames and we sat there watching the sheets of rain douse the fire.

We had talked about my intention of camping all summer which he described as "bullshit." Camping was for pleasure, he said, and if I was going to get any work done I needed something better. By then we were drinking out of a schnapps bottle he'd drawn from under the seat and I had become more voluble. We detoured for a mile and he showed me a tar-papered deer cabin I could stay in owned by friends of his from downstate if I would reroof it and shore up the foundation. How to do so was beyond me but he said he would tell me how. A couple of more gulps of the schnapps and I confessed my long-range intentions of being there and he said "get at it, do it, forget it." Otherwise I'd eat myself up with my resentments. He sounded like Riva.

22

It was my second strange night in a row. I fed Carla, then fell asleep with her on the bed, waking about three A.M. to a high solid roar which it took me a minute to recognize as Lake Superior. Now the cabin was cold and I turned on the electric heater, then fried the brook trout and heated a can of beans. Carla loved the crisp brown skin of the trout. It was clear to her that I was her substitute mother.

I took out my notebook and was pleased at the single entry of the stumps I had counted. What a stroke! This number could very well rise to hundreds of thousands. I felt entirely ordinary in terms of mental temperature, say like someone who had graduated from the university and had their first day on a career job. Nothing had any particular focus but I was doing what I was supposed to do. I read in a volume of Sprague's journal I had brought along how early loggers, featuring my great-grandfather, had created leases to cut native property which would be signed by a witnessed "X," then slipped in a land deed and took ownership for the minimal lease price. I passed over Sprague's irate gloss on this matter hurriedly. I was far more interested in what had happened than I was in the emotion of anger, at least for the time being.

I fell asleep over the small desk then awoke after a nightmare in which Polly was making love to someone else. Well, of course, but then the dream memory revealed that her partner bore some resemblance to my father in a younger reincarnation which meant a resemblance to myself but then it was him not me. I straightaway wished him dead in his Florida jail cell.

I took Carla out to pee and to shake the dream out of my head. There was a strong cool wind out of the northwest and in the moonlight I could see huge waves breaking over the pier and questioned whether the village was a bleak outpost or a paradise. The timber was gone by the First World War, and then overfishing and the lamprey had wiped out the large commercial fishery for lake trout by the 1950s. Now the village survived on tourism and by pulp logging of second- and third-growth timber for the paper mills. Maybe it wasn't as bad as I thought because the real money always went elsewhere in an extractive economy.

There was an image of my father being strangled in jail by poor white trash or an angry black. Once in a sober moment Fred had told me that I was unable to have compassion for my father to the degree that I was unable to have compassion for myself. Of course this made me angry. What did it mean that he would get drunk and fuck girls that were too young among various other crimes and misdemeanors? In a dreary introductory psychology course that masqueraded as science it occurred to me that you could explain everything away but the behavior remained. He may have regretted raping Vera but what could this regret possibly mean to Vera? What did he feel when he stole my cabin, or bilked the trust money due to Cynthia and myself? He didn't hit my mother but his language to her was often icily violent so that Cynthia would hold her hands to her ears and scream until she was about ten, and then she simply stayed out of his presence as much as possible. This taunted him because everyone in Marquette who didn't know him well thought of him as gracious, charming, generous. After the Duluth incident I was outside the screen door of the work shed and heard Clarence say to Jesse that my father would fuck a rock pile if there was a snake in it.

How well had I treated Polly? The sound of our marriage had been my subdued whine. I had driven her away as surely as if I had wielded a club. Even on our marriage day I was vaguely aware that I was doing the wrong thing. I think both Cynthia and my mother were also aware but remained hopeful. There was the definite possibility that after the separation when Polly and my mother had continued seeing each other my mother had said, "You must forgive my son." For what? For trying so hard to be unlike his father that he had no idea who he was.

Riva had disturbed me because though she was clinically hardheaded and knowledgeable she had said that there were invisible fibers between certain people and they couldn't do much about it but try to control them. She had said that after I had told her about Laurie from start to finish. This was during our breaks between lovemaking when she asked me about my sexual experience. I wrote it down when Jesse had referred to Laurie as a "plumita" and years later I had asked a Mexican girl who was a graduate student what it meant. She was embarrassed but laughed saying it meant that whomever was a "fast little feather," a girl who could be from a good family but liked "intimacy," not necessarily whorish but "available."

I told Riva all of this and she said people didn't have to be in love to want each other badly. "Look at us," she added.

I was shivering on the porch listening to the implacable roar of the waves so impersonally hostile that I hugged Carla to my chest. After all, I was her parent. I was straining for the first sign of light in the eastern sky so that I could go out to my tar-paper cabin, clean it up, and make a list of needed supplies. I could feel the thump of Carla's heart against my own. I was her parent and the night before I had forgotten her and was repaid with torn upholstery. On a certain level, perhaps the same as my own, she was trying to explain the world to herself. Luckily she lacked the crippling ideals that suffocated my marriage to Polly. Certain of these ideals blinded me to the fact that I was as self-referential as my father who as a tertiary alcoholic saw all existence only in terms that related to him right down to the weather forecast.

On the way out to the cabin I stopped the truck abruptly and said, "When I'm preaching to myself who am I preaching to?" Carla looked around alarmed to see if I was talking to someone else. I continued on distracted, taking a few wrong trails until I found the cabin. I pumped a few pails of water and heated them on a propane stove to mop out the place. I stopped Carla from eating porcupine shit several times. It startled me when a large garter snake near the woodpile struck at Carla who was barking and grabbing at it. I caught the snake and pitched it in the river. I washed some of the dusty dishes suddenly glad to be there. The cabin lacked the pure grace of the one Sprague had given me but it was more than serviceable for my minimalist intentions. There were three kerosene

lamps to light my journal writing and a Coleman lantern to walk
with to the outside toilet with the usual quarter moon cut in the
privy door. I would buy a couple of extra flashlights as I had a habit
of misplacing them. There was a tattered cookbook called *Camp
Grub* that included hearty dishes for hunters, the kind where you
mix a can of beans with a can of corn with a can of tomatoes with a
chopped onion with a pound of ground beef and add Worcestershire
sauce, hot sauce, and a teaspoon of garlic salt. I'd call Jesse to have
him send over some of my mother's cookbooks and an Italian one
Mrs. Plunkett had given me when I went away to college. Under a
coffee table next to a bunk bed there was a large stack of "girlie"
magazines of the most basic sort with a couple of them outright pornography. One of the latter was packed with photos of men ejacu-
lating on the upturned, eager faces of women. This seemed to be a
male delusion. I saw only one woman truly attractive to me in half
a dozen of the magazines and wondered about the specialization of
sexual taste. Looking around the cabin there were places for eight
to sleep including a small rickety loft. My father used to go to a
fancier camp over south of Munising. He didn't really deer hunt
but he had all the equipment. I know my mother had a strong sus-
picion that their hunting trips were up to no good, especially when
he met his old Yale pal Seward from Duluth, a saturnine man who
oozed privilege and bad behavior. I suppose that some men needed
these camps to return to what they thought of as their birthright.

I heard a shrill barking in the distance and rushed to the cabin.
I had neglected Carla and now she was yelping back in the woods
to the east. I found her in a grove of popples with two quills in her
nose and a young porcupine halfway up a tree in front of her. I
snipped off the base of the quills having read somewhere that the
process lets air out and they are easier to pull. The quills weren't
deep in her nose but when I jerked them Carla howled and snapped
at me. I lay down with her and comforted her then dozed off for a

little while thinking I should go to bed at a set time if I intended to do a full day's work.

I had been inattentive and when I awoke I wasn't sure in what direction the cabin lay. I had always been careful about directions when trout fishing in near wilderness because there was always the possibility of becoming fatally lost in the Upper Peninsula though this mostly happened during an especially cold deer season in November, or to snowmobilers who ran out of gas.

I wasn't fearful when I struck out in what turned out to be the wrong direction but I knew there could be the possibility of discomfort. My jacket with a compass was back at the cabin and I had only a jackknife and no matches. Even my pocket watch was in the jacket pocket. You can keep a fairly steady heading with a watch if the sun is visible. It was a coolish June midmorning but I had a good twelve hours of daylight in front of me at this latitude. I looked in vain in the immediate area for any ferns I may have broken when I came to retrieve Carla but found none. The biggest problem for those lost in the U.P. is the density of the foliage in some areas. You are literally without a point of view except that offered by the sun which you must remember is moving.

After an hour it had become unpleasant. My bug dope was also back at the cabin in my jacket pocket. Carla was tired so I had to carry her. She couldn't have weighed more than twenty pounds but she was ungainly. She may also have sensed my worry and wiggled a lot. I couldn't seem to get out of a low boggy area which made the mosquitoes and blackflies worse. I put Carla down and climbed a pine tree for a vantage point and she wept thinking I abandoned her. I couldn't get high enough to see above the tops of neighboring trees. I tried to maintain a straight line north knowing that there was a county road within five miles. At the beginning I had tried to move too swiftly and that made me thirsty and my ankle sore.

I finally broke through to a clearing of about twenty acres. I was so relieved to escape the claustrophobic density of the woods that my eyes teared and I flopped down against a stump. Carla was also relieved and fell fast asleep. After a few minutes my worried mind and eyes cleared to the degree that I could see that I was sitting on the edge of the grandest collection of white pine stumps I had ever seen. They were simply immense with several so large that three men with hands joined couldn't have encircled them. I had inadvertently discovered a stump shrine. I counted thirty. The soil must have been perfect for white pine and one could only imagine them rising a couple of hundred feet toward the sky. My skin tingled though my heart and mind felt sore.

After a half hour's rest I picked up Carla who consented after walking a mere fifty yards or so. On the far side of the clearing there was a gully that seemed to lead in a more westerly direction. I knew that the sun was farthest north this close to the solstice and the gully pointed to a downward drainage so that it had to finally lead toward a creek or the river from which I had departed. I turned around and stood there a full ten minutes, my enervation and fatigue now gone, until I could again imagine what this patch of forest had looked like. I can't say how but the massive stumps now seemed alive and reassured me that my work had a great deal of meaning. My ankle still hurt but the ache seemed as insignificant as a mosquito bite.

Scarcely a hundred yards down the slow pitch of the gully I came upon a stunning surprise. There before me was the largest of all white pine stumps, the great mother of stumps, straddling the gully like a ten-ton spider supported by roots so massive I couldn't get my arms around them. I had put Carla down and she had scurried around to the other side sniffing the ground. Suddenly she was inside the stump and I was looking down at her through an opening between two contorted roots. There was a slice of sunlight shining down on her face and she regarded me gravely. I scrambled around to the other side and there was an opening large enough to crawl in and I joined Carla. It was sufficiently high enough for me to sit up straight and there was light to see the ground which was a mixture of cool sand and gravel. Carla was shivering in fear but I knew it was the scats on the ground left probably by bobcat and coyotes and a larger piece of dried fecal matter that was likely from a bear. I was enthralled, and there was a distinct feeling similar to when I had been baptized. I thought that this was as close as I could come to finding a church for myself in our time.

The gully did lead to the river though I guessed it was a mile or so, and I had to half-crawl through a dense alder thicket with mud up to my elbows and knees. The important thing was that I could hear the river and it was a joy to slide over the bank into the moving current as if I were a dead man. I released Carla and we floated at the same speed with Carla gulping the water. I was painfully thirsty myself but waited a hundred yards or so to make sure that there wasn't a dead animal in the river that might cause me to get giardia, an intestinal disease that lasted for months.

23

I spent ten days surrounding the Fourth of July weekend laying low while the village was crowded, continuing to work out my grid in the areas where white pine had been present. I could now walk up to four hours a day on my bad ankle, and Carla quickly got stronger too. I rigged a sling and pouch out of a day pack to carry her on my back in the manner of a papoose when she became tired. I had certainly had my doubts at first but Cynthia was right about Carla being a companion. Every midafternoon when it became too warm for comfortable walking we would drive over to Au Sable Lake to bathe and row a couple of hours before making dinner. Jesse had sent along my mother's *Joy of Cooking* but I soon found out that it would take a while for cooking to become a joy. I was distressed by my ineptitude and my first so-called triumph was an elementary dish of scalloped potatoes. The bottom of my meat loaf was burned and the top crumbly. My spaghetti sauce was acrid. Mick helped when he brought out roofing supplies and suggested that my oven temperature was off. I bought a baking thermometer and found that the propane was over fifty degrees higher than the dial read. I had also discovered on the day we were lost and so happily waded and swam downstream that Carla couldn't handle a whole large tin of sardines. We were on our way to town for a drink when she gave me a curious look and her bowels loosened on the front seat. I reminded myself to buy paper towels.

I checked the post office every day and had received a letter each from my mother and Cynthia. In my mother's there was a hundred-dollar bill and a P.S. saying "have a nice dinner." For that amount I could eat at the tavern twenty times. I kept away from the tavern in the evening to avoid getting involved with a local girl despite my imponderable horniness. I wanted to put in a solid month's work before I frantically sought diversion. I still had hopes for Vernice but my thoughts kept returning to Laurie whom I knew was married, and Riva who had left Fred. I got a letter from Fred in his Columbus, Ohio, clinic that said, "Riva has left me in the hour of my need. I can't say I blame her."

Then on the Friday after the Fourth I got a postcard from Vernice that said, "Maybe. Love, Vernice." I smelled the card in the post office lobby and an old crone laughed at me. Incidentally, there was no odor. The card was postmarked five days before and I idly thought that maybe she was on her way north. My heart sped up and my dick twitched in my trousers. My willpower slackened and I went to the crowded tavern for a drink. There were at least a dozen acceptable women in there drinking beer and saying such inimitable things as, "I gotta take a piss." One next to me on the bar stool said to me, "Buy me a beer, cutie." She was from Germfask and her large tits swung in her halter top. My ears burned. I was a leg and butt man but for a change the sight of these big stretch-marked breasts enlivened me. Luckily her pulp-cutting boyfriend showed up and my thoughts turned to Shirley who was playing pool with a burly older man who Mick had told me was a downstate writer. A commercial fisherman I met earlier had given me five undersized lake trout about a foot long apiece and I left after my two-beer limit despite saying to myself "who gives a fuck?"

Outside near the tavern entrance two girls were doing a dance step. They were clearly underage, I guessed them at thirteen or so, but physically attractive. One of them was beautiful in fact. They wore only shorts and halters in the late-afternoon warmth and moved gracefully to the music that came out the tavern's screened door. Both of them grinned at me and I felt blood rising to my face as it occurred to me that this was the kind of desire that had caused my father so many problems, but then he didn't accept the social contract to the degree that he denied himself anything. The other question that came to mind was why didn't I ever dance?

I made the mistake of leaving each day at dawn and spending three days to the west over near the Big Two-Hearted River area hauling the boat and fishing several lakes in the afternoon. I didn't care much for Hemingway who was a twentieth-century icon to my father. Some of the early stories were fine but as a nonveteran I had no fascination with war. I preferred Willa Cather and Faulkner both of whom my father considered "soft in the head." He had made several fishing trips to Cuba with Seward in the late forties and early fifties and had met Hemingway several times, doubtless at a bar. I suspected later that the main purpose of these trips was the sexual tourism so popular under Batista.

My mistake was not checking the post office because I got back in Grand Marais after the lobby door was locked. On the third night after two A.M. Carla was barking, not unusual because she always barked when she heard coyotes or smelled a bear, but then there were lights sweeping through the cabin windows and I thought of the revolver that I had abandoned to make sure I didn't use it on myself.

It was Vernice. To put it in mild terms she was furious. I stood there at the door in my skivvies and she asked why I hadn't met her "fucking plane" in Marquette as promised. In the background Mick waved, outlined by his pickup lights. I was shining a flashlight and there was a cloud of mosquitoes around her head. I tried to brush one off a cheekbone but she hissed, "Don't touch me." She stood at the half-opened screen door as I quickly lit two lamps. More mosquitoes were coming in so I retrieved her blue suitcase and she stepped inside far enough for me to close the door. She flinched when Carla started licking her ankle but then stooped and petted Carla who rolled over on her back. She spoke in a low tight voice saying that she wanted to fly back to Chicago in the morning and had made a reservation when I hadn't met her plane. She had taken a bus from Marquette to Seney, then paid two teenagers at the Seney Tavern twenty bucks to drive her to Grand Marais where she arrived at midnight at the tavern. She had to wait two hours for Mick to close up because other men in the bar were ugly drunks. She had assumed that my cabin was on a beach not "a shack in the fucking woods." I apologized and said I hadn't been able to check my mail for several days. I heated her some water to wash up. She said her plane back to Chicago left at six-thirty A.M. and I said that meant she'd have an hour to rest then we would have to leave for Marquette. She yelled "fuck" so loud that Carla scooted under the bed. She got down on her hands and knees and coaxed Carla out from under the bed and I thought how unlikely it was that I'd ever

get to touch that butt sticking up in the air in a soft denim skirt. I
asked if she was hungry and she nodded while calming down Carla.
I heated her a bowl of my chili which I thought was pretty good
but when she sat down she stared at her bowl and said, "Chili is
not made with kidney beans, tomato, and hamburger." She looked
at me so closely as she ate several saltine crackers that I wished I
had put a shirt on. Her hair was swept back in a single braid which
was curled into a bun. She said she was too tired to leave on a
morning plane and when she had a night's sleep she would make
up her mind. She carried my sleeping bag to a far corner single bed,
took off all of her clothes except her panties, smiled and gave me
the finger, and was fast asleep in a minute. Carla stood on her hind
legs scratching at the sleeping bag trying to get in bed with Vernice.
This made me feel childishly jealous but I helped her up.

24

I had eight days with Vernice that rattled and bruised my world. The damage was permanent in fact. The effect was unintentional in that she had no streak of the missionary. In accepted terms she wasn't a very nice person but neither was she unkind. Except for Cynthia she was simply who she was more so than anyone I had ever met including Riva or Clarence. She tied me in knots neglecting to untie the more difficult ones. Late on our first day together I had the somewhat spooky science-fiction notion that we did not live on the same earth, or how could we live upon the same earth when our perceptions were so radically different? Her world was a procession of aesthetic perceptions and considerations. She knew the contents of my kind of world fairly well but had rejected them

as insufficient to maintain life. Of the hundred or so poets, novelists, painters, and composers she mentioned in the eight days I had
heard of only four or five, and then in passing. She said that I was
a trapezoid while she was a vulnerable and inclusive circle. She bet
that I had done especially well in geometry which was true. I defended myself saying that I had been an excellent student of history but to Vernice history was only an integral part of what she
called the "Big Lie." While we ate tuna fish sandwiches the first day
she quoted a sentence in French, then translated it, "Everything
we are taught is false." This was a difficult position from which to
begin an affair.

I didn't fall asleep until first light. She smoked cigarettes and I
smelled the leftover smoke in the dark air, but also that nearly un-
detectable scent that Polly left in the bedroom when she undressed
at night. It was so captivating that I was restless and got up to smoke
one of her cigarettes, my first since surviving flu during college. At
one point she whimpered and Carla made a similar noise. I thought
of opening one of three bottles of my father's wine Jesse had packed
along for my duffel when he retrieved my camping gear from the
house I no longer wanted to enter. At the moment of putting out
the cigarette the house no longer seemed haunted. Why? Maybe I
had already walked and rowed it away. I left the wine unopened
because I remembered from the Chicago tavern that she had spent
her junior year in France and Italy and she might like it. I drank a
beer from the Servel propane refrigerator and smoked another cigarette, admonishing my penis that stuck its head straight up from
my skivvies saying "the odds don't look good, son." The beer put
me to sleep wrapped up in an uncomfortable wool blanket.

When I awoke Carla's face was peeking in the paned window
near my head, impossible because there was a downward slope on

that side of the cabin but Vernice was holding Carla up. She came in and within minutes she had made us a big cheese omelet. To explain the speed she said she had worked for two years in a mediocre French restaurant in Evansville while going to college. I was impressed because she flipped the omelet over on itself in thirds without using a spatula. She had started cooking quite young because both her parents worked, her father as a small-time contractor and her mother as a legal secretary. She had three older brothers: a "Nazi" school principal, and career chief petty officer in the navy, and the youngest worked with her father. He was a cabinet maker and a "problem drinker" but she liked him the best. Her father was in AA but her mother was often clinically depressed and that was why she had learned to cook so early. She asked me about Cynthia and among other words I used "captious" which Vernice liked. I didn't tell her that it was a word my father had first used for Cynthia. She especially liked the way Cynthia had run off with a mixed-blood at barely sixteen and still finished college.

When she probed further about my parents I said I'd talk about them later but we had to get going before the day became too warm. While I packed some water, sardines, crackers, and cheese she joked that when she awoke she suspected that I was snoring so loud to draw attention to my dick that was sticking out. I blushed and turned away which she thought was charming. While I checked the straps holding the rowboat firmly in the pickup bed she said that when she met me near the Newberry Library she thought I was probably a rich guy due partly to Fred's accent which she said was North Shore Chicago. I wasn't aware of this kind of thing but then she was a poet. She added that I also seemed like a "pleasant prig" and I said "oh fuck you" as we headed down the two-track. "In your dreams," she responded and a lump formed in my throat. I had developed a trace of optimism when she hadn't mentioned flying back to Chicago. I had also told her it was okay to wear shorts

instead of the jeans she should have worn because of the insects as
I wanted a clearer view of her legs and fanny. I felt low rent about
this but not after she had used the dreaded "prig" word. Throughout the day she used words as rare as "epistemology, phylogeny,
and otiose" but in the same sentences did not hesitate to inelegantly
tell me I was "full of shit." I never lost the feeling of being caught
off guard.

I changed plans because it would be getting too warm by midmorning to head inland. I decided on the Grand Sable Dunes. When
we passed through Grand Marais Vernice had me stop by the post
office to retrieve her ill-fated letter announcing her arrival. There
was also a note from Cynthia I stuffed in my pocket to read later.
Meanwhile Vernice was talking about the suicide of Cesare Pavese,
then a poem of Valéry when she saw the lovely harbor in the daylight, and when we came out the west side of town it was the poets
Ponge and Corbière. I memorized the names for when I might be
in a good library in the late fall. When we parked near the dunes
she was launched into a regretful spiel about how she had missed
being in San Francisco in the mid-fifties because she was only five
years old at the time.

Off she went with Carla up the steepest part of the dunes after
shrieking "fucking beautiful." I was peevish because I couldn't keep
up and took a slower trail and because neither of them looked back.
Her legs were smooth but obviously well muscled under the decep-
tive appearance. I remembered quitting tennis at thirteen because
my mother ran me ragged around the court and easily reached any
pathetic junk shot I made. With Vernice the consolation was her
butt and bare legs churning up through the deep sand. I met them
on my circular route about fifteen minutes later on a promontory

covered with beach grass from which you could see Au Sable Lake
far below and Lake Superior in the distance to the north basking
in its cerulean glow.

Vernice was in tears over the beauty of the place, staring to
the west where the dunes ended twelve miles away near a light-
house. She was sweating and when I sat down next to her she leaned
against me for a moment. I started to put my arm around her but
she was abruptly up and off and far enough away so that I yelled
and pointed to a green covert in a valley about a mile toward Lake
Superior. This time Carla didn't follow and was relieved to be put
in her papoose.

When I reached the covert, about an acre of thick aspen and
white birch, Vernice was hiding so I put Carla down and she quickly
found Vernice leaning against a birch tree eating wild strawberries
with one hand and holding a coyote skull in the other. It's amazing
how long people in their mid-twenties can keep up a bantering
quarrel. It was nearly noon and we were to continue well past midnight. Sample:

"Your body is so stiff you might break. You're herky-jerky."

"I am? I haven't broke," I lied.

"Haven't you read the *Tao te Ching*?"

"I don't think so."

"If you had you'd remember. In the Tao it says you must become supple and pliant. Whatever your obsessions might be they're
making you stiff as a board."

"And your obsessions don't?" I gave Carla a wild strawberry
which she spit out as if it offended.

"Poetry isn't an obsession, it's a calling. It's a river you jump
into when you're called and you spend your life floating along immersed in it."

"Until you float to poetry heaven?"

"You're fucking right."

"How about the rest of us?"

"You do what you feel called to do, if anything. Poetry doesn't assume virtue. I'm no better than that group of crows way over toward the lake."

"They're ravens. They're following a bear that is doubtless eating beach pea and wild strawberries."

"Are they dangerous?"

"Not if you leave them alone. They're ironically less contentious than you are."

"With three older brothers I had to fight for my territory. They even tried to screw me."

"Your brothers? I never thought of Cynthia that way."

"You repressed it successfully which is what you're supposed to do. My parents were terminally disappointed in life when we were young. No guidance. You should do some reading in the area of incest."

For some reason, perhaps a plea for sympathy which might lead to the act of love, I confessed my life in an abbreviated form though I included the worst material. It took a half hour and I sweated profusely though the covert was shaded and cool. I finished with the whys and wherefores of my project.

"You can't do that," she fairly exploded.

"What?" I was startled by her vehemence.

"You can't spend your life writing a family history when there's no one who will want to read it. You can't spend your life in reaction to your family, mostly your father, because that means you're still his wounded little boy. You say you're essentially Christian but you're hanging out in the Old Testament when you should be in the New. He rose up and slew his father with the jawbone of the ass, that sort of shit. What a stupid way to lead your life. Do you think you'll have a number of lives or what?"

I rolled over on my face and watched infinitesimal insects walking to and fro. "Why stay if you're going to be such a hard bitch?" I asked the live green grass and the dead brown leaves, also the insects.

"We're sort of attracted to each other. I'm thirsty." She took off at top speed. I loaded Carla in the papoose wondering at the improbable demands that desire can put a man through. My brain felt peeled. Was I a wounded little boy? Partly, but my head ached with anger to admit it. The storytelling hour from the Club returned. Maybe the miniature bad animal wrapped around my spine was my father.

We swam at the launch site and then I rowed down the lake and in order to keep what we were missing in her mind I showed her the sandbar where I had lost my virginity with Laurie. She was amused but then told me a melancholy story about losing her virginity to her first love when she was in the tenth grade and he was two years older. She loved him horribly right up until she entered the university and he suddenly married her best friend because her family had a little dough and he could manage one of their hardware stores. After he was married she returned home and seduced him, making sure her former girlfriend knew, but that had accomplished nothing. She was still sad that she had done such a cheap thing.

"That's a terrible story," I said, watching her take off her wet bra and panties, draping them over the gunwale of the rowboat to dry. "Jesus Christ," I said as she leaned over the back of the boat to slosh cool water on her face.

"Relax," she said. "It's good for you to work up a head of steam." She laughed when she turned around and saw my hard-on in my wet underpants. "Is that for me?" She tickled it with a big toe while I rowed. What an extreme game, I thought.

❀   ❀   ❀

I sat in front of the IGA grocery store while Vernice ran in to buy
a chicken to roast. I began to open Cynthia's letter when my mind
suddenly reenvisioned Vernice leaning over the back of the rowboat. I was no longer looking at Cynthia's letter or out the wind-
shield for that matter but at the well thought out structure of the
vagina and what a problematical theology student had called the
"divine perineum." When my fifth-grade class had made a trip
down to a Trenary area farm a bright little girl had commented
on cows, "They're terribly exposed." The livestock metaphor wasn't
helping so I read Cynthia's letter only to find out that Laurie had
breast cancer, but then there was the usual addition that they seem
to have "caught it early enough." I quickly put away the letter
when Vernice came out of the store.

"I can't remember seeing so much brown lettuce," she said.
"What the fuck do they eat this far north? You're the religious one
and I haven't been in church since high school but the dispensa-
tion of the New Testament is forgiveness. All that bullshit about
the sins of the fathers being visited upon the sons no longer applies.
You're not Moses. You didn't cut down every fucking tree in the
Upper Peninsula. Your cheapness didn't let miners die in unsafe
mines. You didn't rape that young girl. You admitted that she was
attractive but you didn't do anything. Do you think you're going
to get even with dead people?"

"My father's not dead."

"You know I meant your ancestors. Your father sounds like a
dried-up piece of dog shit. He's no longer harming your mother or
sister, just you."

It was too warm in the cabin to roast a chicken until later so we
split a tuna sandwich. I got out the three bottles of wine that Jesse

had packed for me. I never had been much interested in French wine because my father had made a fetish out of it. The wine made Vernice irritable because the bottles were from the early 1950s, very valuable, and I had them standing up in a cupboard in a warm cabin.

"I could sell those bottles in Chicago and have a nice month or so in France," she said.

"Go ahead. It sounds like a good idea for you." This comment didn't please her though I meant it.

She went over and unpacked her suitcase which encouraged me, but then she discovered the stack of porn magazines in the dresser drawer and glared at me.

"They came with the cabin," I shrugged.

"They just feature women as a target and men forget there's a woman attached to the target."

She stripped down to her bra and panties, flopped on her bed, and was asleep in a minute. I didn't want to look at her so I went out on the rickety porch, put on mosquito dope, and fell asleep in a rocking chair.

I awoke in the early evening with the mosquito dope not having worked very well. Vernice was sitting at the table, still in her bra and panties, writing in a journal and drinking coffee.

"Don't say anything. I'm in the middle of a poem."

I poured a cup of coffee, then took a bar of soap and towel down to the river to bathe. Carla had rolled in something dead out in the dunes so I soaped her down which made her wiggle with enjoyment. There was something eerily pleasant about standing naked in a cool river drinking a hot cup of coffee. I soaped down, then grabbed an alder branch above a deep pool letting my body trail off and rinse in the current. It was nearly sunset and Carla made a sharp dog shadow sitting on the bank.

Back in the cabin Vernice was getting the chicken ready to roast. I impulsively told her about Laurie's breast cancer, adding that I was sure she would be fine because she was young and could fight the disease. Vernice told me gravely that it was just the opposite, that her youth would give the disease more energy and that her chances of long-term survival were less than if she were older. This caught me unawares and I got tears in my eyes which I unsuccessfully tried to hide. She looked up at the ceiling to cover for me.

"O fuck it. I never got to taste anything like this before." She opened the bottle called Petrus and poured two glasses. "Your father might be the ultimate asshole, and you might be one too, but I thank you." She took an ample sip, held it in her mouth, and shivered.

I took a taste and admitted it was pretty good which irked her. Fred had been amused when I chose Michigan State over Yale and now I had hit another of many of my rejections of my so-called class. Vernice teased me that a lot of girls who had been in the restaurant business or to France would be glad to fuck for this bottle of wine. I said, "You must be kidding," and she stood up and took off her clothes. I said weakly, "I don't want you to fuck me for a bottle of wine." And she said, "You've been nice while I was being an insufferable prick tease."

And that was that. She smelled like fresh lake water and sunburn the same as Laurie had so long ago. The difference was that she laughed a lot throughout the rest of the evening. It was the opposite of anything melancholy. The fact that she was so orgasmic had nothing to do with my minimal skills. In the last light through the windows I looked into her eyes and they virtually weren't there. I was momentarily spooked. I pushed back and heard our sweaty skins separate. When I pushed away she nearly "saw" me but when I came back close she disappeared into herself again and I had to assume that her "self" at that point included me so that the first time in my life while making love I experienced total union with another. Inside my chest and head I felt on the verge of weeping but didn't. I was mystified but then my mind gave up and I became as lost to the room as she was.

We had our roast chicken at midnight. She had put lemon, thyme, and blanched garlic in the cavity and surrounded the bird with carrots, onions, and a few new potatoes. She closed her eyes while drinking wine. I had a cold beer myself which she didn't object to. This level of food pleasure was new to me except that she as a cook was obviously a few steps up from Mrs. Plunkett. The aesthetic principles involved in her poetry obviously also applied to her cooking. In addition I had noticed the way she bobbed her head slightly to frame the outdoors through the small panes of the cabin windows. I caused the only slump during dinner by suggesting that her superb cooking would enable her to get a good husband. There was a deep flash of anger and I had no options for retreat. She actually said that she had grown up Catholic and was a "nun for her art." To marry would be a blasphemy against all she wished for her life. I tried to withdraw by saying mildly that it was natural for me to think that in biological terms the kind of lovemaking we had just experienced might lead to mating. She laughed and reminded me that I had told her that my separation from Polly had come about because of my refusal to have children. I backed off by saying that she had drained away all of my intelligence. "We've just gotten started," she said.

It was a warm night and we took a dip after dinner. There was a heavy thrashing in the brush across the river and Carla scooted back toward the cabin. Vernice was alarmed and I said that it was only a harmless bear that was doubtless attracted by his or her first whiff of garlic. When she asked how I knew it was harmless I said that if it was the one rogue out of a hundred thousand black bears it would have been in our laps by now. Without the sun we shivered in the cold water and began to make love again but the mosquitoes drove us inside. I was disappointed when she wouldn't sleep with me but she said that on no condition would she sleep overnight with anyone. It was grand to make love with bodies made cool by the river water, though when I drifted off to sleep there were painful memories of Laurie. Everything is attached and nothing is free, an odd thought for a geometrical man.

25

Despite the range of this pleasure we were a little slow and depressed in the morning, perhaps a trace of the sadness in knowing
that despite our better human instincts we would push everything
we had away and follow our own courses that we had embedded
in ourselves so deeply, the willful loneliness that we could not be
deterred by the possibility, maybe the probability, of loving each
other. Maybe people used to fall in love despite having invented
such barriers. Maybe the culture had begun to subtly teach that
this servitude to ambition was the highest hope. Maybe at one time
more people were just people, but perhaps neither of us had ever
tried to be simply people. And maybe we were the kind of people
that it was easy for the culture to denature. When we were children

we were errant enough to wish to be birds for the day but there's nothing easier to lose than playfulness.

There was a brisk south wind early in the morning. I stood at the window watching Vernice drinking coffee on the riverbank, the breeze fluttering her hair, with Carla leaning against her leg. I knew the strength of the south wind would bring thunderstorms so I was packing my light rain jacket plus a poncho for Vernice. Breakfast had become a near disaster when I took out my largest map with its superimposed meticulous grid lines covering the entire Upper Peninsula. There were shaded areas and stickers to identify all of the family's logging and mining activities. After showing it to Vernice I folded the map and took out another which was a more detailed blowup of the central U.P. area where we were now, superimposed on state police county maps so I could navigate the area.

She nastily made it clear that she wasn't a map person, teasing me without humor for being an anal compulsive or an anal retentive, I forget which. I was pissed off but kept it under control. My map work had made me quite proud of myself. Then without asking she began to read the newest of my stack of journals. I felt like I was watching a professor read a term paper dear to my heart. She read without comment a full fifteen minutes and I started packing for the hike out of sheer nervousness.

"Well, the actual stories and details you've collected are fine, but everything else you've written is in that ricky-ticky old-time historical talk. You're pulling all of your punches before you even throw them. Why be so timid? You're setting up some dead people to murder them. At this rate you'll finish in fifty years just before you drop dead yourself. Here's an idea. Watch now." She drew a lateral line though the center of adjoining grids which were partly based on townships, many of them totally unoccupied. Her forefinger followed log roads as much as possible. "Everything you've done so far meanders or vaguely resembles concentric circles. You'd be better off for effect just counting stumps, and adding severed limbs and crushed bodies from the stories. Thirty bucks a month and one day off to 'burn out the grease' in the closest tavern. That's a nifty detail. Why the fuck call whorehouses 'houses of ill repute'?"

"May I read your poetry?" I asked petulantly but immediately regretted it.

She poured another cup of coffee while considering the question in its highest form rather than in the mean spirit in which it was asked. "No. I'm curious about your world and you're not curious about mine." She went outside and I finished packing. I couldn't help but smile at the mental battering I had taken in the past thirty or so hours. I was waddling like a duck through a gauntlet of my own possible irrelevancy. There she was out the window, the Queen of Poetry, an answered prayer to be sure, and I was looking at her wondering how many years it might take for me to digest everything she had said to me. At least I had told her to wear long pants today instead of shorts.

I retraced the path I had taken when I got lost only backward, skirting along a ridge near the gully so we could avoid the swamp. The deepest thickets distressed her so I tried to stay on higher ground while still keeping my bearings. Vernice wanted to carry Carla to see "what it felt like." After about an hour when I could see my great mother of stumps in the gully in the distance I skirted it to save it for last, and we entered the clearing which I thought of as a shrine of gorgeous stumps. Naturally I was testing her but once more she was ahead of me. The clearing had released her from the claustrophobia she had felt in the dense forest. She danced around, with Carla barking from the papoose.

"Fabulous! Sell your dad's wine collection and buy this field, what is it, forty acres? Build yourself a cabin. You've already told me how we've destroyed religion and nature. It's time to save your-self, kiddo."

She sat down against a stump, took her shoes and socks off, and rubbed her feet in the soft green grass. I sat down beside her and did the same. I couldn't remember doing so since childhood and the feeling was exquisite, the grass bunches rubbing against your bare instep so that you felt your toes might cramp from pleasure. I was only mildly troubled when I glanced at Vernice's face and saw she had disappeared again God knows where. Evidently being called to be a poet in her terms was similar to being a religious ec-static like a pillar saint or a Sufi whirling dervish. The southern breeze was brisk enough to keep the black flies and mosquitoes away so she took off her shirt and bra and itched her breasts and tummy against the grass, then off came her trousers and panties. I was becoming aroused but when I leaned toward her she shook her head no. "I'm just having my first grass bath," she said.

Carla heard the thunder first which frightened her, and within a few minutes we heard it too, the alarming violence that often ended a heat wave this far north. I led the way to my mother of stumps the size of which delighted Vernice. We crawled in dampened by the first drops of rain and then the sky truly unloaded so that look-ing out through the cracks between roots the world had vanished in the sheets of rain. Vernice held Carla, who was horrified by the thunder claps, tight to her chest. Luckily the stump's protection had allowed the earth to mound up compared to its sides because wide rivulets of water were running down the gully on both sides of us. Vernice talked about a tornado she had seen at her grandmother's near Springfield, Missouri, and then wondered aloud just what Carla thought the thunder might be. After fifteen minutes or so the storm lessened somewhat but I pointed out we were lucky we weren't in the path of a bank of clouds to the west which were pitch-black with intermittent wide streaks of yellow lightning which exploded toward the ground. I curled up with my head in her lap and began nuzzling her belly but she said, "Stop it, you can't fuck in your church." My disappointment was alleviated when she thanked me ever so slightly for showing her "another world." We talked then about how we think of ourselves as Americans but there are many worlds in the United States if you stray very far from freeways and stay away from television.

26

We had only one more quarrel and that took place the next afternoon. Vernice wanted to work on what she called her "stuff" and I
needed to get started on the roofing job and Mick had brought
everything but a hammer. I was surprised when she said she as the
daughter of a small-town contractor could easily show me how to
do the job. She had worked with her father and youngest brother
for a couple of summers during high school and had roofed many
houses. I supposed that was what made her body so illusively strong
remembering what a summer with a shovel had done to my own
body. She gave me a grocery list and off I went.

There was a letter from Cynthia and also one from Fred.
Cynthia said that our "beloved" father had won early release, re-

turned to Key West, then broke parole (he was forbidden to go to
bars) and was back in the slammer for ninety days. It was obvious
to Cynthia that he would have to seek greener pastures by getting
out of the state of Florida. The letter from Fred was much more
troubling. After a month he had "jumped over the convent walls"
of the alcohol clinic. He was fucking sick of therapy of any kind
and wanted to go home after a trip north after which through the
influence of his Columbus friend he intended to enroll in a Zen monastery in Japan. The very idea boggled me. I suspected that he was
back on the booze but he said he wasn't.

When I got back to the shack with two hammers and a bag of
groceries she was irked because I had bought plain beer rather than
the dark beer she had written on my list. She was making a Belgian
beef stew called carbonnade and though the dish was still a possibility the dark beer would have been far better. During this lecture I could see the girl who when pushed had whipped her brothers
into shape.

She was just getting started. In my absence she had flipped
through my whole stack of journals, which I had begun at sixteen.
They covered nearly ten years but it was plain to her that rather
than progressing I was moving backward in the manner of a junior
Frantz Fanon. I was obviously "too dry behind the ears" to be dealing with such large material. I was preaching a half-baked senten-
tious sermon to myself as if I wasn't quite convinced. I sounded like
I was writing about Cortés's invasion of Mexico. Her trump card
was that thousands of people had probably known the evidence but
saw the story quite differently. Trees, iron ore, and copper weren't
people. Why had I glossed over the destruction or the removal of
the indigenous population, the Indians? Again, the details and the
stories were interesting but I was approaching the material like a
not very intelligent Lutheran minister. I saw that she was only halfway down the list she had made so I bolted.

*   *   *

I fulfilled my genetic promise by getting drunk at the tavern and falling asleep down on the beach where some locals were having a bonfire and party. I tried to make love to Shirley but I had had too much to drink. I went into Lake Superior with my clothes on to sober up but it didn't work. When I woke up cold and wet it was nearly dawn and my head had cleared up enough to drive back to the cabin. Carla barked wildly but Vernice pretended she was asleep.

When I got up at midmorning she was off somewhere with Carla. There was a note on the kitchen counter saying, "I've been too hard on you. Sorry." I was feeling too ill to care but warmed up some of her beef stew, then went to work tearing off the old tar-paper roofing by scraping it up with a shovel. I barely made it down the ladder to vomit. This drinking takes practice I thought while brushing my teeth. I wasn't up to getting back on the ladder so waded the river and took a hike in fresh territory in country my family hadn't timbered. Only I couldn't tell because the same stumps were there, cut by the ancestors of a family who lived down the street from us in Marquette. I could imagine what kind of ruthless quarreling had gone on between our great-grandfathers.

In the next five days before we left for the Marquette airport we had a good time dealing with nothing. This was her idea that she finally admitted she'd gotten from her parents who, when pushed to the wall by the larger issues of this life that they were powerless to resolve, retreated into the lower range of day-to-day obligations.

We finished the roof late on the first evening. In the following days we had left I taught her the rudiments of fly-fishing which she enjoyed. Each early morning we drove farther south to hike out a fresh grid for my project without mentioning the possible absurdity, then when we finished by midafternoon we'd row and fish. We continued to make love at least twice a day but on the lighter side and no longer as though the act were the last source of oxygen on earth. At my insistence she gave me a short reading list that might help me connect with what she was all about. On our last evening when she was a bit rosy with wine she said she thought she might have a child someday without getting married, and I dumbly repeated that I had read that every child needs a father. She didn't say "like you" but we sat there in silence for a full minute before we started laughing. She said that a more ill-suited couple than we were couldn't be invented. I pretended that I agreed but I didn't. I now thought that I loved her far more than during our first wilder days. I thought it was unlikely I'd ever again meet a woman who was so totally alive and I wanted to hold on though I could see that she was more than ready to go.

By chance Fred showed up late the next morning only an hour before we had to leave for the airport. He looked frail but appeared quite happy. When Vernice came around the corner of the cabin Fred acted for a moment like he was seeing a ghost, then looked at me as if I had pulled a fast one, though he was pleased when she hugged him.

"Your nephew is a fine young man except that he wants to fuck all the time," she teased.

"How ugly. You must visit me in the monastery. A free trip to Hawaii."

Since the letter Fred had changed plans, deciding to study with a roshi named Aitken in Hawaii. If he decided to change his mind Japan would be too far away. He said that he was permanently fatigued with religion but wanted to achieve consciousness before he died. Ever the virago, Vernice said she had read that many Zen people were in favor of Japanese conquest during World War II.

"I don't expect more from any form of religion than I expect from people. Grandeur wallowing in smut."

Vernice took out her notebook and wrote this down. I realized it wasn't so much that Fred had become frail but that his face had lost weight except for his bulbous nose.

"Riva said she'd come back to me if I were dry for a year, but then on and on into eternity. I thought of camping on Everest but the permits were too expensive."

"Should I take the beer in the refrigerator?" Naturally I was concerned.

"No, I carry a full bottle of whiskey just to remind me of my past. It's to be drunk if my plane starts falling from the sky. That sort of thing. By the way, have you finished your history of America?"

"Not quite." It dawned on me that I was being traded male abrasiveness for female. I stood there staring across the river at a birch tree with a peculiar shape. I had found a woman who could gracefully handle what I was but then I wasn't enough for her. At that moment I lost several degrees of my inner temperature as if my brain were beating a retreat back to my life before Vernice. I didn't have to look far for what was lacking in me because she had been so explicit. The sudden question of to what extent was I a correctable item froze me in place until Vernice waved a hand in front of me to bring me back to earth.

Halfway to Marquette I had developed full-blown jitters, a jumping stomach, a lump beneath my breastbone, a mind fixed on the idea that you don't really know what you have until it starts to go away. Vernice was revising my reading list with the shoe off her left foot diddling the radio dials with her toes. She was wearing the light floral summer skirt that I met her in and it had fallen up her thigh to the degree that I kept my eyes on the road to avoid a collision.

We had left early because Vernice wanted to see my father's wine cellar. I felt no urge to talk early in the two-hour drive but it irritated me that she was writing in her notebook rather than speaking to me.

"What are you writing?'

"Piths, gists, images, speculations on the nature of nature. I wish we hadn't left Carla with Fred. I already miss her."

I couldn't think of a single appropriate thing to say. When we pulled up in the alley behind our home Clarence was tending the flower bed. The peonies were lavish.

"I didn't think it would be this fucking ritzy." Vernice bounded out and shook Clarence's hand.

"You're a beautiful woman," said Clarence in his flat, even voice. She was a little taken aback as many were by his directness. He said Jesse had gone back to Veracruz early.

She was slightly nervous in the house, identifying certain pieces of furniture and early American landscapes I had always ignored. I would never have known where the key to the wine cellar was located except that Cynthia had shown me where she had found it when she was about twelve, though she told me her boyfriends had complained that French wine wasn't sweet enough. The key was kept on a tiny hook behind my father's framed Yale diploma. Magna cum laude, indeed.

She was impressed by the wine cellar to the point that it embarrassed me. There were a number of cases of brandies and ports from before World War I that my grandfather had left, also wine from that era that Vernice thought might have gone bad. I admitted that I hadn't been here since childhood. Once more her interest in something well outside myself irked me. I suggested that I ship the whole collection to her in Chicago where she could sell it and we'd split the money, and then she would go live in France for a year or so which was her avowed intention.

"Actually several years. But it's not yours to sell, it's your dad's."

I reminded her that I had told her about how my cabin near Ontonagon had been stolen out from under me, adding that much of the money from a trust for Cynthia and me was also missing. I didn't want to say the large amount.

"How much?" she asked, wiping off a label with a tissue from her purse so she could read it.

"The last I heard about three million bucks is down to a few hundred grand. It was to be split with Cynthia when I reached thirty."

"What were you going to do with it?" She seemed to be cherishing two particular bottles so I stuffed them in her big purse. I didn't answer the question clearly because I didn't know how. There was dirty and clean money, or real dirty money and relatively clean money.

I finally said, "Everybody needs enough but nobody needs too much." I had never been confident of my social theories which Fred described as being unrealistically left wing. I finally couldn't understand how the government historically could justify the destruction of many people for the gain of the few but then I was too emotionally preoccupied to be lucid on economic subjects.

We went upstairs so I could show her my room. She looked around in a state of amusement at my library while I made a stack of nature guidebooks to take back to the shack. I was about to ask her to send me a conclusive book on the nature of nature but what came out rather timidly was to make love one last time. She laughed and came into my arms saying she didn't want to mess up her clothes and we didn't have much time. She lifted her skirt and leaned far over my desk. I had the distinct, joyous feeling that my desk was being consecrated though I comically fell backward when I came, looking up from floor level at what I thought was the loveliest bottom in the cosmos.

At the airport she looked off at the lovely green hills north of the runway and said, "You live in a beautiful place and you don't act like you know it." This was the rawest of points because when I looked at U.P. landscapes I often tried to imagine them through the eyes of Schoolcraft or Agassiz before the landscape was fatally violated.

At the gate I saw several businessmen trying to conceal their stares at Vernice. I suppose that technically she wasn't beautiful in the manner of magazine models or actresses but she drew the immediate attention of both males and females. She was full of "élan vital," a life force as described by the French philosopher Bergson. When she kissed me good-bye before boarding she said, "Well, Quixote, I hope your god is with you. Write when you wish and remember I hate the phone." That was that. I went out in the truck and wept. I had my project and my dog with her unstable allegiances.

On the way back I stopped and got a turkey sandwich to go, glancing over at a corner table where I used to sit with my father and Cynthia. I suddenly recalled how in the third grade a little red-haired girl named Martha, the daughter of a visiting professor at the college, controlled my life. They were from Boston and she sounded strange to me but I was smitten and she authoritatively guided me through every aspect of the third grade. When I went to her house to play her mother who "loved the dance" wore leotards, smoked cigarettes, and played classical music very loud. I stole a diamond ring for Martha from my mother's jewelry box but her parents returned it that evening when they saw her wearing it at dinner.

I stopped and hiked the beach near Au Train not wanting to rush home to the company of Fred. I wondered at the attraction of one human for another that could start so early in life. An eight-year-old boy is overwhelmed by a red-haired girl so that when she leaves in June he stands in tears in their driveway while her parents pack their car. In the days after they leave he continues to walk past their rented house in the mornings as if her departure was a horrible mistake that might have been corrected in the night.

Clearly love was as inscrutable as prayer. Naturally I didn't expect this gut feeling of abandonment. Vernice had half turned her head and fluttered a hand and then was in the plane. Why was I rehearsing this over and over if not for love? And all of those roots of desire beyond meaning. There certainly was no evident thread to connect the few women that overwhelmed me—Laurie, Riva, Polly, Vernice. With the exception of Polly who made the attempt the others certainly didn't want to live with me. The idea of finding out why hadn't yet occurred to me to any meaningful degree.

When I got back to the shack in the late afternoon Fred surprised me by saying that he intended only to stay the night, then head for Marquette and up to the Club to see his relatives for a single night. He needed to get to his Zendo destination before he "delaminated," a favorite word. It distressed him that he had to take tranquilizers for the time being. Meanwhile he admitted that he had thoroughly snooped in all of my journals. He enjoyed the detailed maps because they gave a patina of rationality to what I was doing which then became thoroughly distorted in reading the journals. I wasn't upset because I had already gone through a period of painfully explicit

criticism of my life, character, and work and Fred didn't offer anything new. Far more meaningful was the wretched casserole he had
made out of a can of beans, a can of corn, a can of tomatoes, and all
of the leftover splendid pot roast that Vernice had cooked the night
before. He proudly said he had added a full tablespoon of rosemary,
an herb that became dreadful in that quantity. I mourned my lost
pot roast but kept my mouth shut. He had already said, "I got to get
out of here because the woods make me want to drink," so I figured
he was too tenuous for my food carping.

Fred rambled on throughout the short evening in a manner that
reminded me of my mother's Judy Garland stage in the months
immediately preceding the disintegration of the marriage following my father's rape of Vera. I supposed that the tranquilizers were
better for him than being drunk but the results were charmless,
slurred, disconnected, and totally self-referential. He was oddly
conscious of this and said he looked forward to nothing but water.
The evening was utterly bleak until he began to speculate on my
uncle Richard's drowning and the fact that my mother and father
were the only witnesses. Fred was sure that it was an accident but
was equally sure that everything hadn't been admitted by my
mother and father. I lamely responded that I imagined it was disastrous when two brothers loved the same girl, adding the stew
would have been overthickened if there had been two Adams and
one Eve in the Garden. This delighted Fred who said it certainly
would have changed the history of theology. He continued to mull
this over with pleasure, then asked if I had noted the profound
religiosity of my great-grandfather and grandfather, a penchant that
had lost its strength with my father. I said I had but couldn't draw
any conclusions other than the usual hypocrisy. He then made an
observation that despite his muddled mind would both haunt and

aid my project. He told me that I should note in my reading of journals, monographs, and texts how all the great predators were theocratic, that if you were going to rape the land and people, whether
it was the original Indians or the working class that followed, it was
important to think that God was thoroughly on your side. "John
Calvin is always under the floorboards during America's board
meetings," he added.

A loon flew up the river in the moonlight uttering its querulous cry. I'd learned that after the male loon sits on the nest for a
month and a half to give the female a break he goes crazy. I didn't
intend any conclusions when I described this but Fred warmed up.

"Maybe it doesn't matter if you're nuts, you're keeping yourself busy. Fuck everyone including me. Continue full bore. Kick
ass and take names." He then got up and took the whiskey from
his bag, unscrewed it, and poured it out in the sink. "Nature, improperly understood, makes me want to drink. It's incomprehensible. When I was in the booze ward there was a flowering crabtree
outside my window and I lay there sedated watching it bloom with
the full knowledge that I hadn't the foggiest notion of what was
going on beyond badly remembered details from high school biol-
ogy. There was a rummy landscape architect in our ward and he
was quite helpful on the nominal level of how trees functioned but
not beyond that simple level. I had spent years studying the religious nature of man but hadn't got very far in figuring out the origins of the religion, say, looking at a tree and stating, 'What the fuck
do we have here?' Now I have to start all over with nothing."

I learned later from my mother that it took Fred over a month to
reach Hawaii what with a relapse after a delayed flight in San Francisco and a taxi into the city. Meanwhile, the morning he left he
was up at dawn looking at birds with my binoculars. When I called

him in for breakfast he said he had been in the Audubon Club in grade school and should have stayed there. "Seventy-seven roads diverged in the woods and I took half a dozen." At this point Carla woke up from her nap on the rug and jumped in his lap. He was pleased and spooned scrambled eggs into her mouth. "You must learn to eat like a proper young lady."

27

Beginning with Fred's departure I buried myself in my work, a habit that over the years I grew to think less than admirable. In down periods I reminded myself of those ragged, geek street-corner philosophers I had seen in Chicago mouthing their contorted perceptions with a sense of confidence that no one would possibly understand them. I became friends, sometimes sexual, with Shirley from the tavern. Like millions of other jerk males I hoped she was uncomplicated but it turned out not to be so. She was on the run from a questionable situation in Ann Arbor and merely acted the tavern tart as a satisfactory role that nobody questioned except herself in private hours. We filled some sort of modest lacunae for each other though I often doubted that she would have maintained her interest in me without her affection for Carla.

I completed my reconnaissance of my mid–Upper Peninsula grid by mid-October with no thought of what I would do in the winter. I had to move out of the shack because the owners were coming up to try to spot a big buck well before deer season, deer being creatures of territory and habit. When the male is in rut he loses his ordinary sense of caution. Carla and I were sitting on the front steps when a male passed, nose to the ground, not ten feet away and in such a state of sexual charge that he merely glanced at us. Due to his size Carla only growled her lowest growl.

I wanted to see Laurie whose condition distressed me but Cynthia had written that Laurie and her child and mother were staying in Minneapolis with an aunt where they had access to oncologists who specialized in Laurie's peculiar form of breast cancer. She had also developed a melanoma on her lower back and Cynthia admitted the long-range prospects weren't promising. I allowed myself to pray for her. People in their twenties are mentally inexperienced with the prospect of the death of a young friend or lover.

My guidebooks and Vernice's reading list saved my emotional neck that summer and fall along with rowing and fishing. Guidebooks on trees, wildflowers, and birds preoccupy you to the degree that you become more vulnerable to the landscape than yourself. You see a flower and say "daisy" to yourself only to discover that there are more than a hundred types of daisies. White birches were common but where did the yellow birch come from? What did this area look like before the time of the glaciers twelve thousand years before? The larger issues of human history that had always absorbed me didn't so much become smaller but faded into the landscape on many days. At the same time my statistical approach to my white pine grids had become less interesting than the human stories accumulated from the various historical societies in different villages. Each village was obsessed with the history of its own immediate area and infinitely less so than in the history of the village a mere thirty miles away. Later in life I learned that human geographers called this "geo-piety," which also applies to larger units and fidelities like the Michigan State–University of Michigan football games. On the local level, however, very few of the codgers I spoke to seemed particularly interested in the larger picture. "My grandfather lost a leg below the knee at the log slide and carved himself a new one. He was back at work in the camp horse barn in six weeks. He had kids to raise." That sort of thing mostly without questioning any company obligation.

Vernice's letters were without emotional content unlike my own. I wrote her absurd little book reports that I slaved over. Yeats and Paddy Kavanaugh and William Carlos Williams were engrossing but I had problems comprehending Ezra Pound, Charles Olson, and Robert Duncan. Vernice assured me that it took time to absorb the language of poetry. By mid-September I hadn't heard from her for several weeks and her forbidden phone was disconnected. Finally I got a postcard from London where she admitted she was on her way to France with a "prominent poet" who was on a Guggenheim Fellowship. That was that for the time being. Birds of a feather, I thought, sitting in the pickup next to the post office in a blustery rain.

I moved temporarily back to a tourist cabin in Grand Marais when I had to leave the shack. I was short on money and substitute-taught for three days but found the job grueling and not suited to my temperament. I called my mother and asked if it would be okay if I moved back to Marquette for the winter and she said, "Of course, it's your house. I don't want the goddamned place," and she laughed. This was curiously pleasant as I didn't recall my mother swearing. Over my objections she said she would have Mrs. Plunkett move in to take care of me. When I said I could take care of myself she said that Cynthia had told her that I was thin and ragged and I could consider Mrs. Plunkett my Christmas present. Cynthia had stopped by a few weeks before on her way to see Laurie in Minneapolis. She said I could pass for a pulp cutter. I said the closest clothing store was sixty miles away and that's why I had learned to sew up tears in my clothes. She stayed for only a couple of hours. She cried about Laurie and after she heard the story said that Vernice was the best thing that could have happened to me. She asked to what degree I'd ever join the human community.

Back in Marquette Jesse and Clarence were glad to see me though both asked about my health. I had barely reached the alley before a late October snowstorm hit and we sat in the work shed before the woodstove sipping glasses of whiskey. I told them I had lost weight from cooking for myself and walking several hundred miles or so. It was then that Jesse said that my mother had given me the house though she continued to take care of the bills. She had paid off my father in a deal that involved her taking care of his legal bills. They both liked Carla. Jesse followed me into the house to help me with my duffel and cartons of journals and books. I idly said that I hoped one day to visit Vera in Mexico and apologize for my father and he simply said, "Nothing is your fault. You can't apologize for your father." I didn't know how to pursue the subject so let it drop, though I wondered how he had continued to work for him. Fred had told me rather ominously that Latinos have long memories.

I managed to spring some additional education funds by driving to East Lansing and agreeing to do some work for a history professor in researching logging folktale sources and for an anthropologist named Cleland on early Native settlements in the western U.P. This would enable me to buy snowshoes and the short, wide cross-country skis I would need in winter, also to stay in motels when I wandered because I scarcely wanted to camp in winter when forty below zero wasn't unheard of.

My father showed up just before Thanksgiving. I had been at the Marquette Historical Society and Peter White Library and come home in the near dark at five to find Jesse and Clarence helping a man load the contents of the wine cellar in a large truck. Jesse rolled his eyes and when I walked into the house my father was just finishing packing up what he wanted from his den. My mother had told me on the phone that this was going to happen but not when and I had hoped to be away. He was in his "northern gentleman" mode and shook my hand with a smile. He had gained a good deal of weight but carried it fairly well. He refilled his whiskey glass and asked if I'd have a drink with him. After ten years without seeing him I didn't have the heart to refuse. I was overwhelmed by the nothingness I felt. It suddenly occurred to me that I was taller than he was. He told me he admired Carla and that it was sad that we hadn't had a bunch of dogs and that he would never see his grandchildren because Cynthia was so unforgiving. Mother had told him that I was writing a history of logging and mining in the Upper Peninsula and he hoped I wouldn't be "too hard on the family." He added that I looked like an out-of-work logger and he was sure I owned more decent clothing. I found myself unable to say anything until he said he was sorry to hear about my divorce and I said that I was sorry about his own. "My brother Richard was a good person. I'm not. Nearly everything I've touched in my life has turned to shit except your mother, Cynthia, and you. I congratulate you on your survival." And that was that. I knew he wanted to hug goodbye but that was out of the question. I watched him walk down our front sidewalk and slip but Jesse caught him by the elbow.

✳   ✳   ✳

By luck I went down to Chicago for Christmas with my mother. I say "luck" because I didn't want to. I was loving the bleak clarity of winter and the only acceptable reason to go would have been to see Vernice whom I hadn't heard from in three months. The whole trip turned out wonderfully with only one bad event. Cynthia and Donald came down with my nephew and niece and I had forgotten what this holiday meant for children. The bad event was early one morning when I was having coffee with my mother and said that I was thinking of going to Mexico to see Vera and she began to sob. It took a while for her to calm down and then only when Cynthia came into the kitchen with her children. A little later when we were alone Cynthia told me that Vera's son, our half-brother, had been hit by a car while riding his bicycle and had been operated on. Mother had paid for the operation through Jesse. Cynthia showed me a photo of Vera and her son and the beauty of Vera was overwhelming. Her son had my father's jaw and had a rather fearsome look about him for so young a boy.

The luck of the trip came about when I met the boyfriend of my mother's housemate. His name was Gerald Coughlin. He was in his mid-forties and from Ireland though he had been in Chicago since right after the war. He was introduced to me before dinner by my mother as a "mind scientist" because she had a complete aversion to terms like psychiatrist, psychology, psychotherapy, psychoanalyst. Fred had told me that in the milieu in which they were raised everyone was expected to be of sound mind even though they were slowly eating their fingers. After a cousin had committed suicide he was described as having suffered a recent case of the flu. Coughlin put me off at first by saying, "So you're the young man who is bent on saving the past. Quite a job."

After we got over this awkward statement we discovered we shared an obsession for fishing. As a bachelor he had been able to rig his practice in such a way that he trout-fished the entirety of

August and September every year. Years before he had fished many
of the rivers in northern Michigan but now his passion was brown
trout in Wyoming and Montana. He was very impressed when I
told him I had caught a three-pound brook trout while fishing with
my friend Mick on a beaver pond the summer before. Our conversation got around to fathers teaching their sons to fish and I said in
my case it was my father telling our yardman Clarence to take me
fishing. He said, "That's better than most," and told me how his father was a music hall pianist out of Sligo but when he played up in
Belfast in the 1930s some "Orangemen" had smashed his hands with
a mallet for playing the wrong song so that when they fished together he had to heavily tape his father's hand to the rod handle
and tie on his flies. This peek into another world made me nauseous
and I pushed away my food plate. Coughlin was startled at my reaction and skillfully turned the talk in another direction after saying that hatred eats the soul with the energy of a dog at dinner. I
was delighted when it came about that I could name a Yeats poem
and he would quote the whole thing. We were at the far end of the
noisy table but Donald overheard and said, "Ben Bulben" was the
best collection of words that had ever entered his ears.

In the next two days before I left I saw Coughlin twice more.
We met at a tackle shop outside the Loop and had lunch, and then
he came for dinner my last night in town. I had no doubt that my
mother had at least made the seating arrangements but I didn't care.
What was important was that I was getting a dose of oxygen in a
life that badly needed fresh air. The whole trip to Chicago had been
pleasantly unsettling with an ordinary sense of what Christmas was
all about, something that I had never experienced growing up.

On the plane back to Marquette a seat mate asked what I did
for a living and I blithely said that I was a spiritual and economic
historian. This was out of character for me but I wanted him to
commit first. I guessed right when he turned out to be a banker from

Escanaba. I was surprised when he had three heavy drinks in quick
succession but he said his wife was picking him up in Marquette
for the long drive home. He had been a marine captain in Vietnam
and "lost" seventy of his original one hundred and twenty men. I
reflected on how different it was to talk to someone who had been
there compared to the suburban abstractions, the easy blather, the
sheer logorrhea of television and newspapers.

Most often that winter the snow was too deep to take Carla along
so I left her with Clarence who would walk her around a couple of
blocks. She would bark wildly when I walked to my truck but
Clarence assured me that she quieted down the moment I left the
alley. One afternoon in February I made a careless turn for a short-
cut between Sagola and Northland. I was thinking about a text I
had been reading that morning by Louis Agassiz that had been published in 1850, "Lake Superior: Its Physical Characters, Vegetation,
and Animals, Compared with Those of Other and Similar Regions."
Agassiz had corresponded with Charles Darwin on the Upper
Peninsula's uniqueness. This made me feel that my project, however minimally, had a part in a grander tradition of inquiry. The
eye of Agassiz was breathtakingly concise and lucid.

Meanwhile the storm that had been predicted had arrived and
I began to have doubts about making it to Route 35 from my side
road. After a couple of hours of very slow driving I churned to a
stop in a drift a scant quarter of a mile from the highway. I sat there
for an hour and saw the dim orange lights of a single snowplow pass
and knew that I should sit tight. I had less than half a tank of gas,
not enough to keep the heater on all night, but had had sense enough
to pack an emergency kit and take along a sleeping bag for such
possibilities. The kit included two boxes of candles of twenty each.
I had read that a single candle would give off enough heat in a

stuck car to keep an occupant from freezing so I lit three. Within
a half hour I was warm enough to douse one, and then a second,
keeping the third in a tin cough-drop container on the dashboard.
I wrote in my journal for a couple of hours and ate two awful
"nutrition" bars I had bought at a camping store. I also wrote a
note to Coughlin with whom I had been corresponding once a
week since Christmas.

> Dear C.,
>   I'm stuck in a snowbank for the night in a remote
> location. This is not a suicide attempt similar to the one I
> mentioned long ago. I've confidently decided over and over
> to see this whole life item through to the end. I'm heating
> my truck cab with candles and it would be nice to have a
> bottle of red wine but the closest drinkable one is seventy
> miles and trillions of tons of snow away. Three days ago I
> made love briefly to a youngish librarian in a storage room
> and we were both pleased with ourselves. This act stood
> clearly on the side of life and against the guilty self-
> laceration you've seen in my character. To be sure I'm
> stuck in a truck all night in a zero-degree blizzard but not
> making more of the situation than simply being stuck in a
> truck in a zero-degree blizzard.
>   Yrs., Jack London

Coughlin had told me that as a boy in Ireland he had read all
of Zane Grey and Jack London and couldn't decide whether he
wanted to fight Indians or be a hunter and trapper in the wilderness. Becoming a psychoanalyst in Chicago had presented a different sort of wilderness and less visceral but equally daunting
challenges. Now he wished simply to become a master at untying
human knots.

❊   ❊   ❊

That spring and early summer it became clear that Laurie was dying.
Her husband even glared at me at the funeral. When I walked down
the hill to Gertz's to buy some clothes they told me I hadn't been in
the store in a decade and I had shrunk a bit. After the funeral I sat
up with Cynthia until she fell asleep against me on the sofa. Laurie's
moronic husband had insisted on an open-casket wake so that when
mourners passed by they looked down at a skeleton barely covered
by skin in a blue dress that she never would have worn. Walking
past was walking in the darkest air possible despite the bright June
sun coming through the stained-glass windows. A single fly circu-
lated above the casket like a miniature bird. The organ droned. The
flowers wilted.

Part III
1980s

28

I'm in the den and it reminds me of a huge pack rat nest I helped a biologist dismantle in the desert in the Southwest last winter. There are thirteen labeled cartons of papers along the south wall, and a thousand or so books on the north, all of which will be trucked over to Northern Michigan (now a full-fledged university) in a few days, ridding me of all the material of my nearly endless project, my skirmish with the unknowable that intermittently seemed so obvious. All I'll have left save my memories are seventy or so of my own journals, and a few of Sprague's, in which there are many items of a personal nature. Above all, what I've discovered is that certainties aren't appropriate to the evidence.

I've been sitting here since before dawn when Cynthia called from Chicago to say that Mother had died of a pulmonary embolism, not really a bad thing because she had a severe kidney disease, nephrosis, that required daily dialysis and when I visited her a week ago she could not envision continuing to live in this manner. She was matter-of-fact and accepting rather than unhappy. Not ever having been that ill I couldn't understand her mood, her quiet state of suspension behind which there must have been all sorts of mental activity she was unwilling or unable to share, though Cynthia told me that after Mother had emerged from a semicoma of several days' duration she had told Cynthia that during the entire time she had actually been sitting on a big boulder in midsummer up near the Huron River Point and that she had been ten years old again. She had also seen the most spectacular northern lights of her lifetime. I immediately read a copy of Kübler-Ross Cynthia had given me and learned that this near-death state was frequently quite forgiving except for those left behind.

I've closed the den door but in the kitchen I can hear Mrs. Plunkett making breakfast at midmorning for Polly's daughter Rachel who is thirteen and has been staying in Cynthia's room for three days because of a quarrel with her mother. Rachel stayed out late with her boyfriend after the ceremony in which he was a graduating senior. I can't really follow the lingua franca of these mother-daughter quarrels so have been carefully noncommittal though thirteen seems radically young to have a boyfriend.

"La-tee-fucking-da. You can tell that little bitch I'm not loaning her my favorite blouse." Rachel is as brash on the phone as Cynthia used to be. I hear Mrs. Plunkett say, "Your language, young lady," and Rachel say, "Sorry."

Polly lives down the hill a few blocks west of the old Coast Guard station. Last month when she came back north I prepared a special dinner for her with the help of Mrs. Plunkett and "popped the question," as they say locally. She laughed and said that she wouldn't remarry me at gunpoint. I was more startled than hurt. We're lovers and she insists that I'm far better off as her boyfriend. Perhaps that's so. Her daughter Rachel is beyond my capabilities but I've been helpful raising her son Kenneth who is nine. I mean I take him fishing whenever he wants, maybe twice a week, and buy him things he thinks he needs that are a bit beyond Polly's teacher's salary, the most recent being an expensive racing bicycle that alarms me and Polly too who fears that his penchant for speed is the same as his father's, who died on a motorcycle outing in Wisconsin. He was in all respects a good husband and teacher but on Saturdays when the weather was good he and his friends, all Vietnam veterans, would take off on their motorcycles and blow off steam. I'm not trying in any way to replace Kenneth's dead father but was amused when Polly said he was sent home from a scout meeting for fighting with a friend who had referred to me as a "high-class fuckup." I had called Donald over in the Soo for advice on Kenneth, but Donald only said, "Make sure he likes you so that when he needs advice he'll ask you." I impulsively bought him a dog but with the kids busy figuring out Marquette and Polly teaching summer school the dog who is named Sally mostly stays with me. She is a yellow Labrador, the kind of dog I wanted as a kid. She has been enough of a problem so that I have fenced in the entire backyard where she has dug large holes in Clarence's once peerless lawn and flower gardens. Clarence died two years ago at the age of seventy or so when a boat hoist strap broke and the sailboat crushed him. I own a small landscape company that employs two of Clarence's nephews full time. In the winter the nephews plow out driveways.

Jesse retired this late winter and returned to Veracruz after suffering a slight stroke. Before he left I asked him how long it had been since he had received a regular paycheck from my father. He

said he had always been able to take care of himself and had recently sold three small apartment houses he owned up near the
college having bought them many years before at a bargain. Had
he kept them a secret or had I failed to notice? He also owned a
combination auto wash and gas station and a self-service laundry.
I began to wonder to what extent his exile had been a true exile
but then my rationality in regard to Jesse had been totally corrupted
by my father's rape of Vera. A few days before he left for good I
asked him about the coffee plantation land he had purchased with
my father when I was in the ninth grade. He was pleasantly noncommittal and said there had never been enough capital to properly develop it. I also asked him why he had driven hundreds of
times back and forth to Duluth instead of moving there and he
answered that my father didn't like to be under close observation,
and also that it was expected of him to keep track of me. For instance, my father had predicted that my marriage to Polly wouldn't
last because I was too restless and angry for any woman to stay with
me. This naturally angered me but Jesse laughed and said that
proved the point. This calmed me down and we sat and had a drink
during which I asked him why he hadn't shot my father that evening.
He said that would only be punishing himself and hurting Vera
further, not to speak of many others. He had come from a large
family and he was the padrone to many younger brothers and sisters and their children. He had missed his homeland but what could
he have done for so many people if he had stayed in Veracruz? And
my father had given him two months off each year to spend back
home. I naturally said nothing of the number of times my father
had drunkenly said something about his "brown embezzler."

It was at this point that I felt foolish wondering if I had ever
truly seen this man other than as someone who had helped me
countless times. We sat there for hours and I apologized for not
having had the curiosity to understand him. He said that very few

people bothered understanding each other, even brothers and sisters, husbands and wives, though he thought that Cynthia and I had done a pretty good job. The point was that through working for my father so far from home he had liberated his family from generations of acute poverty, and now forty-five years later his job was finished.

He withdrew a bit when I asked him about World War II and the immediate aftermath but then threw up his hands as if to say why not tell me everything. My father didn't enter the service until 1941 when he graduated from Yale. He was Jesse's immediate officer and right away Jesse could tell that here was a man who wished to die and needed someone to watch his back. They became uncommon friends and the night before they shipped out of San Francisco they had become quite drunk and my father had told him why he didn't care if he died. The summer before he had had an argument with his brother Richard about a woman and Richard had committed suicide by jumping off a cliff in the wrong place. There was only one good place to jump and knowing this Richard had intentionally jumped off the cliff into the water. My father had liked the young woman but Richard had loved her. My father had known since he was very young that he would never be a good person but still he loved his brother and because he caused his death afterward he and the young woman, my mother, had decided that the only good thing they could do was to become married.

Of course I could have guessed much of this if I had paid attention to certain things Fred had said, but then if you hate someone you don't want to know their details.

Two years ago a lawyer called from Grand Rapids, Minnesota, to say that my father had been beaten up and might go to jail and needed my help. I was in Grand Marais at my cabin but Mrs. Plunkett tracked me down. I called the lawyer to see if I couldn't avoid the trip by sending a check but it wasn't possible. Someone from the family was required by the local judge. I left at dawn and got there in the evening and went directly to the lawyer's home. It was the usual only this time my father had gotten himself thoroughly trashed by a man his own age, mid-sixties, who owned a small logging operation. My father was in the area grouse hunting with some "swells from Duluth," the lawyer's description, and had "diddled" with a girl who was a little too young, the logger's granddaughter, whose parents were divorced. The logger had found out, tracked down my father, and beat him with a tire iron. The logger would be charged with assault to do great bodily harm and the jail time would ruin his business. My father would be charged with statutory rape which would look "terrible" for a man of his name (our family had done business in the nearby Mesabi Iron Range). I wanted to walk out immediately after I told the lawyer that my father had a long history of this crime. The lawyer asked me not to mention that again and that I should have some "Christian compassion" for my father. We drove over to the hospital where in a private room he was sipping whiskey and chatting with a nurse through swollen lips. He looked like a wrinkled purple prune from the facial hematomas. "Hello son. I'm so happy you could come over. My friends have abandoned me."

We had a meeting in the judge's chambers at six A.M. to avoid untoward observation. The judge who was my father's age clearly wanted to rid himself of the problem. The sheriff, a mammoth Swede, said nothing at all. The logger grandfather glowered and righteously puffed. The judge actually congratulated my father on his distinguished armed services record and our family's record of having brought so much employment to the area. The mother who was brassy in her Sunday best wept throughout the fifteen minutes it took. My father sat there in his expensive sporting clothes, a vicuña shirt and pressed chinos, as if everything had been a regrettable mistake. The potential charges which had not yet been filed were dropped. It cost me two grand for the lawyer who also orchestrated the five grand I gave on the side to the girl's mother. The mission was accomplished, a minor foray into the banality of evil.

On the way to Duluth and before he dropped off to sleep from the pain medicine he mumbled how sad it was with upcoming important engagements that he would not be able to appear in public until his face lost its purple hue. He fiddled with the radio trying to find a news program. He had always been a news junkie and the Walter Cronkite news program that immediately preceded our dinnertime was a sacred half hour during which no one was allowed to speak except during the commercials. Both Fred and Coughlin have mentioned that they have never met a human being less interested in current events than I am. I suppose this is a simple reaction to my father's obsession but there is the natural extension that the news of political mayhem and business corruption flowed inevitably from his class of men. I had been observant enough to note that most high members of the State Department, cabinet appointees, and major CEOs seemed to be cut from the same questionable roll of cloth and were engaged in the same level of discourse whether they were talking about political opponents, war, or economic recovery.

I cut off to the east rather than drive on a straighter line toward Duluth, unable to draw any conclusions over the fact that both Judy Garland and Bob Dylan had been born in the Grand Rapids–Hibbing area. I passed an iron mining theme park that was not well attended this late in the fall. All of the preposterously huge antique machinery loomed on the hillside. I slowed near a gas station to watch a tiny woman smoking a cigarette climb up the ladder and into the cab of a truck that could carry a three-hundred-ton payload of iron ore. I had heard that the immense tires cost forty thousand dollars apiece and it was so bizarre that the child in me wished to drive this truck down a country road.

When I finally hit Route 61 traveling south along Lake Superior toward Duluth my father began sighing and groaning in his sleep, his face a livid contrast to the glories of mid-October in the landscape around me, the yellow aspen and red-leaved hardwoods and the blue sea stretching infinitely to the east. Carla who had died at age twelve had always been such a grand traveling companion and she belonged in the seat beside me, not this ancient deviant. I was then reminded unpleasantly of the backwoods lawyer chiding me about Christian compassion. Coughlin had told me that my father was a nympholeptic which at least seemed a step up from a pedophile. His brain was obsessively fixed on young women around the ages of thirteen to fifteen which is proper only if you're also that age. The etiology of this disease is less than certain and the best revelation of its nature is in Nabokov's *Lolita*, which I don't know if my father ever read. It might emerge from a missing period in a young man's development, or some professionals have suggested that it is partly the mammalian urge to "cover" young women before other males reach them. A percentage of men, small fortunately, cannot accept the culture's "no" when it concerns young women any more than others can stop committing murder, robbery, or simply beating up their fellow men. Coughlin even suggested a genetic possibility, though it seemed remote. Of course the fact that you had begun to understand it had nothing to do with the behavior itself. Out of curiosity I had fished for answers to Richard Nixon's behavior and despite a hundred explanations there was still this peculiar and isolated monster on the hook.

I've put this nasty little incident on paper only because I learned something solid about my father's nature when we reached his place which was the ample-sized carriage house next to Seward's Victorian mansion on a stunning hillside. I helped him in with his gear but before we left the pickup he handed me his 20-gauge Parker shotgun having decided he wouldn't hunt again. Coughlin had come

north twice to grouse hunt and I had only a battered old Fox
Sterlingworth I had bought at a Seney gas station. Grouse were
delicious eating and Coughlin thought it might do me some good
to walk without looking at the landscape critically. My father was
happy at my evident pleasure at having been given the gun.

The inside of the carriage house was uncomfortably immacu-
late with a two-story living room looking out over Duluth harbor
far below. The kitchen and his bedroom were toward the rear, with
a dining area to the left and a den area partly enveloped by Chinese screens on the right. Above his desk there was a portrait of
Cynthia and me standing forlorn in front of our house that mother
hadn't liked and had stored. There were at least a dozen photos of
us as children, his wedding photos with Mother, a photo of Mother
in her dreaded moon costume at the Club, and a recent photo of
Cynthia and her children where it was easy to see that Donald had
been cropped out of the frame. There was also a photo of Richard
on his graduation day at Groton.

What I learned in a few minutes of forced pleasantness was
that my father saw himself as the aggrieved one, the insulted and
the injured, as if the family were a collective pope that had excom-
municated him without good cause. He referred to his shortcom-
ings as "foibles." My sense of my own mental balance felt a tremor.
It was easy to see that to him his victims weren't quite people or
human any more than the loggers or miners that had worked for
his father and grandfather were human, or if they were vaguely
people it was altogether sensible to ignore them. It was appropriate to ignore them. It was just to ignore them. When I got back in
my pickup after relenting and giving him a good-bye hug it occurred
to me that as surely as Europe we Americans had developed an ar-
istocracy whose merit depended on how long their money had allowed them to largely ignore the rest of the human race.

29

Now, standing in the den at midday, I'm eating my favorite Plunkett sandwich, aged provolone and mortadella on a hard roll. In a day and a half I'll go to Chicago for my mother's memorial service, returning with her ashes to distribute these bits of bone and vertebrae near the Huron River Point, her semicoma dreamscape. I have always wished that Laurie had been cremated. I've read that the cement vaults that enclose coffins, built somewhat like septic tanks, often leak so that the caskets float in the darkness. I've never researched why so many people resist the idea of cremation. Anyone who has come upon a dead animal in the woods on successive days has noted the alarming rate that we deliquesce. Fred had written in one of his not very interesting Zen Buddhist notes that "ashes don't return to wood."

With mother cremated I would remember how she truly was but my occasionally berserk imagination will still see Laurie's remains in the vault after a decade. Cremation liberates those left behind, but at the point I made up my mind on the subject I admitted it seemed natural that Clarence had been buried in a plain pine coffin without benefit of a vault in a Chippewa graveyard. In the following November I had attended a Ghost Supper for Clarence with Donald and Cynthia and perhaps a hundred relatives and friends. There were several roasted turkeys and a big kettle of corn and venison stew that was delicious on a cold clear afternoon. In front of Clarence's old shack there was a big bonfire and you dropped tobacco into the fire in order to release the souls of your loved ones who had died. Without the desire of your grief holding on to them they were able then to travel to another world. It was easy to release dear Clarence by crumbling the tobacco into the flames but when I did so with the multifoliate images of Laurie I began to weep. Of course many wept, and when I went out a hundred yards or so to my truck and leaned against the hood I heard a group of old ladies wailing and chanting an Anishinabe death song. Within a few minutes of standing there I had an image of Laurie out on Presque Isle when I had helped her up on a boulder and she was standing there in a yellow summer skirt and brown legs in the warm twilight looking toward the west. This is how I now see her most of the time and this is why the Ghost Supper is a unique experience in my life in how religion can work. However, if I'm enervated, exhausted, petulant, or angry she returns to the vault and its dank water.

I sense that my mother will remain whole in my imagination. I will not see her drunk and crying where she had fallen in the backyard after a quarrel with my father. I was hiding with Cynthia in the grove of lilacs along the alley and peeking out while Cynthia was arranging her collection of keys from her red purse. Probably every child in the world has hidden from their parents. Once she had left her "mad dog" husband my mother said she only gradually could focus on her children and felt panic that it was too late to be of any use to them. I said it hadn't been too late but it was, though there is a question of how much parents can do to change the behavior of their children once the teens have been reached. Once Coughlin got to know Cynthia he remarked that she had been able to use the improbable willfulness of her family all to her own good purposes. Her doubts in this direction about me gathered around the iron hand in which I had established my life's work at age sixteen because most of what had forced my decision was against something, a reaction to the incomprehensible rather than for some possible life force. My father had closed the windows to the world and I was spending my life struggling to open them. The question was whether I should have taken a club to the glass, jumped out, and burned the house down which is what Cynthia had metaphorically been able to do. And that's what my mother had been able to do, albeit late, so that one evening in Chicago when she seemed unable to overcome her sense of having failed me I answered that with a question, "How much could you do when you were trying to save your own life, and the prospects didn't look good?"

This was about a year after Laurie died and I had become a full-time hermit. Mother wanted me to start a "professional" relationship with Coughlin which was difficult because we were gradually becoming friends having fished together for three weeks in Wyoming and Montana the September before. Coughlin thought it would be awkward and unorthodox but was willing to give it a try. I resisted because I valued the idea of a friend more than a human confessional. That winter I suspected that my mother was using Mrs. Plunkett as a virtual spy but when I finally found out it was true while we were drinking too much wine and playing double solitaire I thought "Who gives a shit?" My mother's worries were well founded and well intentioned so why should I care if Mrs. Plunkett made daily reports? The compromise by spring was that I agreed to write a letter a week to Coughlin about my mental state but by that time the storm was nearly over. The idea of the term "depression" had always seemed an inept psychologism to me and that by the time you recognized this state in which all oxygen had left your life the oxygen begins to reenter.

My downfall began in November when I received a manila envelope with Vernice's first book of poems without a return address, a letter, or even an inscription, just the book published by a university press with a sepia photo of a stump on the cover, not a grand stump but an ordinary stump. I eagerly read the book looking for a sign of myself which I didn't find. On the back of the book there was a blurb by a man I took to be her prominent poet lover saying that this volume would establish Vernice as one of the "leading young poets of her time." Her stump poem led the volume and I readily admitted that it was fascinating and elegant. An obviously lonely girl wanders in the forest of the north and finds an immense stump straddling a gully under which she crawls, sits up, and redreams the world.

I had been banished from her work though once my anger subsided I assumed it was an aesthetic decision she was privileged to take. She couldn't very well say that there was a lover under the stump trying to go down on her. What goaded me was that another man had brought her life into bloom. It was sheer raw jealousy. There was no way for me to viably respond though I did write a letter in care of the university press to which there was no response that entire winter. Was she with this man because he was a better lover, a better companion, or, in short, a better man? Did she send the book as a knife, or an offhand announcement to me along with copies to dozens of other friends?

I tried to console myself with the obvious idea that she had taken up with this man merely because he could facilitate her ambition but I knew perfectly well it wasn't that simple. People rarely do things for singular reasons. Our motives are clumsily multiple. With Vernice she had pursued and seduced a man who could directly help her and this man wasn't me.

It wasn't an appropriate conclusion but it was at this point I began to doubt if I could do my project by myself with only my mountains of books and monographs and a few chats with a waning supply of old loggers for company. My fishing friend and tavern owner in Grand Marais, Michigan, had helped me outside of the books, and so had Vernice's abusive clarity, not to speak of Cynthia's sisterly prodding and the gift of Carla. The trouble was that it took so long for me to take advantage of what they had freely given. And now I had Coughlin to help steer me if I had the sense to listen. The September before when we were camped on the Yellowstone River near Big Timber, Montana, Coughlin had said that it was altogether sensible to separate oneself from the human community in order to get my particular kind of work done, but that was assuming you knew the human community in the first place. You couldn't simply be an inexperienced dog (he was kind enough not to say "pup") in the manger peeking out between the barn slats at the world.

That winter words failed me. I should say scholarly words failed me. I came upon a sentence in a treatise that reported, "In 1923 Michigan realized it had to deal with ten million acres of stumps." I threw the book against the far wall of the den and the sleeping Carla barked wildly. What the fuck could this sentence possibly mean? "The west had to deal with the absence of seventy-five million buffalo," would be another version. For months after this incident all scholarship seemed a moronically skewed version of the reality of history. The words dropped like turds in an outhouse. I could read

early environmentalists like Ernest Thompson Seton, James Oliver
Curwood, Thoreau, Sigurd Olson, or Aldo Leopold, but any material that wore the veil of scholarship became egregious plodding. It
had no nurture. It was dead as a canned sardine.

I was completely numb for a few weeks in January where all I
did was snowshoe out portions of Dickinson and Baraga counties
with the firm sense that I was full to the gills with bullshit. I wrote
Coughlin about my dismay and continued snowshoeing in the daylight hours until the winter landscape drew off my poison. By early
February my world had considerably lightened because I spent all
day "seeing" rather than reading or thinking, the latter of which comprised mostly of shortsighted rehearsals of questionable conclusions.
This all could easily be allowed to dissipate into the landscape because I was exhausted by the fraudulence of my hard work.

In early February there was the delight of a three-day thaw
and when it turned cold again I was able to take Carla along. She
loved running on the snow's thick hard crust rather than flounder-
ing in softer snow which made me leave her behind with Clarence.
For a break from physical exertion I'd stop in villages and small
towns and it was easy to find someone who had a collection of what
they would call "old-timey" photographs of the early days of logging and mining. Since I was so vastly overloaded with background
information it was wonderful simply to look at the photographs and
people my abstractions with human faces. A camera held while men
are at work draws forth the tender absurdities of pride. When
Cynthia was about ten she used to wander around Marquette on
summer evenings with a Brownie camera taking pictures of people
walking their dogs. Dog owners were happy to pose with their
mutts. Even my father was fascinated with Cynthia's scrapbook of
these photos.

On a Friday in mid-February I had a stroke of luck which
carried on for twenty-four hours and which helped me to radically

change directions. I got home by dark after a bright glistening day
with Carla snowshoeing the McCormack tract, a large area of old-
growth timber over west of Champion. While taking a rest I had
lain with Carla in a thicket of firs and watched a redstart coming in
and out of its nest. Other than ravens and chickadees the redstart
is the only bird that could survive winter up here. It lines the interior of its nest with a cushion of animal hair and grouse feathers,
the warmest cocoon possible. I was only a few feet from the bird
which had decided not to be troubled by our presence. Carla
watched it for a few minutes then napped curled up in the snow. I
was curious about how many thousands of years it had taken the
bird to evolve this survival behavior, then I idly wondered what
kind of survival behavior I had evolved in my own short life. I let
this preposterous question go with a smile at its insufficient interest.

When I came down a long hill toward the truck Carla growled
and barked because there was a small group of men standing near
their vehicles. I loped down the hill on my snowshoes and they turned
to watch. I found out they were setting up a course for a race the
next day, Saturday morning. One of them was a young lawyer for
the firm that took care of my family's business. He said he was surprised they hadn't heard from me and I admitted that I opened business mail that came my way only on Sundays. My father was finally
selling some land and the court-ordered lien would return to me the
amount for which he had sold my cabin. It was a little over a hundred thousand dollars and I stooped and petted Carla not knowing
how to respond. Another man came over and said he watched the
speed at which I came down the hill and he thought I might want to
enter their ten-mile showshoe race the next morning. The idea normally would have been alien to me but I agreed.

When I got home Mrs. Plunkett was sitting in the kitchen drinking red wine and not cooking and I remembered that I was taking
her out for her birthday dinner. There were two letters for me, one

from Coughlin and one from Fred in Hawaii. Fred had taken to sending me cryptic notes once a week, most of them irritating. This one
was no exception with a quote from a Chinese poet saying that we
must find ourselves in the shallows. I saved Coughlin's for after a
shower and a glass of wine but it was disturbing. He said that I
sounded as stale as hundred day old bread and that I likely should
do something dramatic to get out of my current "septic tank" which
of course reminded me of my poor dead Laurie. Perhaps he intended
to. He suggested that I track down Vera in Mexico and present my
apology, the idea of which had become a kind of cyst in my mind
and it was time to relieve myself of it. Another option was to find
Vernice in Europe, or wherever, and see if she wanted anything more
to do with me because even a definite "no" was better than brooding
about her. Ideally, I should do both because I was clearly suffocating myself. He added that he normally didn't give direct advice to
patients but then our contact wasn't in that category. This was a sore
point because Mother had tried to make a gift to him of a "fishing
vehicle," a 4WD, and he had turned down the gift, chiding her not
for her generosity but for trying to interfere with a matter from which
she should keep her distance.

The only good outfit I had were the clothes I had worn to
Laurie's funeral, unworn since then, and I found I had further
shrunk. It's hard to keep up when you're spending six hours a day
on showshoes. While I dressed I pushed away, for a change, an
unpleasant thought, this time how much I'd rather have my cabin
and property than a hundred thousand dollars. I didn't know at the
time what a good step this was. A mood can be a mud puddle to be
jumped over.

We had a fine time at the supper club, what the better restaurants
are often called in the great north. Mrs. Plunkett ate a large very

rare T-bone which seemed odd for a lady in her seventies and then criticized me for eating broiled whitefish. She was absorbed in the problem of putting more "meat" on me. I told her that maniacs often became quite thin which she didn't think was funny.

At first the dinner was awkward because our waitress was a high school classmate of mine named Susie. I didn't recognize her immediately because when I used to try to help her out on her atrocious grammar in the ninth grade she was very large but now only mildly so. When she asked what I was doing I said that I was writing a history of the Upper Peninsula and she said "the whole thing throughout time?" She laughed at herself and we chatted for a few minutes and she said she was the "usual" for our class, divorced with two children and working two jobs. I couldn't help but look at her fine fanny in the starched pale green waitress uniform. Mrs. Plunkett watched it all carefully and when Susie walked off to service another table she said, "That young woman is fresh for you."

I dropped off Mrs. Plunkett back home then retrieved Susie from the restaurant. She asked if I minded if we stopped at a bowling party. I was already aroused but managed to conceal my lack of enthusiasm. At the bowling alley there were at least a dozen of my classmates but none with which I had more than a passing acquaintance except for Glenn who was sullen and barely coherent. There was general silence after Glenn bellowed, "This big shot is slumming and he's after Susie's pussy," but then Clyde who I remembered as an effective tackle on the football team told Glenn to shut up. Despite his state I sat down beside him and had a beer and he warmed up talking about our fishing and the summer working in Iron Mountain. He was sorry about Polly and said he had lost two wives who thought they could wean him from booze. Of course I didn't know how to bowl and we left after I shook hands with everyone. In the car Susie remarked that "they weren't going to let you be a person like everyone else." I already knew I was largely regarded as a nut case around Marquette, though a much more benign type than my father. Before we got out of my truck at Susie's house she asked if I minded if we made love and I said I sort of had it in mind. I had detected that our pass through the bowling alley had been to make one of the men at the party jealous, hence more interested in her.

I didn't get home until three in the morning and when I got out of the truck in the wintry alley I was happy indeed. Jesse's light in the garage apartment came on and I waved up at him.

I won the ten-mile snowshoe race though I was nearly ten minutes late at the start. There were a dozen other competitors and I was plainly the only entrant who had been on snowshoes for most of the last ninety days. I passed the surprised young lawyer at a dead run about a mile from the finish line. It was all a fresh emotion to me because I couldn't remember having won a contest in my life. Actually it was by default in that throughout the course I was overwhelmed by a series of strange insights and wasn't conscious of the race. It occurred to me that I was three people instead of the one I needed to be. This had started in a dream and was revivified in the race. Along with this there were the images that the destruction of God, nature, and love were a living tradition. In the dream we ate them up and shit them out in a desiccated form. All of this was blurred by the texture of dreaming and I wasn't really convinced there was a meaning. Three-quarters of the way through the race when I was soaked with sweat the world appeared to have expanded again as it had done that day with Fred after leaving Cincinnati and

driving along the Ohio River. For a long stretch I didn't remember
my snowshoes touching the ground. I had read about athletes feeling that they were "in the zone" and that must be the experience I
was having. I became fully conscious only when I passed through
a length of pink yarn stretched across the finish line. There was a
small group of the wives and friends of the entrants and they clapped
and an older man handed me a can of very cold beer, the best one
of my life. I wavered back and forth between thinking hard and
shaking hands. How could all of this have been precipitated by
taking Mrs. Plunkett out for a birthday dinner, a bowling party,
making love to Susie, and a snowshoe race? I loved the comic aspect of it. When I went over to my truck and wiped off my sweating face with paper towels I returned to a waking sense of the dream
where my first and lowest person was an ugly howling boy trying
to somehow detach the animal from his spine and wanting to kill
his father. The second and middle person wore welder's goggles and
was a whiny drudge who read and wrote around the clock with false
passion and an air of phony kindness. The third person was a
smaller version of the second and the facial features were too sanded
or burnished as in a not quite finished painting. This third person's
mind whirled with images of Polly and Vernice and Cynthia and
remembered beautiful landscapes, even from youth, that I hadn't
noticed when I saw them. Obviously I didn't know what to make
of it. How could you eat God or nature or love and shit them out?

The young lawyer, Ted by name, tapped me on the shoulder
and I barely had the sense to recognize him. I wasn't sure I wanted
to be alone so I invited him and his wife over. Mrs. Plunkett was
merrily hungover and made us lunch. Ted mentioned that he kept
an eye on the family paperwork dealing with Cynthia and I and was
sure that since my father was guilty of fiduciary malfeasance or some
legal term like that he could get a court to put some sort of lien on

any future property sales until the matter was resolved. Ted's wife criticized him for talking business on a Saturday. I let the matter drop because I couldn't imagine being in a courtroom with my father. I would certainly rather go without the money than do further damage to myself.

30

On a Monday morning I got Mrs. Plunkett to call Vernice's university press and pretend she was a sick aunt who needed to get in touch with her niece. Vernice and her poet were living in Aix-en-Provence where he was a guest professor at the university.

I got out the world atlas only to find locations weren't quite where I expected them to be. My mother was spending two months in Tucson and I thought of stopping by to see her but Veracruz was well to the east down in Mexico, almost on a vertical line south of Houston. I also remembered my mother's tearful reaction when I had mentioned going south to ask forgiveness of Vera. France was another matter but then there would obviously be a plane from Mexico City. For the first time I felt absurdly sunk in the Upper

Peninsula. When my parents wanted Cynthia and me to join a trip to Europe organized by a cousin from Lake Forest it was out of the question primarily because they wanted us to go. I decided not to dwell on this because it painfully recalled Vernice's schoolmarm lecture on living my life as a reaction to my father. I got an early start.

I had breakfast with Clarence and Jesse before going to the travel agent. I had decided not to tell Jesse that I was going to visit his daughter because I mostly didn't want to be dissuaded. I told them I was on my way to the travel agent to book a flight to France to see a woman and they were delighted at the idea, having briefly met Vernice. Clarence had been up most of the moonlit night following his trap line and I watched him eat three pork chops with his eggs and potatoes, then fall half asleep. I had an idle insight on greed. If there were six hungry people at a table and one man grabbed all six pork chops for himself that would be greed. If Clarence had three pork chops by himself that was hunger. I didn't want to think about how many people he was supporting or Jesse for that matter. When I was young I was puzzled by what to answer schoolmates when they asked what my father did for a living. My mother told me to say "investments." This didn't seem clear so I turned as usual to Jesse. He was a famous poker player in a local Tuesday night game and explained it in those terms. An investment is like a card you bet on and you hope this card helps you win money. I was a little disappointed that that's all my father did.

At the travel agent's I had to listen to an older man who was said to be gay, or "light in his loafers," as they say locally, reminisce on how much my family used to travel "hither and yon." Rather than listening I looked at travel posters which ended up costing a lot of extra money because the agent assumed I wanted to travel in the manner of my parents. Later on I felt limp with stupidity over this matter. Clarence was always saying "it pays to listen" but I hadn't learned this lesson. I hadn't thought about the passport question but remembered I had gotten one in Chicago with Polly for a planned trip to the Holy Land with a group of theological students but then our divorce interfered.

I felt a little manic and flighty but still sure of myself. There was a slight thaw and when I took Carla down to the beach she found a half-frozen rotting fish in the heaps of drift ice and I couldn't get it away from her. I supposed that with dogs greed was a survival mechanism. I would also have to bathe her because after a few tentative bites she rolled on the stinking fish. When I chased her off she had the attitude of go ahead and take it, it's yours. She slept on the end of the bed so I'd have to do something about the smell.

I called Coughlin on his lunch hour and told him I was going on a Mexico-and-France trip but held off on my puzzling dreams. I had described one to him the week before about falling off a cliff on Presque Isle with all of my journals in my arms. I had ended up nearly dead but my journals were okay. This was charmlessly obvious, like another where I dreamt there were three blockages in my spine preventing the free flow of whatever. We talked a few minutes about our plan to tow a johnboat, or strap it on the camper roof, to Montana the following late summer to fish long stretches of the Yellowstone and upper Missouri. He had found out this wasn't safe because of turbulent waters and we agreed to split the cost of a high-prowed Mackenzie drift boat. He then posed a question I hadn't thought about. How did I feel about all of the people in the burgeoning environmental movement who were also examining the logging and mining past in the U.P.? One group had successfully sued to stop a mining company from dumping millions of tons of taconite ore waste into Lake Superior. I said I had had some correspondence with other people in this category and it didn't bother me. I had no feeling that they were poaching on my territory because the prominent difference was that it was my relatives that had done the dirty deeds. The subject was intimate to me. I was trying to subdue the family trait of megalomania and limit my inquiry. "What comes afterward? History is taking place in your head. Life is outside." I answered that he was talking to a man who had gone to a bowling party, slept with a waitress, won a snowshoe race, and was about to bathe a dog. He thought that was a pretty good list.

While I was bathing Carla Riva called and Carla jumped out of the tub and crawled under the bed which I had come to think of as an intelligent way for any young mammal to deal with an unpleasant reality. All kids have looked up at those coiled springs and out at the shoes of the searcher. Riva said she had misplaced Fred's address but after talking to her for a few minutes I doubted a lost number as her excuse to call. She told me that she had gone home for two weeks and run into her first love who had been violent with her in high school. He seemed to have changed dramatically so she slept with him and had become very distressed with herself. I couldn't quite believe that she seemed to be asking me for counsel. I was sitting at my desk and looking at Carla staring at me from under the bed. I couldn't bear to ask Riva how her evening had turned out though I suspected poorly. We talked about how errant human behavior could become. I said I was going to Mexico to see Vera and she said I still felt badly because I had probably still "wanted Vera's ass." I had long since admitted that to myself but said, "I didn't do it. What you don't do is pretty important." She laughed and agreed, then thanked me for listening. She was working in Washington, D.C., but had a chance for a job she very much wanted in Memphis. I questioned this and she said that there was more oxygen at the scene of the crime. Washington was too metronomic for her taste. The men were "dumpy bureaucratic fucks." I

suddenly remembered a line I had read from one of Vernice's
favorite poets, the inscrutable Rilke, "Only in the rat race of the
arena can the heart learn to beat." Riva liked that but then asked
why I was still hanging out in the woods.

Carla wouldn't come out from under the bed so I brought her dinner up. Susie's sister was taking care of her kids so she came over
for the hour she had off between her jobs as a typist and waitress.
She was a little nervous and told me that when she was a kid all
her friends thought our house was haunted because my ancestors
were bad. She was polite enough not to bring up any gossip about
my father. Carla didn't want Susie in my room. She growled so
loudly when we sat on the bed that I closed the door on her and we
went to Cynthia's room. When she was taking her clothes off Susie
asked me to keep an eye out for someone she could marry. She was
tired of working seventy hours a week at two jobs. This managed
to cool my erotic energies and I was struck by the idea that within
an hour I was being asked to help out two women, not including
Carla who was still pissed at me. If you step out in the daylight you
are called upon. For Susie I thought about Clarence's nephew who
had moved back home from Detroit after learning how to become
a top Chevrolet mechanic.

"Does he have to be lily white?" I asked.

"Who?" She was nude on her back and running a finger down
my spine.

"This husband I'm supposed to find for you."

"Indian or black or what?"

"I think his dad was part black from Sawyer and the mother
is mostly Indian with a bit of Finn thrown in." Sawyer is the local
air force base.

"That doesn't sound too bad. Is he cute?"

"Not to me but probably to you. He played the trumpet and basketball. About six feet with good teeth. You'll have to check out his dick yourself. I know he's looking."

She laughed which enlivened me. We could hear Carla baying in the other room.

I had a strangely revelatory evening when Susie left. It was Mrs. Plunkett's night off in which she took part in a senior's bowling league. She was proud of the gold-colored bowling ball I had bought her for Christmas though she admitted it hadn't improved her score. All of the "girls" on her team envied it. While I heated up some meatballs and sauce I wondered at the idea of seventy-year-old ladies still referring to themselves as girls. But they were. In December I had gone to a game dinner with Clarence. He said, "Us boys are going to cook up some deer meat, partridge, and ducks."

I went into the den for a few minutes and leafed through a thousand pages of notes I had typed up on my old manual Olivetti for my project. I had abandoned them this winter in favor of simply "seeing" what had been done. I had stood on top of the false mountains of tailings in Republic with Carla and seen a long way. She didn't like it because there was no animal scent up there.

I now saw clearly why the thousand pages were meaningless except as a nominal background. I recalled how when young I had dropped out of Scouts because I didn't like learning to tie knots and march. In winter we'd march up and down the gymnasium ten abreast in each row. Once I carried the American flag. Marching was embarrassing and so was group singing when my mother forced me to join the boy's choir at the Episcopal church, or in school when we had to sing "Give My Regards to Broadway."

It was all mechanistic. And so were my thousand pages of material, all technical in detail except for a sprinkling of anecdotes from old loggers and miners. There were surveyor's details, township and county grids, production graphs, shaded tree species maps, latitudes and longitudes, numerical rows of millions of board feet per family area.

Back in the kitchen I had to cook a fresh batch of noodles because the first had turned to putty. This time I stared at the boiling water and got them perfect.

I speculated that maybe my project was a spiritual problem though I cautioned myself against leaping to conclusions that might negate years of work. All of the numbers were not so much lies but irrelevant in terms of the history of my family, not to speak of the history of other dominant families. At base my battle against my father, and consequently my battle against my grandfather and great-grandfather, was described in the wrong language. Their language of conquest was the language of war. And my vocabulary, the language of my project thus far, was on the same level of discourse which perhaps made it hopeless. I was abruptly sure that this was what Vernice had meant. I was dealing with the language of the enemy. Greed was a spiritual problem that gradually overwhelmed the economic realities of the area. My great-grandfather's warlike language of conquest fluidly drew God into his business tribulations.

I stopped eating my spaghetti to find a passage of his in the den: "With God's help I will beat Felch to that thirty thousand acres south of the Ford River." The fact that he failed in this particular case goaded him to further religiosity. A month later he won out against Felch by bribing corrupt surveyors who were supposedly working for the state of Michigan. If you won the right to timber something as minimal as a section, 640 acres, you invariably tried to cut the contiguous sections without the theft being immediately detected. The obvious spiritual crime was involving God in the predatory violence as if He were directly cooperating in your theocratic trance. In reference to my awful dream, their behavior was obviously turning God into mere human shit. This all lacked the subtlety of my spaghetti and meatballs, my glass of red wine. I reminded myself to recheck Sprague's journal of his 1920 trip to France where he compared many post–World War I landscapes, the massive carnage of the natural world, to the timbering areas around Ontonogan where the landscape had been "shredded" of beauty. He had also compared an area of France, I think it was called Belleau Wood, to his own father's reminiscences about the great Peshtigo fire that had killed twelve hundred people near the Michigan-Wisconsin border. It couldn't accurately be called a forest fire because the area had already been timbered. What burned with inconceivable intensity were the leftover tops of trees and logging detritus. Local rivers were said to boil around the poor souls who jumped in and a train full of escapees caught fire. Kegs of nails in a local hardware store turned solid after their molten state and flaming birds crisscrossed the sky. The bones of many were no more than ash heaps.

At times when I read Sprague's journal I thought of Vernice's aesthetic principles that allowed hyperbole if it read well. In contrast to my own notes and prose, and certainly including the journals and ledgers of my grandfather and great-grandfather, Sprague's journals reflected his interest in painting and art collecting. He had clearly placed himself by choice in a different category than anyone else in his extended family and I supposed it was partly our similarity that caused him to will me his cabin.

Sitting there with an extra glass of red wine my brain began to get a little sore when I thought that people like Sprague, myself, and Vernice didn't deserve the compassion that one must generally apply to other people. We set ourselves aside. What were Riva, or Susie, for that matter? How could I think of Susie as a "waitress"? Or what to call Riva whose obsession was to help the poor? Susie

and Riva were drawn into their lives with open hearts. Sprague cast
the coldest eye on everything and everyone except his dead wife,
while Vernice insisted that her calling was poetry and the essence
of the act of language, and her obsession with the intrinsic playfulness of words dominated her life. I was startled reading in a
Sprague journal a quote from the Constance Garnett translation
of Dostoyevsky that said, "Two plus two is the beginning of death."
At Michigan State my professor of European literature named
Adrian Jaffe had quoted us the same sentence and told us to write
a one-page explication. Jaffe spoke in ornate and convoluted para-
graphs and intimidated all of us. Some class members met in a coffee shop and discussed the assignment until our heads ached. He
dropped all of our papers in a wastebasket without comment. The
quote became what Fred in a recent letter had called in his new
practice a koan. When I read a note on "35,000,000 board feet from
Baraga County" (which translates into immense acreage) I ran into
the same wall.

 I put on a coat and took Carla for a late-night walk. It was in
the mid-twenties and windless with the largest snowflakes possible
softly falling and when I looked up at them falling out of the darkness under a streetlamp Carla also looked up. The snow made a half-
inch of icy film on the sidewalk and, no longer worried about my
ankle, I would trot and glide thirty feet or so. Carla as usual ran
ahead to check for imaginary dangers. We went down to the harbor and looked at the mountains of ice piled up over the breakwater.
The harbor was enshrouded with ice that wouldn't begin to break
up until April when from the city you could hear the ice break far
out in Lake Superior like shots from big cannons. The lights of the
business district two blocks away were baffled by the snow so that
the old brick and stone buildings were blurred in their outlines
except the granite Cohodas bank. It was all quite lovely and for a
change I felt attached to my home place as if I were recognizing

that some of the works of man were good indeed. It was easy to imagine the population as a Greek chorus commenting on one another and certain purported woeful citizens like my father and perhaps myself. I could see our house on the hill but quickly turned away and walked down an alley to a boat barn. We used to store our basically unused sailboat here. Through a window's yellow square of light I could see Clarence putting away his tools. I opened the door and Carla backed away repelled by the smell of varnish. Clarence was at the end of his sixteen-hour workday and was pleased to see me.

It was midnight and we decided to have a nightcap in a working-man's bar where Clarence was sure Carla would be welcome. After I left Clarence would take her there for a cheeseburger. According to Clarence, because of their short lives dogs were due a birthday every two months or so. We drove to the bar in his ancient DeSoto which seemed to float through the snowy streets like a boat. At the tavern Clarence had his ginger ale and ordered the cheeseburger for Carla who drooled on the floor. I had a shot of cheap whiskey that reminded me of a childhood cough syrup. Clarence advised me to have a bouquet of flowers ready when I met Vernice.

"You shouldn't let your father steal from you the pleasure of having children," he said.

My stomach jumped at this but I let it pass. Jesse had told him that day that a doctor in Duluth had advised that my father be put away for a year. According to the doctor my father showed signs of being fifteen years older than he was. Clarence speculated that my father got out of college "fit as a fiddle" but then four years of World War II began the long slide.

"Over there they got so hungry on them South Sea islands they fried up snakes. I guess that was Filipino country." Clarence's faraway look was amusing.

My mind drifted away to my Mexico trip and something Fred said in his cups in Grand Marais years back when I admitted that Vera had shown me her bare butt. "Girls flirt," he said. "When we were young we went on dates and French-kissed for hours, dry-humped and pawed. That's a tradition with young people. Then your dad comes in as an anti-Dante closing the deal and destroying life's poetry. I was eighteen when I finally got to make love. She was a Boston secretary in her mid-thirties and I got a thumping that put me on the right course. Sad to say there's a hundred things that can go wrong with sex. If you avoid it you feel left out and that's not a good motive. Who knows?"

"Could she live in the U.P.?" Clarence asked.

"No." It was moments before I realized he was talking about Vernice.

"Well, I doubt you could live anyplace else. There's no point thinking about how you let Polly get away."

31

When you get on a plane just before daylight it is easy to be filled with the Great Doubt, again the obvious question of "What is it that I'm doing?" For an ex-theological student there is the fourteenth-century English devotional work *The Cloud of Unknowing*. As I've said I haven't traveled much. I was the first one in line at the departure gate, a full hour early, and moving backward I could remember Montana and Wyoming, Chicago many times, New York City once, and then Ohio. Legally I was a hick or a bumpkin. In an American literature course at Michigan State I had read Mark Twain's *Innocents Abroad* and the memory of it gave me pause.

By unpleasant luck one of my mother's ex–bridge player friends sat down beside me and quickly detached a price tag from the cuff

of my new sport coat and a pin from the back of my new shirt collar. I pretended not to notice and when she began to gab at top speed
I looked out the tiny oval window as if preoccupied with the dawn.
My mind flooded itself with obtuse questions. What would I be
doing if I didn't have my project? Did I have a higher opinion of
myself than was merited? When my Baptist preacher so long ago
sucked on his lemon drops after hearing a complaint about my father
why did he say, "The sins of the father are visited onto the sons until
the seventh generation"? The plane trembled as its engines revved
and the woman blabbered. Her son was on one-quarter disability
as a Vietnam War veteran. I was 4–F due to my problematical ankle.
Her son was the biggest jerk in high school. Everyone knew that
he used to get blow jobs from a retarded girl. Once at a swimming
party Donald had held him under water until he apologized for
being alive. "You boys are still having problems," she added.

I looked down at the glow of the rising sun on the frozen Ford
River and recognized the woebegone village of Sagola, the white
landscape with the woods looking like chin bristles, and the few
dark lines of roads. Of course once you're on a plane it's absurd to
question if you belong there but I felt a deep sense of my awkward-
ness as if my parts might not be in their proper places. Coughlin
called this "dislocation" but the word seemed fragile compared to
the physical sensation. Maybe dislocation falsely assumes that
there's a place you should be other than my shrine of stumps or
under the largest stump in the gully.

"Something stinks," the bridge player said.

"It's my sandwich made of Italian cold cuts."

"I was so sorry about your parents' divorce. They were such
a handsome couple." She was trying to cut to the chase from a
distance.

"Win some, lose some," I said as a petulant goad.

"So many of our grand families have fallen into disarray."

I faked a yawn and slumped in the seat. I thought how easily hell can become other people. Or ourselves, I corrected. I struggled to remember our coffee shop quarrel about Marshall McLuhan in theological school. My favorite professor preferred an anchorite's approach. How could you be of any help when you hadn't worked out your own salvation with fear and trembling? McLuhan claimed that we had put our nervous systems outside ourselves. My professor claimed that you were lost if you joined the long, winding trail of civilization into this particular hell, but what was the choice? If I hid in the woods it was because the woods fit my character. The U.P. was a virtual hotbed of cranky hermits to whom the public culture was unacceptable or unendurable. I had met one in my wanderings who had cut and stacked three hundred cords of wood. He was at least fifteen years ahead on the heat supply for his shack, somewhat like a nuthatch who stores more than a dozen times its required food supply each year. "I like to split wood," he said.

I dozed and dreamt of some Objibwe friends of Donald's over on Sugar Island. One evening we had stopped by and they were in a garage practicing a dance for an upcoming powwow. They had an old phonograph on which to play their drumming songs. I had been amazed at how well and intricately these large men danced, but in the dream the men were moving so fast that they were nearly invisible and when Donald and I turned to leave it was a previous century and we couldn't find my truck, and there were no roads so we walked back home on a path. There were far too many birds in the air.

When I awoke we were coming into Chicago. A few years before Clarence had shown me a coin from the 1893 Chicago World's Fair his Chippewa grandfather had brought back after dancing there. I thought again of Peter White having the Indians dance at the Episcopal church and then the idea that since the Indians were part of the land they also got cleared away when the land got cleared.

I had been amazed at Michigan State and at theological school about how no one seemed to know anything about American Indians except my professor Cleland. Out of sight, out of mind. History is the story of what men in suits did, said a radical friend. When the plane landed I thought that there was a specific etiology of the disease but then the disease quickly became an accepted economic reality.

Trees could be regenerated but not forests. Indians could be exterminated or driven onto paltry reservations but they were strong and resourceful enough to remain tribes. Of course they were widely scorned for being poor but so were Jesus and his disciples and followers.

When I got off the plane I walked up the concourse behind a pretty woman in a tight skirt. Invariably a religious thought was accompanied by earthly concerns. If my hearing were as fine as Carla's I could have heard her butt cheeks squeak as she walked. I pulled abreast to make sure she was old enough for me to look at. Yes. She had a Roman nose and a few gray hairs. I faded back until it occurred to me that I was on a mission. I had a fresh journal and needed to sit down and rehearse what to say to both Vera and Vernice.

32

Chicago, March 2 (from travel journal)

Mexican airline lounge. An elegant Mexican businessman drinks a rum and coke and tells me I must fish in Zihuatanejo where there are marlin, Pacific sailfish, roosterfish, etc. "It's cheap for you rich Americans," he says, again it's the travel agent's fault I'm in this fancy lounge where my stomach and brain quiver.

"Vera, I'm sorry for what my father did."

"Vera, I apologize for what my father did to you."

"Vera, do you need some money?"

"Vera, so this is my half brother."

"Vera, my father should die for what he did to you."

"Vera, I still love you."

"Vera, I have no idea what to say to you."

Only five people in first class. I'm embarrassed as usual but who else gives a fuck. Reading *Black Elk Speaks* which Donald sent as his favorite book. I'm back inside *The Cloud of Unknowing*. Also *Wildlife in America* by Matthiessen. Grim as the missing trees. The stewardess glows with a flowery scent.

Mexico City airport: lost, confused after sleeping. At customs I say I'm here to see friends in Veracruz. American Mennonite family who farm in Mexico direct me to Veracruz connection. As I get closer my stomach eats itself.

On the Veracruz plane there are only three passengers up front. A big fancy Latino woman covered with jewelry and across the aisle a Mexican man who is a version of my father wearing casual, understated, but elegant clothes, drinking coffee and reading *U.S. News & World Report*. Other than a few porters at the Mexico City airport there hasn't been anyone, including on the plane from Chicago, who looks like Mexicans, mostly farm laborers like those I've seen in Ohio and near East Lansing, though I've seen a number of prosperous Mexicans in Chicago. I've had two shots of delicious tequila. I've fingered a Spanish phrase book until some pages are softened with sweat. I've made several copies of the three addresses Cynthia has given me for Vera who sometimes stays with relatives near Jalapa, or in Alvarado, though she mostly lives in Veracruz. I also have phone numbers though I don't want to give her advance warning for fear she'll run for it. The stewardess took my hand and showed me Mount Orizaba out a far window. It is somehow frightening with its peak covered with snow and descending to the greenest jungle with the top catching the twilight sun and the jungle in darkness. The stewardess writes down the Aztec name "Citlaltepetl." I'm pleased to translate her meters into feet. The mountain is nearly nineteen thousand feet, so much larger than those of Montana and Wyoming, looking that way partly because it begins nearer sea level. She points ahead to the dark azure of the Caribbean and the lights of the city of Veracruz. She tells me that the jungle below us is full of jaguars and snakes and an eagle that steals babies. The businessman smiles and rolls his eyes. "Don't believe that peasant bullshit," he says. She flounces off insulted. When I enter the terminal I see that there's a plane boarding for Havana and immediately want to go there. A man who is dark, short, thick, and muscular sidles up to me. He introduces himself in Texas English though he is clearly Mexican. I am suspicious, of course, but he gives the name of the Marquette travel agent. I am still suspicious and wonder if the travel agent told Jesse I was coming here though I asked him not to. I ask the man if he knows Jesse and he shakes his head though not convincingly. He calls himself Bob or "Roberto" if I wish. He says he is there to show me around. I decide to go along with it. I intend to call the travel agent in the morning though it occurs to me that Jesse goes through all of the bills that come to the bank for Cynthia and me. I give up. It is hot and humid and Bob's car has air-conditioning. The soft music on the radio also softens me thinking of summer nights and the music coming from the window of Jesse's garage apartment. Bob tells me he was a cowboy near Corpus Christi in Texas and that a horse pitched over and crushed his hips and he became a cook. He swerves off from the main road to the city and when he reaches a shore road he points to a place where the first cows were unloaded on the continent by Don Gregorio de Villa-Lobos in 1521. I see nothing but dark water. At the hotel I show Bob the three addresses for Vera and he is noncommittal but then affects bluster and says he can find anyone in the province of Veracruz. We will meet in the early morning.

Out the window to the southeast the city lights I think I see turn out to be an enormous ship being loaded with semitrailers driving inside. I stand on a balcony with a table and chairs and am incapable of thought except that I've never been in a place so "elsewhere," so without familiar signs except the ship which would be too large to pass through the Soo Locks. I call Jesse. He is evasive but then admits Roberto is a friend. Jesse says I would be "lost" without him. I give up and ask about Vera and he says he doesn't know where she is because she's angry with him as he won't let her marry a man he dislikes. I read Cynthia's three addresses and he says that they are all good possibilities. "Good luck," he says.

Vera must be thirty-one years old. I have a lump in my throat. There is a vase of unrecognizable flowers beside a bowl of unrecognizable fruit. I'm homesick and my sentimental bullshit repels me. My father got me here. A ship's horn blows far off. I go to the balcony and there's another enormous ship being escorted by tugs a mile out. This is where Cortés the invader from Spain landed for his conquest of Mexico. Cattle and Cortés.

At dinner I examine the tentacles of an octopus. The waiter asks if something is wrong. I say that I've never seen an octopus. He can't quite believe me. I eat a wonderful fish that is called snook in Florida. It is roasted with garlic and lime juice. It's called "roballo" here.

Back in my room someone has brought a bottle of Cuban rum, limes, and a bucket of ice with three beers. The card says "Jesus," Jesse's real name. All the furniture is old but nice. I want to take a walk but I'm falling asleep. My shirt is wet so I take a shower and have a drink. In an ideal world I would call Vera and she would come sleep with me. This is my ideal world, not hers.

Veracruz, March 3. I get up at four-thirty A.M. to escape my dreams. I call down and a young waiter who looks very much like a Chippewa brings me coffee and fruit. I sit on the balcony and watch the loading of the second ship. I'm trying desperately to be honest if only for reasons of clarity and balance. I want the equilibrium of dozing against a stump with a hand on Carla. The question is whether I'm here to see my first love or to apologize for my father's behavior?

An hour later and the first glimpse of light in the east. The answer to everything is everything. She's sitting on my chest on the beach out near Presque Isle. She presses her sandy toes against my ears. Cynthia glances over, laughs, and stares at the sky. Then there is the screaming and Mother and Cynthia are in the hall and my father stumbles out with his wagging bloody dick. Now I remember he fell to one knee, not with wild but with dead eyes. It's odd to remember something new.

When it's light enough I leave my hotel Emporio making sure I know where it is. It's only six A.M. and the city's not really awake. I walk south along a black sand beach for a half hour then reverse myself to watch the ship being loaded while sitting on a bench on the *malecón*. Suddenly I am struck by the enormity of what I don't know. Sometimes I think I know a great deal but now on the bench it disappears. It is possible to loosen up and tighten at the same time. Bits and pieces of unconnected knowledge flow out of me and into the questionable water of the harbor. If the first cattle on the continent were unloaded here it spawned hundreds of thousands of cowboys and much of the culture of the American West. For a long time there were more cattle than people. The alpha mogul, the ur-predator, my great-grandfather and his cohorts drag along a hundred thousand loggers and miners who now have a livelihood. Our young lawyer said they taught human geography at the University of Chicago. Where people are and why and how they got there. Coughlin says our bodies are our truest homes. I'm here in Veracruz within my one-hundred-eighty-pound home. I have eyes and a memory and I'm looking for Vera. I'm unsure of how my parents got the way they are, but I'm pretty sure about myself. I understand Cynthia and Polly fairly well, less so Vernice and my dead Laurie. Clarence has stacks and stacks of gardening magazines and seed catalogs. He can recite ornamental shrubs and flowers by the hundreds. "It's my line of work," he says. He and Mother would spend hours deciding what to plant next. Every time I've thought I had Jesse figured out I didn't. Why didn't he quit when his daughter was raped? There is the idea that this maze I live within is not designed to be escaped. It's life. The stevedores, the dock workers that I watch, are earning their daily bread as they used to say. My body is absurdly relaxed. I'm not even one of the smallest of the household gods the Greeks invented. I can't see far and wide.

Roberto picks me up at ten. He prefers "Bob" as a jaunty man of the world who speaks laconic Texan. He rolls his cigarettes in a moment and spits thinly and well. I don't tell him that I talked to Jesse on the phone. We drive south along the coast toward Alvarado where Vera might be staying with an aunt. Bob says she is angry with her father because she wants to marry a schoolteacher and Jesse wants her to marry a coffee farmer. I'm still relaxed and quite happy with the scenery. Now I remember when Jesse and my father bought a coffee farm and Jesse came back to Marquette with a cloth sack of coffee beans and my mother ground them fresh in the morning. The coffee this morning had the same thick smell, not acidic. Jesse told me that when he was a boy he worked on a coffee plantation for twenty cents a day. On our left are wild lumpy dunes forming a barrier to the Caribbean which can have wild, preposterous storms in the fall just like those off Lake Superior now mostly under a tight lid of ice. Bob says his brother died in a fishing boat one autumn.

❊   ❊   ❊

Alvarado is of surpassing beauty, a fishing village on a riverine inlet, maybe a thousand people living in pastel houses of pink, pale
blue, even faded orange, with fishing boats tied up along a small
road encircling the village. I would come here to hide if anyone were
looking for me. We walk through a miniature cathedral and out the
back door, down a cobbled street. Bob knocks on a door and a
middle-aged woman answers. She looks over Bob's shoulder at me
with penetrating eyes that are incredibly unfriendly. No, Vera hasn't
been here for nearly a month. I am suspicious and ask Bob why he
didn't call. She has no phone, he says. We stop at a tiny restaurant
and I eat a bowl of chopped-up octopus pickled in lime. A man rows
across the estuary, narrow at the mouth but expanding inland farther than I could see. We share a fried snook the waiter says was
caught this morning, "over there." I want to row and when the man
ties up Bob makes the deal. Some fishermen are amused that I don't
want a motor boat. Off I go to the west, rowing so hard that soon I
am soaked with sweat. I weep for one minute and then I think fuck
the past that isn't really past and am suffused with the beauty of
the place. The woman at the door looked like she must be Jesse's
sister. Behind her was a small courtyard full of flowers. She was
dressed nicely. On the way back to the wharf the tide begins slipping
toward the neck of the estuary, which in the distance is rumpled
with a rip current with wind from the east. I can see I'm not going
to make it but will be swept under the highway bridge and out into
the Caribbean. I like the idea but a man comes in a motorboat and
tows me in.

On the way back to the city of Veracruz we stop at a stand and I
buy one each of thirty-one kinds of fruit, the only one I recognize
being a banana. In my room I arrange them on a table and stare at
the fruit while I drink a large glass of rum. Bob has gone off to cook

at a restaurant in Boca Rio, a fancy area we passed through on our
way south. Well-heeled Mexican tourists come there but not Americans who prefer the Pacific coast. Tomorrow we'll drive north to
Jalapa to look for Vera. I'm placid because I'm going to stay here
until I find her or die trying. I am quickly drunk on the rum which
the bottle says is fifty years old and from Havana, Cuba.

I wake up in the early-evening dark and follow a trail of music to
the *zócalo* downtown, passing a crippled man who reminds me of
Polly's father. He's playing a marimba and I impulsively put the
equivalent of five dollars in his collection basket. Maybe he worked
in a mine. In the city square about a hundred old couples are dancing to a uniformed orchestra. I read about this "danzon" in a hotel
brochure which Jesse and Vera also demonstrated so long ago.
There are many spectators including the adult children of the danc-
ers and also grandchildren. Some of the old women hold fans. It is
lovely until I think that my old parents will never dance. I turn back
to the hotel and within a block of the Emporio a young prostitute
asks me if I wish company. I say no but when I reach the hotel
entrance I turn around and retrace my steps but she is gone.

Jalapa, March 4. We've come here on what I detect is a back road
that takes hours longer than the possible route I studied on the map.
Once more I don't care. This charade is obviously directed by Jesse
and, after all, I have the rest of my life. Of course it isn't a charade
because he might only want me to see and understand his home
ground. He's been with our family nearly thirty-five years. When
we swerve around a donkey-pulled wagon full of firewood tended
by two boys and I ask Bob if that's how Jesse grew up he nods.
Before we descend the mountain range we stop so that I can see

Orizaba a hundred miles distant. Far down the mountain a huge
bird swoops across the road. It is an eagle that feeds on the local
monkeys and I remember the odor of the lovely stewardess. "Where
are the jaguars?" I ask, thinking of the jaguars and snakes the stewardess also talked about. "Up there," he says pointing northwest
when we stop on a bridge over a large turbulent river. I lean against
the rail and think there must be such a thing as beautiful anxiety.
My brain is peeled by the gorgeous landscape as if all other considerations are deafened by the water. It is a mythical valley with a
sheer mountain wall to the northeast. I wish Vernice were here. She
teased me that all of human history was a slaughterhouse and that
I would finally give up my obsession with greed in favor of her own
aesthetic preoccupations or something similar, otherwise I would
shoot myself. I didn't tell her about my close call. She said, "Sin-
cerity is so cheap," whatever that meant, though I have suspicions.

We descend until we pass shaded coffee plantations so humid
that grass and plants grow in the air on telephone and electric wires.
We are twenty miles or so from Jalapa and Bob still pretends that
this was the only possible route and I tell him that he is full of shit.
He laughs but finally admits that Jesse wanted me taken this way
to show me that he came from a beautiful place. What do I think?
The best, I admit. I say it is mythological and he agrees. On our
descent into Jalapa which is also built on hills he swerves off to stop
at a gatehouse of an imposing estate. An old man tells him that Vera
was here three days ago to visit her friend. Even the gatekeeper
knows that Vera is angry at Jesse about who she should marry. Bob
tells me that Jesse owns a small coffee farm ten miles to the south
near Coatepec which I saw on the map.

We stop at a pleasant apartment building in a suburb of Jalapa.
I lean against the car and when Bob comes out fifteen minutes later
he tells me that Vera was there last night. He says he has a little
business to do for Jesse for a couple of hours and perhaps we should

go "home" in the morning. We find a modest hotel and then he drops
me off at an archaeological museum that I must see. I'm overwarm,
tired, and a little pissed at being led by the nose. I sit on a bench in a
garden surrounding the museum and calm down immediately, admitting to myself that the day had beat the hell out of my nondirectional
snowshoeing. The beauty took me to a peculiar unfamiliar place in
my brain. An attractive girl passes me and smiles. I suddenly remember a hot day on the beach when my ankle was in the itchy
cast and I was lying on my side reading Dos Passos's *Manhattan
Transfer* which a teacher insisted I'd enjoy. Vera comes out of the
water and through her legs I see Picnic Rocks in Lake Superior.
She sits down beside me and shakes the water out of her hair. For
no reason she stands and jumps up and down. She stops and places
a cool sandy foot on my stomach and slides it down my bathing
trunks with a quizzical look. The arch of her foot is on my penis
and I lift her foot off. She flops down beside me and nibbles my ear.

I'm not ready for this museum but then it is questionable what
I'm ready for. Professor Weisinger used to lecture on "otherness,"
and here we have it. Walking through the door I ache at my silly
deficiencies. At the end of an early March day in the U.P. I might
note down "eleven ravens, four kinglets, three chickadees" while
this morning between Veracruz and Jalapa hundreds of species of
birds were visible, not to speak of different sorts of wildly flowering trees. My Calvinism is possible only in a wretched climate. A
one-directional mind is impossible in this climate. Professor Grabo
read aloud from the Puritan bombast of Jonathan Edwards's "Sin-
ners in the Hands of an Angry God." Here his parishioners would
have muttered "what a fucking nitwit." My brain is melting. There
are so many statues and figurines of the faces of women becoming
the faces of jaguars. I have no idea what this means but they definitely remind me of Cynthia. The museum isn't large but I wander
for a couple of hours with my inner being becoming absurdly liquid.

I keep returning to a twenty-ton Olmec head that was dug out of a swamp near the estuarine area I visited near Alvarado. The question is how they hauled it there from the mountains four thousand years ago. There are several of these Olmec heads and none of them have the reassuring quality of Fred's serene Buddha. The only thing I can imagine them saying is "you are born, you love, you suffer, you die." But maybe not that much. Their answer is nothing and they make you feel foolish for asking a question.

Out in front of the museum Bob is asleep in his car. At the hotel I call Cynthia from the desk because there are no phones in the room. She's harsh with me and says that tomorrow at five in the afternoon Vera will meet me in front of the hotel Emporio and then I should leave Veracruz because Vera has been weeping since I got here.

I keep this to myself and have a large glass of rum in my room. Near the hotel there is a canyon in the middle of the city and Bob pointed out the women washing clothes by hand in the river down in the canyon. I wake up in the dark when Bob knocks and we have a glass of rum and go to dinner after which we meet his girlfriend at a nightclub that has no roof and vines and flowering bushes are growing out of the walls. There are several hundred young people dancing to a fifteen-piece Cuban band which is deafening but also sensuous and melodious. A big woman in a tight green satin dress sings according to Bob's translation, "This world is full of sharks so you must learn to swim." Bob says most of the young people are medical students from the local university. There are no geometrical moves in their dancing. All the motions are fluid as if they were made of running water. Bob must be fifty years old and his girlfriend is a nurse in her twenties who reminds me uncomfortably of Vera. It's hot and I drink too much rum and count thirty-seven

beautiful women as if I'm counting stumps. I won't leave until four
in the morning which pleases Bob who disappears for an hour with
his beloved. They return glistening with sweat. I sit there like an
Olmec head until I nearly piss in my pants. I've watched one girl
who has danced nearly two hours without stopping. When the band
takes a break she continues without music. The crowd cheers her
on. When I fall asleep back at the hotel I still hear the music in vivid
dreams of the cold north.

Jalapa—Veracruz—March 5. Woke up shivering with a cool north
wind coming through the windows, amazed that I hadn't vomited
and rather happy still hearing last night's music in my head. We
left at midmorning after Bob did some business errands and people
on the streets wore coats and sweaters though I guessed it to be in
the sixties. I'm not saying I felt good only that I lacked the overall
wretchedness that I expected. I had long ago guessed that my father
maintained a certain level of alcohol in his system or had generally
inured himself to the discomfort amateurs felt. Or maybe the semisick
feeling comfortably matched the way his soul felt.

   I decided to test Bob by telling him I had managed by myself
to arrange to see Vera though I didn't say where and when. He was
obviously miserable from lack of sleep and I teased him about mixing business and love. He admitted that Jesse was a hard "boss"
and that he might have to give up love to keep his job of looking in
on all of Jesse's little businesses plus the coffee farm. Bob always
used a diminutive to define the nature of any of Jesse's interests. I
can't say I was very interested but I probed further as if I were only
filling up our driving time. Bob was a nephew of Jesse's by marriage. Jesse's father had died leaving many children when Jesse
was sixteen. They were poor but not "dirt poor" and Jesse had tried
to assume leadership of the family but knew the only way it would

work was if he went north to the U.S. He got his citizenship in World War II and became friends with a kind, wealthy man, meaning my father. In the two months he had off every year he was able to oversee "little" businesses run by extended family members. I let the subject slide away with the cool north wind that was so vigorously brushing the green landscape and whipping up dust devils in the streets of the small villages we passed through. I didn't mentally disagree that my father could be kind having heard of his Christmas noblesse oblige in Marquette and other incidents. I had had few close male friends and couldn't quite imagine what kind of closeness could build up during four years of World War II in the Pacific. In this remote landscape I was able to achieve a clearer view of my family so that despite the vulnerability of my hangover I didn't feel any of the physical repercussions, the usual lump in the throat, the tingling buzz of rising blood pressure.

I idly asked why Jesse was so obstinate against Vera marrying a schoolteacher. After all she was old enough to be entitled to freedom of choice. Bob became morose. Of the eight Sundays a year that Jesse was home the extended family gathered at the coffee farm for a generous picnic. Out of Jesse's earshot the families referred to these days as "Sundays from hell." Account books were opened for the dry-cleaning shop, the café, the butcher shop, taqueria, the auto bump shop, and so on. Exact plans were made. On the weekdays Jesse inspected without notice every business he owned. Anything that didn't contribute to the family had to be corrected or expunged. Vera's schoolteacher lover didn't fit into the larger plan while the older man who owned an adjoining coffee farm was a positive choice. It was important that he was neither rich nor poor because the rich were untrustworthy. Naturally everyone enjoyed the prosperity but they were relieved when Jesse returned to his fine job in the north. Everyone in Veracruz knew that Jesse was money loco and that was why his wife had run off to Mexico City with another man. Jesse had then taken his daughter north where she had become regrettably pregnant. Vera was as beautiful and unstable as her mother and her son hadn't been quite "correct" mentally since his bicycle accident. In fact he had beaten a school-mate so severely that the boy spent a week in the hospital.

I wasn't sure I wished to know all of this but here it was and I reflected on how it contrasted with Clarence's family. Jesse had turned out to be not quite benign in regard to his own people and I wondered at the complications when you lifted the lid off any par-ticular family. When we were still short of Veracruz I asked Bob to detour so I could see in daylight where the first cattle were un-loaded onto the continent. Of course someone was going to do it but the enormous consequences were intriguing. Coughlin had told me that China was now almost completely denuded of trees from logging but once had been heavily forested. I was in the anxious position of never having had to completely support myself except when I chose to out of stubbornness. Many others shared this van-tage point which did not make it less questionable. Throughout his-tory there had been economic conquistadores that made everyone nervous, even on Jesse's minor scale. It made you wonder about the word "livelihood."

I sat at the window looking out at the harbor for several hours waiting for my meeting with Vera. The north wind made the har-bor choppy and I could hear the waves slapping against the wharves and watched the small boats bobbing restlessly. The large ships were impervious at least within the confines of the harbor.

I was settled into an uncomfortable "nothing" state of think-ing about Vera and how her father had brought her to northern Michigan for a better life. The mother had fled. Her friendship with Cynthia. My controlled infatuation. My father raped her. She had a son. Her father trading in his probable rage for money, pure and simple, but again, what would I know about being the means of support for dozens of people? The waves I was looking at were not Lake Superior's and I had a jolt of insufferable homesickness that was followed ironically by not wanting to go home and resume my normal life. I had used it up. I had worn it out. So much that I thought I had found in the depths had disappeared in the shallows of this trip. I had become too narrow too early. I couldn't understand my family's part in the whole because I didn't have a clear enough view of the whole. I recalled something I had read where Einstein mentioned that he had no admiration for scientists who spent their lives drilling holes in a thin piece of board.

When twenty years ago in Marquette I had resolved in one of those mockingly intense teenage rituals that I would not spend my life thinking about myself like everyone else seemed to do, I got religion. It went away or transfigured itself into a nonconvincing form, I played the fool because I was a fool. Over and over. I was a mere parody of my best intentions. How can you be both slave and captor? It's evidently easy. Reading many of the books Vernice had insisted on had made me feel quite ordinary. I liked William Carlos Williams because I could understand him and Rainer Rilke because I couldn't understand him. I suppose it's better to accept the mind's disorder rather than make a daily wild attempt to screw the lid on tight. For instance, right now down on the *malecón* a priest with windswept hair is gesturing and lecturing to a group of inattentive ten-year-old boys. I am convinced that Catholicism is best suited for this rather ornate culture and habitat. The next step, of course, for someone who has occasionally disappeared up his own asshole, is to wonder what sort of religion, if any, is suited to my own habitat. At this point I remember a childhood radio program starring Edgar Bergen the ventriloquist with either Charlie McCarthy or Mortimer Snerd sitting on his lap, or both. I smile thinking I am all three.

❋ ❋ ❋

About ten minutes to go. I have my wristwatch, the pocket watch
from my briefcase, and the room clock on the table before me, all
within three minutes of one another. My mind and body are full of
butterflies. I go down early in hopes of settling myself before her
arrival but she's already there across the street from the hotel entrance. She's leaning against a spiffy new car and dressed very nicely
in a pale green dress, a slight man in a trim blue suit standing beside
her. The son with my father's jaw sits half out of the back door glow-
ering. She sees me and crosses the street with the wind whipping
her dress. I step off the curb as she approaches. She is still unbear-
ably handsome but her face is taut, her eyes furtive and unfocused.
"You can't be here. This is impossible. I know your heart is good
but this is impossible." I take her hand but then she withdraws it.
"I'm so sorry for what happened," I begin to say but my voice
catches in a cold knot. "Yes but you did nothing bad. I wanted you
to be my boyfriend but I was too young. This is impossible. Embrace Cynthia for me. Good-bye," and then she turned and walked
back across the street.

Mexico City, March 6. Of course I wept, so much so that my eyes
were swollen and I didn't want to leave the room. I ordered a fish
to eat, a snook again, but didn't touch it. I thought absurdly of
taking it with me, this mysterious creature that led its entire life
underwater.

    I made a few calls and left the hotel abruptly. I spent the night
on the top floor of a hotel in Mexico City where they were playing
tennis on the courts above me. I fell asleep on a bench in the gardens of the hotel next to a bush with blue flowers that had a strong
odor of the sea. A guard woke me around midnight and I had a nice
bowl of soup in a café where young, well-dressed Mexican couples

were drinking French wine and laughing. A girl of surpassing love-
liness looked like she could be a younger sister of Vera. I was naturally thinking of the fatal structure of life that allowed people who
cared for each other to separate forever. The idea somehow achieved
a latitude above my father being the cause. It was haphazardness
of love that doesn't overcome the rest of life. I thought of Polly and
how love conquers itself

I didn't leave my room until I went to the airport, amused that
the whole trip was costing me more than I ordinarily spent in a year
and the sheer idiocy of my visit to the travel agent, which was as
uncomfortable as going to a lawyer, into a bank, or visiting a doctor. On the plane, an Air France flight, I devised three different
letters to Vera before it dawned on me that it wasn't allowed. There
was no way to reenter her life. The only solid relationship I had with
a female was my dog Carla who seemed to equally adore Clarence.
My mother was mostly a pleasant ghost in Evanston and despite
the fact that I was older I would always be Cynthia's "little brother."
Polly was married with two children and a second chance was unlikely. When I was dropped off at the Mexico City airport and had
passed all of the airline desks it occurred to me that my upcoming
attempt to solidly connect with Vernice was comic at best. One
down and one to go. I could board a flight to Los Angeles and become a movie star or a flight to Montreal and become a French
voyageur and fur trapper. I didn't feel the least rejected by Vera,
only that I didn't belong in her company, not even as a memory.

A stewardess in a pale blue suit kept pouring me a delicious
red wine that I recognized as one my father liked. He couldn't very
well be wrong about everything. He had lived for a year in Paris
when he was five. It was a fatuous story. My grandfather had sent
two local Marquette men to North Dakota to shoot several hundred pheasants for an enormous feast he was planning. When they
returned late one October afternoon he had posed in hunting clothes

with the pheasants as if he had been on the hunting trip. This struck my grandmother as disgusting and off she went to Paris with my father and Richard, who was an infant at the time, and Mrs. Plunkett's mother who worked for her. I liked this story because it bespoke the careless freedom of adults and had confirmed my early convictions of their untrustworthiness. Gradually, when I would come upon the picture of my grandfather with the lawn full of pheasants in a photo album, I admitted to myself that this man looked like the consummate asshole that he was. When I heard he had lost more than three-quarters of the family fortune during the Depression I was pleased. My father said that all the land couldn't be lost simply because no one wanted to buy it. It was "lucky" for the family when World War II began and the price of iron ore went way up.

Paris, March 7. Cold and rainy. Perfect weather for the dipshit romantic on the last leg of his not very romantic grand tour. We landed right after dawn and I quickly perceived why certain people love this place for reasons of an ineffably sweet melancholy. The taxi driver had spent a year near Atlanta, Georgia, as an exchange student and consequently his language owned southernisms, "What y'all doing here?" Before I could answer he stated a fee to take me on a sex tour that evening to a place called Pigalle. Without thinking I said that the next day I had to attend a funeral in Aix-en-Provence. I realized at this moment that I was still infused with a dream I had had just before landing. I had fallen asleep after drinking a red wine from a place called Beaune. In the dream I had an involved memory of a seminar at theological school where a professor from England had spoken of the historical aspects of the concept of forgiveness. Some of us thought that this man's Oxonian accent made him sound more intelligent than he was. Anyway, he talked of the idea in early church history that if you couldn't forgive someone you became their slave mentally. This had irked and rattled me. After the seminar I had taken a long walk. It was February and there had been a heavy snowstorm in the Chicago area and people were shoveling out their cars in Evanston. In the dream no matter how far I walked I was still wading through deep snow on the same street in a state of being pissed off at this professor. This was at a time when I still actively fantasized about shooting my father in the same manner that Lee Harvey Oswald had shot President Kennedy.

The dream was obvious but when I got to my hotel I called Coughlin in Chicago and by luck caught him when he wasn't busy. We talked about my trip to Mexico and the palpable early spring itch to go trout fishing. I brought up the idea of forgiveness and he said that for it to work it had to be a complete experience rather than just an idea and that perhaps when I got home I should visit my father in Duluth or wherever. Forgiveness wasn't excusing the offender but unburdening yourself of the tyranny of the offender by seeing him in a full human perspective. I said that this sounded a little abstract to me but he countered with the notion that if I considered all of the worst things I had ever thought of I might look at my father as a man who enacted them. I paused, recalling that after I had seen Vera's bare butt in the upstairs hallway I felt lustful for days. Coughlin then said that his own father had told him he had forgiven the men who smashed his hands mostly to avoid traveling back north to Belfast and shooting them. If he had shot them he would have lived a life of rage in prison far from his family and also from the pleasure of trout fishing.

At the hotel my room wouldn't be ready until noon so I drew a grubby rain parka from my duffel bag and got a map from the desk man who marked the location of the hotel, looked at me closely, then wrote down the Hotel de Suede's address and phone number for my wallet fearing I'd get lost. I set off on a four-hour rain-soaked stroll

of the Left Bank from my start near the Invalides up the Seine to the
Jardin des Plantes circling back through the Luxembourg Gardens.

At the outset I was a little blind to my surroundings because
when we closed the conversation Coughlin had advised that I try
to be slow and judicious with these feelings about forgiveness because there was no available safety net. He said he could liken the
process to carrying a heavy backpack for twenty years then suddenly tossing it away. To do so would be to abandon much of the
energy, however faulty, for a large part of my life. For instance,
would I give up the project that had been central to me for so long?

Jesus Christ, I thought, walking swiftly along the Seine. No,
I wouldn't give up the project because for nearly a year I had been
walking or snowshoeing in the outback without my vision becoming self-referential. What "is" overcomes what "was." I didn't func-
tionally believe the humdrum drone of "knowledge is power" but
gradually I seemed to be acquiring a topographical view of the maze.
It had become more important to me to understand the entire maze
than trying to limit myself to comprehending my family's part of it.
In January near Sagola I had been lost in a snow squall for a brief
but modestly frightening half hour just before dark and then I suddenly teetered on a snowbank and slid down onto the county road
on which my truck was parked to the north of me. In the driving
snow I nearly walked into my pickup before I saw it.

The long wet walk in Paris lifted another layer off my confusion. Some rich and powerful men obviously had a firm aesthetic
sense. This was far less apparent in urban areas in America than it
was in Paris where you came close to not believing your eyes and
your skin prickled as if you were looking at a great painting. There
was something historically troubling in America's geopiety that
allowed her to become proud of the destructiveness of her creation
of ugliness. The capacity to cut all of the virgin timber in the state
of Michigan became a source of pride.

Somewhere in the puzzling streets between the Jardin des Plantes and the Luxembourg Gardens a little fresh air entered my mental wanderings. Vernice had tried to peel away the filmy blindness of my own sense of beauty and hadn't quite realized, as I didn't earlier, that my obsession with the landscape was more aesthetic than scientific. This idea was fresh enough to me that I tried to push it away for the time being. In the midst of my obsessiveness I had rejected many of the forms beauty can take. My depression over my father's wrongdoings and consequently those of my ancestors had prevented me from living a life of wholeness as surely as greed had blinded them.

It was now about noon and my pants were soaked and my shoes squished. The wind had clocked to the south according to my map and when I passed a restaurant called La Closerie des Lilas I stopped and asked myself, "How can we be so wrong?" This feeling was a little bit silly but the restaurant reminded me of my father's admiration for Hemingway and his book *A Moveable Feast* which I had read. I never cared for Hemingway but that was beside the point at this moment. In college the young men I knew who loved Hemingway tended to wear flannel shirts and seemed to affect a heartiness I never felt. I didn't know it at the time but I recognized it later that I was too possessed with questions to think that manliness was an answer. Besides, when you came from the Upper Peninsula you were scarcely mystified by the "big woods" because you were born and raised within it and with proper caution it wasn't threatening. My father presumed to see a different Hemingway than I did. When I read his early work the writer seemed as fragile as I was. What was nagging at me now like a virus was that what the war had done to my father wasn't simple and literary. When you added the history of family malfeasance the war had pounded my father into a monster. My grandfather had been an officer in World War I but never left Washington, D.C. He had made war

on Germany as surely as he had made war on the land. The Fourth
of July marching music that I dreaded helped us forget the dead
and maimed. I had been at war with human nature so long I had
forgotten to live a life.

I was walking splaylegged down Montparnasse because my wet
pants were chafing my crotch now. The rain had slowed to a trickle
and I took off my parka and pushed back my sopping hair. Now many
people were in the street including lovely, fashionable women and
pert shopgirls. There were glances at the wet dog, the idiot American, meaning me. I went into a bistro and ate a whole roast chicken,
though it was relatively small, and drank a bottle of red wine, leaving when I began to doze over the question of how to live a life.

I slept half a dozen hours waking at twilight. There were birds in
the large garden behind the hotel but I didn't recognize them. When
it was dark I called down for coffee and the name of the owl I was
hearing in the garden. The desk girl said "chouette," a nice name
for an owl. I sat there and questioned whether greed always overwhelmed the aesthetic in life but then quickly dressed because I had
done enough thinking for one day. I was tempted to try to call
Vernice to set up a meeting but dismissed the notion because I was
beginning to enjoy the slapdash quality of my trip. If she had left
town I could always sit there and wait for her return or pursue her.
If I met her lover I'd introduce myself as her cousin from Indiana.
Fort Wayne, to be exact.

March 8. I'm on a fast train south to Marseille where I'll change to
a local for Aix-en-Provence. I'm understandably nervous about
seeing Vernice but any sort of trepidation is not in the league of Vera.
When I was about twelve I envisioned women falling into my arms

when they met me. First it was Ingrid Bergman, then Deborah Kerr, then Ava Gardner, then Grace Kelly who probably drank iced tea and wore white cotton underpants like a girl named Nancy in seventh grade who would lift her dress and show you her underpants for a dollar which seemed expensive at the time.

Last night after a long walk I had a herring snack at Café Select and talked to some people at the next table who were graduate students at the Sorbonne. One was an attractive young Jewish woman from Thessaloníki in Greece. It boggled me as I had never heard the word Thessaloníki outside of the Pauline epistles. I didn't get to talk to her because her companion, about my age, kept quizzing me about American Indians. I explained that I mostly knew only about the Chippewa which he properly called the Anishinabe. He was studying Native religions and asked what chance there was if he came to the Upper Peninsula of meeting and talking to a shaman. I said that from what I knew this was unlikely. I had known Clarence's cousin Harold for twenty years before I learned he was a shaman. I explained that it wasn't really an open society when it came to religion. I added that my brother-in-law Donald had wished to talk to a shaman who wouldn't have anything to do with him until he sat for three days and nights without food, water, or shelter. Donald had made it two days but intended to try again. I added "no wine" which they thought was funny. The girl from Thessaloníki who was studying the Sufis teased her boyfriend that he should try it. She reminded me of Vernice and as they quarreled in French I reflected on the accidental nature of affection. Laurie was Cynthia's friend. Vera arrived from Mexico. Polly was at a hamburger stand in Iron Mountain when I worked on construction. Vernice approached while I talked to Fred outside the Newberry Library. It was all so random. The Jewish girl was so attractive and witty I would have run away with her. To cap it all off a beautifully dressed middle-aged woman in the far corner of the café bore a passing resemblance to my mother. The scholarly couple asked me if I wanted to go with them to an American jazz club and I said I couldn't because I was leaving early in the morning for Aix-en-Provence to look for someone. They advised that I simply sit at a café called Deux Garcons and I'd eventually find my prey. Untypically I changed my mind and went to the club where the jazz band turned out to be from Detroit. The young woman sat between us and when he went to the toilet she put her hand on my leg and gave me her phone number. Sweat popped out on my forehead. I realized again how comparatively inexperienced I was for a man of my age but then I was unaware of the statistics. You meet very few women in the woods plus what affections I had were manic and limited. I left after an hour and on my way back to the hotel decided that the main problem of cities is that you couldn't see the stars up in the dark.

After a splendid train ride and checking into a fancy hotel I'm sitting at the Café Deux Garcons. I have this idea of returning to France at some point with a small suitcase and spending a couple of weeks riding trains.

It's two in the afternoon now and I'm prepared for a long wait despite not quite knowing what I have in mind. What would I do if Vernice threw herself in my arms screaming "I want to have your baby"? Though this is indeed unlikely anything is possible except world peace. I have started some sort of log rolling down a long hill. For instance, this morning I decided to visit my mother and see if she has forgiven my father, and then visit my father to see if he is willing to explain his life. I suspect this elementary idea was caused by the movement of the train. Time is passing.

But Vernice. Once I was sitting on the deck of our unused sailboat and my father and some friends were on the slip dock. I

was attempting to ignore their talk about a pretty young woman
who had just walked by and boarded a large cabin cruiser down
the wharf. She was a daughter of what they call a "leading family"
but had been spotted in the arms of a black man in a Chicago nightclub. My father and his friends were busy agreeing that this woman
was "high octane" which puzzled me because the term referred to
gasoline. Later that day my buddy Glenn explained that it meant a
"high-powered crazy bitch."

What would I do if I won her away from her poet? I had read
his book called *Études* (not the real title but close, to protect identi-
ties). He was one of those improbably tortured souls and what's
more he made a living at it. There was a long poem about how much
he missed his young daughter Lila in California. It was a lovely
poem but raised the question of why he didn't go visit her. "Destiny has swept me away from you," he wrote.

Vernice was clearly high octane and I was perhaps low octane, at least in my own mind. Or I had chosen that path. Sprague
in his journals had seemed a little nervous about what he called the
"privilege of idleness." After his young wife died he had dedicated
himself to a life of "service" by school teaching. He had donated
his checks but after a number of years he had become so repelled
by the lack of curiosity in high school students that he quit to pursue his interests on the art of the Pueblo peoples of the Southwest
which struck me as an interest as far as possible from the family. I
had never been idle which was not to say my preoccupations were
truly worthy. The idea of privilege was another matter. I have heard
that some realtors refer to clients with inherited funds as "lucky
sperms."

Sitting in Deux Garcons from two until seven became comic.
After a large number of customers left following the late lunch hour
the outside tables were largely empty because a chilly wind had
come up. I was a little anxious about taking up space so I kept

ordering a bit of this and that after eating delicious chicken with lemon for lunch. Wine, fruit, coffee, cheese, tea, more wine, chocolate cake. Finally my waiter, a pleasant older man, told me that it was permissible to sit there without constantly ordering things. I had been thinking about Polly's father whose legs had been crushed through improperly maintained machinery, a cost-cutting maneuver. Twisted into fleshy pretzels.

I had read very little detective fiction so I couldn't come up with a gambit to isolate Vernice. Wait until dark and see if there's light in their window? Keep calling until she answers? Hang up if he answers or say I'm a cousin? I was hopelessly inept. A girl with an armload of schoolbooks sat close by drinking coffee and chain-smoking. I ordered a pack of cigarettes, the first in a long while. Her legs were lividly bare in her short skirt and I got an erection. Had I come this far to fuck Vernice? I loved her but that didn't preclude the former. Was I a vampire that could get life only in the company of women? Probably. The company of men only exacerbated my own sodden concerns.

I stood on a dark street across from their apartment which was 2A. The lights were on. The lights went out at eight o'clock. Vernice emerged with her tall, thin poet. They got in a tiny car and drove away. I had taken the bull by the horns, as it were, and bought a packet of stationery. I wrote, "Dear Vernice, Meet me at the Hotel Pigonnet at 10 A.M. to discuss what to do with Aunt Louise. Your cousin from Grand Marais. D.B." Silly, of course. When I approached the darkened doorway to look for her mail slot there was an old lady glaring at me. What would Cary Grant do? I bowed deeply and gave her the envelope along with ten bucks in francs and asked her to give it to Vernice in secret all in jumbled French though she grinned when she got the gist.

I walked back to the hotel with my stomach unsettled from the afternoon out. I sat before the open window as I had in Veracruz hoping to see the stars but they were dim from the ambient light. I sat there hoping that Vera would marry her schoolteacher lover and that Riva and Polly were doing fine at whatever. I was frankly lonesome and wondered why other than Polly my affections had sought such unrewarding possibilities. Unwilling tears formed when I thought about Laurie. They dried and then the same thing happened when I thought about Polly. This tear thing was new and I had the notion that new parts of my brain were becoming apparent to me without my help.

I went down to the desk and asked if they might find me a taxi to take me out in the country to see some stars. "But, of course." The idea seemed logical to the woman at the desk. She was about fifty and trim with a shy smile. There was an urge to jump over the desk counter at which point she would wilt into my arms, and after that would ensue one of those scenes that I read about in Henry Miller's *Sexus* in college.

The taxi driver took me up a valley on a narrow road that led into the mountains. He paused a moment and pointed at a small darkened house saying "Cézanne studio," at which point I remembered why the name of the city of Aix-en-Provence was familiar. When I was young I used to leaf through my mother's art books looking for nudes but still managed to read the text about the exciting but tragic lives of artists. Cézanne had managed to live a long life by staying down in Aix-en-Provence.

The stars themselves were so close when I got out of the cab that the Milky Way was a filmy white blur. I was exhilarated in this bowl within the granite mountains that rose in slabs of gray. I walked along the road in the cool night air with a swelling heart half expecting the northern lights. I thought of nothing but the grandeur of the universe.

❁   ❁   ❁

Farther up the road there was a fancy restaurant and when we began to turn around to head back to town I suggested we have some wine to celebrate the stars. The cab driver had begun to absorb my buoyant mood and agreed. He turned off the meter and we walked through the half-full parking lot into the bar part of the restaurant where I ordered a Côte Rôtie from the wine menu, another wine my father admired. We were halfway through the bottle when I turned to see a group of eight diners come into the bar for brandy and coffee, among them Vernice and her poet who spoke in a diffident, chortling basso to their friends. Vernice immediately spotted me up at the bar. She approached as if not quite sure of herself. She was much thinner and quite pale.

"What in God's name are you doing here?" she said in a whisper.

"Do I know you?" I was trying to joke but it didn't work. She looked like she might faint so I added, "I left a note with an old woman at your apartment." She nodded and left. I waved at her lover who was looking at me with subdued curiosity.

Woke up at dawn after the sweetest sleep imaginable though decidedly nonspiritual in terms of dreams. I was sharing a roast chicken with Carla who was sitting in a baby's highchair. I walked the mile downtown and sat on the back steps of the cathedral watching a large group of country people setting up a market in the square. A sign said the baptistry of the cathedral was established in 357 when the Romans were along the Mediterranean coast. The back doors of the cathedral were open and someone was up in the organ loft practicing Bach. The dense, thrumming notes hummed in the granite under my butt. My brain tingled with the music so that when I closed my eyes I thought I could see music. I descended into the marketplace and watched a man tending a tall vertical rotisserie with rotating rows of chickens and ducks dripping their baste down onto a three-foot-deep pile of vegetables and sausages. I thought that Marquette could certainly use one of these gizmos.

Back in my room I sat before an open window wishing I had a French bird guidebook. It was two hours before Vernice was due assuming that she intended to see me. Both optimism and pessimism seemed irrelevant though I doubted if she did come that she would fall into my arms.

I meant to put my entire house in order but to leave all of the doors and windows wide open. If I had a Bible and a concordance I would look up all of the entries for forgiveness. I would see my mother first and then my father. I had noted that Cynthia and my mother, and the few other women I knew well, appeared not to think in geometrical terms or in linear notions of junctures, halts, firm positions, specific numbers of days or months. As a man I had a great talent for order that was unrelated to reality. If I threw away my wrist- and pocket watches it was likely that I'd still always know what time it was. I seemed to lose my questionable abilities regarding time only while trout fishing or during one of my thankfully rare trances.

At nine-forty-five my mind began to burble but not with the dread with which I had anticipated seeing Vera. Life was chockfull of errant possibilities. I would marry Vernice immediately but that was as likely as my climbing Mount Everest naked. She had the same iron self-determination as Cynthia. During a drinking period in college I had read for an assignment for a religious course Idries Shah on the Sufis and despite my supposedly high intelligence the experience was like sticking my head in a snowbank. Later in theological school I tried again and made minimal headway but

Vernice may as well be a Sufi. Our eight days in the cabin had been
a succession of alarming surprises and I now began to think of her
as having been my unlikely savior. She gave me a violent shove in
the dark. Did I want another or need one? Naturally I would have
given anything, as people say without knowing what they mean, to
retrieve that physical ecstasy but I could see in the bar last night
that it wasn't going to happen.

And it didn't. The meeting was unclouded with desire except on
my part. The desk woman called up and then there was Vernice at
the door looking thin and brittle in slacks and a shaggy cardigan,
her face a tinge of gray as if she had used ashes in her makeup. There
didn't seem to be a trace of southern Indiana left in her. Anticipat-
ing my concern she said she had had the flu twice since October
which allowed her childhood asthma to return. She was discouraged about life without cigarettes. It was harder to write. Her lover
preferred her skinny but she sensed their affair was nearly over. In
two weeks he was going home to visit his children, one each by three
marriages, and do a "very important" reading at the Library of
Congress. They still loved each other on a "certain level" but he had
decided poets shouldn't live with poets. They both had known this
when their affair had begun but thought they might be an exception.
    I was naive enough to ask why and she said it was because
poets were essentially competitive and got on each other's nerves if
one was working well and the other wasn't. He felt his star was a
bit in decline while hers was ascendant though that hadn't been very
apparent to her. There were so many poets compared to the amount
of attention available. The two of them were really quite poor because so much of his income went to child support plus alimony for
the last marriage. She was always tired because she privately tutored
French students in English for six hours a day. She had won two

prizes of five hundred bucks apiece for her first book. Aside from her poems she was trying to write a sexy novel "in the manner of Djuna Barnes's *Nightwood*" in order to make some money. As an afterthought she said that even the great Apollinaire had written a little pornography to support himself. She wouldn't come back to the States until the fall when she had a tour of seven readings and a part-time teaching job in Columbia, Missouri. When her lover left she hoped to move over near Arles to join a quasi-lesbian friend from Chicago who had an apartment there assuming she could save enough for her share of the rent and food. She said she wasn't complaining just "describing." She loved living in France. She abruptly stopped talking and looked at me as if I were a stranger, then smiled and said, "I haven't asked about you."

She was sitting by the window and seemed to be noticing her surroundings for the first time. She got up and looked at a small placard at the door to check the price of the room. "So?" she said as a cue for me to explain myself.

I told her I had gone to Mexico to see Vera and then came here with the remote idea that we could begin seeing each other again. She was pleased with this thinking it quite romantic. I then blurted out that she had helped me a great deal by making my world so much larger than it had been before I met her. I became cautious about what I wanted to say next not wanting to offend her pride but told her I had been lucky enough to get the worth of my cabin back and wanted to help her out financially. I said I had no idea what she needed but I was going home the next day in order to straighten things out with my parents and had two thousand dollars left in traveler's checks. It wasn't much but I could send her something every month until she got on her feet and perhaps sold her novel.

Now she was looking at the wall a foot in front of her face. "Why would you want to be my patron?"

I repeated that she had enlarged my life and I was in her debt, plus I didn't give a shit about money and it pained me to see her in distress.

"You really mean that, don't you? I forget how matter-of-fact you are." She walked over and looked into the bathroom. "I haven't had a shower in six months. We only have a tub. Do you mind?"

I sat there embarrassed that a relatively small amount of money could mean so much to someone so deserving. I didn't bother rehearsing the extravagances of my family. It had been rare for me to have the chance to do someone else some good. I opened a bottle of wine I had stowed in the closet in an ice bucket for a possible aid to seduction. My face burned and my fingers trembled. I stupidly thought of Mickey and Sylvia singing "Love Is Strange" but my mind heard Cynthia and Laurie singing it. Had I intended to stay in France if Vernice had consented to be lovers? I thought far ahead about the wrong things. I ruminated like a cow while Laurie and Cynthia jumped around singing and dancing. Now I trembled over a love that was out of the question.

Vernice emerged from the bathroom fully clothed, spied the wine bucket, and laughed. "Where are the roses?" I momentarily felt huffy and it didn't help when she gave me a chaste kiss on the cheek. "You'll have to wait until October. One at a time is more than enough."

She drank a scant ounce and then we walked to her bank because the desk didn't have the cash. "Why don't you just go to a college bar in Marquette and pick someone up?" she teased. I said that my tastes were too specialized and they didn't include college girls. After the bank we held hands a few minutes, then kissed goodbye. It was cool and breezy with the wind seeming to push her down the street away from me.

❆   ❆   ❆

Back in my room I packed in minutes in order to take a cab to Marseille to make the connection for Paris. I felt a little murky but at the last moment I called the young woman from Thessaloníki in Paris. Her name was a variation of "Mary" that I couldn't quite catch, Meriam I think. My morale rose when she said she had hoped I would call. She would stop by the hotel when she got her work done in the evening.

On the train out of Marseille I figured I had to see my mother and thought I might drive all the way to Tucson with Carla. My mother thought of herself as Christian and I would ask her if she had forgiven my father. It was clear that she had been far more sinned against than me but that was on an abstract level and there were no scales on which to balance the matter. I had recently developed an urge to go against a culture which wishes to come to conclusions in order to rush on to what's next. "We must move forward" was pounded into us. This, however, was radically different because I was now almost thirty-five years old and I wasn't much more than a child when I perceived that something was terribly amiss. My entire project had been pure stuttering and I was slowly learning to speak.

While waiting for Meriam I looked out in the night garden and listened to the chouette owl. The desk girl told me that sometimes the garden is visited by a larger owl called the "grand duc" who comes there to feed upon the ample supply of pigeons, an angel of pigeon death. I drifted away in the glow of the ambient light above Paris, receding from my past life as if I were easing again out of the hospital room before my planned ankle surgery. After I completed my parent mission I needed a long dose of nothing before determining if my project, minus the considerable anger at my father, was worth completing.

By the time Meriam arrived after ten I had drifted away far enough so that when she entered the room I hadn't quite returned from the hummock in a particular swamp down near Seney. Carla and I had struggled out there on a hot afternoon in August. Beaver had dammed a creek and while we sat there on the hummock a family of otter was playing on the far shore. Having failed to catch one in numerous attempts Carla affected boredom with the otters. We were more than a dozen miles from any other human sign and I doubted if anyone had sat on that hummock before.

Meriam carried a small picnic hamper and I thought my last French chicken would have to wait. Maybe I could raise round, plump French chickens in the U.P. I told her that I wanted to take her out for a nice dinner but she reminded me that I had paid for the cover charge and bar bill at the jazz club. Though she looked exotic in my terms her speech was very direct but slow. In fact she opened the wine and laid out our food in slow motion. She averred that she was a liberated Middle Eastern woman and knew that her casual boyfriend had a wife in Lyon but had never admitted it. I was at the same time famished and sexually excited. There was bread, several kinds of olives and cheeses, hot peppers, and some kind of Greek marinated fish. She tried to be pleasant about it but was negative about the U.S. because the American students at the Sorbonne talked to her very fast about their country but didn't seem curious about her own other than to inquire if they could live cheaply there. She had a tiny battery-operated transistor radio in her purse and tuned it into what sounded like Arabic music. She lit a joint and handed it to me. I took a rare drag and helped her clean up the table and then she went into the bathroom for what seemed like a long time but it was probably the effect of the marijuana. I was paralyzed with a daffy concern that I'd never get to make love again. I thought of lying on the bed but suspected the move might be too presumptuous. She came out fully clothed, turned out the lights except for the bathroom light peeking from the door, turned up the radio a bit, and said something to the night out the window, in her own language I presumed, and led me to the bed. I asked what she had said. "I'm telling my awful mother that I'm going to make love to an American," she laughed. After a couple of hours I wondered why I was leaving Paris but I did.

33

In Chicago while waiting for my plane to Marquette I called my mother in Tucson. She said to sit still for a week and she would be back in Chicago to see her doctor. She didn't say what was wrong with her but then as a reaction to her own hypochondriac mother she never mentioned her own illnesses excepting her earlier "phantom pain." On the flight north to Marquette I was impatient enough to decide to visit my father in Duluth first. Despite all those wretched childhood lessons on being patient, usually to the advantage of the teacher, I was compelled to get on with it now no matter how ugly it might get.

Mrs. Plunkett was ready for me with a batch of lasagna. Clarence wasn't feeling well and had gone home at noon which was unheard of. I went out to Jesse's apartment and for a change he invited me in. He refused my invitation for dinner but immediately opened the fine bottle of brandy I had bought him at Orly. He was tired, pissed off, nearly distraught, dropping the guard I was familiar with since I was a child. After I had left Vera had run off to Oaxaca with her schoolteacher and her son had decided to stay on the coffee farm with an uncle and aunt. Jesse admitted he was cash strapped because my father hadn't paid him in nearly a year. His businesses were fine but he wished to help Vera and her husband to get set up in Oaxaca despite being angry with her. He was surprised and nonplussed when I offered to loan or give him some money for Vera. He asked how Vera looked, pouring us another brandy.

"Beautiful. I would have married her in a moment even though her son is my brother." It was hard to be light about a matter of which we had never spoken but thought fuck it and barged ahead. "I was surprised you didn't quit." It was a long time but that night was palpable in the room.

"Taking care of my family was more important than my anger." It was all he would say.

"I wanted to kill him. I thought about it for years. I loved her."

Jesse nodded in agreement as if my impulse to murder my father was the most logical thing possible. The idea of "what might have been" brought us into a long silence. I turned down a third brandy which any fool would want considering what we were talking about. "Please call him and tell him I will be there in the afternoon. Tell him he must be honest with me or I'll take his land in court." Tears rose in my eyes but I didn't know if they were from anger or from finally doing something about it. I realized many sons simply ran away but my mind would have been too heavy to carry along.

While eating too much lasagna with Carla by my side I opened a note from Mick over in Grand Marais that said he thought the deer

shack would be coming up for sale pretty soon. The hunting group
had suffered quarrels and were splitting up. He thought I could get
the shack and ten acres on the river for about fifteen grand cash.
To the disapproval of Mrs. Plunkett I called Mick during dinner
and said I wanted the place very badly and to keep in touch. Carla
was drooling on the floor beside my chair so I made up a saucer of
lasagna. She always had a hankering for Italian food and I supposed
that garlic struck her nose affably. In Sprague's journals he mentioned how his dog liked the Cornish meat pies called pasties. The
only other piece of mail of any consequence was a book from Fred
in Hawaii, *The Gnostic Gospels* by Elaine Pagels which concerned
itself with the Nag Hammadi papyrus manuscripts dug up in Egypt.
Fred's note said, "This is you. Read it slowly." If he got anymore
cryptic in his Zendo he would end up saying nothing at all though
the majority of our talk is made soundlessly to ourselves.

I was abruptly tired but figured it was four A.M. in France so went
to bed with my Elaine Pagels book. I suppose that few would think
a book called *The Gnostic Gospels* was bedtime reading but Fred's
note intrigued me despite the fact that my eyeballs were hot and
grainy and there was a trace of Meriam's murky perfume on my
skin. Of course it was midwestern childish of me to still think of
sex as some sort of perverse opposite of religion, a schism that the
Baptists and most other denominations seemed to encourage. The
fact that I was in tears by the time I finished the book's short introduction was the rawest reminder possible of my own fragility, which
was untouched by my recent feeling of decisiveness:

> Jesus said, "If you bring forth what is within you, what you bring
> forth will save you. If you do not bring forth what is within you,
> what you do not bring forth will destroy you."

I thought I would levitate with this quote that early Christian leaders had decided to leave out of the Gospels from the discarded Gospel of Philip. I read on to a quote from Theodotus who said that a gnostic was one who had come to understand: "who we were, and what we have become; where we were . . . whether we are hastening; from what we are being released; what birth is, and what is rebirth."

A following quote by a gnostic named Monoimus indicated that you had to find God in your "self":

Abandon the search for God and the creation and other matters of a similar sort. Look for him by taking yourself as the starting point. Learn who it is within you who makes everything his own and says, "My God, my mind, my thought, my soul, my body." Learn the sources of sorrow, joy, love, hate . . . If you carefully investigate these matters you will find him *in yourself.*

I paced the room like a forlorn geek in my underpants with sleet beating against the window. This was a form of Christianity where the church was not allowed to become a remote and dictatorial parent. My spine was still curved into a question mark but there was the suggestion that remedies were close at hand rather than a matter of galactic communication. Carla was irritated at my restlessness and I petted her good night with the quizzical sense that the earth was a far more fascinating place than I had allowed it to be. I was not inclined at the moment to blame anyone else for the number of ways I had been single-minded in the wrong direction. I put myself to sleep by thinking of trout fishing and my favorite stumps but not far away was the proposition that a woman's ass was also the glory of God.

34

Before heading to Duluth I had breakfast at the diner with Clarence and Jesse. They got there first and I could see that Jesse had told Clarence that I was headed to Duluth to see my father. They were both in their mid-sixties and quite suddenly they looked as if life was wearing them out. Clarence said the doctor had told him that his heart was weakening and he could no longer work sixteen-hour days. What worried him more was that his mind was "loosening" and he had made the same order twice for shrubs to be planted in April. My mother hadn't been around for twenty years but they still consulted over the phone about landscaping. Jesse was frail but I suspected he would recover now that he had lost his marriage quarrel with Vera. I knew that they were both curious about my intentions for my trip to see my father but I couldn't say anything other than that I hoped to settle some matters. On the way out I slipped Jesse a check to get Vera and her husband settled in Oaxaca. At the last moment Clarence wondered if I had time to drive out to Presque Isle and though I was impatient I couldn't say no.

We parked and walked the last half mile through crusty snow that would support us for a few steps and then we would break through. We reached the grave of his great-great-grandfather who was said to have lived from 1798 to 1901, Chief Kaw-baw-gam. Clarence said a few Native words, then turned to me and said it was bad medicine for me to go too hard on my father. "He's too old for you to kick his ass. You might have done that way back when and left town but now it's too late." And that was that. I drove him back home where he intended to spend that afternoon with Carla and his flower and shrub catalogs.

I was halfway to Duluth when I recalled a line that Vernice liked from some poet I hadn't read, "The days are stacked against what we think we are." Everything was in question and the feeling reminded me of the day Carla had found a dead wolf in a dense thicket over south of Republic. Her hackles rose and she retreated growling. The wolf's muzzle told me that it was very old. At the time I wondered how a dead animal could seem so much more than a dead animal but then wolves were rare enough to seem heraldic and a dead one in a thicket resonated the idea that the natural world is far more, rather than less, than we think it is.

Coming into Superior, Wisconsin, I recalled the goofy remarks Fred had made after a visit to the Club about what a harebrained nitwit my grandfather had been. Given a certain amount of drinks Fred was an across-the-board expert on economics, especially the historical aspects. Great-Grandfather was the prime mover, the great acquisitor, and grandfather, the solidifier of the holdings in timber and mining but also one who thought his expertise was unilateral. By the time he died, however, late in the Depression, he had managed to diminish the family wealth by three-quarters mostly by pompously thinking that his expertise in mining and logging was easily spread into other areas.

The trouble with this in my own mind was not my grandfather but Fred's notion of "really rich," that the primarily theological bent of Fred's mind was still making numbers sacramental. He had taken another path but was easily, in his cups, drawn back into the fact that he was a "dud" in my mother's family and that his early interest in literature had made it plain to his own family that he was cut from the wrong cloth. Fred made a fetish out of pretending he was poor though I knew it to be otherwise. It took me a long time to figure out that the church pension for his mental breakdown was fiction. What struck me there in the car was his struggle to find a comfortable way of being that did not include his relentless sedation with alcohol. He had enough of his mogul father in his system to wangle grants with the flick of the wrist as Riva had pointed out, but that still left him in a world in which he was ultimately uncomfortable. His latest attempt at Zendo life made me wish him success.

Naturally this thinking narrowed itself in my case to hoping my own liberation would become more complete. Drawing closer to Duluth I felt strong enough to know that I couldn't create a life in terms of reaction to the father I was about to visit, that bringing forth what was possibly within me was not a matter of rebounding off someone else.

Coming up Seward's driveway I saw my father teetering out of the woodlot behind the carriage house in brightly colored exercise clothes. He looked absolutely silly as he waved to me. Of course I wanted a concision in reality that it was never prepared to offer. It was in the mid-fifties and he should have been sitting in a lawn chair in a warm coat looking out at Lake Superior with an air of receptive melancholy. I followed him inside and he poured himself a midafternoon drink. He looked rickety, the only word my mind could raise. His bruised leather luggage was by the door and he said he had delayed his annual fishing trip to Key West by a day in order to see me. I was aware that his luggage cost more than my own extravagant trip and taking a close look at the big room there were all the accoutrements of a rich gentleman, most of them old, which struck me as pathetic in terms of his diminishing capital. I cautioned myself against sympathy because no one really knew how much land he had left. The challenge at hand was to break down his impervious posture of control, his laconic attitude that no matter how fucked up life is he sees it clearly and just as clearly is in the driver's seat.

"You shouldn't have driven all this way. If you would condescend to visit the bank and our lawyers you would know that for each piece of land sold you and Cynthia get your share. Some of my investing went awry and I was a bit careless dipping into money not explicitly my own."

"I'm not here to talk about the money you stole. I want to know why you tried to fool with Cynthia when she was a girl?" I had hoped to pour out everything in the manner of a Russian novel but this clumsy question arrived first.

"She's an insufferably cruel girl. She won't let me see my grandchildren."

In other words, a blank. It was far too warm in the room and I was already down to my shirtsleeves. I noted that his formerly athletic body was now overthin though there was a small pot belly. The loss of facial muscle made his jaw seem even larger.

"How did you become so sexually perverse?"

He considered this question for a few moments though there was no emotional sign. "I was always a bit questionable. What's the point? I'm still assuming this is about money."

"It's not. I'm trying to forgive you."

"Why bother? I mean really, why bother?"

"I wanted to kill you for raping Vera."

"There's nothing new in that. I wanted to kill my father. He was a mean-minded, self-righteous asshole. The ultimate bully to Richard and me. After being raised by him World War II was a relief. He was in his late forties before he fathered us. We were inconsequential. He was busy losing money. We'd all ride down to Chicago in his private railroad car and he'd never leave his desk, never look out the window."

"What about your mother?"

"She was an expert at leisure. She died when I was twelve of a supposed heart attack but I think it was suicide. Pills and booze."

"What keeps you alive?" I had no idea where to go with my questioning.

"I love each day. You will too when you reach my age." He said this without irony.

"Why did you rape Vera?"

"I recall that I was drinking."

"It has to be inside you when you're not drinking. I mean there were many others."

"Well, I've wondered. Maybe it started in the Philippines during the war. Younger girls were less likely to have syphilis. We all seem to have errant desires in us."

"It's what you *do* that counts."

"True, but where are we going with this? Few of us have more than nominal religious feelings unlike you or your uncle Fred. I wish you well. I'm actually proud that you seem not to have followed my behavior."

My throat filled up. There was nowhere to go from here. He averted his eyes from my obvious discomfort. He wasn't going to say "Forgive me for raping your girlfriend" any more than he could ask Vera for forgiveness. I was the odd man out. The language I wanted from him didn't exist in his world.

I got up to go. I couldn't talk and I couldn't swallow. I wished then that I had brought Carla along so we could take a recovery hike though it would be a long one, maybe a year or so. I marveled that we were both speaking English.

"Is this your old Jesus thing? I mean I now think you drove over here to try to forgive me. You're worn out with thinking about it. Jesse said you went all the way to Mexico. You can't forgive what I did. Don't even try. You could forgive me for being a bad father. It couldn't have been otherwise."

We went outside and looked at the receding sheets of Lake Superior ice in the distance broken by blue water. On the porch there was a large bowl of dog food he said he put out for the stray dogs that hung out in the woodlot. He leaned against the railing and his legs looked spindly. Age.

"The people in Chicago say your mother is having a glorious life without me."

I couldn't summon a response. There was the child's feeling of the first time swimming over one's head, a possibly bottomless lake.

35

I had some diversionary luck. On the way to see Mother in Chicago I stopped in Kalamazoo to close the deal on the river shack. Sensing my eagerness the price had gone up to twenty thousand. I was amazed at the purchase meeting with the two principal owners to see a Native name on the original deed, also to hear of the inane squabbles that had broken up the deer-hunting group. The younger members wanted to stay up late playing cards or would come home late from the tavern making a lot of noise. One of them had puked on a wood-burning stove so that it stunk the entire, cold November night. The younger members cooked carelessly, couldn't split wood but bought it, and didn't do their share of the chores.

Both the older men worked in a furniture factory and were giving up a cabin they had owned for thirty years out of sheer spleen.

I had brought Carla along and rewarded her hour wait in the pickup with a cheeseburger. The recovery from the meeting with my father the week before had been fast and bracing, aided by an hour's phone conversation with Cynthia who thought my attempt both courageous and naive. I had sent her a batch of jaguar-woman postcards from Jalapa which irked her as she viewed herself as a soft and compassionate woman. When I reminded her of her combative past she viewed it as only "defending herself," a quality her brother hadn't learned. She said it was likely that our mother had a degenerative kidney disease but would live a long time. "Why couldn't it be Father?" I asked. "You know that's not the way it works," she said.

Rush-hour traffic in Chicago was a tonic because it obviated thinking about anything else. Carla insisted on protecting us from the hundreds of semis with barks and growls which drove me daffy until I drowned her out with a good rhythm-and-blues station. As cities go I like Chicago though the congestion approached the incomprehensible. When we got out of the truck in front of Mother's house in Evanston Carla flattened a male dog who tried to sniff her butt. I swung my duffel bag at her then grabbed her by the collar. She had pinned him to the ground by the throat. I apologized to the owner, a fey young man, who said, "Zeke hasn't learned that some females don't care for him."

I sat down in the kitchen with a glass of wine. Mother was inexpertly frying chicken and dumped in a can of mushroom soup for "sauce" before I could stop her. She was tanned from the South-west but underneath her color wasn't good.

"How is he?"

"He thinks he's fine but he looks terrible, you know, rickety and spindly with a bulbous nose. It all makes his jaw look larger."

"Cynthia told me you wanted to forgive him." She was drink-ing water and averted her eyes. I could see that I'd have to avoid anything rough.

"Have you?" I asked.

"It never occurred to me. I think of myself as Christian but then he never asked. On most days it seems long ago but then I always remember how long it lasted. I was never able to touch gin again." Now she smiled which was a relief.

"Well, I had to try it but he was as impervious as a good rain-coat. He told me to forgive him for being a bad father but not for what he had done. It's hard to separate. He said it never could be otherwise."

"His friends, you know, his classmates were all like that when I'd meet them here in Chicago, or in New York, or even up at the Club. They all seemed to think that everything about them was inevitable. They saw themselves as princelings but when I talked to their wives away from them it was peacocks that came to mind."

"I suppose that's the money," I offered.

"It's everything that comes with it more than the money. None of his friends accomplished anything in particular but that didn't stop them from feeling superior. They sputtered about the nasty world and went on their way. Maybe I'm not a big exception." She stopped on the verge of tears and paused to regather herself.

"I don't think of you that way," I said.

"I was only prepared for a certain kind of life and I never had the ability to really step outside it like you and Cynthia. When I visited Donald and Cynthia last fall I couldn't see a single trace of her parents. There was simply nothing of me or your father in her life. I was pleased. As you know I'm the eternal docent but when I tried to help out in a children's oncology clinic I only lasted a week. I'm not tough enough. I'm irrelevant except among the type of people I grew up with. My only outside friends are Polly and her two children who call me 'Granny.' Don't you ever miss her?"

"Of course." I found myself pleased to see she thought of my father as a dead duck. There was a specific anemia to the so-called upper class that boggled the mind. All of the paths were proscribed with centuries-old cobblestones. She had told me that early in their marriage Chicago had been their headquarters with Marquette and the Club reserved for the pleasant months from May until mid-October, then they decided that Marquette was a better place to raise children.

"It was so sad when you broke up." She wasn't going to leave the subject of Polly. "I don't really understand why you refused to have children."

I got up and stirred her gelatinous chicken. There was a question of how to withdraw from the immediate situation which seemed to resemble the beige mud puddle in the frying pan.

"I think Dr. Coughlin feels that you want more from life than it can offer. Jesse told me you went to Mexico. That's a good example."

She had me there. I had read about the point at which parents could become querulous children and it was a mistake to think of them as more than older versions of our own questionable selves. It had to be enough that I, along with Cynthia, had successfully escaped living their lives which despite the secure place in the culture seemed utterly deranged. As an escape route I fed Carla. Looking around I was struck by the idea that that sort of life was an expensive kitchen in which nothing could be cooked because you had everything but the proper ingredients. I remembered how sloppily Fred made bologna sandwiches for the poor kids but he was trying.

"You're avoiding me," she said.

"I haven't seen what life has to offer. I've been too busy think-ing. I've been trying to get through the used part." This was lame but all I could offer. I couldn't humanely pursue certain things with her as I had my father. Part of me might wish to be a spotlight but a penlight would have to do. The point was not to feel lighter by sinking someone else. For instance, there was no reason to ask her why she hadn't grabbed us and run for it far before our lives had declined to the point that Vera could be raped. A point had been reached where further examination of wounds would be fruitless.

I looked down amused at the chicken glop I had been stirring. This was clearly a case where a pig's ear couldn't be made into a silk purse. Carla sat beside my mother's chair looking at me as if the delicious fumes rising from the stove were unendurable. Mother was entranced with petting her. It was almost a still life. I loved my mother and I felt as if I were taking off my imaginary judge's cloak and tossing it in a Dumpster. I walked over and embraced her. I followed an absurd impulse and asked her if it was okay if I called out for a pizza. I hadn't had a good Chicago pizza since I had left theological school. She was pleased with the idea.

36

I fell into a state of serene collapse. After dinner Mother went to bed and Coughlin came over so that we could begin mapping out our trout expedition later in the summer. He had previously teased me about eating too much of the world without spitting anything out so when he arrived and asked me how I was doing I said I was busy spitting out my excess world of which there was a lot.

I had intended to leave the next morning but my sense of urgency had fled and I spent it with my mother and a neighbor lady digging holes and planting shrubs. At one point I found my mother beginning to call me Clarence but then she caught herself stopping at "Clare."

In the afternoon I went down to the Newberry Library and
stared a long time at ethnological maps of the northern Midwest
but I couldn't concentrate because I was still full of the pleasure of
digging holes and the notion of following in Clarence's footsteps.
When I left the library I stood for a moment in the place where I
had met Vernice. There was a cold wind off Lake Michigan whipping through the streets so I couldn't quite re-create her summer
dress.

When I left at dawn the next day Mother got up to fry me eggs
solid as a tennis ball and see me off in her old blue robe which she
used to wear wandering around our early morning yard talking to
Clarence about what to plant where.

I drove hundreds of miles out of my way in order to look at the
Mississippi over near La Crosse, Wisconsin, my progress slowed
by Carla's toilet stops though it was still better that she ate Mother's
chicken than if I had. I thought of stopping in Madison to check
out a program in the new academic discipline of human geography
but reminded myself again that I had to pull back and gather some
oxygen around myself. When we were talking about our fishing trip
and looking at maps Coughlin had mentioned my natural cognitive
disarray in trying to figure out why people were where they were
in the United States. It was far simpler in Europe, in southern
France for instance, where a locale was virtually the birthplace of
the Occident.

I found a good place on a pasture hillside north of La Crosse
and sat there on a big rock looking at the ice-laden Mississippi while
Carla roamed a pasture. It was warm enough, close to fifty degrees,
to sit there comfortably and I recalled how a wonderfully cynical
history professor had pointed out that when we came to America
we were always discovering something like the source of the Mis-

sissippi that the Natives were already well aware of, but then our attitude to the Natives was not unlike Hitler's attitude toward the Jews. And the history of my family was not unlike the history of the United States. We were among the leading conquerors of a region and when we had thoroughly depleted its main resources we mythologized our destruction.

But then the river drifted me away from the obvious presumptions I had gathered around myself like a child's favorite blanket. Almost too perfectly there was a group of crows hitching a ride south on a large fragment of drift ice with a single crow at the far end hopping and squawking at the others. I had to smile when I thought how my father hadn't denied anything but thought his crimes of insufficient interest to talk about. This was a welcome mat to his reality. I had read that even crows have specific ethical concerns and, sweeping my eyes over human history, sociopathology was as rife as the common cold.

I sat there for nearly two hours with Carla close beside me having been frightened by a feral barn cat in a nearby thicket.

It was the strangest feeling possible when the primary obsession of my life began to abandon me. Every filament of my musculature began to loosen and it was as though my brain had liquefied and might begin to leak. I was struck by the irritability of my hate for my father and now that it had begun to recede I realized how strongly we wish to love our parents beyond childhood.

The vast river before me became incomprehensible with this perception and I wanted very much to give up trying to understand the world, at least for the time being.

I scratched Carla's ears. She was enervated by the feral cat who had now emerged from the thicket and was glaring at her from fifty yards away. In respect to Carla it was comic to think again of Cynthia's gift for intimidation while I walked through life leading with my chin. On occasion I had unwittingly tripped over life herself on my myopic, solo descent into hell. It now struck me as so simple in that looking backward I saw how fueled by a singular obsession I couldn't see clearly where I was walking.

Meanwhile Carla was stiffening and there was a rumbling in her chest, and then she burst toward the cat who shot up a slender tree at the edge of the thicket. On the way back to the truck Carla was full of herself, prancing absurdly, and she seemed to grow larger. As for myself I was the same size but not quite the same man.

Dinner in the hotel dining room was discouraging but I met and talked at length to a red-haired busgirl who wanted to be a writer. She had pale skin, the grace of a ballerina, a high clear voice, and the vivid speech of a precocious or junior Vernice. She asked if I wanted to get together after she finished work and I became excited at my good luck, but then she said she would call her father and tell him not to pick her up if I would give her a ride home. I asked, "You don't drive?" and she admitted she wasn't old enough to get a license which meant she was under sixteen. My scalp prickled and I said I couldn't see her later. I took Carla for a walk and when we returned I could see in the window from the motel lawn. The girl was finishing up her work and looked a little downcast. I put Carla in the room and then went into the back door of the bar adjoining the dining room and had a double whiskey. The night was cool but my hair was damp and I had difficulty swallowing the whiskey. She appeared at the door between the dining room and bar and waved at me. I swiveled the bar stool and turned my back.

37

I began to flow then, not like a river but at least in a fashion similar to a feeder creek coming out of a forest in twists and turns. It was a few days before I recognized it as a state of serene collapse.

On reaching Marquette there was a morose and discordant note from Vernice admitting she had loaned half the money I had given her to her poet lover. He was expecting a check from the States but when it came they had separated without him returning the loan. She had moved in with the "slightly Sapphic" woman near Arles for the time being who was willing to support her until she finished her novel. She didn't want anything more from me except that when I went to Grand Marais I must greet our stump for her. She was using our affair in her novel but, of course, was changing the names to protect the innocent. Perhaps we would see each other in October.

I couldn't help but wonder if her melancholy state would be permanent. Her profession was pretty much her "self" and that could be a fragile path. My own long-lost impulse to avoid thinking about myself had been a failed effort though I could now see that it was not so much a matter of stopping but letting it drift away. My father had been a perverse anchor and I had cut the rope.

Within a few hours of reaching Marquette I was deep into the pleasure of digging holes. Clarence had bursitis in a shoulder and a snowplow had destroyed much of our back hedge bordering the alley which meant it had to be replanted. His nephews were supposed to do the digging but they were busy on another landscaping job. I was surprised when I found remnants of winter ice a foot down and had to use a pickax. It was a warm late April afternoon and I was soon soaked with sweat and had to put on a pair of Clarence's work gloves to avoid blisters. Clarence and Jesse sat on lawn chairs, drank beer, and watched critically. After a few hours Clarence's nephews arrived and helped me finish the job, and then Susie came by, obviously tracking the nephew, Sam, who had moved up from Detroit. We had an al fresco picnic in the backyard over Mrs. Plunkett's lasagna and questionable red wine. I made a small business decision and decided to help the nephews with their landscaping service which was undercapitalized. Ownership would be split into thirds and I would buy them a used pickup, shovels, rakes, a rototiller, and a couple of lawn mowers. Clarence would advise on the trees, shrubs, and flowers to be planted. A couple of days later when I packed up to go to Grand Marais I saw that Susie had painted on the door panels of my pickup "David Burkett Landscaping Service." I can't say I felt a warm glow but it was pleasant. I intended to alternate weeks at the cabin with weeks of hard manual work. This program would

keep me on earth rather than floating above it. I liked the idea of
mowing the lawns of my parents' friends.

In the morning on the way out of town I stopped at a job site and
ended up helping Sam and his brother Teddy align a group of boulders along a driveway which were designed to prevent snowplow
services, which work with haste, from ripping up the yard. I was a
bit dreamy thinking about the opening of trout season and my in-
attention caused me to get the tip of a finger squashed. I hopped
around howling and then Teddy drilled a small hole in my finger-
nail with the tip of a jackknife blade to release the impacted pressure of the blood which then spurted up through the hole. Because
of the nerve ending in the fingers the pain was more intense than
fracturing an ankle. I felt it more strongly with each heartbeat.

Teddy and Sam sat there drinking coffee from a worn ther-
mos and looking at me with empathy. I rose above my absurd pain
far enough to reflect on how battered they appeared though they
were only about my age. It wasn't just the accelerated aging I had
noted in Clarence and Jesse the day before but the hardness of life
within the lower regions of the economic scale. Teddy had had
considerable experience as a Golden Gloves lightweight and after
that as a medium obnoxious street fighter with cauliflower ears and
eyebrows lumpy with scar tissue. Sam was less scarred but with
the gristly appearance of one who had worked in a Detroit drop
forge, also auto plants. He had lost some of his hearing and came
close when you spoke.

I as a well-heeled ideologue and history zealot was relatively
smooth and unmarked having recovered from my ceaseless winter
walks but then my hardships were those of choice.

On the drive to Grand Marais it occurred to me that you
were not likely to feel compassion when you had become totally

self-sunken. I was obsessed with my family's crimes against nature, less so with the human victims of logging and mining. Maybe the survivors had to mythologize their work to make the past bearable. The implicit ideal of my great-grandfather and grandfather would be to get people to work for nothing as in the practice of slavery in the south. The rich invariably knew how the poor should live. Just show up for work, humbly.

Off the main road and into the cabin on a two-track I had to break through a few crusty remnants of snowdrifts though it was two days before the beginning of May. The woods were still gray but the trees were beginning to bud and the dead grass in the openings showed a little pale green working through the beige. My finger still throbbed but I felt an almost unnerving lightness which I compared to Carla's fidgety eagerness on the seat beside me. This was clearly her favorite place. Early in the morning I had thought of calling Coughlin about this sensation because waking in the night I thought I might levitate. Walking down by the river in front of the cabin I wept freely. One can scarcely question tears.

38

I was swept along with time in a new manner. It was a pleasant form of crazy as if the vacuum left by my father as a primary concern was filled by a repressed goofiness. The river was too turbulent from the spring runoff to fish so I walked with Carla and rowed in the bay or on Au Sable Lake though the cold air rising from the water meant you had to dress warmly. I caught some whitefish from the pier with a group of geezers who shared their bottles of schnapps with the flavor of the snuff tobacco from under their lips. I wrote letters to Vernice, Fred, Coughlin, and Cynthia. I wanted to write Elaine Pagels, the mage of church history, but I was too shy. I pondered the gnostics' insistence on relying on your own immediate experience. It sounded more than a little like Fred's Zen discipline.

One day I skipped like a child until I was exhausted and soaked with sweat. I even tried crawling though it disturbed Carla in the same way a parent's errant behavior bothers a child. I made love to a middle-aged woman I had met a number of times at the grocery store. She had asked me to look at her roses many of which had died during the winter. We made love on her living room floor next to a grandfather clock. I turned her around as the metronomic swing had begun to irritate me. I had rug burns on my knees. Her cat hissed at me. We made love with less energy a second day and on the third I was relieved that her husband was returning from Minneapolis. I think that she was also relieved. She claimed it was her first act of adultery in thirty-five years of marriage. I thought irrelevantly "that's how old I'll be next year" but said nothing.

One day while rowing I fell into a fresh kind of trance while following a loon down toward the west end of Au Sable Lake. It was warmish with enough breeze to keep the bugs away so I took off my shoes and socks in order to feel the water passing under the thin floor of the boat. When I started rowing from the launch site I had been idly preoccupied over the old idea whether there can be individual salvation without collective salvation. This thought arose when I had awakened at dawn thinking about Sprague's journals from his trip to France soon after World War I. After visiting Verdun where eight hundred thousand men had died in ten days he speculated that the battle site raised the largest question mark in the history of mankind, followed by "no answers can be fairly raised." Thus I began rowing in a rather lighthearted state because all of existence seemed clearly beyond my comprehension. With each stroke I'd think of something, say how all religions seemed to imitate and sacrifice themselves to temporal political powers thus allowing greed to wrap itself in a semi-holy mantle, then after each strong stroke there was a long glide when I'd become utterly submerged in the sheer "thingness" of life around me and be incapable of thought let alone comprehension: lake, water, sky, bird, my feet, my breathing. Something similar had happened when I went west to fish with Coughlin and in Nebraska had seen my first buffalo closeup. We had been talking about my project that morning before we stopped at Fort Niobrara near Valentine and I was still distracted when I got out of the pickup and was face to face with a buffalo behind a sturdy fence. A ranger told us that this buffalo was one of the largest in existence. My skin prickled and the rest of the world including myself faded away with the perception of its immensity, its odor and the sound of its breathing, its baleful pinkish eyes. I came back to "reality" when it let out a hollow, thunderous grunt and I jumped straight up in the air in an act Coughlin described as "athletic." From that point onward my brain would imagistically confuse buffalo with logging and the immense stumps we had been discussing before we stopped at Fort Niobrara. As a boy in Ireland Coughlin had been obsessed reading about cowboys, Indians, and popular-culture renditions of the American West and knew that perhaps seventy-five million buffalo had been killed with a remnant of a couple of hundred left to maintain the species' existence. It seemed metaphorically logical that my brain would connect buffalo and the huge white pine stumps I had found.

The loon had circled back east from the Rhodey Creek inlet and with a few hard strokes I was approaching Laurie's beach. This time my mind drifted to my childhood collection of bird feathers, thence to Laurie's vulva. Maybe no one is prepared for how warm it is inside. Glenn and I were about twelve when we snuck up on a couple making love one spring in a college woodlot. We recognized the girl as one we had seen frequently on Third Street when we would ride our bikes past groups of college girls who all looked mysteriously attractive to us unlike our shrieking classmates. In the woods with Glenn in the courageous lead we were appalled at the clear view of merging parts and the groaning sound the girl made.

The man huffed and one of the girl's legs flopped. There seemed to be much more to her than when she had clothes on. It reminded me of a dowdy and rather homely seventh-grade teacher who after I saw her on the beach in a scanty bathing suit achieved an altogether new reality in my mind. She called me over to ask how my summer was going and I could barely speak. She was clearly amused by the effect she was having on me, but nothing in my life had equaled the presence of Vera dancing on the beach, or in the upper hallway when she had exposed her bottom. The unrealized desire was on a different level, closer to physical illness, than I had reached with Laurie, Polly, Riva, or Vernice. While saying my abject prayers against lust I had the notion that if I made love to Vera I would die on the spot. When I reached the launch site I laughed when I discovered I had spent four hours rowing. Carla had slept in boredom on the back seat with one eye open in a squint at the possibility of anything happening. On shore she ran off in the woods for a half hour, clearly pissed at the uneventful afternoon. I made it up to her by taking her back to my great mother of stumps early in the evening. When we crawled under the stump she growled at a small pile of bear feces. I felt the general urge to pray but it seemed too aggressive in that holy place.

39

I alternated a week of work with a week at the cabin until I left with Coughlin on our fishing trip to Montana in early August. At the cabin I fished every evening and continued my somewhat autistic practice of rowing for a few hours every day. When I worked with Sam and Teddy in Marquette I'd fished in the evening on my old haunts on the Middle Branch of the Escanaba near Gwinn or on the Chocolay. One day in Marquette when we had to retreat from our landscaping due to a hard, driving rain I spent the day going through my research papers for my project which were stored, ironically, in my father's study. Who gives a shit, I thought. It was obvious to me that nearly everything I had written save the stories from old miners and loggers was stilted, junky, falsely academic, and fueled by anger. Unlike the stories the writing was purely awful. It seemed that when I tried to be informative I had two choices: write it from a clearly remote angle or as a personal memoir using the tactics Vernice had suggested but informed by my father's disappearance as a motive. After all, what he had mainly accomplished in family history was smugly spending the money.

One afternoon there was an embarrassing moment when we were working in a yard of what Teddy called "rich folks." A brittle-voiced old woman came out of the house chiding us for this and that, then stopped cold and looked at me as if she was dislocated. "David?" she said, and then I recognized her as one of Mother's bridge partners from long ago. "Are you okay?" She regarded me and then Sam and Teddy with puzzlement. I was getting used to this look around town though she was the first to say anything. I clearly wasn't supposed to be working for a living.

I wondered why no one had answered my letters and then it occurred to me to check my Grand Marais box, my original error with Vernice. There were letters from Cynthia, Fred, my mother, and a recently arrived note from Vernice who said that she might come back to the States early if I'd loan her a grand for a ticket. She had finished her "sex" novel and was trying to determine whether she should publish it under her own name but then scarcely anyone knew her own name so why should it matter? She was delighted at the idea of her mother reading the book. She had moved from the house of her "overly affectionate patroness" and was cooking for an elderly couple from Chicago who had a house near St. Remy and entertained a lot.

Cynthia wrote that Donald had finally succeeded at his three days and nights without food, shelter, or water and had returned swollen with mosquito and blackfly bites, cooked his favorite barbecued ribs, became ill, and went to bed. She had heard from Vera in Oaxaca that her marriage wasn't doing well and that she was homesick for Veracruz partly because Oaxaca was full of tourists. Cynthia added that we were due another check because "Dad" had to sell more land in order to resolve a legal problem with a black girl he had met at a quail plantation in south Georgia several years ago. (This explained a letter from the young lawyer I hadn't wanted to open.) Dad probably would have been home free but the girl's parents were involved in civil rights activities.

Fred said that he was still trying to save his "sorry ass" at the Zendo but had lost the spiritual excitement of the first few months. He was working in the vegetable garden which he liked and also studying Hawaiian birds and botany for no particular reason. He was sad because Riva never answered his letters. Had I heard from her? The mention of Riva made me lonely. I wondered if I would become like Sprague who after the death of his young wife never again found a companion.

Mother was at the same time apologetic and vaguely obnoxious. She enclosed a check and said she was appalled to hear that I had been seen mowing lawns in ragged clothes. My upbringing and education had prepared me for something better. She had directed her accountant to send me a monthly check. She felt that she had failed me. Had I given up on my history of the Upper Peninsula? She had finally called Clarence and found out about the landscaping company which was still the equivalent to her of mowing lawns. Would I please come see her so we could fully discuss my future? She had some sort of kidney disease which, though not normally fatal, accentuated her worries about me since Cynthia was doing fine. She actually said that my current manual labor might reflect badly on the family name. She concluded by saying she loved me so very much and would pray that I have a noble future.

❃   ❃   ❃

The night before I left for Montana I asked Clarence and Jesse for dinner and Mrs. Plunkett made us veal parmesan. Clarence had become slow on his feet in addition to his bursitis. I noted he placed his feet carefully. Jesse had developed an almost imperceptible slur. I asked him about the most recent land sale and he said the lawyer was handling it. I also asked him about Vera and he seemed pleased to say that her marriage had become difficult.

That night after eating and drinking a little too much for the planned early departure I had a nightmare based on reality that showed me that though I had neutralized my father I hadn't gotten rid of him. We were out on a raft on a lake at the Club — four fathers and four sons — having a supposed fishing, swimming, and picnic party. I must have been eight at the time. The raft was large and solid with a ladder to the water and was supported by oil barrels. We kids were fishing and swimming while the men were drinking. We ignored them until it was time to eat. My father by then was lying on a mat at the edge of the raft telling stories and then he suddenly groaned and rolled off the raft into the water. Everyone reacted in panic. Two of the men who swam well jumped in to look for him. I was a good swimmer and dove in but when I came up for air I was yelled at and told to get back on the raft. My drowning father might pull me under. After five minutes the two men got back on the raft with one of them crying and saying it was a lost cause. It was then that my father called out in a basso voice saying he was in the land of the dead. He had lodged himself up into a space between the barrels where he could breathe. The men were furious and I couldn't stop crying.

In my nightmare my father never came back up on the raft. I dove down to the bottom where he was holding on to a sunken log and wouldn't let go. Air bubbles came out of his mouth and then there were none. I was hysterical because I couldn't save him. I was too young and weak. I awoke sweating and thrashing. Carla was alarmed and jumped off the foot of the bed. It was four A.M. and I tried to sleep with the lights on but it didn't work. I read some late poetry of Yeats but the elegant cynicism drove me further from sleep. I kept thinking that throughout the world there are sons and daughters with distorted wishes for what their parents should be, or hopeless wishes for what their parents should have been. Some of the most critical of us are afflicted with a paralysis over this, our brains too active with resentment to solidly function. At least I had created my garbled history. The fact that I could be so thrashed in the hands of a nightmare about my father startled me. My reaction had nothing to do with anger or curiosity but a mute acceptance of the human condition, the brain spinning tales before which we are quite helpless.

40

We took a tortuous route west to satisfy Coughlin's curiosity to see certain places he had read about as a boy in Ireland. This included Teddy Roosevelt's ranch in North Dakota, then south to Belle Fourche where we cut northwest on 212 to pass through the Northern Cheyenne Indian Reservation and arriving one early evening at the Custer Battlefield near Crow Agency. I was boggled by Coughlin's knowledge of Native history, trying to imagine an Irish boy in Sligo making his own personal map of history. Coughlin said that whether you are brave or foolhardy depends on whether you win and Custer had lost disastrously so that he stood there not alone in military history as one who had followed his daffy ego rather than sensible strategy.

I brought up the idea that you can seem normal to yourself because you are who you are and have become accustomed to your oddities. You hope to be rewarded for what you are whether you deserve it or not. Even where you live takes on the warmth of a personal nest. Coughlin tended to think of the Upper Peninsula as a "mini-Siberia" pointing out that the forest that begins in northern Michigan continues on through the U.P., Wisconsin, and Minnesota, becoming open prairie only a thousand miles later just short of Grand Forks, North Dakota. He suspected that many people who moved West were claustrophobes. I added that within the dimensions he had described fifty-three million acres of virgin timber had been cut.

"You sound lonely when you say that," he said.

I was embarrassed with this plaintive sensation and asked how I could hope to get rid of it. He suggested that I likely should finish my project but not to dawdle, then figure out what I might want to do with the rest of my life. He sensed that I wasn't really a "natural bachelor" and someone might come along whom I couldn't drive away once I had lost my obsessiveness. Naturally I had told him about my marriage to Polly and had been surprised how completely he had sympathized with her.

We picked up our river boat in Livingston, Montana, and spent a day with a guide named Danny who attempted to teach us to handle the boat in such a way that we wouldn't imperil ourselves on the Yellowstone River. He suggested that we keep to the stretches downstream near Big Timber where the currents of the huge river were less tricky. Unless you're in a dead, relatively fishless stretch you row backward in order to avoid turbulence and protruding boulders. It wasn't easy but then how could you expect to learn a portion of someone's difficult livelihood in a day. Danny was a

caustic ex-logger who turned to guiding after a shoulder injury from
a falling tree in the woods. Later in the evening Coughlin described
him as an "autonomous man," a specialty of America that you see
less in Europe. In the boat Coughlin had suggested that we stop
talking about logging and just fish and learn to row. I had been
appalled to learn that a clear-cut area up in the Absaroka Mountains Danny had pointed out would take three hundred years to
fully regenerate due to the lack of moisture relative to Michigan.

We fished for five days solid including through a violent thunderstorm where we beached the boat and lay flat in a pasture avoiding
the cottonwoods along the river that would attract lightning. I covered myself with a poncho and it was oddly pleasant to lie there in
a warm grassy puddle. As the storm passed a group of Angus calves
inspected us closely to the point that I was able to scratch the nose
of a bolder female. The male weanlings stayed farther back with
little snorts as if we posed a threat.

On the evening of the fifth day Coughlin received and made a
number of calls over the illness of his younger sister in London and
that was that. It was likely that she had pancreatic cancer and I
drove him to the Bozeman airport at dawn after we had talked most
of the night. There is a curious attribute to days of solid fishing in
that you wipe your mind relatively clean and return to ordinary
reality with begrudging steps. Pancreatic cancer is always mortal.
Coughlin's sister lived alone after two bad marriages and as an as-
piring painter she had refused to have children. She was a pretty
good painter but not good enough, Coughlin said, adding that this
put her in the highest category of the "almost" and made her a clear
example of the "wretched" and "mysterious" lack of democracy in
the arts. "Many are called but few are chosen," he concluded pouring himself an amber glass of malt scotch at two A.M.

I had quit drinking earlier in the night out of fear that my mind was spinning backward to a familiar place I didn't want to return to. Coughlin's sister had set herself aside like Vernice and myself. I had asked him before how he could bear to be immersed in the problems of so many people and he had said "but that's my life's work." Now he was obviously distressed to see his vacation end prematurely but that was a very small item compared to his sister's illness. I couldn't quite imagine Cynthia needing me, but if she ever did I'd get there as soon as possible.

Coughlin was far from drunk but had loosened up considerably. He reminded me of my brilliant college professor Weisinger who on occasion would utterly unload on his classes to the extent that we were numb when the hour was up. Coughlin's night speech was the verbal equivalent of the Bach solo I had heard that dawn in Aix-en-Provence. He moved from loneliness to time to death to the nature of our private religions. I got out a journal to make some notes but he asked me to put it away. Other than small pushes in the right direction he wanted me to work out my own path. If I listened to him too closely I would only be a follower. I joked that he sounded like a gnostic teacher and he agreed.

I dropped him at the Bozeman airport close after dawn then drove to Big Timber having decided on a solo trip down the river to clear my head. We had traded the rowing chore while the other fished and now I intended to beach the boat on sandspits and islands to fish certain riffle corners we had passed too quickly. It was a very warm morning and at the launch site I watched a girl help her boyfriend pull a rubber raft off a trailer. I felt nervous when he admired my boat and said he was saving up for one. She was wearing a sleeveless blouse and aqua-colored shorts. Her legs and bottom were uncomfortably perfect as they pulled the rubber raft into the water.

In fact she had the loveliest body I had ever laid eyes on. My heart actually ached and there was a silly tremor in my nuts as they floated off. She had affected my concentration and the bow of my boat glanced off a boulder in the first few hundred yards.

I rowed hard until I reached the first riffle I intended to fish. I was streaming with sweat and discovered that I had forgotten to bring along water or lunch for that matter and it was five hours before I would reach the spot the shuttle service had dropped off my pickup and trailer. After I left Coughlin at the airport I had been sunken in the urge to drive home and trash nine-tenths of my project, clear the deck as it were, and then start again when the autumn's cold weather arrived.

I couldn't very well drink the river water because the cattle along the banks spread giardia into the water. There was a single desperate bag of potato chips in the cooler but that would only make me thirstier. I daydreamt and fished and watched a big thunderstorm to the south. While taking a dip in an eddy I saw a golden eagle chasing a sandhill crane. They passed over a hill before I could see who won. The passing water put mortality in the best possible light. How could it be otherwise? I came around a bend in the full current and saw the empty rubber raft on a beach on the far side. The couple were likely up in a grove of cottonwoods making love. If I had been on that side of the river I could have borrowed a drink of water and seen the girl again. Only I wasn't on that side of the swiftly moving river and would likely never meet her again.

Finally I could see my truck in the distance but due to my ineptitude still overshot my take-out place by a hundred yards. I beached the boat and laboriously pulled it upstream with the anchor rope, my mouth as dry as hot gravel. A young man helped me the last thirty yards or so after watching me fall face-first after losing footing on the slippery stones. He offered me a jug of cold water from his ratty old Subaru. Comically, he turned out to be a botany senior at Yale and was curious about the landscaping sign on my truck. He also gave me a candy bar and I said his accent didn't remind me of my father's. He told me he was a scholarship student from Ohio and the accent I was talking about was in the minority. He was studying weeds and showed me which weeds weren't indigenous in a patch of pasture near the site. When I said good-bye I added that he had helped me to partially remove another aimless prejudice, and he said, "Every day I wonder how many things I am dead wrong about."

41

I was in Marquette only for a day in late August when Vernice called
from her parents' house in Indiana. She had a few free days and
was I interested in buying her a ticket for a visit? Of course. She
had come home early from France in order to try to sell her sex novel
to a New York City publisher but it was hard to pin anyone down
in August. Thus far she had received two rejections with the only
encouragement being a single phrase, "elegant but not very erotic,
too literary." She had been forced to accept a temporary job teaching at a junior college in Indianapolis starting in late September. A
minor lightbulb lit itself in my brain and I said that it would make
more sense if she would allow me to support her for a year or so
with her only duty being to help me edit my project manuscript.

This idea seemed to delight her and she said that we would talk about it.

I went off and helped Sam and Teddy mow and trim hedges for a couple of hours. I was forced to talk for ten minutes to the owner of the home, a prissy old retired insurance man who teased me that it must have been more than a hundred years since anyone in my family did an "honest day's work." I held my tongue but wanted to say that the insurance industry had never filled me with admiration.

That evening Cynthia called me from Rochester, Minnesota, where she had accompanied Mother while doctors did a week's worth of tests on her kidney problems. I could tell Cynthia had been crying and held my breath for the bad news until I was dizzy. It was unlikely that Mother could live more than another year. This didn't seem possible from what I had heard but Cynthia explained that our mother was from the "old school" where a woman could discuss her medical condition with another woman but not with a man. A son wasn't an adequate exception.

It was a warm evening but I felt numb and cold when I hung up the phone. I was swept with anger that my father would likely outlive my mother. At the same time Carla was barking at me because while I talked to Cynthia I had nervously twirled the world globe near my desk. For unclear dog reasons Carla hated and was frightened by the twirling globe and her barking mixed with the terrifying news seemed appropriate rather than irritating.

I left the house with icy guts and walked Carla out to Presque Isle in the dark. It was a starry night with a slip of the new moon and we walked a full hour before I stopped and cried. For a new and curious reason I couldn't detect I didn't think of my situation as unique in regard to the unfairness of who death selects. I had nowhere to go with my childish anger that Mother would leave the earth before my father though there was a split-second urge to drive to Duluth and strangle him but then I remembered Jesse said he was out on the Apostle Islands in western Lake Superior sailing with his cronies.

On the way back from Presque Isle I was soaked with sweat and stopped on the beach to take a skinny-dip with Carla. I was reminded again of the errancy of the human mind because at one moment in the soft, watery darkness I was thinking of the fact of my mother dying and the next moment there were passing images of Vera in her scanty bathing suit on this self-same beach. Vera with lilac scent on her neck. Vera with sand sticking to her wet legs. Vera sitting on my chest. Vera's foot on my bathing suit. And then Mother drunk on the lawn. Mother shaking the toaster so it would work. Mother stooping before flower beds with Clarence. Mother nude in the bathroom. Mother in her moon mask with her breath sweet with gin. I nearly swam out too far in the cold water but Carla turned back and I followed her.

A happy note. Coughlin called from London very early in the morning. He was jubilant. His sister was recovering from a rare pancreatic infection and it wasn't cancer.

I worked brutally hard with pleasure with Sam and Teddy until late afternoon when I cleaned up and drove to the airport to pick up Vernice. She was still too slender but looked healthier than in Aix-en-Provence. It was Mrs. Plunkett's day off so we stopped for groceries like a married couple. When Vernice took a shower before she roasted me a chicken for dinner she allowed Carla to join her, Carla who hated being clean. We had a fair amount of good wine and talked idly about her career. I was quite careful realizing that nearly everything I could say would be either flat wrong or simply uninformed. She was obviously very tired and I was disappointed but not surprised when she asked if it was okay if she slept alone. I said she shouldn't ask and she teased that she felt like a courtesan writer and that it was her responsibility to please her patron. This upset me and she sat on my lap until the blush left my face. I kissed her good night at the door of Cynthia's room and was mildly irked when Carla decided to sleep with her.

Sleepless and alone I recalled that Meriam at the Hotel de Suede in Paris had said that when the French were troubled they often referred to it as "black butterflies" in their brain. On the edge of sleep a butterfly wore my mother's face as if I were still a child who couldn't quite separate the species. Certain dogs in the neighborhood seemed to listen to me carefully when I talked to them though not as attentively as they listened to Cynthia who always carried biscuits with the keys in her red purse, and a Brownie camera around her neck.

Vernice joined me at first light. I heard the door open and she came toward me with a slow-motion lassitude. We made love without much energy at first as I imagined true adults did though my own energies gathered in volume toward the end. Afterward I thought how different we appeared to be compared to our first time together, and at breakfast when I mentioned this she laughed.

"People can learn to love living with their suckhole mental problems and when they get over them they often are lonely without them. Luckily they remember and don't go back." She said this while eating an entire muskmelon.

"I seem to be in pretty good shape for a change," I said.

"So I noticed. My own problems are only professional. Why did I choose such a hard thing to be? Sometimes I wish I was still simply a cook but when I started writing poems the process seemed awfully similar. But with you I still can see a wide streak of melancholy."

I told her the news about my mother and while we packed up for Grand Marais she told me that when she was a child and her favorite uncle died during a stock car race she couldn't believe it even though she was there with her parents. The race was at the county fairgrounds and for amateurs only and the usual safety rules weren't enforced. Her uncle's car had busted through a wood fence, rolled over several times, and burst into flames right in front of the grandstand. Her uncle had turned his head toward the crowd as he was enveloped in fire. She still couldn't imagine that he was dead and when she went into his garage she smelled his work clothes hanging from the door. She stole his lunch bucket and kept it on her desk full of her writing pens and lucky stones and marbles. Her mother had told her that her uncle had gone to a "better place" and she had answered, "No he didn't." With death her favorite man had disappeared.

42

Grand Marais was experiencing a not so rare late-summer heat wave with a slight breeze carrying the heat north from the interior. Lake Superior was dead calm and only dimpled by freshets so that when we rowed near the harbor mouth Vernice leaned over the gunnel and said, "I see big fish far down on the bottom."

Vernice had me take along my bulky manuscript and on our second day at the cabin I went off brook trout fishing with Mick so that she could edit. I was unnaturally anxious about the whole thing for a good reason because when I returned at dinnertime she said she could salvage only thirteen pages of the actual writing and these were covered with red marks. She said that nearly all of my writing was mushy and slurred like a bad scholar's, and quoted René Char, "Lucidity is the wound closest to the sun."

"What the fuck does that mean?" I was hot, dirty, and irked cleaning a few trout at the sink.

"Figure it out for yourself. If you can't you'll always write shit. You're dog-paddling in too much material. Start over. Give me a hundred clean pages called 'What My People Did,' or something like that. You're trying to be a nineteenth-century curmudgeon. You're starting twelve thousand years ago with the glaciers then moving slowly onward like a fucking crippled toad. Get over the glaciers in one page, please. You quoted that beautiful prose of Agassiz. Try to understand why it's beautiful and your prose isn't. You wrote nicely in those thirteen pages because you forgot yourself and your thousand post-rationalizations and let your material emerge directly and intimately."

I had pressed my thumb on the dorsal fin of a trout and now watched a raindrop of blood ooze out. I had asked for this speech and been roundly whipped by a schoolmarm. All these years after the inception and I had thirteen golden pages.

It was too warm in the cabin to eat at the usual time and we took naps in separate beds, awakening in the twilight. I was no longer pissed at her critique. She was the pro and I was the hubris-soaked unenlightened amateur.

We bathed in the cool river laughing at nothing in particular with Carla drifting downstream looking back at us, quizzically unused to laughter in her owner. Vernice got out on the grassy bank and I stood in the river looking up at her nudeness then flicked a mosquito off her ass leaving a little blood smear. I got out of the river and sat on a small deck I had built, the pine boards still warm from the sun. I put my face on her shoulder which smelled vaguely like Carla who had napped with her. I felt her skull beneath her wet hair and saw in the dim light her slightly canine smile. Mosquito whine. She's a little dry as my cock visits her, so warm after the cold river water. The day birds wane and I hear the first owl above the river.

43

Four wonderful days and then she was gone. You couldn't call it love because she wouldn't permit that kind of talk or thinking. With my help she was resigning her Indianapolis job before she started and getting a studio apartment in Chicago. I adored her and she agreed to one visit a month at most. When I took her to the Marquette airport my heart and brain were lumpish with the leave-taking. Much of the oncoming loneliness would be less sexual than the enlivening grace of her company. One morning while drinking coffee on the riverbank I described to her what the river would have been like before its path had been gouged by thousands of giant logs during the timbering era. She said that I was cursed with this knowledge of a pre-Adamic Eden and that the river looked fine to

her and so did the forest. I said that the river had achieved an explicit nature in the twelve thousand years since the glaciers and it
had been shameful to destroy this nature in a few years of logging
violence, adding that she could clearly see what was wrong with
prose and poetry and I could see what was wrong in the natural
world. "I don't exclude people like you do," she had said, adding that
she was pleased with her innocent eyes that were still overwhelmed
by the beauty of her surroundings. I agreed but then said if we don't
identify what we did wrong we'll keep on doing it. "I just don't want
what's wrong to swallow your entire life, then you'd only be a critic
reacting to what others have done badly. You won't have any balance in your life." "Do you?" I asked and she laughed and said, "I'm
not meant to have. My perceptions write my life."

With the departure of Vernice all I did was work at trying to add
to my lightweight base of thirteen pages. With my father torment
largely expunged a great deal of the anger and anxiety in my writing process disappeared. It was as if I had removed much of my
"self" from the process and could see everyone else in a more defined outline whether it was my great-grandfather or grandfather
or Sprague, whose venom could be astounding, and my father whom
all of them would look on with disgust as a mere spender. Sprague
regarded the stock market as a "contemptible poker game" and its
collapse gave him pleasure. My work developed into a kind of neu-
tral freedom that at times became as pleasant as the landscaping
and lawn work I continued to do with Sam and Teddy on alternate
weeks. I was learning to write and when in Marquette I spent hours
with Clarence discovering the subtleties of landscaping. Of the first
thirty pages I sent to Vernice she judged seven as "passable" which
encouraged me. I was thrilled when she marked a sentence I had
labored over as "very nice but irrelevant."

Coughlin came up twice to bird hunt, once in mid-September and then again three weeks later when the foliage had thinned and the grouse were a little simpler to hit. Carla was interested in finding grouse and woodcock for us with her talented nose but didn't really want to give up the retrieved birds thinking of them as her own. Coughlin shot a grouse as it flew across the river and when Carla swam to the other side she stared at us then sat down and ate the bird we were already counting on for dinner. On the last day we hunted Carla seemed particularly weary so that after dropping Coughlin at the Marquette airport I took her to a vet named Randy Ryan who diagnosed her as having a bad heart. I was embarrassed when my tears fell profusely. She would now be limited to short walks.

Coughlin loved the cabin because on the cold mornings when we stoked the fire it reminded him of winter mornings in Sligo. He was in fine fettle with the recovery of his sister. He cautioned me to prepare for my mother's departure by seeing her as often as possible. I didn't mind going to Chicago because I could also see Vernice but the idea of visiting my mother in Tucson irked me. Coughlin reminded me that you get one mother in this life and that the sins of omission loom large with the passing of time. He thought it reprehensible that James Joyce had refused to pray with his mother. How could it possibly matter? Old ladies deserved being catered to even if I had to fib and forget my mother's many years of questionable behavior. What kind of parent would I have been if I had had a child with Polly? This chilled my soul. Any child deserves a better father than the maniac I had been at the time.

It was a melancholy day in early November when I closed the cabin for the winter and churned out through the newly fallen snow. Our landscaping company had closed down with the work left being snowplowing for Teddy and Sam who had attached plows to their pickups. Our first season had been profitable but I reduced my share for the obvious reason that I hadn't worked full time. This move wasn't acceptable to Sam and Teddy who said "a deal is a deal" and that I had financed the equipment. It's inexplicable how poor people are less greedy than the rich.

My work made me boring. I had to learn that those I knew weren't equally fascinated with the subject of my writing. Mrs. Plunkett yawned and turned on the television or shuffled the playing cards impatiently. When we had an end-of-the-season dinner party at the Northwood's restaurant Sam and Susie tried to be attentive to my ramblings but Teddy's barmaid girlfriend Myrna, who wore furry white knee-high boots, told me blankly, "I don't understand nothing you're saying."

At Thanksgiving dinner with Clarence and Jesse, Clarence became abrupt with me as he had done when I was young and drove my bicycle through a flower bed. "How were people supposed to live without work?" he said. "Everyone had to log or work in the mines. People died young because they didn't have enough good food or because they couldn't afford doctors. The Finns and Cornish worked the mines and that way they could afford to get married and have kids which is a natural desire. There couldn't be any people without logging and mining. After those Italian hard rock miners helped build the Soo Locks they needed work. They couldn't just go back home. You can't have a world with no people."

"What about your Chippewa relatives who got pushed out?" I was frantic for an answer without repeating the right-and-wrong-way speech I had delivered to Vernice.

Clarence stared at me thoughtfully, his fork poised above his pumpkin pie for several uncomfortable minutes. He could have said, "You miserable fuck, you never needed a dollar."

"My son Donald tells me that everywhere in the world when white people took over a new country they just killed the natives or pushed them aside. Only God knows why history has to be so mean-minded."

"After Cortés marched from Veracruz to Mexico City he burned down the aviaries. That would be the same as if the Japanese and Germans had won the war and burned down all our zoos and animals. It's that kind of thing that made us fight." Jesse was pleased to offer something.

A week later Clarence was dead, crushed by a sailboat that had slipped from a hoist in the storage barn. I've already mentioned the funeral but not that when Mother and Cynthia and Donald and their kids arrived no one would stay in the house with me. They all stayed at the Holiday Inn which they doubtless viewed as a happier place. Mrs. Plunkett was upset when they wouldn't even come over for a meal. Of course I fully understood their refusal. Cynthia was worried about Vera who was thinking of leaving her husband, and also about Jesse who seemed unhealthy to her. She took Jesse to his first visit ever to a Marquette doctor and it was discovered that he had severe hypertension. He was worried that the pills might damage his love life which Cynthia thought quite funny. "Would you rather die?" she asked. "I'm not sick," he said. I had seen a schoolteacher less than half his age leave his garage apartment early one snowy morning. She held a finger to her pursed lips for our shared secret and I marveled in that Jesse had to be in his mid-sixties.

44

A week before Christmas I packed for our long trip. Carla had been distressed over the missing Clarence and went to the garage work-shop every morning as if he were going to reappear. Since he hadn't she was fretful that she might be left behind. Dogs adore a soft-voiced gentle person like Clarence had been.

I was fearful that I wouldn't be able to write at my mother's home in Evanston but was busy at it within an hour of my arrival. On the way down through Wisconsin on a snowy day with blus-tering winds I would stop and make exhaustive notes on the nature of a single page. I also counted the "cheese" signs as Cynthia and I had done as children on trips south to the Chicago area with our parents. I gave up after counting seventy-one.

Mother looked tired and jaundiced but was merry at the prospect of the arrival of Donald, Cynthia, and her two grandchildren. The day after New Year's I was to drive her to Tucson and stay with her a month after which Cynthia would come out with the children. I thought the long drive to Arizona might be too much for her but she had become frightened of airplanes which she had never liked but had endured.

She knew about Vernice and said she hoped I would bring my "sweetheart" home for a visit, something I couldn't quite imagine. After dinner I set out for Vernice's in Old Town, in Chicago, taking along Carla at Vernice's insistence. I was apprehensive about my single page which was a description of Sprague's peculiar life including two idiosyncratic passages from his journal about his need "to bite the hand that fed him," a matter about which I was no longer worried.

Vernice's studio apartment was small and reminded me of Polly's semisqualid little place in East Lansing near Michigan State University. There was no doorman for the building and I fretted about her safety. She lay on the couch cooing and kissing Carla but detected my disapproval without my saying anything. She called me a "rich asshole" and for a change I did a good job defending myself. If I cared about money why was I mowing lawns, planting shrubs, and living in a deer-hunting cabin? I hadn't earned the money for supporting her so why shouldn't she live in a place with more room? I was thinking about getting an advanced degree in human geography and teaching school. Did that sound like a rich asshole?

She liked my indignation and we made love as we had passionately as on her first trip to the cabin. Afterward when I asked her if she would think about getting a larger place she said, "M.Y.O.B.," which we used as kids, meaning of course "mind your own business." She looked girlish when she said this and I backed away.

We went out to an Old Town bar where I had a calming whiskey and Vernice ate an enormous cheeseburger. She couldn't eat when she was writing, she said, as digesting food stole her imagination. I met a couple of her rather strident feminist friends who reminded me of Cynthia. They were altogether pleasant to me and I thought of all of the groups and organizations men have to remind themselves what they wished to be: Lions, Elks, Moose, Panthers, but never Possums.

Mother was waiting up for me when I returned after midnight. She had been worried about my nighttime trip to Chicago but the true reason was that she had decided to tell me she was dying. She stumbled over her prefatory words so I told her that Cynthia had already let me know. We sat in her breakfast nook in the kitchen and I held both of her hands. An electric clock hummed. Her hands were dry and I had a sense of human mortality that I had never experienced before. My throat filled with tears but then she leavened the moment by showing me her brother Fred's holiday card from the Hawaiian Zendo. It was a photo of Fred leaning against a hoe in a large vegetable garden. There were two attractive women with shaved heads standing beside him. Fred looked tanned and slender though his nose was still bulbous. Mother still referred to him as "my little brother" though he was now in his mid-fifties. He had told me in a recent note that he had one more year of being totally dry before Riva would agree to see him. She had sent him a cryptic postcard from Jackson, Mississippi.

When I hugged Mother good night she said it was strange to think she would be celebrating her last Christmas. She was looking out at the falling snow through the window above the kitchen sink. I couldn't think of a response but was saved when she wrapped a piece of cheese around Carla's bedtime heart pill. It was strange looking at these two females whose bodies had doomed them to early departure. I meant to allow myself to celebrate the birth of Jesus and not dwell on how Christianity had been used as a club to beat the world into shape. I could not collect in a single place what was left of my religion except that I had acquired some compassion by looking outward rather than inward. The fact that I somehow still believed in the Resurrection was neither here nor there. As one among a few billion people I had allowed the world to become much larger and the glittering spray of stars so visible in Grand Marais, though only a memory in the ambient light of Chicago, reassured me that efforts to move away from strictly private concerns was the right thing to do.

45

Driving west toward Arizona with Mother and Carla dozing on the seat beside me I thought of waking Mother to see the Mississippi when we crossed it at Davenport, Iowa, but refrained because I was struggling to regather my equilibrium from the day before. It had been sunny but cold when I took a morning walk with Cynthia down to Lake Michigan. It all started innocently with talk about religion and politics. She felt a little envy for Donald because his religion was based so firmly in his locale where his people had lived possibly more than a millennium. There were a few Christian elements thrown in that didn't bother him in the least. She had warned him when he recently became more involved in tribal politics that he'd have to be careful to avoid the politician's trap of repeating

things that weren't quite true countless times until you believed
them yourself. With Indians as surely as whites the culture demanded its leaders to say things that everyone knew weren't true.

We stood there looking to the gray sky above the gray windy
lake hearing the invisible airliners above the clouds in their landing pattern for O'Hare. The hard part began when Cynthia mentioned that Father was filing a suit against her that would enable
him, if successful, to see his grandchildren. She became suddenly
quite angry and said she thought all of my feelings about forgiveness were the purest bullshit. To understand does not mean to forgive which she saw as a sappy abstraction. When she and Laurie
were twelve she caught Dad "fooling" with Laurie in the lilac grove
near the garage and started to scream. A few days later was when
she had hit him with the garden stake. Cynthia said that girls know
when they are quite young when a man wants them and they often flirt but they also know when it's terribly inappropriate and
how to step aside. It's scary and confusing. She had told Mother
about Dad's attempts on Laurie but Mother ignored her. Cynthia
had been pleased in the eighth grade when she found out Dad was
having an affair with a waitress but it hadn't lasted long. She very
much wanted him to be normal. She had actually thought of cut-
ting his throat during one of his drunken naps on the sofa. One
evening in Rochester, Minnesota, when they were at the Mayo Clinic
and Mother had become sure she was dying she told Cynthia that
perhaps Dad had pushed his brother Richard who was swinging
at him. She had rehearsed so many versions in her mind and now
that it was more than forty years ago she could not feel confident
in any of them. She felt partly guilty because she had slept with
both brothers and with one gone she had felt compelled to marry
the other. Cynthia said that Mother totally broke down when she
said this.

We stood there in the cold wind with the merest wisp of sun shining through on a patch well out on the rumpled water. She then asked me if when I saw him I had noticed anything awry in Vera's son and I answered that he was too far away but that he had looked surly which was nothing special in a boy. Cynthia said Vera had left her husband and moved back to the countryside south of Jalapa rather than Veracruz because her son had become occasionally violent but was peaceful in the country. His nickname was Mañoso which meant cruel, he had no friends, and he spent all of his time exercising and working to make himself strong.

"Why do you create hardships for yourself?" Cynthia had asked, adding that I seemed to spend my life attacking the impossible whether it was my project or women. She admitted that a few days before when she had said she was going shopping down on Michigan Avenue she had met Vernice for coffee and that they had speculated on my behavior. They wondered why I didn't find someone I could marry.

"How far did you go with Vera?" Cynthia asked abruptly.

"Nowhere," I said. "I told you that before."

"I just wondered if you weren't constructing your life as a penance for you and Dad."

I felt helplessly irritated with my teeth clacking in the cold wind. It finally occurred to turn my back to the wind as Cynthia had already done.

"I guess we turned out reasonably well considering the circumstances. Donald said you're a 'mugwa,' a bear, and you're not liable to change directions. You're helplessly what you are. I liked Vernice but when the time comes you're going to get thrown out with the trash." She grabbed my arm and hurried back toward the house when I told her Vernice had pitched me out long ago and both Carla and I were only occasional pets. Cynthia let go of my arm and ran across a small park leaping a park bench. Once a dancer, always a dancer.

It was difficult on a more pleasant level when we reached Mother's house. Cynthia had waited for me a few blocks distant to suggest that I burn down the Marquette house or sell it. She was sure she could get me a job teaching at the Soo or maybe up at the community college in Brimley. Indians liked slow-moving nineteenth-century creatures similar to myself.

There was an older, compact car in front of the house which turned out to be owned by Polly who was there with her two children to say good-bye to my mother. I was stunned and had no idea what to say. Maybe anyone would be on seeing an ex-wife they hadn't run into in more than a decade but I didn't feel like an ex-husband. I just stood there in the dining room with blood rushing into my face. I stooped to pet Carla who approached with a garland of Christmas ribbons around her neck made by Cynthia's daughter. Cynthia, Mother, and Polly sat at the table clearly amused at my discomfort. I'm not saying it was cruel but I had noticed for years that women enjoy a certain edginess that men like myself try to immediately resolve, the lowest example of this being when girls in high school apparently enjoyed boys fistfighting over them.

"Hello, Polly," I said and they all laughed. She looked harder and was relatively thin but then it turned out she coached girls basketball after school and that kept her moving. Despite their age difference I could see that over the years Polly and Mother had become pals and Polly's children on some sort of imaginary level had also become my mother's grandchildren. It was awkward talking to her and it didn't lessen while she was there. I asked after her father and she said "terrible."

Coughlin arrived with a batch of Irish stew and a loaf of soda bread he had made for lunch. It was without excitement to me but passed muster with everyone else. I noticed that he and Polly flirted a bit on the lightest level possible. I also noticed that Cynthia and Donald's twelve-year-old son was following Polly's daughter of about the same age around the house. When he became discouraged by her coolness and turned on the television she would devise a way to get him started again. When Polly slumped on the sofa and I caught a glimpse of thigh there was a tremor beneath my breastbone. It seems no one is exempt before the grave.

I went into the kitchen with Coughlin where we spread out fishing brochures and maps of Costa Rica and Mexico for a planned spring trip. He whispered that Polly was "fetching" and I was cast back to the cold winter morning at the motel in Iron Mountain where she wouldn't let me penetrate her but we had writhed around nudely on the bed doing what she blithely called "the other stuff." When Polly came into the kitchen to say good-bye Coughlin got up from his chair and bowed. I impulsively kissed her hand while devoutly wishing her hand was her ass. She said, "Wow, I heard you made a trip to France."

In Des Moines the weather forecast was a little ominous, cheating me of my intended route through Nebraska. I turned south on 25 and headed for Oklahoma instead. Mother whimpered for several minutes in her sleep like a puppy and Carla awoke and looked at her with concern. Mother had brought along the same pillow that she has taken on trips since my childhood. Cynthia said it had been Mother's pillow ever since she was a little girl. It irritated Father when she carried it into a fancy hotel in New York City.

My stomach was churning and raw from my conversation with Cynthia the day before especially from when she had said Vernice would dispose of me like trash. I had seen her twice in Chicago and

the second evening had been inconclusive at best. When I entered
her claustrophobic apartment she had virtually shrieked that she
had had a "seven-page day" of fresh material to lengthen her sex
novel. She paced in circles and flopped around with Carla. She
hadn't done anymore editing on my own work and I noted a spoon
jutting out of an empty can of baked beans. I had hoped to take
her out to dinner but she was too tired. She drank the nice bottle
of Meursault I brought for her in half an hour flat. She lay on her
tummy on the single bed and told me to go ahead and make love to
her in that position because she was incapable of movement. By the
time I finished she was fast asleep though she was also smiling. I
wanted to leave a note but couldn't think of anything elegant to say
so settled for "Dearest Vernice, Glad you had a good writing day.
Blah, blah, blah. Love, David."

Time began to race when we reached Tucson. After a few comments
from me Mother was embarrassed by the grandeur of the home she
borrowed from her cousin Maude up a mountain on the north side.
It would have been nice if I had kept my mouth shut. She had
thought of buying the house but then wanted to save her money
for Cynthia and me. I said we could have sold it when she was gone
and she replied, "That never occurred to me," and I thought again
how women of her generation and class were mostly taught to be
decorations for the lives of their husbands. Her notions of money
were basically distorted and I knew that her family would never
let any of her money go to my father for his screwy investments.
Like a kid she referred to her income as an "allowance."
    I set up shop in a little guesthouse beside a swimming pool in
a far corner of the yard. Are you living while you're writing, I wondered? Days passed with breathtaking quickness and I invented
errands for myself. I took over the grocery shopping from the

Mexican maid to her delight. The yardman who was married to the maid was from a little town on the border named Patagonia and told me I might like walking in that area. I would try out my clumsy Spanish on him and he was helpful with slang. I would get up in the dark and drive south early in order to avoid the obnoxious traffic, taking Carla only once a week in order to conserve her heart. I'd walk for an hour or so with a guidebook to explain the utterly strange flora, then come back, shop for groceries to avoid Mother's simple cooking, then write for the rest of the day. Except for the grand walks it was monochromatic. I had fallen three times in the first three weeks because a midwesterner is unused to being so careful about where he puts his feet. Everywhere I went on a Bureau of Land Management property known as the Empire Ranch it was either up or down and I severely skinned my ass doing the splits down an arroyo. I was lame for a few days, time enough for my wounds from the catclaw bushes and my cactus punctures to heal. I tried to climb in a small mountain range to the south called the Mustangs and was quite frightened and vertiginous making my way down. I was a flatlander, simple as that. One day I ran across a biologist disassembling a pack rat nest and midden and he said it took years to learn a new landscape.

Years later I can still be brought to tears when I think of a particular morning in early February. It was close after dawn and I was taking a short walk with Carla up a remote canyon. It had rained the day before and small amounts of water had collected in rock pools. Carla barked farther up in the canyon. She was wise enough about her condition to trot rather than run. When I reached her I saw that she was growling having found a fresh set of mountain lion tracks. I beckoned her in the opposite direction back toward the truck and when we were almost there a large, gangly jackrabbit burst from a patch of catclaw. Carla gave chase at top speed and though I yelled she continued on for a couple of hundred yards until she fell and rolled. I ran toward her still body knowing that she was probably dead. She was. I sat down beside her and wept. I remained several hours with a hand on her cooling chest. How could her eyes become so suddenly lifeless? I thought about nothing but my beloved dog and our life together especially at the cabin where she was in full flower. I carried her to the car and found a veterinarian clinic in Tucson that arranged a cremation so that I could bury her ashes at the cabin.

46

The death of Carla was a juncture after which the times became confusing. That night I was trying to read Lawrence Durrell's *Alexandria Quartet* which Vernice had sent in hopes that by my study-ing it my prose would become less "geometrical and herky-jerky." I loved the four novels and had been shocked when Vernice wrote that the last, *Mountolive*, had been written in ten days. When I had questioned this she said I couldn't possibly write better than a good amateur unless I utterly gave my life over to it. This seemed un-likely indeed but that night reading the splendor of Durrell my eyes kept blurring with the sight of Carla skipping across the pages, Carla resting under our sacred stump, Carla swimming in Lake Superior, Carla floating down the river as if sightseeing, Carla

crawling under the bed when irritated with the world, Carla following Clarence as he gardened as if she were helping, Carla's form
of prayer which was watching me as I ate and hoping for a bite of
something more interesting than dog food. How could I not answer
her prayers? How she loved cheese raviolis with a dab of marinara,
how she loved fried whitefish skins or some butter with fried garlic and a sprinkle of good parmesan on her kibble. I sent death notes
to Coughlin, Jesse, Mrs. Plunkett, and Mick in Grand Marais, those
she cared for and especially cared for her. Coughlin wrote back that
my grief was understandable because other than Polly, Carla had
been the only creature in my life that had at least a few aspects of a
good wife or lover. I remembered with inconsolable anger that the
Church had decided in the seventh century that animals couldn't
go to heaven because they were unable to contribute monetarily.
Anyway, I had to give up on Lawrence Durrell for the time being
and return to Elaine Pagels whom I had designated as Saint Pagels,
my patron saint who had reinvigorated the Christ who had died in
my heart because He had been encrusted to the point of suffocation with heinous doctrine.

Meanwhile as February passed into March Mother began to fail
and her dialysis procedure was increased from twice to three times
a week. I did a lot of reading in the waiting room. Cynthia came
out for a week and took things in hand by buying an expensive
(about fifty thousand dollars) dialysis machine and finding a young
doctor rather than a nurse to come to the house three times a week.
I questioned this but Cynthia said Mother could afford it and besides
she hated going to the clinic. Her sense of etiquette had stopped
her from ever complaining to me. At dinner one evening Cynthia
said that I seemed to thrive helping someone other than myself. I
had cooked a crown roast of pork, an old-fashioned dish that

Mother liked. Later, after Mother went to bed, I told Cynthia I was thinking of getting a graduate degree and teaching human geography because I sure as hell had no intention of being a writer. I was already a relatively lonely person and being a writer would only make me more so. She said that if I took a master's degree at Madison or the University of Chicago she was sure a tribal community college would take me on. I looked at my sister in the lamplight that left her eyes in the shadows. We were watching a variety show on a Mexican network. I said, "I love you," and she looked at me with sudden alarm then laughed. "I love you, too, even though we've never said it before."

I flew home the next morning and spent a few days sorting through family papers with an accountant who also kept the household books. I hired my young lawyer friend's wife to keep track of things. There was a fair amount of land left with mine and Cynthia's lien intact, also a few downtown office buildings. Out of lame curiosity I looked at my father's credit card bills and was appalled at the money spent at restaurants and at Big Daddy's wine and liquor store in Key West, and also for shipped wine and special groceries from Palm Beach.

Mrs. Plunkett was becoming forgetful but finally gave me letters from Riva and one from Vera in Mexico. I read Riva's in the kitchen but saved Vera's for my room upstairs. Riva said she was quite happy at her government job in Jackson, Mississippi. She certainly loved the place compared to Washington, D.C. She recently began corresponding with Fred and thought that the "Orientals" had done him some good. She was having a pleasant affair with a bookstore owner which meant that she also got free books to read, his only illusion being that he could cook barbecue.

I admit that I was fluttery when I opened Vera's letter. In the back of a locked desk drawer I had a photo of her in her blue bikini that I hadn't allowed myself to see in years. In an act of daring I looked at the photo before I read the letter and then stupidly wondered how the photo could retain its power after the passage of so many years. There wasn't a trace of romance in her letter but a plea that I intercede with her father to allow her to live in Jalapa rather than out on the coffee farm where he intended to retire. She wrote that these were "modern times" and it wasn't fair that she should be his economic captive. She would rather kill herself than be a farmer's wife and could I possibly loan her two thousand dollars so that she could get an apartment in Jalapa and perhaps find another husband. Her son who had been so unhappy in the city loved the farm and would stay there. She ended by saying that perhaps one day I might wish to visit her in Jalapa.

Of course the last suggestion made my ears hot and my heart race though well back in my brain there was the slightest neural pulse that told me the idea would be disastrous. How could you make love to a woman who had given birth to your father's child? I would send her the small amount she requested but I certainly wouldn't go to Jalapa I insisted to myself.

Mrs. Plunkett wasn't feeling well so I wanted to cook Jesse our last dinner together but he decided he preferred to go to the diner where he had taken so many meals. We had a stiff drink in the den and edged our way down the icy hill with caution. Jesse liked the idea of going home and being truly warm for the rest of his life. By tacit consent we decided to keep the evening light and my father never came up. We ate the simple meat loaf special which was covered with gravy of indeterminate origin, using up a fair portion of a small bottle of Tabasco. We talked of Clarence and Carla and Cynthia whom he admired without bounds though I noted that what he loved in Cynthia's feisty nature he found unacceptable in his daughter's. We had several rum nightcaps in his garage apartment listening to Veracruz music. It was melancholy seeing his packed luggage. There were only two suitcases, nice leather luggage my parents had given him one year for Christmas. We finished a third of a bottle of rum and there was no point in going on. I would take him to the airport for the earliest flight and he would reach Veracruz late in the evening. When I opened the door to leave he did a little jig and said, "I've taken care of my family."

That night I had a revelatory dream that began as a nightmare. I was working deep in an iron mine over near Ishpeming and a bell rang which meant that work was over for the day. I drove home through a forest with stacks of pulpwood along the road and was served dinner (meat loaf) by a middle-aged woman I didn't recognize. I woke up then at five A.M. just a half hour before the alarm was set to go off. It occurred to me that I should have written my hundred-page story from the viewpoint of miners and loggers, but that was out of the question because I had never worked as a logger or miner. In my waking daze I realized this was easily solvable and spending a year at each profession wouldn't be that hard to accomplish. By the time I got downstairs to turn on the coffee machine the whole idea seemed less clear but still possible.

Before I had flown from Arizona Vernice in a letter had questioned if my hundred-page draft might be better in the first rather than the third person with the story now told by a not so old "ancient mariner." The prospect of a new load of work hadn't disturbed me because what else was I doing besides looking after my mother and taking walks in the desert and mountains? The act of writing filled up life until I could find something better. Vernice had liked my idea that when she felt my essay was finished I would merely publish it in a number of newspapers throughout the Upper Peninsula leaving the book form for real writers.

47

Time rushed on as it does when life is full of work and duties. It was easy to see helping my mother as more meaningful than my writing, especially the chore of turning the project into the first person. I wasn't as fond of the word "I" and noted in Sprague's journals how quickly he was able to get out of himself into larger concerns. "I" was the axis or pivot that transferred its energies to the world with all possible speed.

Meanwhile I had bought a beautiful replica of a Hohokam pot at the curio shop at the Desert Museum for Carla's ashes. She had been a dog from the far north but she had died in Hohokam territory where you frequently found small red shards of their pottery. I had examined the ashes fingering the small bits of bone that the crematory fire hadn't devoured. There was nothing left of Carla but in the equally fragile minds of those who had known her. My melancholy letters to Coughlin had brought the response "you better get another dog."

On a warm early Saturday morning in late April when I had nearly finished the packing for our trip home I was sitting out in the yard with Mother trying to figure out what kind of migratory songbirds we were seeing when the maid Inez alerted us to a phone call. It was Polly's mother saying that Polly's husband had died in a motorcycle wreck. I didn't want to tell my mother but of course I did. She stood up, teetered in a circle, and then began to weep. I knew she thought the husband "a bit crude" but then she was crying for Polly and her children.

I checked the options including a charter ambulance plane but Mother rejected that saying she wasn't an invalid. She flew to Chicago the next morning with Coughlin readily agreeing to meet her at O'Hare. I packed us up all that day into the evening wondering at the closet full of my mother's matronly and doubtless expensive dresses. Another part of the code of her class was to look perfect at all times. It took her a full hour to get ready to accompany me to the grocery store. Once when she had quipped "a lady doesn't eat garlic" I asked her who she was going to kiss and she laughed saying the year before I was born she and Clarence had kissed but that was as far as it went. This sounded so unlikely that I had to ask her why and she answered that Clarence was the only "manly man" she had ever known and that at the time he reminded her of her favorite movie star Robert Ryan.

I loaded the truck in the middle of the night and headed for Chicago. I thought of driving straight through but that would only enable me to attend a funeral I didn't want to attend. I reached Mother's house late in the evening of the day of the funeral. Polly was there with her children and her parents the latter of whom were staying with my mother for a few days because it was awkward for her father to stay in a hotel and Polly's apartment was small. Her father moved crablike in his walker but to my relief treated me warmly. We had a drink in the kitchen and he referred to my mother as an "angel." He hoped Polly would move "up home" and get out of the hellhole of Chicago. It had been her husband's hometown and now there was no reason for her to stay.

The next morning I took a walk with Polly on the same route to Lake Michigan I had taken with Cynthia only now it was a warm spring day and the lake actually looked friendly. I didn't have to bring up her moving north with her children. She said that she had been tired of Chicago for several years because you had to make so much money to live decently and that excluded teachers. Their insurance hadn't covered her husband on a motorcycle because he had had three previous accidents. I caught myself saying that it would have been nice if he had been driving a car then blushed at my ineptitude. She looked at me gravely, shook her head, and then smiled. We sat down on a park bench and she said she didn't want to teach in the Iron Mountain area because it would be too close to her parents and her father's bitterness would be hard on her children if the exposure was frequent. Escanaba would be okay and so would Marquette because then her kids could go to college locally. I said that I could buy her a house and she corrected me saying that maybe she could borrow a down payment. She didn't know it but it was a moot point because I knew that she was included in Mother's will in an amount that would more than take care of a house. This was a true daughter-in-law and my mother wasn't abandoning Polly because her son had.

We said nothing for a full half hour though she held my hand loosely before she said that she didn't want me to get the idea that we ever could be married again. Between me and her dead husband she had had more than enough of marriage. I didn't have anything to say to that though I considered that the upheaval of the past four days must have been terribly confusing.

"He had four expensive motorcycles," she said. "Now it's three. We were always making payments on motorcycles. I think he also had a girlfriend up in Kenosha but that's neither here nor there. I think I loved him for a while and he was a good father, or at least a fair one. He certainly beat the hell out of you in the husband category."

"That was a long time ago," I offered lamely.

"Of course you're different now but that's irrelevant. Most women crave a good provider but I'm not one of them. Of course I'll need some affection once in a while and I remember you're not bad at that."

48

Looking backward it was by far the strangest May and June of my life. It was good to see again the slow greening of the Upper Peninsula landscape. Cynthia had taken a leave from her teaching job and assumed my role as Mother's caretaker. On the phone she bridled at spending May in the Chicago area. I opened the cabin and Sam and Teddy got our landscaping business started for the season. Polly quit her job and moved to Marquette in mid-May. I loaned her a down payment on a small bungalow about three blocks from my house. She asked me to steer clear for a few weeks so as not to further confuse her children. She had become so generally angry that she gave the remaining three motorcycles to her dead husband's friends.

Vera wrote that Jesse had intercepted and sent back the two thousand dollars I had sent for Vera's escape to Jalapa which clearly wasn't far enough away in the first place. This was a raw point but I realized that any further interference on my part at the time might be disastrous. She wrote that she might marry the farmer after all because he was kind to her son (my half brother!) and could control him. She prayed that we would meet again someday and she anyway wouldn't marry the farmer until late in the summer just to show her father that he couldn't bully her, all of which churned my stomach and brain. I kept thinking why jump in a bend in the river that had once nearly drowned me?

My biggest comeuppance arrived June first when I published my hundred-page essay, "What My Family Did," in a dozen U.P. newspapers, ten of which I had to pay for its inclusion. Vernice had pretty much given up, describing my last draft obliquely as "so-so." I had simply exhausted her interest. In mid-May she had written that she was moving from Chicago to Boston to be nearer publishing circles and to help take care of her poet lover who had been hospitalized for acute depression in a private hospital in Cambridge.

Nothing of consequence happened after the publication of my essay. I don't know what I expected. Here is the concluding paragraph as a sample of my pomposity.

Nothing is more ignored by the human race than it own historical record. It's as if our forefathers wrote the true story in ink that would disappear in their own lifetimes so that their descendants would not be burdened by the woeful behavior of the past. Our timber barons in the Upper Peninsula virtually denuded the area leaving less than a hundredth of one percent of standing virgin timber. There is the question whether greed may be quantitatively measured because what mathematical figures can add the blighted lives of those who follow? The book is still open on man as the most virulent of all predators beside which the cancer cell is relatively innocent. These considerations are remote to most of us because knowledge of this sort is lost in the netherworld between generations, and lost even in terms of emotional content to scholars who so willingly adumbrate the record to continue to assure their own living. In the course of my study I needed only to unearth the history of my own family and offer it to the citizens of the Upper Peninsula whether they cared to look at it or not. Having done so I can't say that I'm at peace, but only that I have a shred of hope that these dark chapters might offer a corrective for the future.

It occurred to me again that life wasn't going to be what I wanted it to be whatever that was. I received a total of nineteen letters most of them fond reminiscences of the "old days" which totally missed the point. A few were cranky and nasty, "Nice to see a rich fucker crying over spilt milk." I was asked to speak to three environmental groups and one meeting of librarians in Escanaba, all of which I declined. Polly told me that the experience was probably like the postpartum slump a woman feels in the period after she gives birth to a baby. I said that my pregnancy had lasted nearly twenty years to which she only shrugged. When we finally made love one evening the week before my mother died I lasted less than a minute. Fortunately when she dropped off the dog I had bought for her son the next morning we tried again on the sofa and it was wonderful. Her years in Chicago had made her more abrasive and after our lovemaking she patted my sweat-damp hair and said I was a "good little soldier"—perhaps a holdover from being married to a veteran?

A few days later I went to Chicago to say good-bye to Mother who was failing at an accelerated rate but then she seemed to recover a bit so I came back home. Cynthia had her children with her and my main function was to entertain them by taking them to the zoo and the Navy Pier. Cynthia chided me for buying them expensive presents but then I had had no experience with children and didn't know any better.

It was at the cabin in May that I knew conclusively that my life as I had known it was over. I took the same path back to my huge stump and wondered at my route because there were many ways to get there. Even Carla had been habituated to certain paths. Why was I behaving like a train that couldn't abruptly turn right or left?

When I was in the last stages of retyping my manuscript on my old Olivetti I noticed that I did not spring out of my chair like I used to do. I was suddenly discouraged at the speed I was getting older. At my age nearly all professional athletes have retired. One morning I stumbled on a small pile of firewood I had been splitting and I felt a twinge of pain in my old ankle injury. This frightened me but it went away by evening and I celebrated with a mediocre steak and a good bottle of red wine. I was anyway old enough to have my mother die of natural causes.

Some good things arrived when I finished my final typing. I understood again my love for moving water. I stared at the river for hours at a time and resumed my rowing in the harbor and on Au Sable Lake. I seemed to have lost all of my depths of perception in the shallows of busy work but when I finished the project my perceptions began to enliven. So much of my old life had been fueled by resentment against my father and had become vivid only when I somewhat emerged from myself. At the cabin during certain moments the world became so huge I felt vertiginous. I realized that nothing good came to me from the Romantic "I" that apparently had its origins in the Europe of the early nineteenth century, or so I remembered from the university. The wish to separate myself from mankind now reminded me of the way Carla would lick her wounded foot for hours at a time.

One day I got lost south of the Kingston Plains and sat against one of the thousands of stumps in a snit refusing to believe my compass. I thought with regret about making love to Riva while Fred was busy having alcohol poisoning but then grew tired of the regret. The occasion had required love and I was the mammal to meet the challenge. Whomever I loved was totally another being, a private universe that was not me, a simple fact that is hard to learn. When I thought of the women that I had loved — Vera, Polly, Vernice — I understood how I could not be central to their lives considering my character. I had never believed I was in love with Laurie but there was the question that there was no specific name for what we meant to each other.

Sitting there against the stump on a deeply cloudy day without the sun to correct my disbelief in my compass I thought that the natural world wasn't meant to be soothing which was only an abstraction. People were nature too and it was schizophrenic to try to separate them from what we ordinarily thought of as nature. When you allowed your view of world to vastly expand the questions expanded with it.

When I returned to Marquette from the cabin before Memorial Day there was a letter from one of my father's Duluth cronies. A couple of weeks before during a dinner at a local restaurant a waitress had slapped my father and he had "punched her in the nose." My father then threw a wine bottle through the front window. Several employees subdued him until the police came. My father claimed a shoulder injury and the crony had him hospitalized for a week to delay legal charges. A friendly judge advised that if my father would go to an alcohol clinic in Minnesota for six weeks the charges could be resolved more smoothly. The delirium tremens he had in the hospital "suggested" alcoholism. The crony hoped that the family could send a check to cover the hospital stay as he had recently experienced market setbacks. And would the family underwrite the time in the clinic? It was sad that this all had started with an "innocent punch" in a restaurant. Reading all of this I laughed thinking I would skip my father and send an equivalent amount to the Marquette Humane Society.

49

We're back to June 17, 1985. Mother died early this morning, a condition she had looked forward to for months. It's evening now. Polly is here and she's crying, leaving her dinner uneaten. Mrs. Plunkett totters around the kitchen sniffling about Mother whom she described as "a grand old-fashioned lady." I'm fairly peaceful having expected this for quite some time. Polly wipes her eyes and says, "I know she wasn't much of a mother to you but she was wonderful to me and the kids." In Tucson Mother had described herself as "a late developer on the motherhood front."

The next morning Polly and her kids fly with me to Chicago. At the house Cynthia is talking to three local women who had been friends with my mother since her childhood. They are sedate but at the same time a bit garish in their expensive clothing and jewelry. They are a little self-righteous about having refused to abandon Evanston for Lake Forest like everybody else. Everybody couldn't be all that many.

Coughlin comes over and Fred soon after, fresh from the Hawaii Zendo. I must say he looks good with his head bald, his nose still bulbous, in a Hawaiian shirt and frayed linen jacket. The three of us walk several hours until dinnertime. Coughlin had gone ahead to Mexico fishing Zihuatanejo when I had to cancel because of Mother's illness. He had a splendid time catching roosterfish and snook but felt unfaithful to trout. Fred was a little unnerving in his quiet form because I had spent so much time listening to him babble. Coughlin talked about how the death of someone we love comes to us as a jolt but we perceive it as a whole only in the incidents when we feel poignantly their absence and this can go on for years. I said I had noticed this about Carla and had been very accepting for months until I had buried her pot of ashes in her hiding place under the stump and fell apart. Coughlin corrected me by saying that consciousness can't be called falling apart. When we walked down the beach Fred blushed at a young woman bending over in a bikini. It was a very warm day and they were out in numbers. Coughlin asked Fred about Zen attitudes toward sex and Fred said there weren't any which mystified me. That night Polly slept with me but we didn't make love.

The next afternoon when finalizing arrangements for a small private memorial service rather than a funeral Cynthia blanched when she answered the phone and handed it to me. It was Father. He was at the Drake and needed to talk to me before the services the next morning in Lake Forest. I naturally asked why and he assured

me that he was fine having spent the first three of the prescribed
six weeks at Hazelden, the alcohol clinic. I said I would call back
after I thought it over. I drew Cynthia out on the back porch and
she said she wouldn't do it at the point of a gun but it probably was
a good idea for me because I had never been able to quite write him
off like she had. She hadn't told me that he had written Mother the
week before she died asking her forgiveness for his misspent life.
Mother dictated a note to Cynthia in which she'd said, "I forgive
you and hope that helps bring you some peace. Good-bye."

I took a cab to the Drake and was startled at how composed he was.
His eyes were rheumy and I suspected he was on some sort of tranquilizers but he lacked the palsied twitches I had expected. His
request was simple though at first it made my gorge rise. Would I
go to Veracruz with him so he could ask the forgiveness of Jesse
and also Vera if she was there? Asking forgiveness was part of the
twelve-step program he was enrolled in. He couldn't very well expect forgiveness but it was necessary that he ask. He had struck
Jesse when he had come to Key West on business and the memory
was unbearable. We would be gone only two nights and then I could
go home to Marquette and he would return to Hazelden for three
more weeks. As penance he intended to give Jesse his half of the
coffee farm which was in joint ownership. This reflected my father's
typical misunderstanding of making amends. We continued talking through dinner in the Cape Cod Room at the hotel, both of us
drinking iced tea. I was impressed with the gusto with which he
ate his lobster, something I had never seen after he had his martinis before dinner. When we said good night in the lobby I gave a
fateful yes to the Veracruz trip. I was nearly amused when I saw
his eyes wander to a pretty young girl standing near the elevators.
Overnight conversions are unlikely.

❊   ❊   ❊

The memorial service the next morning went without a hitch except for one awkward moment when my father entered the Episcopal church with two of his old Yalie friends. Cynthia and I were standing near the door as the welcoming survivors. Donald and their two children were off to the side. Cynthia stiffened despite her foreknowledge but handled it well. My father was smooth to the point of unctuousness though he ignored the presence of Donald. Cynthia beckoned her children and introduced them to their grandfather. The three shook hands and my father passed into the church after quickly embracing me. I stared at my hands throughout the service and remember little. Afterward I wondered how many of the hundred or so of my parents' friends from Lake Forest, the Chicago area, and the Club could have had lives as difficult as my family's. Not many, I thought, but who knows? After a long afternoon with Cynthia and Donald and their children, Coughlin whose company seemed to soothe everyone, and several of mother's friends, I had a fitful night's sleep of wondering why I had agreed to go to Veracruz. Maybe I only wanted to see how the very long story of my father and Jesse ended. Maybe it was just ill-placed compassion. I had only one father and there was something of the fool in his son. I had to see it to the end, pure and simple.

50

June 21st, the summer solstice. We're off to Mexico City, first class of course, but my father supplied the ticket. Soon after takeoff he dozed and I looked at him and felt the same dislocation I had on my previous trip to Mexico. It is easier to be agreeable and he had hit me with the most sympathetic play possible. Fuck yes, if the plane crashed because the pilots were drunk I should forgive them as the plane sped earthward. This was obviously not a good frame of mind so I wondered how my father was enduring life and a plane ride without a drink. He must be taking powerful tranquilizers.

When the stewardess brought our mediocre lunch (with iced tea) he ate with the vigor of a starving man and finished what I had left on my plate. Several other first-class passengers were drinking

a fair amount but he seemed not to notice. We spoke idly about my
published essay a friend had sent him in Duluth. He wasn't critical
other than over a few factual errors about his own father, nor was
he troubled by my rather scathing conclusions. The tranquilizers
were extremely effective, I thought, but then he added, "Making
money is never very pretty." He was also less kind than I had been
about Peter White, the Mathers, and the Longyears. "They were
better at public relations and our family simply didn't give a shit."
He concluded by saying that if I continued my interest in predatory behavior I might look into banking, oil, steel, ranching, or the
Pentagon and Congress for that matter.

In Mexico City our first flight to Veracruz was canceled and
we sat in a fancy Mexicana Airlines lounge for a couple of hours.
When he went out for a hamburger, a food item I had never known
him to eat, I had two quick drinks. When he returned with a splotch
of catsup at the corner of his lip he gave me a conspiratorial smile
after obviously smelling the rum I had drunk.

He was back asleep on the leg to Veracruz and missed the
splendor of snowcapped Orizaba. Before he slept he flirted dis-
creetly with the stewardess who complimented him on his tailored
tropical suit beside which I felt shabby.

The twilight heat in Veracruz was a moist shock so that you struggled for breath. Roberto was there waiting for us. He was warm
to me but formal and noncommittal to father. He took us to the
Emporio and said he would pick us up at eight in the morning. I
told my father I wasn't hungry, said good night, and went to my
room and ordered a snack and a bottle of rum. It was the same
lovely room I had before and I sat on the porch in the darkness
drinking rum and watching a huge ship depart the wharf wishing
very much that I was aboard.

In the morning my father was far more chipper than I was. I asked Roberto to take us the long way around on our drive up to Jesse's farm so my father could see the beauty of the mountain landscape. Roberto told me again that he preferred "Bob" and continued to utterly ignore the existence of my father who loved the drive which reminded him of certain mountainous areas of the Philippines. The plan was to spend the night at Jesse's then Bob would take us to the airport by the main road in the morning.

Thinking back I'd like to say I had an ominous intuition but the truth is I felt nothing of the kind. Jesse embraced us in the driveway of the trim farm at the bottom of a hillside of coffee bushes shaded by larger trees. He pointed out that coffee was better if it grew in the shade which kept it from being bitter. I looked off to where a young man was working on a tractor near a shed. It was at least fifty yards away but I could still see by his jaw line that it was my half brother. Jesse followed my sightline but pretended Vera's son wasn't there as did my father. Jesse said that Vera was in Jalapa with the farmer to whom she was betrothed but would be back in the morning in time to bid me good-bye.

We had a nice lunch of broiled fish served by an attractive woman in her forties who I took to be Jesse's girlfriend. Jesse had a beer with lunch but my father and I were served iced tea. He said he had had a nice chat with Cynthia in Chicago which explained our iced tea. I wondered if his drinking a beer was a way of sticking it in a little bit. My father and Jesse began talking about the "good old days" (without irony) during World War II in the Philippines. Bob saw that I was bored with the conversation and offered to take me on a tour of the farm.

Outside Bob formally introduced me to my half brother who was still working on an ancient Ford tractor. I can't say he was warm to me but was certainly polite and used the most formal Spanish possible. He had to be nineteen by now and was about my size but intensely muscular and wore a machete in a scabbard. When we got in an open Jeep and drove off up the hill Bob said, "He knows you are not bad but his father is very bad." I nodded without saying anything because there was nothing to say though when we reached the top of the hill and looked at the view I tried to explain to Bob the motive of the trip. It was like giving a mountain lion a lecture on kindness and when I was finished with the idea of my father asking Jesse and Vera for forgiveness he said "bullshit." I stood there flushed with embarrassment. In the silence that followed I tried to imagine that I was the father of Polly's daughter who was twelve and a man raped her and radically changed her. Could I forgive him? This was close to home and "no" came into my mind easily. I tried to lighten the atmosphere by saying that my father intended to give Jesse his half of the farm as penance but Bob said my father hadn't paid Jesse for three years and the amount of money my father owed Jesse exceeded his investment in the farm. It was only at this point that I recognized the absolute absurdity of our trip. The last filament of rationality lay in the idea that my father had to ask forgiveness for his twelve-step program whether it was successful or not. Standing on the hill with Bob and looking at the sweep of fabulous green hills and the mountains beyond my eyes misted with the sense of my own alien presence in this green kingdom. Bob put his hand on my shoulder as if to say nothing was my fault. We drove back down the hill to Jesse's house, entering through the kitchen where an old woman was trussing up a piglet to roast for dinner. I was enthused about the piglet and when Bob showed me to my room I said a rather plaintive little prayer to a small primitive statue of the Virgin Mary. The baby Jesus was peeking out from under her skirt. Even Jesus was a victim of natural childbirth in the way he fell to earth, I thought before I slept.

❊   ❊   ❊

I awoke to a nightmare. Passing through the kitchen the old woman
now roasting the pig gave me a cup of coffee. I heard yelling and
my stomach jumped and I didn't want to go into the living room
where Bob and my half brother Mañoso were standing off to the
side while my father and Jesse sat at the dining table drinking rum
and arguing. I immediately had the faint hope that the rum plus his
tranquilizers would make my father pass out but he was working
in an opposite manic direction. Most of the bottle of rum was gone
and they were yelling about money with my father's hoarse and
slurred speech saying that a classmate was an American consul in
Mexico and he would use his powerful Mexican friends to make
Jesse pay the money owed. I looked helplessly at Bob and Mañoso
who clearly didn't understand what was going on. Bob waved me
away when I tried to approach the quarrel. Jesse was yelling half
in Spanish that when my father raped Vera he had lost his half of
the farm. My father stood up wobbly then abruptly dove across the
table with his hands tightly around Jesse's neck so that Jesse's eyes
bulged and his chair tipped over. They were rolling on the floor with
Jesse's face changing colors under my father's grip. Bob rushed over
and I followed with both of us pulling my father back with his hands
still attached to Jesse's throat so that we were pulling them both
upright. Bob kept hitting my father in the face. I didn't see the blade
of Mañoso's machete fall but it nicked off the end of my thumb and
one of my father's hands at the wrist. The blade fell again and off
went my father's other hand. I fell backward striking my head on
the table's edge and saw my father bleeding gouts of blood from
his wrists and rolling back and forth on the floor. I must have passed
out for minutes because when I woke up Mañoso was gone and Bob
had finished wrapping my unconscious father's wrists in duct tape.
Jesse sat in a chair snoring. Bob wrapped my bleeding thumb and

when I tried to talk he put a piece of tape on my lips and bound my
hands and feet. I sat there until dark with my father still unconscious on the floor while Bob mopped up the blood. Jesse came over
to me with tears in his eyes and then left. When it was dark my father
and I were loaded into the back of a pickup by Mañoso who carried us each without apparent effort. We were covered by a tarp
and I was sure I was going to my death hearing my father's head
thump on the bumpy road. The truck finally stopped in a grove of
mangroves and we were loaded into a rowboat where Bob undid
my legs and hands and peeled the tape from my face while Mãnoso
walked us out into the tidal creek that opened up on water where I
could hear light waves. He gave the boat a good shove, shined the
flashlight on us, and then it was dark.

*Father was wailing. I deduced from the morning sun and moving flotsam that
we were drifting slowly southward with the force of an unknown current. He
slumped on the back seat of the wooden rowboat and I leaned forward grabbing his shirt to keep him from pitching overboard. Both of his hands had been
severed at the wrist and the stumps had been tightly bound with duct tape.
His normally withered forearms now bulged with an unsightly color. When
they had pushed us out from the estuary on a falling tide before dawn I had
been given only one oar. When I clearly noted this at first light the humor
wasn't lost on me. I was equipped to row in circles with my left hand. The
thumb of my right hand was missing and the pain lessened when I raised it
high. In the early light I had seen a green or loggerhead turtle and took the
tip of my thumb someone had stuffed in my pocket pitching it toward the beast
but the turtle had submerged in alarm misunderstanding my good intentions.
By midmorning the shore had arisen and I could see the coastline south of
Veracruz. The current was carrying us toward Alvarado. My father woke from
his latest faint. His face was too bruised for clear speech and now rather than
wailing he bleated. His eyes made his request clear and I pushed him gently*

over the back of the boat. It was quite some time before he completely sunk. I would study the stinking fish scales and bits of dried viscera on the boat's bottom and then look up and he would still be there floating in the current. And then finally I was pleased to see him sink. What a strange way to say good-bye to your father.

EPILOGUE

Obviously I made it home. I was swept closer to shore by the tide that was flowing into the immense estuarine area next to Alvarado. A kid fishing near the bridge saw me and his dad towed me in with a motorboat. I rode the bus into Veracruz and bought some unappealing fresh clothes, then went to the airport. I called the farm from Mexico City and told Jesse that as far as I was concerned my father had disappeared when we were at the Emporio. "What happened?" he asked. "My father was lost at sea," I said. When I hung up the phone I wondered if there would be any further complications but I couldn't foresee any. In my imagination I could see him wandering off down the street from the Emporio looking for an especially young whore. His erratic behavior had prepared the world for anything.

❊   ❊   ❊

At the end of June just before the Fourth of July weekend Cynthia
came over to Marquette from the Soo and we headed up to the Club
to bury my mother's ashes on the beach near Huron Point which
was her request. I had told Cynthia most of the story on the phone
but she seemed not to want to know specific details.

"I didn't want him to outlive mother. He made it only by five
days," she said.

There was a new gatekeeper at the Club and we were momentarily stymied when he said that our father had let his membership
lapse, but then Cynthia gave my mother's maiden name and explained our mission. Her relatives were still active members and
we were waved through.

It was nearly a mile to the Huron Point from our parking place
on the log road. I didn't have bug dope for the mosquitoes and blackflies. Cynthia was lucky because she could still run like the wind
and I couldn't do much more than a fast trot. It would have been
nice if it had been a beautiful day but it wasn't. There was a cool
north wind and Lake Superior was rumpled with whitecaps. We
knelt and dug a hole with our hands. We opened the urn and poured
in the ashes with their small bone fragments. Water from the lake
quickly seeped through the sand into the hole and we paused to
watch as if we were still children. Of course as with anyone else
there was still some of the child in our souls if not our bodies.

ACKNOWLEDGMENTS

I would like to thank Amy Gibbs and also Professor Richard Eathorne of Northern Michigan University for their research help and advice.

I would also like to thank Joseph Bednarik for his perceptive efforts on behalf of this novel.